In America

In America

Nina Romano

TURNER

Turner Publishing Company
Nashville, Tennessee
New York, New York

www.turnerpublishing.com

In America

This is a work of fiction. All the characters and events portrayed in this book are either products of the author's imagination or are used fictitiously.

Cover design: Maddie Cothren
Book design: Kym Whitley

Library of Congress Cataloging-in-Publication Data

Names: Romano, Nina, 1942- author.
Title: In America / by Nina Romano.
Description: Nashville, Tennessee : Turner Publishing Company, [2016] | Series: Wayfarer trilogy ; book 3
Identifiers: LCCN 2015047648| ISBN 9781630269111 (softcover) | ISBN 9781681623832 (hardcover)
Classification: LCC PS3568.O549 I5 2016 | DDC 813/.54--dc23
LC record available at http://lccn.loc.gov/2015047648

9781630269111

Printed in the United States of America
15 14 13 12 11 10 9 8 7 6 5 4 3 2 1

For Nico

and

in loving memory of my parents

Marie and John

In America

CHAPTER I

Marcella

SINCE THE DAY I MADE my First Communion when I was five, in the lacy dress that looked like a wedding ensemble with veil included, I attended Mass with Mamma or Papa or both of them in Our Lady of Angels. The organ music gave me chills, and I knew the religious songs. I adored all music for that matter, and loved to sing. My mamma was partial to that church because her name was Angelica and she believed in those heavenly beings with or without wings that help us human beings in dire need of salvation, and anything else a human needs to survive on earth. Every Sunday, I'd set a match to a candle in the alcove and pray on my knees in the lambent light for one thing and one thing only—to fall in love, the way Mamma loved Papa and vice versa. My thoughts usually went like this: maybe it hasn't happened yet because the saints above aren't listening; or maybe because I don't always drop a coin in the box before lighting the candle—little vixen that I am, Mamma always says. But it will happen; I know it will.

Even though I was only fifteen, I felt as though I was on the brink of womanhood, and in recent weeks, Gianni had been on my mind more than I'd like to think of him—is that love? When I saw him, I'd get this feeling of excitement. It felt like some gossamer sensing in the pit of my stomach wanted to rise, making me believe I could almost fly. But his family was difficult. Were they just protective? No, they appeared to be belligerent and snobbish—although somehow his gentle mannerisms and those soft hazel eyes and sweet disposition made me uncaring of their hoity-toity attitudes. Smart, wiry, athletic, and maybe even a little too handsome, he was entertaining, kind, and humble, not like his older brothers—not one bit. He was always polite and respectful toward my parents, shaking hands with Papa and asking after his health and kissing Mamma on both cheeks—he adored her, and she him. He was the only one I've ever seen rob a meatball or dunk the heel of an Italian loaf in her Sunday sauce and get away with it. Even Papa would get his hand slapped, if he dared try. But not Gianni. He had this knack. First he'd make moon eyes at her and then nod his head toward the pot. Next thing I knew she was handing him a plate and fork or a piece of bread and a napkin. It didn't seem fair, but I loved her all the more for doing it and him for getting away with it. I always thought it was because his mother died when he was so young. It was tragic to think of it.

What I'd heard about his mother was that she had caught pneumonia on the freezing dock, the wind restless and scavenging, while she waited for Gianni's brother Giuseppe, who had left the seminary in Sicily and was coming to live and work with his brothers in their importing business on Stillwell Avenue. The poor woman had the day of his arrival wrong, and when her son finally did get to see her, she was laid out in a bier in the family's living room. What a shock that must have been for Giuseppe. Although I felt sorry for him, I can't really say that I liked him. He was one of those know-it-all bossy types who lorded everything over my Gianni, who doesn't work in the office or store with his brothers. Instead, they sent him out on routes to deliver provisions of olive oil and cheese.

The day after Christmas, Gianni came over and joined Jack and some of the neighborhood kids sledding down our hilly street. After an hour or so, they tired of that, and we all had a snowball fight. We broke into teams. Jack and Val built one fortress of packed snow, and Gianni and I made the other. At the end of the game, Jack and Val, being the absolute winners, quit to go have some hot chocolate.

Gianni and I made angels in the snow. Then he chased me and tried to douse me with snow. I begged for mercy, and he caught me, trying to put snow down my collar.

"You're a more playful kid than Jack," I said.

"You have red apple cheeks," he said, knocking snow off my hair and scarf. "I'd like to take a bite."

"Don't you dare. I'm out of breath—you soaked me."

"All's fair in love and war, they say."

He pulled off one of his gloves and stuck it in his pocket, and taking my hand, pulled the glove off and handed it to me to put in my pocket. We walked back to the house, my hand snug in his.

⋆⋆⋆

RIGHT AFTER NEW YEAR'S, GIANNI came over to deliver a can of imported Simoni olive oil to Mamma. He always came to the back of the house, knocked, and strolled in carrying Mamma's provisions. I heard him from the front porch, where I'd just picked up the late mail, so I walked to the back kitchen to say hello. The day was biting cold, and the frigid air came blasting in with him. He shook.

I pointed at him. "Why did you wear such a light jacket?"

He unzipped it and said, "I've got a sweater on, a shirt, and an undershirt. Thought I'd be warm enough."

Before he took the packages upstairs, I offered him a cup of hot chocolate to warm up as it was no trouble and I was going to make one for myself before starting my homework. The days were so short and the light faded fast toward late afternoon. The sun had never peeked out that day, so I lit a little lamp on a table by the window in the dinette off the yellow kitchen. The atmosphere seemed suddenly warmer, and I had him take a seat.

"Take your jacket off, or you'll be even colder when you go back outside."

He took off his jacket, and as I prepared the cups and then served, we talked about the weather. Mamma always said never talk about clothes, men hate to hear it, and always sit up straight, and the list went on and on. So I asked him if he heard anything of late from his sisters in Italy.

"Funny," he said, "I was just thinking I should write them. When my mother died, we felt like orphans. They were four and six, and I was eight. I was in school and used to rush home to them and bring them candy whenever I could. I lost out on a lot of games and playing baseball, but it was always worth it when their tears turned to smiles as they stood at the window and watched me from behind the living room curtains. They'd see me running toward them, and they would literally start to jump up and down. Good girls. I miss them." He cleared his throat.

Oh, my heart. My hand went to my chest with his telling of this story filled with emotion. Yes, in my secret heart of hearts, I stored this information. Never had I heard of such an unselfish boy, kind and considerate, leaving play and sports to rush to little sisters.

We made chitchat for quite a while, me gazing into his soft eyes, looking at his sweet mouth, wondering what it would be like to have those lips pressed to mine. I leaned over and picked up his cup. We were so close. I couldn't resist, and on impulse, kissed him. His lips yielded to mine exactly as I thought they would.

And then Mamma called down for Gianni. He grabbed the box of goods and practically bolted to the bottom of the stairs. I followed him with my eyes and watched his lean yet powerful legs pump into action as he took the stairs two at a time, his arms loaded.

He came downstairs about twenty minutes later. I knew what Gianni was up to—ingratiating himself in a loving and caring way because he wanted my mother's approval. He didn't realize it, but he didn't even have to try with Mamma. I had turned on the overhead lamp and was sitting at the dinette table with my books spread all over. He sat down and wrote the rest of the list that Mamma wanted in two weeks, in time for my sixteenth birthday.

He stopped writing, pocketed his notepad, and looked at me for a long time. Then he shrugged into his jacket. "Walk me to the door?"

I didn't answer so he took my hand and led me. His hand felt warm and strong, and I had lightning bugs all aglow in the pit of my stomach. Could this be romance?

⸙

PERHAPS FALLING IN LOVE WAS the thing I'd need later in life to settle down, and maybe that wasn't going to happen for a long time, which was fine with me because what I truly wanted in life was to become a singer. My voice was not operatic, but I sure could belt out a tune. Of course, Mamma and Papa thought only loose women went on the stage to sing—or a professional, perhaps selling more than a song. This kind of "singer" my parents classified as a *puttana*.

I noticed that some of those singers drew on their faces what I had naturally above my lip—a birthmark, although Mamma always called it a beauty mark.

But I'd been blessed. God had given me a gift—a great voice—and I sang all over the place, especially in the bathtub, and especially "I'm Forever Blowing Bubbles," but also all the songs I heard on the radio and in the movies. I sang on my way to school, sang at Mass, and sang walking down the street to go to the stores for Mamma. My favorite songs of the moment were "Marie," "Singin' in the Rain," and, of course, Eddie Cantor's "Makin' Whoopee," which naturally scandalized half the old folks in the neighborhood, including Mamma, when I left the windows open and sang at the top of my lungs, doing the Saturday cleaning and dusting. Mamma preferred "Tiptoe through the Tulips," but Papa adored "Whoopee" when I sang it, not to mention his favorite with the great beat, "Lullaby of Broadway."

My hometown of Bay Ridge, Brooklyn, existed as a lovely little hamlet near the city. How I loved movies at the RKO Dyker Theater on Eighty-Sixth Street. How lucky to have a cinema in walking distance, and even luckier to have a Papa who always had spare change for me on Saturday. The movies were fun, but the music and songs were what I loved best. When Papa had something on his mind, was distracted, or said I couldn't go for whatever reason, I somehow managed to get him in a better humor and wangle him into giving me the two bits for a double feature. I'd say, "Just the entrance, Papa, I don't need a nickel for candy." He'd sigh, pinch my cheek, and reach into his pants pocket and fork over the exact change and most times that extra nickel as well.

Not so with my poor dear sister Valentina, younger by a year, who'd scrub and clean and do Papa's bidding, but those nickels in his pocket stayed put. Valentina not only didn't succeed with Papa but always tried to shine in Mamma's eyes and make herself the adored one. Why? Mamma only had eyes for our eldest sister, Pina—it was beyond the beyond. Thank Heaven for Pina, who was always looking out for Valentina, not a jealous bone in her skinny frame and never realizing what envy glared at her through Valentina's eyes. Pina was married now to Bruno. They had a darling baby girl, Elena, and lived nearby in a rented apartment. Then there was my younger minx of a brother, Jack, two years younger than me. He was handsome, with a devil-may-care attitude from day one, our mascot, loved for his endearing approaches to life and knowledge that he'd always survive, tolerated for his wacky ways with a dimply smile to melt the frostiest midwinter heart. I could tell Jack admired Gianni, who never fluffed him off as a kid. They played catch, and sometimes on weekends, even baseball together. If Jack ever saw Gianni driving around the neighborhood, he always ran home to tell me, so I'd be sure to go outside in time for a glimpse of him that usually turned into a chat.

⋒⋒⋒

IT WAS A COLD SUNDAY morning, and I walked to church with the family, hating the hat I had to wear, and under my wool coat, the light gabardine pinafore top with a huge white collar that Mamma liked to see me dressed in. Always navy blue, black, or charcoal gray outfits and big white collars—round or square—she loved keeping me looking like a baby, afraid someone might really take notice of me and whisk me away. But what about me? I felt like Baby Snookums in the comic strip "The Newlyweds."

I knew I'd get distracted during the Mass. Sometimes I'd just drift off from all that Latin. How much *Dominus vobiscum* does it take to understand "The Lord is with you"? And I figured He wasn't going away anytime soon, because I had wonderful, loving parents who doted on me—particularly my papa. I was fortunate enough to understand a great deal of the Latin Mass because I speak Italian. I wasn't a saintly girl, nor do I have those kinds of leanings, although Valentina was trying for sainthood in Mamma's eyes. Something I was not, nor aspired to become, and what's more, I doubt saints ever sang—and certainly Valentina is tone deaf. How could any saint in that kneeling position, looking beatifically up at the Madonna, manage anything but a croaking Hail Mary?

Almost every Mass I went to I was faced with that holier than thou, simpering, pious creep of an altar boy Danny O'Donnell holding the Communion plate. I couldn't bear it—it was almost impossible to control myself from being sick right into the plate. I never liked him, the prissy blond, and I pitied his sweet sister, Eileen, not only because she was twice his weight, but also because she had to live under the same roof and eat corned beef and cabbage at the same kitchen table, knowing her brother was not only a villain but practically a murderer. Maybe he did what he did to impress his friends, or as Mamma later suggested, maybe he had a crush on me. A crush? Frightening me the way he did!

Ever since that scary night all those years ago, a silver streak had appeared in the front of my hairline. Mamma said it was a reaction to fear. I thought it would go away, but as the years progressed, that swath of silver remained.

How could I forget that night? I remembered it distinctly even though it happened when I was eleven. I was reminded of the incident earlier in the day while I readied myself for church. I couldn't find my hatpin, and so I searched in Valentina's top drawer of the bureau, and sure enough, there it was. I scolded her, mildly of course, as it does no good—she has sticky fingers and will take what she likes. It was a dark and overcast day, which prompted me telling my sister, who takes in and delivers laundry in the neighborhood and does fabulous alterations, to be careful walking at night.

What I said to her was that I remembered the mild Indian summer days we had in late October the year I was eleven and she was ten. What made me think of it now was I looked out the window at Papa's garden, and the Chinese long string beans had all withered on their vines, those pink and white and lavender flowers that I loved were all gone, now blanketed in early snow. No one in the neighborhood had these, and Papa gave them to everyone and anyone who asked for them, even the O'Donnell family—how could he! I thought back to the evening I'd picked those beans—they could grow to three feet long. Papa always harvested them when they were a foot to eighteen inches long throughout the long, hot summer and the last ones right before the first frost. I'd bring them up to Mamma in our second-floor whiter-than-white kitchen, where she'd wash and cut them into two-inch pieces and quick fry them with olive oil, hot pepper, and *zenzero*. I only learned that *zenzero* was ginger when I went to Chinatown one day for lunch with Papa.

❦

REMEMBERING BACK TO THE DANNY O'Donnell trauma, I had started home late that evening from buying a loaf of Italian bread at Ferrara's Bakery on Thirteenth Avenue. It was, as they say in some of the delicious novels I read with a flashlight under the covers, a dark and stormy night. Papa always asked me where his two-cell black and chrome flashlight had gone to: *You know, Marcella, the one I take fishing in Sheepshead Bay early in the morning. The one with the boat switch and ring hanger?* Of course he knew I always took it, but I'd play innocent, hoping he'd buy me my very own. I was a voracious reader, and I never had enough time in the day to get through all the books I coveted.

It also happened to be the night before Halloween, but for some reason, the kids in our neighborhood liked to dress up in costumes even before the Eve of All Saints.

The days had grown shorter. The sun set way too soon. I walked home with a loaf of seven-cent bread under one arm, and in the other hand I carried a paper bag filled with persimmons, my mother's favorite fruit. I stopped in my tracks, realizing that nothing was moving. Not a car, not a bicycle, a cat, or a dog. There were no kids on the street playing stick ball, war, ringaleavio, or the bottle cap sliding game of skelly, and the only sound I heard for half a block was this eerie whistling through the partially denuded plane trees that line my street.

I picked up my pace. All of a sudden, a bunch of boys whooping and hooting, yelling, and running swooped in around me. I was completely surrounded by pirates brandishing knives and swords. The swords were phony, but the knives were real and glistened in the lights streaming from the wrap-around porches, gardens, and a few already lit gas lamps. The knives were just like the ones Carmine the butcher used to carve up the meat. I counted the boys—there were six of them. All had blacked their faces with burnt corks and wore half masks, but I saw their eyes, like runaway dogs that had run hard and long. One slipped up and called out to Danny, the coward. How could you disguise that platinum blond hair and those hunched shoulders? As if that bent position would detract from his height—the tallest boy in his class. His hand shook as he held the long knife not even two inches away from my stomach. I looked up, and in that instant, I felt fear crawl into my belly. Did this skinny kid have to prove something to his friends? Would he really stab me in the stomach? I started to scream at the top of my lungs, and at the same time, I shoved his scrawny shoulders away from me, swinging the bread and fruit, breaking through a narrow space in the circle. I must have dropped the things I carried and ran hell-bent for home. I think what happened was that the gang dispersed and ran in different directions. But I kept up my blood-curdling howl until I reached my front doorsteps.

I have often wondered why the stinkers never followed me home. My brother, Jack, more brave than cautious, went in search of the bandits, bread, and fruit. His scouring of the neighborhood produced two objects: a bag of squashed fruit and bread broken in half, still wrapped in brown paper but quite creased. Jack threatened to bash Danny, a head taller than him, in the nose the next time he saw him. In that moment, I loved my brother as no other—an absolute hero dressed in knickers and jaunty cap. And to make sure the family knew this wasn't some theatrical show I'd invented, I told everyone the story time and again until they begged me to spare their ears, so finally I let it go, although I felt obliged to compensate my hero, Jack. I'd begun to boast about him as my champion. The second time he heard that he said, "Drop it, sis, but you owe me."

The next afternoon, we walked down to Paulie's on Twelfth Avenue, where I treated Jack to pink bubble gum and penny candy. I even splurged for a chocolate egg cream, but since I'd spent all my money, I couldn't join him and get another for myself, but sweet Jack gave me a sip of his. I used my own straw.

My dream is one day to have a family with this much love.

CHAPTER 2

Giacomo

GIACOMO CAME HOME EXHAUSTED FROM helping Mr. Green put finishing touches on his back porch, doing the lion's share of the work to spare the old man because it was so cold. Giacomo had quit his job in the Navy Yard some years earlier and was doing construction permanently, but times were tough. Last summer he had taken on the extra job of pouring cement for a patio in the old man's backyard, and the job went on too long because two of his helpers had not shown up for work. Of late he'd been hiring out as a brick layer until some other, more favorable job came along. He had his sights set on construction, as he had learned quite a lot working at the Brooklyn Navy Yard. Since the layoffs began and he quit, he'd taken on almost any job in any capacity in construction work to gain experience and expertise. No job intimidated him.

The weariness he felt in his broad shoulders this evening, he knew would pass as soon as he was greeted by his loving family and a hot meal from Angelica. Thinking of her delicious cooking, he had a fleeting memory of when they were first married in Sicily and his mother-in-law, Rosalia, made him one of his favorite dishes, *pasta con le sarde*, with fresh, feathery fennel tops, raisins, and pine nuts. From there his mind traveled to China during the Boxer Rebellion, where he had been the cook on board his ship, the *Leopardo*.

Tomorrow would be Marcella's sixteenth birthday, and he wanted to exhibit a cheerful and sunny disposition for his daughter despite his backache. As he walked along the snowy street going home from the late indoor carpentry job he'd picked up from Mr. Green to help defray the cost of the party, his thoughts brought him back to the year when Marcella was born.

~CX~

HIS WIFE, ANGELICA, HAD COME from Sicily to America with his firstborn daughter, Pina, when the baby girl was one year old in 1909. Angelica had miscarried the following year. The year after that she'd carried a baby girl to term, but lost her in childbirth. Angelica was strong in spirit, and it was difficult for her to reconcile these two great losses despite her faith. She prayed a continuous Novena that she would be able to give Giacomo another baby soon.

When she had found out she was pregnant once again and told Giacomo, he was deliriously happy and begged her to take extra care in everything she did and to make sure that she wouldn't strain herself or pick up anything heavy. He made her promise to put her feet up as often as possible. To this end he bought a used French chaise longue on Mulberry Street and had it reupholstered by a friend of his in gold and green silk brocade from China that he bought in Chinatown, using what he remembered of Mandarin along with Italian bargaining powers for a better price.

When Giacomo had been late or detained for some reason, he knew he would find Angelica stretched out on the chaise, propped up by pillows reading or listening to the radio, but only after she had dinner ready for him and had already put Pina to bed. The front door to their home was always unlocked so neighbors who wanted to visit could knock and enter without forcing Angelica to come downstairs to open the door. Giacomo knew he didn't have to scold and she'd take extra care, not rushing to do any unnecessary household chores. He wanted her activity limited. And for this reason, he even helped with the cleaning.

He despised the number seventeen, like many Italians, but his lucky number was thirteen and, sure enough, his daughter Marcella was born in the first month of the year 1913. The feeling of explosive joy surrounded him—so incredible he wanted to stuff it into a bottle and carry it around with him and open it up only when he felt blue, to let his personal magic genie out.

He went in to kiss the newborn child, marveling at the wonder he helped to create. Angelica and he were careful because life is so precarious and it was winter. They watched the snowflakes on the immature branches of the denuded dogwood tree they'd planted in spring and decided to wait a few months before having her baptized. When Marcella was a year old, they would have a photograph taken of her as was the custom, bare bottom up.

How he doted on this child. He changed her diapers and, when Angelica had finished breastfeeding her, would take her in his arms and croon Italian love songs.

When Marcella was one year old, Giacomo took her to be photographed at Pietro Galli's studio at 181 Bleeker Street, where the motto in Italian was *Si lavora anche contempo piovoso e di notte*: We work also in rainy weather and at night. They guaranteed to keep the negatives as well. When the naked photo of his baby girl on a bear rug was ready, he purchased two of them backed on sepia-toned stiff postcards. At age five, Marcella developed the croup so badly that her breathing sounded to Giacomo like a dog barking. He carefully measured out two drops of kerosene on a teaspoon of sugar, gave it to her, and left her gagging in Angelica's arms. He moved her rocking chair into the bathroom where he ran the hot water until it steamed, fogging up the entire room until sweat ran off the tiles. He rocked and rocked his Marcella, massaging her little back until her breathing was restored to something almost human and she fell asleep in his arms. Then he carried her back to bed, sitting nearby until he was sure she would stay asleep.

When she was six he brought her to public school and told the teacher to watch out for her, as she only spoke Italian at home and a little English with her sister Pina. At seven, he'd bring her to the seashore so she could run in the sand and breathe in the strong salted air. When she was eight, he sent her to private school with the nuns of Visitation Academy.

When she was eleven, he would trek all the way to Riis Park just so she could breathe in the fresh air and also meet up with some of the longshoremen he worked with and their families.

One night he thought he heard a mouse and was about to catch the little rodent red-handed but instead found his thirteen-year-old daughter cutting a thick slice of Italian bread. He watched as she smeared it with her mother's homemade apricot jam. So intent on the task and the succulent taste of the sweet preserves, she didn't even notice blood dripping from her cut hand onto the white linen napkin she'd used to hold the bread on the cutting board. Giacomo washed and bandaged her wound, then sat her down to finish eating her bread while he poured her a glass of milk.

⋘⋙

SIXTEEN YEARS. HAD THEY REALLY gone by that swiftly? Giacomo was pensive, but the minute he walked into the large foyer and Marcella came bouncing down the stairs, his mood lifted.

"Mamma made you something special. She had a feeling you'd come home tired and said she bet those *malscalzoni* that work for Mr. Green didn't show up again." Then she kissed her father's cheeks, pulled the scarf from around his neck, and tossed it onto the coatrack before bounding up the stairs again.

He sat on a wooden bench that also served as a trunk for outer wear, pulled off his galoshes, and hung his navy pea coat and hat on the coatrack. Then he followed the aroma of a simmering sauce with meat and mushrooms up the stairs, thinking, *Nothing like a dish of pasta, a glass of red wine, and the company of my women to restore good humor.*

"*Buona sera, tutti,*" he said, entering the upstairs kitchen. He inclined his head to his wife, Angelica, and his three daughters, Pina, Marcella, and Valentina, then went to the sink and washed his hands, noting that Jack was once again missing.

Angelica smiled and handed him the *mappina,* a tea towel, to dry his huge hands. She kissed him lightly and pointed to the table where his solitary plate awaited him. "The iceman delivered today, so I restocked and packed in everything I could. We need two of them, the way Jack eats."

"Ah," he said, "and what's that delicious sweet aroma?"

He walked over to the pie safe and opened the door as if peeking at a gift before Christmas. "You baked, I see." He counted three *crostate*. "I love the cookie crust—sweet but there's something—"

"Mamma put in a gallon of vanilla," Marcella said.

Angelica knocked Marcella's elbow down and said, "Slight exaggeration. The girls were starving and couldn't wait and Jack, our little rascal son, wolfed down a sandwich for his dinner and went out. He piled on a pound of salami and provolone—enough for a grown man, saying he was on a mission of mercy. God only knows what he's got up to—"

"His idea of a mission of mercy probably had something to do with a girl." Giacomo sat down and ripped the heel off the loaf of bread. Marcella poured him a glass of red wine from a raffia-wrapped *fiasco* and set it down on the table next to his glass. Despite Prohibition, Giacomo always had homemade vino. Pina and Valentina both stopped their preparations and kissed their father. He indicated for his wife to sit, and she did.

"Never need to worry about Jack. He's probably out collecting salvage material for Lester Sussman," Marcella said.

"Who?" Giacomo asked.

"The secondhand man, you know—the junk dealer over on Bay Eighth. He pays pennies for the copper, iron, and wire scraps the boys bring him—weighs it on an old scale, but he's accurate. I've been there myself," Marcella said.

"What's he do with it all, Papa?" Pina asked.

"He takes leftovers, sometimes repairs—maybe not, but either way—he resells everything. Sometimes for triple or more what he pays the boys. What're you doing here at this time of night, Pina? Why aren't you home with Bruno?" he asked.

"Don't you remember? He left this morning on a ship with his brother Pietro," Pina said and finished draining the pasta, pouring some of the meat and mushroom sauce on top, not too much because Papa liked *past'asciutto*, dry pasta.

"I thought he was leaving tomorrow. And the baby?" he asked.

"Elena's asleep, thank God. Cried something awful—she's teething. Mamma used your trick and rubbed some anisette on her gums. She'll sleep for a while now." Pina sprinkled some grated *pecorino* on top and laid the plate in front of him. Her shirt cuff slid up and she pulled it down to cover a black and blue mark.

He tucked a white napkin into the collar of his work shirt, lifted his glass in salute and thanks, and took a long sip. He wiped his mouth, sniffed the dish in front of him, and said, "A little bit of Heaven on earth." He stuck the fork in and twirled the spaghetti expertly. After his first mouthful, he asked for a little more cheese, and Valentina obliged, after which she excused herself saying she had to study as there wouldn't be much time tomorrow because of the party for Marcella. Giacomo caught Marcella shooting her a glance, meaning, *who are you kidding*, as she watched her sister sidle out of the room and head upstairs to one of the attic bedrooms they shared.

Giacomo asked Marcella about the things they'd done that day in preparation for her party.

"We cleaned everything—dusted and scrubbed until our fingers almost fell from our hands. We've been cooking as if we owned one of your favorite restaurants in Coney Island. Lucky it's so cold out. If you look out the window, you'll see on the balcony Mamma's serving platters. Let's hope it doesn't freeze and break them all."

"No school?" he said in a nonjudgmental tone.

"Mamma let me stay home so I could be her 'right arm.' Pina helped too, in between watching the baby."

Giacomo winced slightly at the thought that his eldest daughter had married so young and was already a mother. Angelica shot him a recriminating glance—he knew she'd not been happy about Pina's marriage to Giacomo's distant cousin, Bruno, whom Angelica considered a thug.

He watched his wife clear the dishes and clean up the kitchen as he lingered over a last glass of red wine. Marcella said goodnight, although he doubted she'd sleep from her excited demeanor.

Pina took off her apron, kissed her parents, and said she'd see them tomorrow. When Angelica and Giacomo were alone, he said that he'd been thinking of looking for a part-time position on Sundays. Angelica's questions were worse than being shot. He pictured a mob hit with a *mitragliatrice*, a machine gun. "Why ever would you? How could you? Where? What kind of job?"

"I'm unsure. It's only an idea. Nothing set in stone. We could use some extra money. We'll talk about it after the party."

"Why not now before I wilt completely?"

"Because I'm too tired, too."

Angelica kissed him. "Time for bed. To sleep," she said with emphasis. He smiled and kissed her back, taking her hand and leading her to their bedroom and sanctuary.

cCØDↄ

AFTER BREAKFAST THE FOLLOWING MORNING, Giacomo was barely out the door when he lit a cigarette. His mind had begun to recollect the year 1909, when he had been working with a crew finishing building the USS *Connecticut* for President Theodore Roosevelt's flagship—they called it the Great White Fleet. He remembered that there were twenty-six vessels all told that were to sail the globe on a two-year tour—this was going to mark the inauguration of the United States as a global power.

Giacomo recalled standing on the Brooklyn Navy Yard's dock looking out over the water. The wind hit, ripping through him like a dagger hewn of ice, only sharper. It reminded him of China and an ice storm, distant lands, other shores, other ship tie-ups.

It was too hurtful and dangerous to remember the past, so he tried hard to toss away his thoughts as if they were dying embers from a cigarette. But his memories persisted, insisted, and suddenly it was as if Giacomo was standing once again on that dock looking out over the slate ocean on a foggy winter morning.

Back then, Giacomo had gotten to know pipefitters, marine painters, crane operators, and shipwrights as well as many of the welders and ship fitters. He had worked with these different men on various occasions and met to confer with both the superintendent and the marine project manager.

The foreman, Piero Monfalcone, was hired because he was from a shipbuilding family from Monfalcone, a few kilometers northwest of Trieste. He'd told Giacomo that his family was Jewish and that they took the name of their town, which was a common practice for generations.

Giacomo remembered that he'd been smoking the last of his cigarette before the horn blew. Piero leaned on a wall, holding tools in one hand and chits in the other. "My family worked in shipbuilding. I also worked in the *Stabilimento Tecnico Triestino,* which had been restored." Since that conversation, Giacomo heard that during the early '20s, STT built the heavy cruiser *Trieste* for the Italian Navy and the luxury commercial liner SS *Conte Grande.*

From the time he was hired, Piero always spoke Italian with Giacomo. That morning Piero had warned him over a cup of hot coffee in the shelter that the *irlandese,* Michael O'Malley, with a mop of red hair and beard to match, was mouthing off about Giacomo's inability to sire a son. Piero said to ignore the man who was only stirring up trouble to get Giacomo's goat—whatever the hell that meant—and it certainly didn't warrant Giacomo's attention. He had other concerns to worry about. Piero had warned O'Malley for a week and told Giacomo the bosses weren't going to put up with O'Malley's disruptive behavior any longer and had to let him go.

Each morning after coffee, the men broke up into groups and headed over to the cantina. Giacomo's unit was the most expert in carpentry. When they'd finished working on all the details, they broke up into twos and threes for lunch. Each man had his lunch pail stowed in one of the lockers near the latrine and went to retrieve it. They sat on benches, planks, two-by-fours, logs, under the cantina's overhanging eaves for a bit of shelter as there were no tables where they could eat.

As time went by, Giacomo discovered that these minor things weren't the only things O'Malley was saying. He had voiced complaints to many of the men that Giacomo wasn't holding up his end of the job, that his men were idlers, and worse, he blamed Giacomo for missing equipment, of stealing tools, and pilfering implements necessary to complete the job, pointing the finger of accusation at him to take the blame off himself, where it belonged. Giacomo might have been able to live with insults and accusations, but what he wasn't capable of tolerating was a man who drank on the job, endangering everyone else including himself.

Before heading home, O'Malley usually stopped at The Shamrock, a nearby underground speakeasy that for some reason never was raided, mostly because cops out of uniform were customers. Most of the guys who had change jingling in pockets and weren't feeling the pinch, or didn't need a smidgeon extra for the family, joined him for a beer. A short stop at the bar after work was one thing, but another was when O'Malley started drinking heavily on the job after his wife and three kids left him. His wife had taken up with their wealthy landlord, Giacomo gathered from the rumors that circulated around the building area. The foreman had no choice but to lay him off, telling him to sober up, and even found him a temporary job in Flatbush, but O'Malley kept drinking heavily and lurked around the yard, getting kicked out more than once.

A blustery day two weeks later, dark settled in quickly when the last whistle blew. All the men had cleared the area and headed home. All but the Irishman, who shouldn't have been there in the first place and had entered with a cloche of men changing shifts. He hid in between two rolls of cabled wire, hunched and at the ready to attack Giacomo, who always made a final check to see if any tools were left lying about that were his responsibility. Giacomo changed his clothes and put on his jacket to leave. He'd been distracted, thinking of his family, when a foghorn sounded in the distance. It shattered his reverie and brought him back to where he was presently walking toward the exit on the grounds, about to pass through the gate at the front of the work zone. He hadn't checked the scaffolding. For some niggling reason, he didn't feel right about it, and decided to go back to check. He climbed up on the scaffold above the cement mixer and heard the whirring of the machine winding down, so he knew he wasn't the last man to leave. He looked down and saw the cement guy walking off. Piero waved to the guy and then waved to Giacomo, who gave a mock salute in return. Giacomo turned and continued his investigation for lost objects in a welter of tangled ropes and discarded tools. No need to hurry. For him, there wasn't anything to rush home for, as Angelica had told him she'd be visiting her cousin on Staten Island. He and Angelica had argued last weekend over the shapely redhead with the hourglass figure who continued to sashay past the front door of their respectable house in their very proper neighborhood. The woman used to own the boarding house where Giacomo had stayed when he'd first arrived in America, and Angelica, pregnant, had stayed behind in Sicily. How could his wife be jealous over something that had happened so many years ago? That night, he knew he'd be going home to a big empty house and would miss the welcoming chatter of his daughter, Pina, a nice hot meal, and the warm arms of the woman he adored.

Something was wrong. Giacomo was wary. With animal alertness, he bent down to pick up a hammer partly exposed by a piece of planking and a snagged rope. His heavy padded pea coat absorbed most of the shock of a knife blade as it tore through material and muscle, stabbing him in the upper right shoulder. In one swift, fluid motion, Giacomo straightened, whirled around, and flung his leg at his assailant as naturally as if he'd sneezed, kicking him in the ribs, hurtling him backward onto coiled ropes, the same motion he'd used when he was attacked by his lover Lian's husband, Lu, in China. Giacomo didn't have time to think back on that event, but his body had learned the rote lesson of where and how to strike and hit fast.

O'Malley, all hooched-up, hunching and weaving, flung himself at Giacomo again. But Giacomo ducked and gripped the hulking man by his shoulders to send O'Malley hurtling, flipping backward over the pipe rail. The Irishman plunged headfirst downward, twisting like a ballerina or a tightrope walker strung up by an ankle rope. But there was no rope, although he seemed to dangle midair as if there were one, until he pierced the center of the cement mixer. Giacomo knew his assailant was dead. The shock hit Giacomo only when he peered over the railing and saw only his attacker's legs sticking upright.

Giacomo pulled the stiletto out of his shoulder with his gloved left hand and stared disbelievingly at the upside-down body in the cement mixer.

Not five minutes later, in back of Piero's over-crowded office, Giacomo took off his pea coat. He was bleeding profusely. Piero indicated a chair and handed Giacomo an unclean cotton rag, which he ripped into two pieces, wadded up, and stuck under his shirt. Piero lit a cigarette, smoked for a while, and offered a drag to Giacomo, who bent forward to take it in his mouth, not using his hands. He inhaled. Piero took the cigarette back.

"Think I should go to the police?" Giacomo asked.

"Cops are all bigoted Irish. White and Christians. They hate Italians and Jews," Piero said matter-of-factly.

"Why is that? They're immigrants like us." Giacomo winced.

"They think they own New York and now no longer feel they're immigrants—like entitlement. They were here first and resent us. They belong here and we're what? Upstarts. Newcomers. They're bitter and afraid we're taking over what's theirs." Piero put the cigarette out and added more wadding to absorb the blood. "It's not working. Let's bind the rag to the shoulder and apply some pressure."

"But we're here to stay," Giacomo said.

A few minutes later, Piero said, "Get the hell out of here. Now. I'll report this accident and meet you at the speakeasy. Don't say anything about being late to anyone."

"Not thinking straight, what if someone asks?" Giacomo stood.

"If any of the guys want to know what took you so long, say you met an old friend down on his luck, had to give him a helping hand. You listened to his tale of woe, but he kept running off at the mouth, chewed off your ear about his hard times—kid died, wife died—he married her sister, a hooker."

Giacomo replaced his jacket. "How did you come up with that so fast?"

"I memorized that handy excuse in case I ever needed one. But I never dreamed I'd actually have to say it to someone." Piero opened his hand. "Give me the knife for a sea burial."

⌐C✱D⌐

ALMOST AN HOUR LATER IN the speakeasy, Piero Monfalcone told everyone of the unfortunate accident that had occurred to O'Malley, and it was general consensus the man had it coming. Drink was his ruin, and he was a nasty SOB to boot.

Piero bought Giacomo a drink and slapped him on the shoulder. Giacomo grimaced, and Piero said, "Oh, sorry. Drink up. Looks like you've seen a ghost." Giacomo's hand shook as he took the whiskey jigger and tossed back the drink.

Piero told Giacomo he'd sworn to police earlier in the yard that he'd seen the whole thing and it was an accident, leaving out the detail that Giacomo had been there. Now Piero raised his glass and said in English for all the men to hear, "Too bad you weren't there, *paesano*, to see the poor hulk slip, fall, and kill himself. He wasn't supposed to be anywhere near the property. Wonder what devilment he was up to?"

"Big Mick. May he rest in peace," fellow worker Oskar said.

"And maybe find a bottle of good Irish whiskey on the other side," Danny said from behind the bar. They all raised their glasses and toasted the dead man, even two guys thought to be undercover cops. Giacomo was silent. Overwrought by all that had occurred, he was drinking, but it seemed not to hit him.

They stayed at the bar, and Piero leaned in, speaking Italian, and told Giacomo he'd read about a famous lawyer named Clarence Darrow who had said, "I have never killed anyone, but I have read some obituary notices with great satisfaction." Piero wore a grim smile. "I have to agree with Mr. Darrow. But I can tell you one thing for sure: No one will miss that SOB. Now drink up."

Giacomo noticed Piero had placed a brown paper-wrapped package on top of his coat. Piero looked at it now, picked it up, and nudged his head toward the lavatory. When Giacomo entered the men's room, Piero locked the flimsy door. Giacomo stripped without a word; Piero washed the wound with brown soap. "Looks bad. Deep laceration. Still bleeding. I've got to sew it—it's not going to tickle."

Flinching, Giacomo said, "Hurry."

Someone knocked on the door. "Got to take a whiz." The banging became insistent. Piero yelled through the door, "Piss in the alley." He poured some whiskey from a flask onto a threaded needle and began to sew. Giacomo bit into his pointing finger's knuckle and drew blood.

When they came out of the bathroom, Oskar said, "Hello, girls, had yourselves a good time?"

"Sure were in there long enough to get some satisfaction," Danny added.

Two of the guys laughed and the barman chuckled at his own remark. Piero and Giacomo joined them at the bar. Piero sat next to the stool with his coat.

"Hey, Jocko, take jacket off. Stay," Józef said with a heavy accent.

Giacomo buttoned the top button of his jacket. "Nah. Been having chills all day. Not feeling so hot."

"So what you ladies do back there?" Józef asked.

"I was offering a side job to Giacomo," Piero said.

"Something inside your pants?" Józef said.

The guys snickered.

Piero stood, and Giacomo put his bulk between the foreman and Józef. Giacomo said to Piero, "Perhaps you can offer an extra job to them, too," with an expansive wave of his hand, indicating the guys at the bar.

Piero sat down. "Yeah. If the deal solidifies."

"What?" Oskar asked.

"Building a warehouse near the cantina. You're good with tools, Oskar. You too, Brodzik—interested?"

"Could be. After work lets out?" Józef said.

"Exactly," Giacomo said.

"When? What money?" Oskar asked.

"Not sure yet. Two months—maybe three," Piero said. "I'm working on permissions now. If you guys would rather hang at the bar, making lewd accusations instead . . ." Piero trailed off, knowing the language went over both of their heads.

"*Va bene.* Let's cut it. I'm heading home after this last shot." Giacomo offered his two coworkers a peace-making draft beer.

⚜

GIACOMO MADE HIS WAY HOME in drink-doused pain. He walked with his lunch pail in his left hand, listening to dogs wail at the moon some blocks over. The lights were on at his Seventy-Ninth Street walk-up. *I must have left a light on this morning. No, too many lights. A thug? Thief? Was she home?* Giacomo had his key out, ready to open the door, when it swung open, and there stood Angelica.

Without a word, she threw her arms around him and gave him a kiss that begged forgiveness, at once tender and yielding. "I'm home," she all but sang. "Surprised?"

"Ah," he sighed. "Easy on the shoulder. Should have warned me," he teased, "I might've been arm and arm with the old red-headed hussy you accuse me of liking so much."

They kissed some more. She led him in and shoved him gently onto a kitchen chair and sat in his lap. "Have a hard day?"

"You playing with me?"

"I missed you—couldn't stay away. Felt guilty not to have left you dinner. Look what I made? Beans and escarole, and there's fresh bread."

"What I need and want is you. You're my sustenance."

"What's on your mind?

"*Cara mia,* I wish I had the energy for the thoughts running through my mind. *Amore mio,* today was bad. I can't even—"

Her demeanor changed and she became serious. He knew her so well, and smiled, knowing she was thinking, *If he doesn't want to make love, there's something terribly wrong.*

"What happened?"

He picked her up, scrunching up his face in pain, and deposited her on the other vacant kitchen chair.

"*Tesoro,* you're hurting—what is it?" she said.

He took off his pea coat, the wadding, shirt, and more cloth soaked red. Her eyes became little round moons of worry.

"Look at the wound. You'll do a better job than Piero."

"Giacomo! *Dio mio!* Why did Piero bandage you? Sew you? It could be infected. How long ago? Why didn't you come straight home to me?"

"Thought you were still away."

A tiny "Oh" slipped from her pretty mouth, and her guilt showed in a shake of her head, agreeing he was right, already moving toward the kettle to fill and boil water.

"Who did this to you?" She reached underneath the sink for a small dark-green satchel, her medical kit.

"Some goon attacked me. Must have been drunk. Ended up badly."

She made him strip to the waist and administered to the wound. He already felt better with the mere feel of her touch on his skin. First she cleansed it, washing it with a clean dishrag soaked in boiling water and soapsuds, uncaring of the heat on her hands.

"Why did he assault you?"

"Don't know. Hatred maybe."

Then she rinsed it with rubbing alcohol and he flinched. She blew on it to dry it and then poured in peroxide. When it foamed, she pursed her lips. "This could go to gangrene." She doused her sewing scissors in alcohol and began to snip the dark thread. "You must see Dr. Amanti tomorrow, first thing."

"Ouch!" Giacomo wailed. He exhaled and said, "What should I do? Go across the street, bang on his door, and say I was stabbed? A bit unbelievable, no?"

"You could say I had a knife in my hand and turned around abruptly and accidentally—"

"*Amore*, that excuse might work if I'd been stabbed in the front, but not in the back."

"Of course. But it doesn't matter what he thinks as long as you're cared for properly." She threaded the white cotton into the needle and began to sew. She tended the wound using the homemade offerings the first-aid kit possessed. "This kit's not worth a tinker's damn. If this heals, you won't be picking up anything heavy for a spell. Tell me what happened. The truth." She laid gauze over the cut and used adhesive tape to make a square patch.

"Not a bad bandage," she said of her handiwork.

❦

THE NEXT NIGHT AT THE same speakeasy, a most sober Giacomo said in a hushed tone to Piero, "Can't stay late. Angelica wants to redress the wound."

"She's back?"

Giacomo nodded. "When I got home, she rebandaged me. Thank God she was there. Said it looked red, probably infected. I've been thinking . . ."

"Knife probably wasn't clean, for sure. You should see a doctor."

"Not about that."

"About what?"

"His kids."

"Whose?"

"O'Malley's kids—and what about his wife—maybe I can send his widow some money."

Piero signaled Danny for a refill. "Good thought," he said, and added, sotto voce, "don't you think that'll cast the briefest shadow of guilt on you? Leave it. Heard his wife took the kiddies and made off with someone who could rub two coins together in his pocket and finally buy milk, not booze."

Giacomo thought back to the fight last evening. His stomach soured. How could he not have defended himself? It was a physical attack on his person with his back turned. He reached across and touched his sore shoulder.

Giacomo wondered how he'd ever repay Piero for telling him to leave and meet him last night. Would he always feel indebted? Piero had reported the "accident" to the police, something that happened all the time on the docks. No shiv, no signs of a brawl—just one drunk laborer who'd looked for trouble and found Death for company.

But Piero had also told Giacomo that some of the policemen on duty last evening had known O'Malley, had said he wasn't a bad sort, felt sorry even that he met an untimely death, him being so young and all.

"How dangerous is this situation?" Giacomo took a pull of his drink.

"Not at all if you play it smart and keep away from his family. Remorse at this point, *amico mio*, can only land you in prison. You never know how this story can get twisted. I'll bet it wouldn't be in your favor. Keep your nose out of it. Now scram."

⌐≺✦≻¬

WHEN GIACOMO GOT HOME, HE heard a conversation going on in the upstairs kitchen, and it wasn't a child's voice speaking with Angelica; it was a man's.

Giacomo entered the kitchen surprised to see Dr. Amanti sitting at his kitchen table sipping espresso.

"*Buona sera*," he said.

"Ah, Dr. Amanti came by to see if Pina was all right after a fall—she slipped out of my arms like a slippery eel."

"Is she all right?" Giacomo asked with a scowl of concern on his face.

"Fit as a fiddle," the doctor said.

"*Dottore*, while you're here, would you mind looking at Giacomo's shoulder? I whirled around with a sharp knife in my hand and stabbed him yesterday. I patched him up, but the knife was dirty, as I'd been cleaning a rabbit."

"*Ma sicuro*," Dr. Amanti said, standing up. "Take your shirt off."

Giacomo closed his eyes and shook his head. "It's nothing, really," he said, but stopped objecting when Angelica raised her eyebrows. He started unbuttoning his shirt.

The doctor complimented Angelica on her stitching. After he had cleaned the wound and dressed it, Giacomo, shamefaced, said, "Please let me pay you."

"*Neanche per sogno*." Don't even dream about it. "Instead, why not come and replace that kitchen cabinet my wife is always complaining about. Sunday?"

"I'll come after six o'clock Mass. Is that too early?"

"Not at all. We're early risers." He stood, washed and dried his hands at the sink, and put on his jacket.

"It may take a month of Sundays," Giacomo said.

"Fine. You sit, Giacomo. Angelica is going to see me to the door."

"You're not leaving without my biscotti for the children," she said, handing over a paper-wrapped package tied with twine.

To Giacomo he said, "*A domenica.*"

Giacomo shook his hand.

When Angelica returned, he said, "What's going to happen when the good doctor runs out of invented chores for me to fix?"

"He never will. And if he does, he'll send you to a friend."

CHAPTER 3

Marcella

MY BROTHER JACK USED TO find scrap metal and sell it to traders around our area—one was located on Bay Eighth Street at the entrance to the parkway for Long Island. He became a collector and brought his found goods home. He searched refuse and thrown-away articles in trash bins, alleyways, and vacant lots. These he sold or pawned off to one of the neighborhood junk brokers, who in turn sold the merchandise, always by weight, to others. The salvaged material that Jack mostly dealt in was almost anything metal: aluminum, brass, ferrous metal, steel, and other sundry items. He never picked rags or bones, though there were some that did in the poorer sections. Although his clothes came home unclean, they were never marred by grease or blood.

On Saturday mornings, Jack also delivered newspapers, and afternoons he worked delivering groceries on a beat-up old bike from an Italian *salumeria,* a delicatessen, that sold everything, including the replacement parts for Mamma's coffee pot.

Jack was saving to buy his own Schwinn bicycle with a price tag of seven dollars. He could have bought a used one already, but he was going for the bright new-and-shiny black one. Jack was always going on about how he was going to fit out the handlebars with an extra bar in front and a big basket on the back for carting and toting parcels.

At Gennaro's Italian delicatessen, where Jack worked and where we shopped sometimes, his favorite thing was filching a black olive here and there. The owner's daughter was a pretty little girl named Sofia, fifteen, a year older than Jack, who had a mad crush on him. The truth was that snobby, squat Sofia wasn't his type. Jack did all he could do to discourage her, and when he succeeded he found out that he got sacked—kicked in the can by Mr. Gennaro and he hadn't even laid a finger on the prissy miss, but that's precisely what she'd wanted poor Jack to do.

He was home early, so I asked him what had happened. He explained and I felt terrible for him, but for some reason I couldn't contain my laughter, thinking of chubby Sofia puckering up for Jack. After my laughing seizure, I asked him how he was going to save for the bike now.

"Simple," he said, his cockiness bolstering every word, "I went straight into Carmine's and asked if he needed an errand boy, an apprentice, or anything. I already got a new job from the meat man. The only bad part about that is I'm going to have to wear a sissy white apron that'll get all bloodied."

"Small price to pay, if you get your dream bike."

"Dream, huh? Here's what I'm dreaming." He undid the button of his back pocket and took out a billfold to show me a folded page from the Sears Roebuck catalog with a picture of a 1929 Elgin Cardinal motorbike. Price: $30.95. He looked at me, his eyes gleaming. "Can you image how fast that model can go? Why, that beauty can fly."

"A fortune! You'll never be able to hoard that much, but your enthusiasm isn't lost on me. It'll take forever to save for—when do you start at Carmine's?"

"Next week. How come?"

"Thought you could save me a trip and bring home five pounds of sausage, two sweet, three hot—"

"Sorry, sweet sister, not till next week."

"Oh. I'll ask Mamma to make something else. Maybe we can wait until next week. That way you can make sure he puts in enough fennel seeds."

"And also gives us some soup bones. Sure thing, but let me tell Mamma about getting sacked and the new job."

We left it at that.

LATER THAT SAME DAY, I had a bit of a pinchy throat, not quite a sore throat, but I decided to walk to the avenue intending to buy a box of Smith Brothers black cough drops. The minute I stepped outside I thought of ways to describe what I was seeing: patches of fog, banks of fog, pockets of fog. It was so thick I could slice through it with a dull knife. My throat was scratchy, as if I'd swallowed some straw, but I didn't want Mamma to know for fear she'd cancel the party. I took my time going to the drugstore and sat at the counter and ordered a chocolate egg cream, and then I bought the black cough drops. I couldn't afford to be sick on my birthday. The advertisement on the box was: "The cheapest health insurance in the world." Did I believe it? Who cared? I had to trust in something; I couldn't do anything else but suck on those lousy cough drops one after the other. I had the feeling that by the time I got home I'd have polished off half the package. Lucky for me, I'd purchased a tin of Sucrets lozenges as well. I'd start on those later.

I was expected to sing at my party, and was on my way home to gargle with warm water and salt, when I caught a mirror image of myself in a storefront window. I tugged at my long, dark hair bunched up with a pink bow at the nape of my neck. What was I thinking? I needed a new look— in fact, a new-fangled me suddenly became vital to my future tomorrow. I entered the beauty salon. Upon opening the door, a tiny bell rang. Several heads turned my way. I greeted the lady in an apron close to me and asked for a bob. "Are you sure?" the blond hairdresser with short hair asked. "You've got such thick, wavy hair. Why do you want to cut it?"

"I'll be graduating in June and want a more sophisticated style," I said, thinking that sounded reasonable.

"You're so young."

"I skipped a grade."

"But June is six months away. Will your parents approve?"

I nodded, crossing my fingers behind my back, as she ushered me to the wash station. I had never had my hair washed by a professional. I looked over to the wall with a price list. I'll just make it, I thought, with the change from Mamma's shopping, but I didn't know if I had to tip or not, or how much. I'd be finding out soon enough. She placed a towel around my shoulders and then put me in a cotton smock. She shampooed and rinsed my hair twice and led me to another chair where I sat while she showed me some pictures. I picked out a style I thought would suit me. When she began to snip, I thought I'd cry seeing my long tresses cascading to the floor. Oh, boy, I thought, I've really done it now.

When I got home from my wild spree at the hairdresser's, I wanted to remember forever the sequence of the dreadful happenings that occurred before my sixteenth birthday—I guess I have some impulsive traits I never knew I possessed. I wrote the following down in my history notebook because I didn't have one of those fancy five-year diaries—they cost a dollar! Of course, I wished for one with all my might, but knowing my family didn't waste money on what they thought were frivolous items, all I could do was dream about something like that—real-life drama, that's all my parents thought about—in fact, lived!

Although I still hoped that maybe someone would purchase a diary for my birthday, I resolved that in the future, when I desired something, anything at all, I'd be smart enough, thrifty enough, clever enough, ruthless enough to earn it on my own or get it by whatever means it took. What a revelation! Who knew this about me? Certainly not me.

I wrote in the notebook that on the evening before my sixteenth birthday, January 25, 1929, Gianni and I had been sitting in Mamma's upstairs kitchen, the hour of day when the sunlight streamed through the window above the sink and the other window by the bread drawer. Papa always had a loaf of Italian bread in the drawer, and I was always the mouse who stole a hunk in the middle of the night, buttering and swabbing it with one of Mamma's tasty homemade jams—fig, my favorite—but anything she made was nectar for the gods. I'd read that phrase in a novel recently, and it sounded heavenly, so I added it to my growing vocabulary.

We had been enjoying a delicious afternoon cup of espresso— Mamma laced it with anisette—what's not to like? But Gianni had preferred his with a lemon peel. I watched him rub the lip of the tiny cup and then set the lemon peel on the dish. He'd always pour in a heaping teaspoon of sugar, though. He loved sweets. I often thought this was somehow a great need, as he lacked the true affection of his mother. How lucky I was to have two parents who adored me. Maybe adored was a little strong, but they cared for me and loved me and tried to give me all the things in life that would make me not only happy, but a better person facing our world, our society. After these soapbox thoughts, I stepped back into the reality of the fading afternoon.

Sitting in the upstairs kitchen were Mamma and my older sister, Pina. Mamma had set out a plate of cannoli, freshly stuffed with her magnificent ricotta filling. She always used powdered sugar, never granulated, and she always shaved in fat curls of dark chocolate, which she knew Gianni and everyone else in the family loved, except her—she was a milk chocolate lover, although she never admitted it to anyone but me. Mamma was afraid that if she did, she'd be inundated with it for every birthday.

Mamma had made some anise biscotti and biscotti with almonds, a little harder and meant to be dunked into white wine or Vin Santo— these were delicious. She was a fantastic baker as well as a cook, and this must have come naturally to her from her mother, but I hated the kitchen! Such servitude and then to watch as everything you slaved over for hours was all gobbled up—the entire meal in twenty minutes—the very same meal you'd prepared with love, special ingredients from the old country, and caretaking and stirring it for hours! Could I ever be a good Italian-American wife here in the wilds of Brooklyn, New York?

During the course of our conversation on that lovely afternoon coffee, Gianni somehow let it slip that I'm a little on the wild side.

Mamma sipped her coffee and put down the cup. "How do you mean?"

I must have blanched white, my usual rosy complexion going specter pale.

He said, without blinking an eyelash, "Marcella let me kiss her last time I delivered the gallon of olive oil you ordered."

Beast! Savage! Betrayer! Without even thinking, I swiped the cannoli off of Mamma's good Florentine Ginori cake plate, got up, and broke the dish over Gianni's head.

Mamma screamed.

Gianni said, "Ouch," and rubbed his head, now dusted with powdered sugar.

Pina shouted, "Marcella, are you out of your mind?"

I glared first at her—then at Gianni. Without another word, I stormed out of the room, calling back over my shoulder to the kiss-and-tell guy, "Don't you dare come to my party, Gianni; you are uninvited."

❧

LATER THAT NIGHT AFTER DINNER, Papa asked me if I'd consider relenting. After all, it was only a little kiss, and he'd already seen me holding hands with Gianni and never thought much about it. I knew he wanted Gianni to attend my birthday party.

"Relent? Papa! I'm your daughter. I should have whopped him with a horsewhip."

He smirked, so I continued having the stage, front and center. I made a fist and shook my arm. "I should've knocked him to abbreviation with this African soup bone," a direct quote from my Papa, who laughed despite himself, his mirth bubbly as champagne. "You should agree with me, not side with Mamma this time."

He nodded. "*Va bene*. But it's an entirely different matter to cancel his relatives."

So I knew I was doomed to have to face *i suoi parenti*. Of course, I should have known that Mamma and Papa would insist on inviting the traitor's brother, Franco, and sister-in-law, Grazia, who were like parents to Gianni. And of course Mamma's dear friend, the revealing bigmouth's quasi-grandmother, *la signora* di Maggio, Zia Grazia's mother. Worst part of that invitation? I was expected to behave civilly to all of them. Did Papa think I'd actually break more of Mamma's good dishes over the guests' heads? I just hoped I wouldn't get cornered like a rat by the old lady who adored precious Gianni.

⌒◈⌒

THE DAY OF MY BIRTHDAY Mamma let me take off from school, and I helped her with all of the last-minute things we hadn't attended to, and then ran to the store for her. I was petrified when I walked into the house in my new hairdo, but it seemed everybody was busy at something and nobody noticed as I ran upstairs and grabbed my dress off Mamma's bed and went up to my attic room. I threw off my coat and set to work, taking up the hem of my dress, which was a bit tricky. Then I went to the huge bathroom where we had the ironing board and iron set up and wet a handkerchief and steamed the whole new hemline. Mamma was going to have kittens. But what could she do to me in front of a thousand guests, except to say the shorter hem showed off my fine-looking calves? I prayed that's how it'd go.

Next I threw half a bottle of bubble bath under the tub faucet and waited till the water was boiling hot and then adjusted it with the cold tap. Lounging in the upstairs cast-iron bathtub covered in white porcelain with claw feet pedestals made me feel as if I were a lovely lady from some Gothic or nineteenth-century novel. I loved to soak in the tub with the lion's claws—along with the bubbles, I used some of Pina's bath salts she had in the closet. Val would probably want to strangle me for using most of her bubble bath, but at this moment in a tubful of suds, blowing bubbles off the top like a kid, I wasn't a bit worried. It was worth the risk.

I daydreamed of meeting a song publisher on Tin Pan Alley who'd want to write a special song just for me. Then my thoughts hopped over to the real world of my home, where I knew I'd done my best to help Mamma with all the cleaning and cooking preparations. Now that my work was done, I looked forward to the party this evening. My newly hemmed dress was laid out, shoes and silk stockings at the ready. I told Mamma I wanted something made of a light material because I intended to dance my head off. The dress was navy blue with a huge white collar— she wanted me sophisticated but still didn't want a FOR SALE sign on me! But with my new haircut and shortened dress—watch out, world, here comes Marcella *bella*, as Papa calls me.

Music from the radio drifted down the hallway from the living room to me in the tub above. My sister Valentina had tuned in to a wonderful song, and since she knew I loved it, rotated the dial all the way round as loud as it would go so I could hear it. I began to sing along with "The Very Thought of You" when I realized it wasn't Ray Noble but Bing Crosby singing the song. I liked his voice a lot. Of course I stopped short midsong, thinking of Gianni. I would need to get over him and start some new romantic adventure—after all, as Papa would say, I'm sixteen now.

My parents had invited so many people, I was sure I wouldn't be missing Gianni. What's more, I promised myself if at any moment I dared to think of that scoundrel, I'd pinch myself. Hard. The way Mamma does in the soft part of your underarm so you know you've been tweaked. He wasn't going to be the only boy in my life. Why, they'd be coming in hordes, droves of them down the path to bang on my door.

Valentina knocked on the door, just as I'd envisioned some dashing lothario ringing our front doorbell, and Papa with a baseball bat behind the door. "Are you ever coming out? You're going to shrivel up in that tub. It's late and you need to get dressed. Come on out and tie my sash. You always do it perfectly."

My answer to her through the closed door were the wonderful lyrics to that song, sung louder, but then I realized she was right, and I'd want to fuss with my hair. I got out of the tub dripping wet and dried off with two towels and threw on a terrycloth robe, cinched it at the waist, and washed out two pair of silk stockings with Val's Palmolive soap, saving my Ivory. Then I rinsed them in cold water and hung them on the towel rack over the tub.

I came out to dress and Val squinted to see if it was really me. She shook her head. "Oh, boy. I can see tomorrow's headlines: *Mother beheads daughter, holding up her trophy by short hair!*"

"You like it, right?" I puffed up my hair a bit on the side.

"Love it, but I'll miss you."

⋙✣⋘

JACK CAME HOME FROM SCHOOL, late as usual. By the time he came in, everyone was dressed and he looked like a ragamuffin. I figured he'd gotten into a baseball game, but it was so cold out, how could he? Instead he had been dawdling with his friends and was now enthusiastically telling me he'd been rummaging around in a neighbor's waste and was in possession of some strange objects—a diary—now wasn't that odd, as I'd just been thinking I'd never get one? I couldn't wait to look inside and see if there were some empty pages for me to scribble my wild thoughts and possibly even get to read someone's personal inner musings. I smiled from here to Kansas as he handed me the diary, which he probably thought was a great bore. Besides, he wasn't the voracious reader and writer I was.

"Happy birthday, Sis," he said and took a 78 RPM record from inside the back of his shirt and placed it into my hands.

I shouted, "Lucky for me you didn't break it! Both gifts better than store-bought." I put the record down on the catch-all bench and hugged the urchin for the sweet gesture. He possessed the most adorable and winning smile. Dimples any girl would pray on her knees for, never mind a head of luscious, thick brown waves. No wonder every kid on the block wanted to be friends with my brother. He was born on All Saint's Day, a year after Valentina. My parents had named him Giacomino Santino, but everyone called him Jack if they wanted his attention.

He also had toted in someone's old, hardly used cast-iron black skillet—why would someone throw that away? He flashed and fanned himself with three Action Comics, comic books of the superhero Superman. These, I could tell, Jack was thrilled to have found and was in no way going to part with, unless of course he found a sucker deal where he would have the advantage of a trade.

He was so excited by his found treasures and put on such a contrite face as he handed the fry pan to Mamma that I knew she wouldn't even scold him. Mamma asked, "You didn't steal this, did you?"

"Mamma, I just told Marcella I found it in someone's trash."

"My son! A garbage picker! Like the bums on the Bowery!"

He kissed her cheek, never answered, and dashed downstairs to his bedroom where I knew he'd devour those comics. I called after him, "Jack, take a bath and get dressed. Party's in an hour."

He yelled back, "By the way, who scalped you?"

It was then that my mother actually looked at me and had a conniption fit. I thought she was going to pass out. "What on earth have you done to yourself?"

"Got a haircut." I twirled around and showed her the back. "Great, isn't it?"

"*Mio Dio*! Wait till your father sees you cut off all your magnificent curls. What were you thinking? Your birthday party!"

I thought she'd start crying. "Mamma, please! They'll grow back. It's just a phase—I needed a perk after that unscrupulous person deceived me."

"Oh, *figlia mia*, how you do go on. You'll never be an actress. And you'll never sing on a stage—I guarantee you will only over my dead body." She slapped my cheek, and with that she turned on her heel and walked back into the kitchen.

It didn't even sting, so I knew she liked it. All she said was, "March. *Vai.*"

I sprinted upstairs with my loot. I placed the record near the Victrola, dusted off and wrapped the diary in a washcloth, and stashed it under my mattress to have a good look at it later. I wouldn't want Valentina finding it before me. I washed my hands and face and pinched my cheeks, then I heard Mamma banging pots so I scooted down to the kitchen.

"Need any help?" I took an apron down from the hook behind the door. Mamma said no, but if she needed help with anything else, she'd let me know. I watched her scrub the pan. I tied the apron around my waist and dried the pan.

"Not good enough. The Lord only knows what it's been used for."

She lit the gas to high. I handed her the pot and watched as the redolent flame cleaned, scorched, and heat-sterilized it. Mamma should have been a doctor. I was proud of her midwifery skills—something I knew I'd never succeed in becoming. And she was handy with a knife; she could actually dice an onion in her hand.

She finished sterilizing the pan and then washed it in sudsy hot water. She'd been quiet for a long time, and then she said to me, "Skills like singing or trying to act for Hollywood won't help you keep a family."

"What if I succeed? Couldn't I do both?" I picked up the pan to dry it.

She wiped her hands on another dish towel and sat at the table. "Most of us can hear only one whistle at a time."

"Meaning I can't do two things? You did. You're a midwife and a wife and mother." I turned to face her.

"Not at the expense of my family. Performing will eat up too much of you—time, energy. You'll be overwrought with a desire to do your best. Your family will suffer. Children need a mother in the house, not someone running off to a stage set in some other city. You're young yet. Please don't rush headlong into something. Give yourself the gift to grow and stretch into womanhood. Remember the old adage, Rome wasn't built in a day." She brushed away a tear.

I put the pot down and sat next to Mamma, took both her hands in mine, and kissed the palms.

CHAPTER 4

Giacomo

THE LIVING ROOM FURNITURE WAS pushed back along the walls to make room for dancing. Angelica had prepared a long table with a dozen different appetizers and what Giacomo called *spizzichi e bocconi*—nibbles and bites that could be eaten with the fingers or speared with toothpicks. She had set piles of napkins on every table. She uncovered the sofa and chairs, and now the room was alive with the color of green-and-gold brocade upholstery, festooned with curling, swirling crepe paper in colors of gold and green and blue that crisscrossed the ceiling in a bright array. Balloons appended from twisted crepe paper at various junctures. Sprigs of holly encircled red and green candles on all the small end tables. In the middle of the green onyx coffee table sat a dazzling arrangement of red roses. Giacomo looked at the card, extravagant to say the least, and saw it was from Gianni. He smiled and then glanced around the room. He wouldn't permit white flowers, white candles, or white anything anywhere. Ever since his time in the Italian Navy in China, he always considered white the color of mourning. He had worn white when he arrived in Sicily from China.

⟨✿⟩

GIACOMO HAD ASKED HIS MUSICIAN friends to come and play and was thankful he wouldn't have to pay them. The party was an enormous stretch for Giacomo's lean wallet. He'd taken on two night jobs to cover some of the expense and would look for some extra jobs next week. The band was already warming up. Some toasted Marcella and the family, and others abstained until their gig was up. Giacomo had offered to pay the men, but they wouldn't hear of it and instead had brought along a wife, a friend, or a child to join the festivities.

When Marcella walked into the room, Giacomo did a double take. Where was his little girl in a pinafore dress with her long hair tied back in a bow? Her rosy cheeks and winning smile were no longer those of a child, but of a girl on the verge of womanhood. He looked her up and down, noticed the shapely legs in the shortened dress, and was about to say something when Angelica appeared at his side and leaned toward him. He bent down to hear her whisper, "*Per favore, amore mio*, don't make a fuss. You know your daughter, and she'll make a ruckus or create a scene worthy of one of those films she's so fond of."

Giacomo let out a sigh, straightened, and shook his head. Then he faced Angelica. "*Bella da vero*. She's really beautiful. Why couldn't Gianni have stuck around to keep her on the straight and narrow? God knows what alley cat she'll bring home to us next before she settles down."

As they walked downstairs to the front door to greet the guests, Angelica said, "Our darling girl is too smart for her own britches, and too much like my sister Rina, that other vixen."

"And where is Marcella's friend Lucille?" Giacomo asked as he hung up one of the guest's coat and hat.

"All the guests have arrived." Angelica folded her arms.

"What do you mean?"

"I mean your daughter and her long tongue had words with her friend, and I couldn't convince her she'd be sorry later or to change her mind. 'Off the list' is what she said to me." Angelica let out a long breath, unfolded her arms, and put on a smile to greet the guests.

Giacomo wondered what was amiss, but didn't have time to dwell on it. All the guests went to the upper living room and were milling about. Giacomo had brought up from the basement cases of homemade wine and filled everyone's glass, whispering, "Prohibition be damned. Try a little of my grape juice." When everyone had a full glass, they all raised them.

Giacomo pointed toward Marcella with his goblet, saying, "*Cento di questi giorni!*" and everyone in the crowd shouted back, "A hundred years!"

Giacomo noted that Marcella beamed but barely sipped, recalling the episode of three years back when she'd explored the basement with her friend Lucille and found the wine-making equipment along with several corked bottles of his red. After drinking their fill and feeling quite ill, Marcella, seeing double, had dragged Lucille out of the basement to the backyard where Mamma was hanging laundry. He remembered she yelled as loud as she could, saying, "Mamma, Papa! Come quick. I've killed Lucille!" before fainting. Both girls ended up in the hospital having their stomachs pumped. Marcella abstained from wine ever after, although she still did like the taste of a little anisette in her espresso.

"Music, maestro," Giacomo said, coming back to the present. Then the dancing began. At one point, Marcella stopped for a minute. Giacomo sat on the sofa and patted a spot next to him. His daughter sat, and he asked why Lucille was so late.

Marcella went from rosy cheeked to bright red. "Not coming. Some friend she turned out to be. But it's my fault—I stupidly told her about Gianni. You know what she said?" Not waiting for an answer, she plowed right on. "If a baseball player drops his seasoned glove on the field, another player might just pick it up and claim it. She's not coming to the party, and I wouldn't be surprised if she has invited him to take her to the movies."

Giacomo patted his daughter's leg. "You'll make it up with her, I'm sure."

"Will not. Ever. And Gianni, too."

"You'll see that she doesn't hold a candle to you—Gianni will be back in your life—he's got eyes for only you. I know that boy's heart," he said and tapped his own.

"Papa, you think you can read people. We both mislaid trust in that little viper, Lucille. She comes across as a sweet patootie, but she's not. And as for Mr. Tell-All, Gianni Simoni. *Basta.* Enough. Now let me enjoy the rest of this snazzy shindig you and Mamma are hosting. I don't need either of those two. Dance with me," she said and pulled him to his feet.

After several dances, Marcella joined the band and sang a repertoire of all the latest songs. Everything so far was lovely. When Marcella sang the last lines of "Ain't Misbehavin'," Jack came in to announce dinner was being served downstairs, and the group started filing out by twos and threes.

⌒ϾͷϿ⌒

JACK AND GIACOMO HAD SET up the dining room table, along with the upstairs and downstairs kitchen tables and several borrowed long picnic tables. They'd put them together end to end and then made an "L" shape from the foyer to the windows of the downstairs parlor. The table was elegantly set with several of Mamma's hand-embroidered linen tablecloths and lace runners. On top of these were candleholders of different varieties—silver and cut crystal, each one adorned with a red candle and a circlet of pine. Here and there were small poinsettia plants, and in between these were tiny salt dishes with itty-bitty silver spoons, red pepper flakes in small ceramic blue-and-white bowls. Wine decanters and raffia-covered bottles were set near water pitchers.

Giacomo said to all three daughters standing near him, "You've made us proud, *care ragazze.*" Marcella kissed her father and said, "*Grazie mille.*"

Giacomo was careful to seat Franco, Gianni's older brother, and his wife in a place of honor and not too close to the wine, as Franco had a reputation for liking alcohol more than he cared for his sweet wife. Giacomo was relieved to see that Gianni didn't follow in his brother's footsteps in this, although Franco had to be admired for his business head. Jack and Giacomo filled the glasses as people began taking their seats. Naturally, Giacomo asked the priest, Monsignor Baggio, to sit at one of the table heads and to say a prayer of grace, hoping it wouldn't turn into a homily.

Giacomo recognized two of the pretty neighborhood girls in Marcella's class. He'd seen both girls, tall for their age, playing basketball with Marcella, who considered herself a star but was lackluster in some of her moves. She was better at swimming and baseball, but she loved basketball, so Giacomo and even Jack had tried coaching her. What she really was good at, he thought, was singing and writing for her school newspaper, but no daughter of his was going to sing for a living or become a journalist. For a few moments he tuned out of the gathering and thought how much happier Marcella had been since she started Bay Ridge High School. He thought back to her elementary school days at Visitation Academy with the cloistered nuns that were so strict. At least she had learned a little French—and a great deal of etiquette and neat cursive handwriting.

Franco served himself another hefty glass of wine, spilling some on the immaculate tablecloth. He tilted the glass toward Giacomo. "*Cin-cin.*"

Giacomo looked over at Angelica, whose eyebrows reached her hairline, and she shook her head slightly. Giacomo reached for the bottle and put it out of harm's way and Franco's long reach. Many of their acquaintances were exchanging comments and congratulations for the wonderful organization of the party.

"The party girl herself looked captivating in her new bob and shorter hemline," said a neighbor, Mr. Zaidan, receiving a sharp elbow to the ribs from his wife, who had graciously brought a platter of *kibbeh* to be served as antipasto before the dinner. These were shaped like tiny torpedoes, fried and served with mint that Angelica had given to her. The herb always blossomed in her garden, and she brought plants indoors or dried it for the winter. The plump lady, dressed in black from neck to toe including black pearls, had also brought one of Marcella's favorites: Lebanese *fatayar,* spinach cakes made with onion, lemon, cumin, and pine nuts. Marcella wasn't a great cook like Angelica or interested in cooking like her sisters, but she learned to make these from scratch with their neighbor because she loved them. Giacomo knew his daughter had a knack for learning anything she wanted in the kitchen. All she had to do was watch once, and she had it to perfection.

The dinner proceeded with baked lasagna, pasta with wild mushrooms, grilled lamb chops, pork sausage, little quails stuffed with a combination of white and wild rice, and *melanzana alla parmigiana,* baked eggplant, another of Marcella's favorites—this one prepared by her two days earlier. When Angelica started to dish out the portions, Giacomo heard Angelica say to Marcella, "For some reason this always tastes better a day or two after it rests." A mixed salad abounded with fresh bread, and then after conversation and *digestivi*—digestive dinner drinks—were served, Valentina brought to the table a huge birthday cake with sixteen burning red candles.

Marcella closed her eyes, made a wish—and Giacomo knew it was the same one she made at every Mass—to become a movie star, a singer, or both, and of course, to find true love. Then she blew out the candles to cheers. Angelica handed her a knife, and the way the light caught it, Marcella flinched, and Giacomo wondered if she was thinking back to that scary night with Danny and his gang. The moment passed, and she cut the cake and wished. Giacomo leaned in and said, "Make a couple more—can't hurt."

After homemade *limoncello* and anisette had been served and a second cup of espresso had been offered, Giacomo realized Franco had drunk too much. Franco faltered in his steps getting up from the table and tried to steady himself as Giacomo reached over to assist him, just seconds late, and the man went down face-first into the cake. Angelica screeched and everyone gasped.

Marcella rescued the situation. Giacomo couldn't have been prouder of the quick-thinking girl as she said to the company, "The cake was way too filling and fattening for our slim hips, ladies, and besides, Mamma's made mouth-watering nut cookies. And Papa brought home confetti. Let's have these upstairs and enjoy more music."

Giacomo helped Franco up and escorted him to the downstairs powder room to clean up. He nudged his head to Grazia, meaning *take your mother upstairs; I'll take care of him.*

That's when Giacomo saw Marcella cornered by the fireplace by Grazia's mother, who had engaged her in serious conversation that he was sure wasn't about Franco's drinking. He knew the old lady was lecturing Marcella about the incident with Gianni. Well, maybe it will bring the girl around, but he doubted it because he knew she couldn't be persuaded easily. He murmured to himself, *testa dura*—hard head.

CHAPTER 5

Marcella

EVERYONE HAD GONE TO BED except Pina, who had volunteered to help do the rest of the cleaning. Pina and Val had done the majority of the work already, and now it was late. I didn't want to face the rest of the clean-up in the morning, and I was still way too energetic after the last guest departed. I changed out of my pretty dress and threw on a pair of comfortable beige crepe-de-chine wide-leg pants and a boatneck sweater and came into the kitchen to find Pina at the sink washing serving dishes. "You just got that outfit for your birthday and you're wearing it to wash dishes?" Not waiting for an answer, Pina added, "Where's Valentina? How come she's not helping?"

I put an apron over my head and tied the strings in back. "She threw up. I think she drank too much when no one was looking. I told her to go to bed and we'd finish. Mamma wanted to help, but she was exhausted, so I nodded to Papa to whisk her off to bed, too."

"The slacks look great. You look like a movie star, but you can get that idea out of your pretty bobbed head."

"Thanks for the beautiful wool felt cloche. The ribbon is perfect. You must have paid dearly."

"I had help from Mamma. You're just dying to know how much I paid for it."

"Well?" I picked up the dish towel and started drying.

"Mamma saw it in a catalog from Bedell Co. and ordered it with postage included—just under three dollars."

"I'm going to wear it to church." I set the dried platter aside.

"Sorry about your cake." Pina rinsed a stack of soapy silverware and placed it in the wooden drain board.

"I could have died," I said in an exaggerated tone. "Zio Franco ruined it! I didn't even get one tiny morsel to taste."

"You said it was too fattening anyway." Pina finished washing the last dish. "Here, put this in the cupboard."

"I only said that so Zia Grazia wouldn't keel over from embarrassment. He was three sheets to the wind. Papa had to clean him up and lend him some clothes. How does Zia Grazia put up with him? All that work. Poor Mamma. Then, on top of everything, Signora di Maggio grabbed me aside and lectured me about all the attributes Gianni has—her 'caro ragazzo.' Well, her dear boy shouldn't have snitched and said I kissed him."

"But you did, didn't you?"

"Whose side are you on, anyway?"

"Where was Lucille? I heard you talking about her to Papa when you were sitting on the sofa."

"She admitted she was going after Gianni. Do I need a friend like that when I've got a sister like you who really cares for me?"

Wind rattled the window above the sink.

"No." I shivered not from the cold but from the thought of losing Gianni to my best friend. I pictured our kiss and was sorry I hadn't relented—I missed him at the party. "Bet it'll snow tonight." The snow had come early this winter, before the trees had lost all of their leaves, and I hoped tomorrow would bring streets garlanded with snow and ice, looking like fairytale picture book images. "How I adore snow," I said, remembering how only this morning the sighs of the branches somehow softened the gelid air.

"Make up with her—she couldn't get Gianni if she stripped naked on Forty-Second Street."

"Pina!"

"Don't look so shocked. *Credimi.* Believe me." She fluttered her eyelashes. "He only has moon eyes for you. The truth. You need a friend outside of the family. I wished I'd had one."

"And about Gianni?" I dried the boat dish Mamma used to serve sauce.
"What do you mean?"

"I'm confused. How could I be in love with him one minute and then never want to see him again?" I placed a dried platter on the sideboard.

"Maybe it's not love, only what's called 'puppy love.' You like him, but still aren't sure of yourself or where you're going. You've got your whole life ahead of you."

"Not to be able to do what I want—sing."

"I'm not sure you've got the ambition, or the back-stabbing qualities, it takes to claw your way into that kind of business. As much as you crave the limelight, *sorella mia*, you need stability."

"Maybe," I said.

Pina said, "Look at the stove, will you? I forgot a pan." With a vengeance, she took hold of a Brillo pad from a little soap dish that had once been a ceramic ashtray from Hotel Taormina and scrubbed the bottom of a lasagna pan.

"What makes you so worldly? Hold your thought. I'm going to get the rest of the glasses."

I came back with a loaded tray. "Heavier than I thought," I said, placing the tray on the opposite side from the drain board. "I asked you—"

"Not mature enough. If I'd been more experienced, maybe I wouldn't be in the position I'm in now. I'm sleeping over again. Time enough to go home tomorrow. Bruno won't be back for another week, and I thank God for these trips he takes."

"Wait a minute. Don't you like being married?"

"Thought I'd gain independence, but all I did was exchange one kind of tyranny for another. Dry some of these dishes. I'm running out of space."

"You mean domination?" I wiped a lipstick smudge off one of the glasses.

"Papa. Adores. You. But all I felt was drudgery and sometimes like a slave." Pina started washing the glasses.

"Papa made you feel like that?" I whipped the dishtowel around.

"Easy with that weapon. He's never been strict with you, apple of his eye, but I'm five years older."

"So what? You're his firstborn."

"You can't change who you love best. There's no inventing a pattern to say, 'Love me, I'm your first child.' God bless Papa, he tries not to show it, but he always expected me to be Mamma's helper, and I never resented it. Just as he loves you, I adore Mamma."

"No reigning in your heart, I guess. What about Bruno?"

"Marriage without love is brutal—I can't begin to tell you the little things that make my stomach turn." She kept handing me rinsed glasses until the drain board was filled.

"I thought you cared for him and the baby?"

"Elena's my greatest joy. The trouble is he wants another."

"So soon?"

"That's not it. Swear you won't tell."

"I'd never betray you." I raised both arms with open palms, like a priest at Mass.

"I don't want another baby." She took a long breath. "Not with him. He's not always," she hesitated, "kind."

My hand shot to my mouth and slipped to my throat. "My God. He mistreats you?"

"I shouldn't discuss this with you."

"Pina. Consider me this wall." I made an expanding motion with my hand. "Tell it to the wall," I said and made a cross over my heart.

Pina put down the dishrag. "He's rough. Gruff. He paws and manhandles me violently. Even when I beg him to stop. I read this book about lovemaking before we married—it's supposed to be—God forgive me, but I've listened at the door when Papa is with Mamma—it's gentle. They caress. Papa kisses her till she moans. With Bruno, it's brutish. Probably my fault because I don't try." She rinsed her hands, took the dish towel out of my hands, and dried hers.

"Of course, isn't it always the woman's fault for everything? Have you ever talked to him? Outside of the bedroom? Explained how you feel?" I stacked three dishes and carried them to the table.

"Are you crazy?" Pina sat down at the table, and shook out one of Papa's cigarettes from the pack and lit it.

"Since when did you start smoking?"

Pina inhaled and blew the smoke out in ringlets. "Since the bastard started taking out his frustrations on me and beating me."

"Pina! Papa will kill him!"

"Lower your voice, wall. Papa can never know."

"My darling sister's being thrashed by a brute and I can't tell Papa. Then Jack."

Pina gave a soft chortle. "Jack's a lamb, like Mamma—"

"You'd be surprised. He's got strength of character," I said.

"You're like Papa. Maybe I should hire you to do the hit."

"Dear God—you want him dead?"

She didn't answer. I thought a moment and then spat out a name. "Carlo Albano."

"Not really dead, but thanks for reminding me Papa has a Mafioso friend."

"Who doesn't? This is Brooklyn." I became conscious of the fact that Carlo wouldn't get involved. Why would he? He doesn't owe Papa or us a thing.

"Want more names?" I asked with bravado. The question was barely out of my mouth when it hit me; I really didn't know anyone else in this line of work. I wondered if Gianni did.

"Hey, calm down. Too late for a little more coffee?"

I untied my apron and hung it behind the door. "Not if we lace it with Papa's anisette. I never heard you talk like this." I walked to the stove and heated some leftover coffee.

"Make sure you're madly in love before you marry, or like Mamma always says, I'll break both your legs." I thought of Gianni and knew he'd never hurt me, not willingly.

"You're only twenty-one and have a baby. What're you going to do for the rest of your life?" I set out the cups and sugar.

"For one thing, I'm going to talk to that handsome new Irish priest, Father Gallagan. Bet he's been around the block a few times, and with some pretty short-skirted cutie-pies, too."

I almost poured the coffee onto the table. "And here I thought I was wild. You're going to seduce a man of the cloth? What closet have you been hiding in?"

"The upstairs one before I moved in with Bruno." Pina reached for the liquor housed in a milk bottle. "Where does Papa get this stuff?"

"Little Italy. Chinatown. Not sure. Careful, you can get addicted."

"Nah, it's not opium."

"What're you going to do?"

"Haven't decided yet. One thing for sure, I can't tell Mamma, and you swear you won't either."

I crossed my heart with my thumb and brought it to my sealed lips.

"Did you know a few days before the wedding that she gave me some money and said, '*Scappa*,' run. What a fool not to have listened. Then again, I don't possess your courage, wall."

I got up and threw my arms around my sister's lean shoulders. Pina cried and I cried with her. But my tears weren't just for my sister's brutal plight; they were also for me and were in part for the gentle soul Gianni possessed, for my big mistake of losing my temper, and for banishing him from my life. Where did I get off having such a superiority complex?

Mamma had warned me numerous times to keep my haughtiness in check. Her words came back now. "You can't walk over people and hurt them. Many will bow their heads in submission because they don't know how to fight back, but there will come a time when things even out somehow. On that day, one of the sheep will retaliate. The tables will be reversed, and you, precious girl, will feel the crack of the whip over your bent and humbled shoulders."

I saw myself doing what I did then: tossing my long hair back over my shoulders, before I cut it, snapping at my mother with one word—"Never." Mamma shook her head, wiped her hands on her apron. "We shall see."

Mamma had said sheep will retaliate. I wondered if Gianni was a sheep with his brothers in order to keep peace. Will he someday become a gladiator and stand up for himself and what he believes in?

"You've got to do what Mamma always says—lay your cards on the table with Bruno. If you want me present for courage, I'll be there. Name your time and place. Pina, seriously, this can't continue."

"One more cigarette. I'll be up in a minute. Check on Elena for me—she kicks off the covers. I put her in the cradle in my room, but she's getting too big for it."

I kissed her goodnight and went upstairs with a feeling of regret, our brief hour together absconded like a thief. Val was already in dreamland, so I pulled out the diary and started to write. My thoughts gushed so fast with all the events of the party and my discussion with Pina that my pen couldn't keep up with the thoughts. I took my history notebook out of my schoolbag and copied those infamous comings and goings that I'd jotted down to recall forever. I asked myself: Am I really heartless? Impetuous? Angry? Yes, and miserably, I had to admit and own up to my own stupidity—all of these things I could confess to an inanimate object, but never to Val unless I wanted a lecture. I thought about why neither Val nor I had moved into Pina's old room; guess we understood it was her refuge.

CHAPTER 6

Giacomo

GIACOMO MADE THE DECISION TO leave the Navy Yard in January 1910, and he wasn't sorry. He had too many grieving memories and ghosts that had followed him around while he worked there. Another reason for his final determination was that Piero Monfalcone was leaving to go back to Trieste, figuring he'd always be able to rely on the family business and all his acquaintances if the hard times were really coming. He invited Giacomo to go with him. Back to Italy wasn't what Giacomo wanted under the best of circumstances. They parted friends, but more than friends, and once more Piero reminded Giacomo he'd never betray him or reveal what had happened the night O'Malley died. Who did Piero remind him of? Unexpectedly, he thought of Gianni. Yes, Piero's quiet strength was like Gianni's. "I never doubted it—I trust you completely," Giacomo answered.

Giacomo gave his friend a parting gift. He didn't understand the significance of it, but Angelica had sworn it was the best thing Giacomo could give Piero to always remind him of his sworn promise and their friendship. At the end of the workday, as Giacomo walked toward the office, he murmured a confessional prayer: "Forgive me, Father, for I have sinned."

He knocked on the window, and Piero opened the door. Giacomo handed the small package to Piero. It had been the same kind of blustery, ice-fringed day that the other gloomy day in his past had been. He reached his left hand to touch his right shoulder, an ever-present reminder. He wasn't the innocent man he purported himself to be, and without warning a sharp memory pierced his conscience. Besides O'Malley, Giacomo had murdered his friend Enrico's killer in Sicily. His hands were sullied forever, and he'd pay in the afterlife—of this he was certain. Giacomo watched his friend open the package.

Piero looked up stunned. "A *mezuzah*," he said, as if a small miracle had just occurred. "I'm so touched."

Giacomo hunched his shoulders. "My wife's people were from Spain before immigrating to Sicily. She bought it from our salesman friend, Mr. Blitzer, who swore it was from Jerusalem, but I wouldn't be surprised if he made it himself in his own backyard." It was wood, painted sky blue, and had a three-tongued flame and a Star of David beneath in hammered silver. "Anyway, she said it's made the right way." The scroll in the protective case was rolled left to right, so that God's name, *Sha-dai*, faced front.

"But you're not religious."

"I've got a wife who swears her family is Jewish but prays beneath a wall image of the Sacred Heart of Jesus every night. She says He, too, was Jewish. Sometimes I'm afraid I'll burn in Hell just for looking at her, not even touching her. I'm not a religious man, but I learned a lot of spiritual things about Buddha in China, and I've seen much, heard much, but believe, like the Apostle Thomas, in only things I can see and feel. Angelica and my family—that's my religion."

"What'll you do?"

"I couldn't abide working under Sean Connor, the Irishman's best friend; he's going to be the new foreman. He's always suspected foul play in O'Malley's death. Besides, I'd miss seeing your ugly face every day."

Piero embraced Giacomo. "Found a job yet?"

"Construction."

"You know where I'll be, if you ever need a friend."

"Likewise, *fratello mio*."

"Giacomo, one more thing. You can put your mind at ease about the widow O'Malley. I paid her some compensation from the company coffer with the blessings of the higher-ups."

Gicomo nodded and shook Piero's hand.

⸎

YEARS LATER, WHEN GIACOMO WAS doing some odd jobs in Coney Island and looking for something more permanent, he often thought of Piero and his time working as a longshoreman, facilitating the transportation of cargo from ships and doing all the other maintenance jobs he did.

Summer days, mostly on weekends, when he wasn't working, he went fishing with Jack in Sheepshead Bay. Sometimes Gianni went along, never failing to ask about Marcella.

Jack loved to go with his father, and Giacomo said his son brought him good luck, for the days that Jack went along, they always took in a decent haul and were able to bring home a nice catch of fresh fluke or summer flounder. They caught other fish sometimes; it depended on what size boat they went out on and how far out they went.

After dinner one evening, when he had finished eating, Giacomo smacked his lips. "This fish didn't die in vain."

⸎

THE FOLLOWING TUESDAY, GIACOMO HAD driven out to Point Lookout, where his friend Dario Marchese owned a cottage. Dario was going out of town with his family for the last two weeks in August and the first two of September. He gave Giacomo the keys in exchange for caretaking and doing some upkeep work with Jack as his assistant. They'd make several trips, a joint male venture. When Gianni joined them for handyman jobs, he made them do ten minutes of stretching before commencing, which was good for Giacomo's back. It became a family affair only on the weekends, as everyone loved the beach.

Giacomo parked inside the unlocked gate in the alley. Most of the houses were vacant because it was late in the season for summer residents. They'd cross a large expanse of land in back of the house to get to the sea. The sandy lots were littered ghostly white with a million broken clamshells, and Jack would invariably take off his shoes and socks to see if he could stand the torturous walk to the huge rocks where they would fish. Giacomo and Jack fished for an hour or two, and when they tired or were bored from no catch, they'd always snare a few pounds of mussels. Sometimes

Jack would dive in deep for these and yank them from their hairy beards where they clung to the rocks. Giacomo always preferred to snare the submerged ones, thinking they were healthier than the ones that had been only partially under water. Every once in a while Jack would find a starfish, but he'd outgrown the desire to collect and dry them. In summer, on occasion, they'd drive to a different spot along the coast and take a dip in the ocean. If Marcella was with them, Jack would tease his sister doing a dead man's float, which would agitate her until she begged him to stop. In the muddy shoals, Jack and Marcella would dig with their feet, then dive to bring up clam after clam until they filled a net bag full.

On their way back after fishing, sometimes Giacomo jiggled the back door, so he wouldn't have to use the key to gain entrance to the newly painted kitchen, noting he'd have to fix it later on. He would sauté the mussels, and they would feast on the pink, pulpy flesh of the salty, tasty mollusks. Giacomo would bring the clams to Angelica to make with spaghetti.

When Giacomo and Jack were by themselves, the boy always cleaned the kitchen and left it spotless. If they were in no hurry, Jack would read magazines or play solitaire, and Giacomo, like a great papa bear, would occupy one of the beds or sofas for a *pizzolino,* a tiny siesta or nap before the drive home.

In summer he'd bring the whole family, except Pina, who couldn't swim. On a Sunday after early Mass at the end of August, the family stayed for the whole week. It was during the summer church festival season. They'd often stay up late for dinner with friends, usually corn on the cob; fresh garden tomato salad with garlic, freshly dried oregano, and olive oil or with red onion and basil; and some kind of fish with white wine and a splash of olive oil or lemon, capers, parsley, and butter.

After dinner, the men would sit and talk and smoke on a screened-in porch or play cards. The women and children walked over to the ice cream parlor and bought sugar cones, or they'd go to the little Catholic church nearby for the summer bazaar. Angelica always brought a cake to raffle off as a donation.

Once, Marcella won a teddy bear in a raffle, and another time she won an alligator purse, but back at the cottage Valentina had made such a fuss about never winning anything that Marcella said, "Here, if it means that much to you, I'd like you to have it." Giacomo's heart swelled with pride to see Marcella's generosity.

September, when it was too blustery to go out fishing, Giacomo would go to the Fulton Street Market, where all the fisheries were controlled by the mob, but if you minded your business and only bought fish, you'd be pretty safe. His friend Dario also worked near there, and when Giacomo had time, they would natter about this or that and sometimes have a coffee together. Dario always had a thermos, and it seemed it was always spiked with what he called "the hair of the dog." On Saturday mornings when Giacomo wanted to get his shopping done early, he bought the fish and had the vendor pack it in newspaper if he were heading straight home. When Giacomo had to delay going home because of work, he left the fish with Dario, who packed it in a bucket of ice. Giacomo would pick it up later when he finished his job. A slight but wiry guy, Dario had a pushcart and went about pretty much minding his own business but hustling little old ladies for sales. On this particular day a mobster tried to hustle Dario, and Giacomo, seeing the action, came from behind with the bucket of ice to stand next to Dario. The "family man" became intimidated by Giacomo's brute size and walked off. Dario said, "*Grazie, amico.* How long do you want the cottage for next summer?"

Giacomo laughed. Then he said, "How often does that happen?"

"Not very."

"What if he comes back?"

"Nah. Never the same guy. They manufacture these little bastards by the dozens, and besides, I've got a companion." With that, Dario inched out a billy club from behind the pushcart.

"Where the hell did you get that?"

"A cop lost it in the neighborhood. My son found it."

Giacomo smiled and patted him on the back, wondering how dangerous it would be to retaliate instead of paying the "vig," meaning vigorish. Giacomo had to laugh at himself, knowing the Russian word for profit: *vyigrysh. That's what comes from working on the docks.* He had another thought on the way home: The day caressed by hours sifted by—a fleeting dream when all went well. But how many hours would Dario have to work in order to pay the next guy off when he came around for the vig?

NOT TOO LONG AFTER MARCELLA'S birthday party, Giacomo began working a new construction job. He'd been hired as part of a crew for a contractor under the architect Frank Buchanan, who was going to build a new club in midtown Manhattan.

Jack Kriendler and Charlie Berns moved their Club Fronton from 88 Washington Place to 42 West Forty-Ninth Street and called the new place The Puncheon, but it had a multitude of pseudonyms, basically to confound federal tax agents. As soon as the doors opened, the owners received a notification that Rockefeller Center was going to be built on the site. The owners were offered $11,000 from the landowner to vacate, and vacate they did, all the way to 21 West Fifty-Second Street, with their fists and pockets filled to overflowing.

In 1929 the club moved to its current location and changed its name to "Jack and Charlie's 21." For most of the year, Giacomo worked on the construction of Jack and Charlie's 21. Because he was dark and swarthy, he was nicknamed Jocko—for lawn jockey, which were usually black—but the name didn't offend him, and it didn't stick. He chuckled to himself remembering his buddy, Bulldog, from his Navy days. "Jocko" was easier to pronounce than Giacomo, which so many people got wrong anyway.

Prohibition caused club owners to go to great lengths to hide illegal liquor. Jack and Charlie hired the architect to design a complex system of camouflaged doors, invisible chutes, revolving bars, and a secret wine cellar to hide or destroy evidence. Giacomo helped complete the assembling of this system.

Having worked on building the place, Giacomo knew it was a speak-easy, and before it would open in 1930, he received a nice bit of change to keep his mouth shut about the inner workings of the joint.

Although raids by police were ongoing and plentiful during the years of Prohibition, the owners were never seized—nor ever caught—and Giacomo knew why. When the barmen were tipped that a raid was about to begin or if they were alerted to a raid in progress, a dependable and complicated assembly of what Giacomo knew to be pedals and treadles would slant, angling the shelves of the bar in such a way that all the liquor bottles would skate and swish off through a channel-type chute and baptize the rats in the city's sewer system.

The bar also included a secret wine cellar, where one could gain access through a concealed entryway in a brick wall that opened into the subterranean vault next door at No. 19. Therefore the wine cellar wasn't a component of the 21 building at all, but the basement of No. 19. When the authorities interrogated the staff if any liquor was on the premises, they honestly answered, "No!"

Before the doors opened at 21, the wrought iron gate, with the help of a few patrons, was unhinged from the doorway of No. 42 and installed three blocks north at 21 West Fifty-Second Street and 21 was officially opened. The gate undeniably became an intricate element of this New York establishment—just as much as the secret wine cellar and the eventual celebrity clientele.

⸱⟡⸱

WHEN GIACOMO FINISHED WITH THE construction job, he took Angelica by the hand and walked her to their bedroom and shut the door. He proudly handed Angelica his last pay envelope with the robust bonus and a bottle of Chateau Haut-Brion 1923 from Bordeaux to seal his lips forever.

"So much?" she asked with a stunned expression on her face, holding the money in one hand and the wine bottle in the other.

"*Tu ricordi la parola omertà?*"

"They use a code of silence about criminal activity in construction?"

"Depends on what's being constructed. Think of it this way: I'll probably never be questioned, but they know I'd refuse to give evidence to authorities about what and how it was built. You, too, *amore mio.*" He put his finger over his lips. "This is between you and me and goes no further." With this he gently pushed her in the direction of the Sacred Heart statue. "Now you can confess the perfidy for both of us." Although Giacomo knew he'd do it again to pay his bills, remembering how he'd sacrificed to pay off Marcella's party.

After a few minutes, she said, "As if you had to say that," and chucked him on the chin with a fistful of money. He playfully fell over onto the bed, and she sashayed from the bedroom.

She came back from the kitchen empty-handed and hummed for a little while, then retreated her steps. "This means a new washing machine."

"Only if you show me how much you really love me."

"Jocko! Aren't we a little past this?"

"Never."

Angelica sighed. She threw a shawl over the lampshade on the night table and started to remove her clothes.

CHAPTER 7

Marcella

ON FEBRUARY 28, I'D FINISHED homework and dishes early and was about to listen to the radio. My mother, in one of her I-told-you-so moods, accosted me on the stairs and swiped me with the newspaper, which I never managed to get hold of in our household until very late or the next day. There it was, the *Brooklyn Daily Eagle,* folded and thrust at me. I took hold of it, wondering how she got it as my Papa practically devoured it when he came home if dinner wasn't ready, or later after dinner if he hadn't finished chomping it up word by word. It was folded at the article she wanted me to read.

But after dinner on Thursday, which for some reason seemed always to consist of *pasta coi ceci*—pasta with chickpeas—and fried *baccala*, Mamma slapped my arm with the folded paper and said, "You see, girl of so many pipe dreams, where singing and dancing on the stage leads? To misery, poverty, and death." She told me to read it to see what became of a celebrity cancan dancer in Paris. I envisioned dancing girls on a stage, doing cartwheels for Toulouse-Lautrec and showing their ruffled panties.

I read that the famous artist who'd invented the cancan had died. They called her *La Gouloue*—"The Glutton," but her real name was Louise Webber, which didn't sound a bit French to me. She was the "Queen of Montmartre." It was tragic—she'd become a *chiffonnier,* a rag-and-bone picker, and lived like a poor gypsy and died in penury. A shame. I wondered what had caused her downfall, and there it was in plain old black ink—she drank. *There but for the grace of God go I*—one drinking bout almost killed me—no more hooch for this gal!

My thoughts switched to Mimì, the tragic character in the opera *La Bohème*. Mamma and Papa both loved to listen to opera on the radio, *La Bohème* in particular. I repeated the story later to Valentina after my bath, standing in a pair of Pina's hand-me-down flannel pajamas, and said, "Perhaps they'll write an opera about *La Gouloue*, too."

Circling her pointing finger in a loop of her hair, with a look of consternation frozen on her face, she stared at me for almost a full minute like I'd sprouted a third eye. With that same pointing finger, she released her hair and pointed at me. "You cannot be that hard-hearted, can you?"

"I only meant—" But she had turned her back on me and walked into the bathroom, slamming the door shut.

"What did I say?" I asked the closed door.

⌀

ON SATURDAY MORNING, WE LISTENED to *Aunt Jymmie and Her Tots in Tottyville* on the domed wooden floor radio with the baroque front in the upstairs living room, but we had outgrown the program. So we mimicked and made fun of it, which was way more amusing than the actual show. I had a natural bent for imitating voices and a willing audience in Valentina.

We also had another Zenith wood console downstairs, and this upright was a great source of entertainment and news. We could listen to two different programs at once, if you cared to run up and down the stairs. I think we were the only house in the neighborhood that owned two radios. When we tired of the radio programs, I'd put on records and do some housework singing along to the music.

⌀

ALTHOUGH PAPA HAD BOUGHT VAL a Singer sewing machine for her birthday on St. Valentine's, as she'd said she didn't want a party, he didn't give it to her until he'd paid it off. He bought her a used 1921

Portable Electric 99K model with a knee lever. She loved her electric motor-powered model and started using it the minute he handed it to her in its original wooden carry case. Valentina sewed like a dream, like angels had given her hands knowledge of needles and threads and commandeered her to stitch, and after our Sunday outings on the trolley, she'd come home to sketch garments she'd seen and sew entire wardrobes for dolls—amazing.

On Sunday afternoons in early March, Valentina and I would occasionally ride the trolley and go all the way to Sixty-Fourth Street and back just for fun to watch the people. Val would notice how the ladies dressed. I paid special attention to people's conversations, facial expressions, and body movements when speaking. Once, I swore I saw Gianni getting off and walking away hand in hand with a blond. My stomach did flips. Was it him?

⋘⋙

VALENTINA SAW AN AD IN the *Brooklyn Daily Eagle* on Monday, March 18. This time the news pleased her. We sat on the floor in the living room near the door that went out to the upper porch.

"There's going to be a showing of frocks to be modeled by mannequins wearing McCall patterns copied from Parisian styles at Abraham & Strauss," she said. "And listen to this," she smacked the paper and read out loud. "It'll take place in the Brooklyn store on Tuesday, Wednesday, and Thursday of this week from eleven to three."

"What are you going to do about it?"

She then told me she was going to play hooky to buy some of those new patterns.

"I can't blame you. What're you going to use for money?" I saw a little gleam in her eye and watched her shake her head, and I knew she was dreaming up a scheme.

"You aren't the only one who can handle Papa," she said, her tone sly and meaningful, her hand reaching up to curl her hair. "I made Papa a new work shirt, and he gave me money for material and threads at the notions store, and I squirreled some away."

"You stole from Papa?" I said.

"Don't look so shocked. Mamma's a shopper, so am I, and apparently you are, too," she said, pointing to and referencing my bobbed hair.

"If you go anywhere near that notions store, promise you'll take me with you. Mr. Askenadzy adores my big brown eyes. He'll give you a discount if we're the first customers. It's some Jewish custom or something. Mamma does it all the time downtown when she shops on Delancey, Canal, and the Lower East Side—she makes sure she's the first one in the store in the morning and gets her price. The owners never want to lose the first sale—I think it makes or breaks their day."

Valentina and I went shopping, and sure enough, Mr. A. saw me first as I entered the shop and all but did cartwheels, which would really have been funny to see—he was short, not the least bit athletic, and thoroughly myopic.

My sister stood in front of bolts of material, practically memorizing patterns, while twisting and curling a bunch of her auburn hair as was her habit. When she finally decided, she was able to purchase at a discounted price all the dazzling material, threads, buttons, needles, and accessories she desired. The price for this was three dollars cash, plus two pinches on my sister's pink cheeks, a smile from both of us, and, all right, I admit it, I actually offered him my cheek and leaned in for his kiss! My mother would absolutely murder me if she knew, but I had Valentina's word she'd never snitch, because I'd never snitch on her about going to A&S for the fashion show.

On the way home, the wind picked up, and I buttoned the top of my coat, wishing I'd brought my woolen scarf that Val had knitted. "I had a rough night. Didn't sleep much. The trees kept rattling against the windows—you slept like a baby."

"Didn't hear a thing," Val said.

"The dim moonlight played hide and seek among the branches and made grotesque shapes, which became part of my dreams when I fell in and out of sleep. The truth is, I kept thinking about Gianni. He's never come around since the day before my birthday—always sends that creepy looking salesman, Alfredo. Can't stand to look at him. Thinks he's so smooth; he actually twirls his stupid mustache and gives me the eye—had the nerve to wink once! I can't think of anyone except Gianni, Gianni, Gianni. He's invaded my psyche. I'm sure I just need time to get over him."

"You'd better. He's never coming back. Would you in his place? You're a fool for what you did—and the way you did it. Words could've put him in his place, oh great sage, and you could've kept him dangling on your string."

"Mind your own beeswax! Listen to you with so many boyfriends." We turned down Eighty-Sixth Street. "You don't know everything."

"Let's go to Woolworth's."

"I'm not eating a tuna fish sandwich when I can have Mamma's leftover pasta with zucchini," I said.

"You put the kibosh on everything—don't have to eat at the counter. We can shop." She gave me an odd look.

"What?"

"I think Gianni's seeing someone."

"Lucille?"

"Of course not! Some little Mafia princess from what I've heard. She went to Visitation. A senior at Fontbonne Hall now, with all the rich, snobby girls—no matter how their daddies earn a living."

"*Il n'y a pas de comptabilité pour le gout.*"

"Translation?"

"There's no accounting for taste—the nuns used to say it all the time. And by the by, who died and donated you all this intuition, making you so savvy?"

"I keep my mouth shut and ears open and don't hit a possible suitor over the head with Mamma's good plate."

As soon as we got in the door at home, I grabbed the mail. There was a typed letter for me. No return address. Whoever from? I dashed upstairs to write my feelings about Gianni and his new girl. I didn't like the idea, not one bit. But first I opened the letter. It was like one of those old-fashioned cards of a cupid with wings carrying intertwined hearts and was pasted on a small, round, white paper-lace doily. Printed in red were the words "My Love to You." So sweet and romantic. Could it be from Gianni?

When she came upstairs, I showed it to Val and said, "Valentine's Day has long passed."

"Probably meant for me," she said and plucked it out of my hand. Too shocked, I was left without a retort as I watched her lean it against the dresser mirror.

"But it was addressed to me."

"A secret code—message to you, but meant for me so nobody suspects."

"But I could swear it looks like Gianni's handwriting." I left it at that. I was too tired to argue, and she probably needed a secret admirer more than I.

It dawned on me in the middle of the night that Valentina had been sneaking out seeing that guy. What was his name? She'd been smug because she thought she had it over me, knew what love was really about. I had a feeling she was crazy about the guy, but he was taking advantage of her. I wanted to kick him in the teeth. I started thinking about a plan to meet him in person, but I must have fallen asleep in the middle of it.

⌒⟨✦⟩⌒

THE FOLLOWING SATURDAY, I WENT to Manhattan to shop for a book with extra money I'd gotten from Papa. The library probably didn't have the book I was looking for. It had just begun to snow when I entered the Gotham Book Mart on Forty-Seventh Street. I always loved to read the sign "Wise Men Fish Here." This was the heart of the Diamond District, where men with long black coats and high black hats and side-lock *peyos* curling into long beards were always moving at a frenetic pace. I loved peering in the windows to see all the beautiful jewelry wink at me: rings, bracelets, necklaces, and even tiaras, wondering if someday I'd be lucky enough to have a brilliant stone flashing on my finger to mean I'd found the right guy.

"There's something comforting in the smell of old books and yellowed pages. What is it?" I asked the saleslady.

"Lignin."

I didn't press for more information and decided to research it later because I was a woman with a purpose and didn't want to get sidetracked. I defiantly wanted to buy the book *Lady Chatterley's Lover* and asked for it by its title and author, D. H. Lawrence. The salesgirl, who had stepped behind the counter at the back of the bookstore, looked horrified and said she'd have to speak with someone. Before I could stop her, she went to consult with the store's manager at the back of the shop.

I had seen him a number of times and recognized him. He stepped from behind a curtain and faced me squarely. He hesitated. "I really don't think this book is quite suited for a young lady. Won't you let me suggest something else?"

Not missing a beat, I answered, "Is it because I'm too young or because you're concerned for my moral well-being?"

His mouth dropped open, and before he could get a word in, I continued, "This is most surprising coming from a nonconformist owner who fights censorship with what books are selected for sale, yet you're censoring me and what literature I care to read."

He sighed, turned directly to the meek little salesgirl in a gray jumper, and said, "Sell her the book, but please wrap it up in gift paper."

As he stepped away from the counter, I called after him, "*A sheynem dank,*" an expression I learned from Mr. Blitzer, Mamma's friend, the door-to-door salesman.

He looked over his shoulder and bowed his head, grinning.

I paid for the book, put the bill in my pocketbook and watched as she wrapped it. I asked her for the used book section, and she directed me to a few aisles to the right. The minute I stepped into the first aisle I was struck, as always, by that delightful mixture of vanilla and the curious scent released from old books. I wondered if that could be the lignin the girl had mentioned. That smell comingled with a musty odor, and the dry, dusty air filled my nostrils and senses with a desire for the knowledge of antiquity. I was in a little corner of Heaven to be sure as I leafed through several books. In a 1927 edition of *THE COMPLETE POETICAL WORKS OF PERCY BYSSHE SHELLEY*, I found a dedication in a florid script, and thought of Gianni: "You are everything to me and I wish you every blessing in the collective mind of the world." I copied it on the back of the bill and would later put it in my diary.

❦

AFTER A FEW AFTERNOONS OF reading instead of doing my homework, I finished the novel. I reread over and over a sex scene. How beautiful, exciting, yet quiescent it was. At first, I had to look up the word "loins" in the dictionary. From its meaning, the words that stuck out were "erotic" and "procreative power." These lingered in my brain long after I'd closed the book, like the word "quiescent," which I'd just learned the meaning of, and seemed to be using in conversation, left, right, and in between, just to annoy Val.

About the same time as my sexual elucidation began thanks to D. H. Lawrence, Valentina started staying late after school. She mentioned an older, dirty blond-haired guy was hanging around the schoolyard. I didn't pay attention at first until I realized the guy was interested in Valentina. My sister, who had such a talent with a needle and thread and could sew like an angel, suddenly stopped taking in sewing or doing any alterations for the Chinese laundries and instead started seeing that guy she was so head over heels about—Vic Piccolo. I loathed the term "grease ball," but it suited him to a T. By this time, Valentina had been sneaking out with him for about six months, and I knew by the way my sister jabbered on and on about him she was far more interested in him than he was in her. I discovered that Valentina was smoking, hiding her cigarettes in a drain at the side of the house. That's when I made up my mind to stalk her movements.

I watched her every move whenever possible. I'd make up an excuse to take a day off from school to be early enough to catch her after her school, New Utrecht High, let out. One Thursday afternoon I pretended to be sick so I could take the following day off, which I could ill afford, but this was important. On Friday morning, I play-acted going off to school as usual for Val's benefit. After window shopping for a few hours, I circled back home. Mamma was concerned when I strolled in, but I told her a bold-faced lie and said it was a half-holiday and so we got off early. How would I ever make this school work up?

I made sure I was in stalking distance when school was about to let out. Sure as a schoolboy hankers after a toy six-gun, there was a black Studebaker parked, ready, and waiting. Val came running out, flushed and excited, toward the car. I recognized Vic, who had an awful reputation of being a wolf, sitting behind the wheel, smoking. So that's where she picked up the nasty habit. Oh no! I couldn't believe it, she got into the car. If he drove away, there'd be no possibility for me to follow. I never considered this. And sure enough, he gunned the motor and out he pulled from the curb. I slunk home, tail between my legs, but at least I had his tag number.

Just to be sure, the following week I circled back home and cleverly waited until Pina, just recovering from a miscarriage, and Mamma went out shopping. It was Thursday. Mamma never shopped on Friday because shops closed early for Shabbos, and never on Saturday. They had gone to Orchard Street, and then they were going to visit Mamma's friends for lunch and cards.

I was so nervous I willed myself to stop shaking as I approached Val's school. This time I was on a bike and followed the car to Vic's rooming house a few blocks away. He opened the door for her and took her in his arms and kissed her with eagerness, then grabbed her hands and pulled her inside with him. The bile rose in my throat and I spit up. The bastard was taking advantage of my sister! I'd heard he was married. I intended to find out.

When Val came home, I confronted her. I wasn't looking forward to this part of my investigation, but the minute she came upstairs and started undressing, I said, "The guy's more than seven years older than you. He's using your blind admiration. Gullible, stupid child! Vic's exploiting your innocence."

"He isn't taking advantage of me," she said, twisting a clump of her hair furiously.

"Val, please be careful. If I tell Mamma she'll beat you to a pulp."

"Promise you won't tell Mamma."

"Stop fussing with your hair. Where does he take you?" Not waiting for an answer, I quizzed her on what they talked about and what he did to her. She was like a corpse at the morgue. Not a peep out of her.

"Don't give me that haughty look. I swear if you do it again, I'll swipe it off your face with a slap."

But she refused to talk to me—*punto e basta*. Period and enough. I threatened, cajoled, pleaded, begged, and bullied, but she wouldn't open up, and I knew I couldn't live with myself if I betrayed her and told Mamma.

"This must come from you, Val," I said and insisted that she seek help and guidance, because in matters of sex, I was no expert, except for what I read in books.

She glared at me. "And what makes you think we're making love?"

"Love, is it? More like lust on his part, guaranteed, and you don't know what the hell you've gotten yourself into with your infatuation of an older guy."

With that, she stormed out of the room. I'd have to wait till she cooled her heels before I could broach the subject with her again.

⚜

THEN, A FEW WEEKS LATER, something changed radically. Valentina started getting sick, and I had a terrible feeling it wasn't the flu. She was hiding the fact that she was nauseous and throwing up most mornings. Every time I asked her about it, Val lied, and then began to feign fainting spells to get out of scrubbing the floors and cleaning the bathrooms. Mamma was getting suspicious, but Valentina could never fool her older sister. It was too late. I had warned her, but she was an impulsive redhead that heeded no one.

We were in bed. I was just about to turn off my light. "When are you going to tell Mamma?"

"Tell Mamma what?"

"About all this vomiting. Are you pregnant?"

"You worry too much. I must have eaten something that didn't sit right with my stomach.

"Picked up a bug, eh?"

"Mmmm," she said, like she was already half asleep and dreaming.

"Every day!"

"Shush. You'll wake everyone."

I fumed, but there was little I could do. I turned out the light and punched my pillow, wishing it was that creep's face.

⌒⟊⌒

IT WAS LATE MARCH, AND we had a freak week of snow, a blizzard that threaded the skies with skeins of snow, or sheets of it scattered by winds that kept most people inside. When it was over on Friday, school was still closed because the heat was off, as some of the pipes had frozen. The neighborhood kids were out using their sleds, zipping down the hilly streets. Others took to the parks with ice skates hanging from their shoulders. That was my preference. I had made up with Lucille, trying to be more mature. She said she was hurt that she didn't get to come to my party, but I explained my feelings and she accepted my apology. I wanted to go ice skating with Lucille, but almost got roped into going shopping with Mamma and Pina—I couldn't think of anything less exciting.

We were sitting in the kitchen, Mamma, Pina, Val, and yours truly, deciding who was going where. Valentina begged off because of a terrible headache. Pina had left the baby with a neighbor because she had a cold, and Mamma and Pina were going to go to Abraham & Strauss on Fulton Street, but I reminded Mamma that it was now closed due to the renovations.

"We can go to Silver's—the five and dime. It's got a luncheonette counter and soda fountain," Mamma said to Pina.

I supplied her with "I heard that the supposed grand reopening of A&S will be in July. At least that's the rumor. Why go so far, anyway?" So they opted to shop in the neighborhood and have lunch in Hinckley's, a soda shop on Fifth Avenue between Eighty-Sixth and Eighty-Seventh Streets. They made a great cherry mash.

⚜

WE MADE PLANS FOR THE day. I told Val I'd be home from ice skating at around three because it was already getting dark by then, but Mamma and Pina would be at Pina's for dinner. Mamma was still worried about Pina, who had recently miscarried a baby boy. Papa was working late, and then he'd pick up Mamma on the way home.

Valentina's timing was impeccable—she knew I'd find her—so calculating. She probably waited until she heard me opening the door, had checked to see it was me, spying through the window in the middle of the staircase that looked out onto the covered porch and outside, then she'd run back to the top of the stairs. I found her all right, soaked in sweat at the bottom of the steep stairwell, moaning, and I started screaming. I perceived a quiver in the atmosphere surrounding us, like touching a jack frost web in a window, and realized this was no accident. Then I hushed her sobs. Valentina didn't trip and fall, but that's what she made it look like. Her shoe was caught on the carpet of the top stair rung. That rip wasn't there when I left to go skating. Had she staged it—thrown herself down the stairs? Now I knew for certain she was pregnant and didn't know how to rid herself of the baby. What a catastrophe. Crooning to her, I picked up my sister's head. "Why, oh why, didn't you tell Mamma? You foolish little brat. You could have killed my darling sister!" I laid Valentina's head down. I felt panic starting to rise from my solar plexus. "Calm down," I whispered to myself as much as to Val, thinking, *Use your head.* I flung off my coat and gloves and began to undress her, thinking if she'd only gone away and had the baby, Mamma would've pretended to be pregnant and raised it as her own. No one needed to know.

I'd seen Mamma, a midwife, pack a bleeding woman, and that's exactly what I intended to do to Valentina. I ran to the downstairs bathroom toward the back of the house, filled a basin with warm water, grabbed a bunch of the strips of cloth that Mama had for us girls to use at our time of the month.

Then I washed my sister and packed her to stop the bleeding—which wasn't as much as I thought it would be—the way I'd seen Mamma do it. I fervently prayed Mamma and Pina would be home soon, prayed that Papa wouldn't be delayed at work, prayed as I'd never begged anything of God or the saints in my life. I could not lift her, so I helped her to her feet and made her lean on me and half carried her to Jack's downstairs bedroom that circled the porch in back.

I had acted fast, thanking God none of my companions were with me when I'd opened the vestibule door and found my sister. I placed Valentina on Jack's bed, ran and got some towels, and shoved them under her in case she soiled the bed. Then I thought to get her aspirin for the pain, but hadn't Mamma said that only makes you bleed more? I ran to get some cold coffee Mamma had left on the downstairs kitchen stove, lit the flame under it, and hunted around for Papa's bottle of anisette. In all my nervousness, I missed it on my first go-around, but then I spotted it inside the pantry closet on the top shelf in back of a bag of flour and one of sugar.

When Mamma came in, she was alone. It was getting late and she'd decided not to go to Pina's to wait for Papa. I went to meet her at the front door and asked for Pina, who had gone home to pick up Elena from her neighbor.

"What's wrong?" Mamma said, taking off her gloves and putting them in her pockets.

"Don't worry, it'll be all right."

Mamma took off her scarf and I helped her out of her coat and hung them both up on the wooden coatrack by the front door. "You're white as a sheet. What's happened?"

"Valentina took a bad fall on the stairs. She's resting now on Jack's bed."

The words weren't out of my mouth, and Mamma was already opening Jack's bedroom door. She rushed to Valentina's side. Val had drifted off to sleep. I'd given her enough anisette to knock out a horse.

I whispered to Mamma what I thought had happened. She nodded in such a way and with such a placid face that I knew she'd suspected something for some time.

She touched Val's forehead and throat. "No fever," she said, and then began to grill me. I told her how I'd found Val and what I did. Mamma said, "Bring me more clean cloths, and a basin with hot water and soap." She sat next to Val and started to croon to her the way she used to when we were little.

When I got back to the room, Mamma washed and dried her hands, uncovered Val, and examined my sister. I thought I'd be under scrutiny for the fast and sloppy job I did, but Mamma merely redid everything I'd done but more slowly and with confidence.

"Valentina." Mamma tapped her face.

She opened her eyes. "Am I bleeding?"

"Yes, but not a great deal. You didn't lose the baby. What are you—two months pregnant?"

She nodded, her face registering fear.

"You could have killed yourself," Mamma said as she rewashed and dried her hands and covered Val.

She got up and sat on Jack's desk chair and motioned me to sit at the foot of the bed.

"You are more than foolish. Death doesn't triumph loudly but walks quietly away and fades. You could have killed yourself or broken some bones. Does the father know?"

Val shook her head. "It's useless to tell him. I just found out he's married." She started to cry. I reached into my skirt pocket and handed her my handkerchief.

Mamma sat for a long while, pondering and stroking Valentina's hand. Then she looked at me and Val. "We won't tell Pina, your father, or Jack just yet. What occurred here today remains among us three." Val moaned and opened her eyes. She took one look at Mamma and burst into tears.

"Too late for that, child. Now we must invent a story that will be swallowed whole by the other members of this family. And this stays with us till the grave."

We knew we didn't have to promise, but both my sister and I nodded in agreement.

Mamma and I took Val upstairs to the kitchen, where Mamma gave her hot beef broth *stracciatella*. She beat an egg with some grated *parmigiano*, whisked it into the soup, and set it before Val. "Eat. You must keep up your strength."

I ran back down and tidied Jack's bed and room, closed the door, and flew up the stairs.

Mamma gave Val a swig of red wine, and then made her take another big gulp. Mamma forced her to eat every bit of the soup she'd prepared. She broke off a chunk of bread, dipped it in some olive oil, and sprinkled it with grated cheese. "Eat," she said.

We sat there watching in silence as Val struggled to swallow. When she finished, she wiped her mouth. I cleared away the dishes. She stood shakily.

"Sit." Mamma said. "You had a bad headache, were dizzy, tripped, and fell down the stairs. We'll say you have a fever and need rest, and I won't allow Jack or Papa to come visit you tonight, and maybe not even tomorrow. We'll see. Pina will probably come over tomorrow afternoon, but I won't let her up to see you either, saying I don't think she should be exposed to anything in case it's the flu—I don't want her to expose Elena."

"You've stopped bleeding now, so you'll take a bath with some salts that are in the bathroom closet. You'll not go to school for the rest of the week, and maybe even next week. Did this man at any time ever say he loved you or wanted to take care of you?"

Val shook her head. "But I love him," she said, barely audible.

"I'm sure you think you do, but you will never see him again. Ever. *Hai capito?* Understood?"

I told Mamma about Vic and Val.

Mamma was quiet for a few moments, and then she explained to Valentina that she wouldn't start showing for several months, and when she did, we would send her and Pina away to Lake George, where she'd have the baby. "I'll deliver it," she said, "and Pina will raise the child as her own. After her miscarriage, she'll be thrilled to have this baby to raise, and you'll be able to see her every day of your life and be grateful."

Valentina started to protest.

"You'll never find a husband if this gets out."

"Mamma, remember that girl at school last year who had a baby and nobody even knew she was pregnant? She had watched her diet and done exercise, and when she started to show, she wore a girdle and loose clothing," I said.

"Marcella, please, not now." Then she turned to Val and said, "You, Pina, and I will go to your Uncle Carlo's cabin in Lake George for the last two months. There's no bargaining, Valentina. We do this my way, or you'll leave this house tomorrow. You will be dead to me."

I looked from Valentina's tear-stained face to my iron-willed mother's. Where was the sweet, gentle woman I'd always known? I'd never seen this ferocity in her before. How had she kept it hidden? What other secrets was I not privy to in the family?

Mamma returned my gaze. "You want to ask me something? You knew she was seeing this boy?"

"Man. He's older, but I didn't know he was married until now."

She shook her head. "I see."

"I couldn't keep missing school. She'd be late, but always had an excuse. Then once I saw her get into his car. I couldn't follow them on foot, so the next time I tailed them on my bike. They went to his place nearby. Later, I confronted her. She was crazy in love—I was afraid to break your heart."

"Why? Isn't it broken now? Go on."

"When she started getting sick in the mornings, by then I knew, but it was too late. I pleaded with her to tell you."

"I was beginning to suspect something but—" Mamma's voice trailed off.

"How do you know Pina will agree? How will you keep this from Papa and Jack?" I asked.

"I will. We will. I'll tell Papa when it's time. Pina, too. She's most like me of all of you. She'll take the baby. She'll learn from this. You, too—in life, you play the hand you're dealt."

Mamma looked at me staring back at her, seeing her in an aura of light I couldn't comprehend. "The nature of life is transient, illusive. Grab onto whatever strikes you as real and important, let the rest go." I knew her heart was rent anew. How many trips and falls, rips and tears, could one heart sustain? I thought of Mamma leaving her parents in Sicily, losing babies, bringing her mother over to America when her father died, only to lose her within a few months.

"Marcella, take her upstairs now," Mamma said, her tone forlorn.

I put my arms around Val, took her to our shared attic room. I drew her bath, got her into a nightgown, and put her to bed with a kiss on her forehead and a wish for pleasant dreams.

⁂

HOURS LATER, I WENT TO check on Valentina. We had twin beds, and I sat on mine.

"How could you, Val? Why didn't you confide in me?" I picked up her hand and stroked it.

"You would've tried to stop me from seeing him, but I love him."

"You know what Mamma says about love. When the right man comes along, you'll know it. You're too young. He—" I put her hand down and patted it.

"I'm not too young if I can make love and get pregnant."

"I'm sure Eskimos do it even younger, and not all of them are in love either," I said. "Gianni would never have forced himself on me, and that's what happened."

"Not true. I went willingly."

"You're more naïve than I thought. Are you blind? Didn't you see what he was doing?" I got up and sat down on the edge of Val's bed. I kissed her forehead.

"Not everyone can sit and wait to meet the man of her dreams at twenty-three, like Mamma," Val said.

"Fifteen is ludicrous," I insisted.

"Don't start flinging the English around me."

"Preposterous. Absurd. Ridiculous."

"No one in the family ever treated me the way he did. He gave me chocolates and silk stockings and perfume, brought me to the movies, and we even went to the zoo."

"Bribes. To get what he wanted."

"No, he cared. Paid attention to me."

"He's an adulterer. Are you saying you're deprived at home?"

"Don't be so facetious."

"Now who's flinging English? Don't dare see him again. You've got no bargaining power in this." I brought her shoulders forward and made an attempt at fluffing her pillows.

"Please, Marcella, I implore you. You've got to do me this one favor."

"What?" I pushed her gently back onto the cushions.

"You've got to meet him and tell him it's over. Say it's because he's married. Swear you won't mention the baby."

"Don't you think he's smart enough to get it when you don't show up for your *rendezvous?*"

"Beg pardon?"

"Your meeting."

"You don't understand. He'll come looking for me. I can't stay out of school forever."

We both stopped talking and looked toward the door. We heard Mamma's footfalls on the upper landing coming toward the bedroom.

"Why is Valentina so agitated?" she asked me.

"We were trying to figure out a solution to a problem."

"Don't be cryptic with me. Go on. Spit it out. You look like a croaking frog about to catch a fly."

"It's just that—" my voice trailed off. "If I don't tell this Vic she's not going to see him anymore, he's going to become a nuisance."

Valentina almost screeched. "Mamma, he's very forceful. Someone has to tell him I'm not going—"

"Why do you think this family owes him any such courtesy?"

"He'll never stop coming for me. He's used to getting what he wants. I think he's connected."

"Connected? To Almighty God? The Holy Ghost?"

"The mob, Mamma," she cried.

"Stop it this instant. He's a two-bit nobody who preyed upon an innocent, inexperienced girl. He won't dare do a thing—your father's a mob all by himself. Have you really been on cloud nine? Just who do you think his friend Carlo Albano is? He's never sought a favor, but your father has done many."

"Mamma, you can't tell Papa!" Val said, her voice pleading.

"I never said I would. But don't tell me about what this what's-his-name can do. What is his name?"

"I didn't say," Val said, still sniffling.

Mamma looked at me. "Marcella?"

"Mamma, this isn't the time to discuss this. Please." I thought she'd be angry I'd said that, especially with the haughty tone I'd used. Instead, she said quietly, "You're right," and left the room.

"Val, my darling sister, were I you, I'd tread very softly where Mamma and Papa are concerned. They were raised on an island that saw its share of violence, and although they seem meek and mild on the outside, I wouldn't want to cross either of them. When push comes to shove, Papa's a bull, and Mama holds a red flag."

cᴄ✿ᴐↄ

IN THE KITCHEN, LATER, I kissed Mamma. "Don't fret. Although, I fear Val might do something stupid, like run away."

"What makes you say that?" Mamma put a pot of water to boil on the stove.

"She hinted at something earlier."

"We'd both better be watchful for signs of that. You warn her. If she does something crazy, Papa will really go after him. And God help him."

cᴄ✿ᴐↄ

AT EASTER BREAK, I SAW Gianni and had the opportunity to apologize for my temper and breaking the plate over his head.

He stood in the vestibule and rubbed his head as if it still hurt.

He said, "Here, kiss the boo-boo and make it all better," and with that, he bent his head forward. I rubbed his head and then gently tugged at his hair.

"What, no kiss? Afraid I'll tell again? Not on your life."

And the next thing he did was kiss me sweetly.

"Now you can snitch on me. Go ahead and tell my brothers."

I laughed. "I missed you at the party. Thanks for the flowers. I didn't deserve them."

"You're a diva. Of course you deserved flowers. Bet you sang for everyone, too."

"I did, and one of Papa's friends wanted me to audition, but you know Papa. I still want a chance to at least try. I need to know if I could make it singing in movies."

"Why do you want to break your own heart? Your parents'll never let you go," Gianni said.

"Not now, maybe, but in a year or so—"

"Stop. Please." Gianni shook his head. "Here we are on our way to becoming dearest sweethearts, and you're ruining it by telling me you want to run off to California."

"Will I see you for Mass on Easter?"

"Sure, if you're still here. By the way," he said, with a hand fluttering under his shirt acting like a palpitating heart, "did you get my Valentine card?"

"A few weeks late." I smiled, remembering Val insisting it was hers, and roughed-up his hair. "But it's the gesture that counts."

We walked to the front porch. I opened the door.

Gianni made a magnanimous fling of his hand to the outdoors. "Spring's in the Brooklyn air and I've got tickets for the Brooklyn Robbins game on April 21. They've got a new Press Box in Ebbets Field and I'd love to see it—it'll already be Daylight Savings at the beginning of the month."

"What day is that?"

"Sunday."

"Who're they playing?"

"Philadelphia Phillies." Hat in hand he put his hands together like he was holding a bat and took a swing.

"Brooklyn Robins. Brooklyn Robins." I scrunched my mouth and shook my head. "I liked their old name better the year I was born—the Brooklyn Trolley Dodgers."

"They changed their name in honor of the manager Wilbert Robinson—a great guy."

"Know him personally?"

"Cut it out." He toyed with his Ivy cap, circling it in his hands. "He's got terrific baseball sense."

"So where's this leading us, Mr. Simoni?"

"To a game, so we can hold hands and rush in with the crowd and you can sing the national anthem at the top of your lungs and at the seventh inning stretch you can pipe out 'Take Me Out to the Ball Game.' And—"

"I love both the Star-Spangled Banner and the Tin Pan Alley song! You've got me almost sold." I hesitated for a brief second. "And you'll buy me a hot dog loaded with mustard and relish?"

"How can you think of food at a time like this? We're discussing our two favorite things—baseball and singing?"

I scrunched up my nose and said, "Because I love hot dogs, too?"

"You drive a hard bargain. Say yes, and I'll throw in peanuts as part of the deal."

"Done!"

CHAPTER 8

Giacomo

AFTER WORK, ON A MILD day in the middle of May, Giacomo walked into the kitchen to see Angelica looking very pale. She sat fanning herself with a cold glass of tea in front of her. She shook her head. "Such a sin."

"What's happened?"

"Sit down. Do you want something to drink?"

Giacomo shook his head. "What is it?"

"Do you remember when Valentina fell down the stairs?"

He nodded.

"I wasn't going to tell you yet, but that was no accident. Stay calm. She was pregnant and thought she could get rid of the baby, but it was too early for such a trick and the infant held on."

"*Mio Dio*," he said, and kept repeating, "my God, my God."

"God has nothing to do with this."

"What a disgrace. What're we going to do?" Giacomo felt a gouge in the masonry of the universe that he'd constructed to protect his family and knew some stonework was about to come tumbling down.

"I had planned for her to stay home and continue school until she starts to show, and then Pina and Elena and I were going to take her to Carlo's cabin for the summer where we'd stay until the baby came. Valentina was going to give the infant to Pina to raise. That would've been the end of it."

Giacomo started to object.

"Listen to me," she said with sharpness. "Why—you think these things never happened in Sicily? You can't imagine how many young girls had to give their babies to their own mothers to raise."

Giacomo's look went from incredulity to shock. He was speechless. His mouth began to twitch.

"Don't say anything. *Ho capito bennissimo.* I well understand." Angelica's look went from disgust to one of hopelessness. "Men," she spat out. She stood up. "You're not grasping what I'm saying. I'm using the past tense because your daughter had a miscarriage this morning. What she wanted to do earlier happened now."

"Good Lord!" He heaved a great sigh and tears filled his eyes. His thoughts went careening back to China, when Lian had told him she'd aborted an unwanted child. "How is Valentina taking it?"

"How else? Like her life is over."

"But she'll live with no repercussions, and nobody knows about it. There's no scandal."

"We know. Her family. All but Jack."

"You mean, only the womenfolk knew," he said, irritated.

"What good would it do, *marito mio*? So Jack can suffer too? No telling what he'd do. He's very protective of his sisters. More than you know. He can tease them, but nobody else better hurt them," Angelica said.

"He'll make a good father and family man. Where're you going?"

"To prepare dinner. Life does go on. She's resting now, but please talk to her later. She's begging forgiveness from everyone. This will be hard for you."

"And the boy?"

Angelica sighed. "Man. Older. *Figilo di puttana era sposato.* I forbade her to see him ever again. That was months ago. By now he's probably back in Boston, I'd imagine. Lucky for him, I told her, or you might have wanted to exact vengeance."

Giacomo's face was beet red and his hands were balled into fists. He started to say something, but faltered.

Angelica came over to him and took both his fists in her hands and pulled them apart and kissed the palms of his hands. "*Mani benedette.* Blessed hands," she repeated.

Giacomo gazed at his wife with an incredulous look on his face. "Now you'll have to invent a story to tell Caterina and Carlo why you can't go."

"Even if she catches on, she'd never betray me. She knows how closed-mouth we are as to Carlo's line of business."

Angelica looked puzzled. "But why? We can still go. Carlo wants to travel this summer, perhaps to Italy, after finishing things he has to attend to in the city. It'll do everyone good to get away. I'll leave as planned with Valentina, Pina, and baby Elena, and even Marcella before she has to find a permanent job. Maybe you could come up for a weekend?"

⌁⌁⌁

GIACOMO SAT AT THE TABLE with Marcella and Angelica after eating dinner. It was so quiet he could hear the sugar crystals dissolving as his wife stirred her coffee.

Marcella said, "It's like a morgue in here. She didn't die, and that's the most important thing, isn't it? She could have died, but she lived and she'll get better, grow up, and have a normal life." She sipped from her water glass.

"Do you think she can wash away the internal stigma she'll carry with her forever?" Angelica said.

"For all of her life?" Giacomo asked. "I think not." He poured a little water in his glass of wine.

"Of course not. But she's alive and will get healthy and lead a normal life unless you cover her in shame," Marcella said.

"She'll shroud herself in it, I'm afraid. Your sister isn't like you—doesn't have, what's that word you always say—"

"Spunk? Pluck? Mettle?" Marcella volunteered.

"Any of them. This discussion goes no further than this kitchen. I know my children from the womb. Valentina wasn't born with the kind of spine to make her character strong. You received many gifts from Heaven—all the verve and charisma, darling girl. My Pina got honesty and courage, Jack guile and horse sense."

"What then has Valentina?" Marcella said.

"A certain charm, adaptability, cunning. She's cagey, not an open book like you, nor generous like you and Papa. I love her, faults and all. We all have flaws, but hers are glaring, and she has to work to keep them underneath her shift."

"And you, Mamma?" Marcella asked.

Giacomo tipped his glass in a mini-toast toward Angelica. "Your mother is a survivor. She's tenacious. Resilient."

Angelica stacked their dishes and set them aside. "I bounce back from hurt and pain. I possess unconditional love for all of you."

"She was born with a capacious heart." Giacomo looked at Angelica, grateful that she was his wife. He thought how later, in the privacy of their room, he'd tell her so.

Giacomo went upstairs with a tray for Valentina, but she barely touched her food.

"Oh, Papa. I'm so ashamed."

"God has a plan for each of us. He always does. You were a weak lamb and preyed upon. You'll never be weak again, will you?"

Valentina threw herself at her father and cried on his chest.

They talked for a long time, and Giacomo comforted her each time she cried. When Giacomo heard Jack in the kitchen, he kissed his daughter's forehead. "Rest."

He carried the tray downstairs and set it down to wash the dishes later. He would not call Angelica but served his son dinner himself.

"Hey, Pop, I can do this. Go inside and read the paper."

"No. You work like a man now, and you're still in school. I want to do this little thing for you." He indicated a seat. "Take your shoes off and sit." Giacomo poured a half glass of vino and added water to it. "This is restorative. Drink."

"Hey, Pop, want to come watch Gianni and me on Saturday? We've got a ball game in the park."

"Sure. Now eat."

CHAPTER 9

Marcella

I EXCELLED IN THE LAST part of my senior year in high school, and although the youngest girl, graduated at the top of my class. I was the valedictorian, and since we had made up, I was pleased that my best friend, Lucille, was salutatorian. We were both members of Arista Honor Society at Bay Ridge High School, an all-girls school. I was coeditor of the school magazine with another classmate, Cara Sant'Angelo, a real dynamo and a great orator for a girl who was only seventeen.

At the graduation ceremony, which was held outside due to the pleasant weather and slight breeze, I made a speech. I knew my family was proud of me by the looks on their faces. I could almost see from the podium where I stood my parents' eyes glistening with happiness. When I finished and was seated, for some reason my mind raced back to elementary school, and I thought of the sacrifice Papa had made to send me to private school.

꧁꧂

MY MIND FILTERED BACK TO when I had attended Visitation Academy with the cloistered nuns on Ridge Boulevard. I loved to play dodgeball before classes started when I got there early in the morning. I was a serious, fierce player and had a wicked arm toss. I also loved to row on the lake at recess and especially in races around the statue of St. Michael the Archangel in the middle of the lake.

In the spring and the fall, sometimes on a dare, I'd climb up to the open glassless archway of a stone summer house with great wooden beams. I'd stand on the window ledge and reach above my head to the high, thick rafter. I'd stretch till I could grab hold and then climb hand over hand across to the opposite wall's window, knowing each of the girls who dared me held their breath, thinking I'd fall, but I never did. I'd reach the other side, then on to the window ledge and jump to the ground.

Once, Sister Marie Therese caught me, and I received detention. Who ever knew she could move so fast? She was crippled and could barely walk. I swore to the girls in my class that I knew for sure she'd been wild in her youth and was in a car accident speeding with a boy. I also told the girls that instead of reading the Divine Office, she had a magazine cut up and tucked inside her prayer book. I always changed the magazine—*Life, Ladies' Home Journal,* or *Red Book.* I usually used a magazine they'd know, because once I said a risqué novel and then had to explain what risqué meant.

At school with the nuns in winter, when there wasn't any ground cover of snow, I'd pit one gang of girls against another. Two captains would pick—I was always elected a captain, and I always made sure I won first draw to pick a girl for the team. How? I cheated or talked fast. Then our opposing teams would "fight" each other to see who could build the largest and best "home" under the secular trees. With the sun streaming through the trees, dappling the ground, my friends would gather pine needles and form them into long, humped borders as if they were large extensions for ten "rooms" or so beneath the ancient trees. These, I vowed to my classmates, held the spirits of dead nuns, and that kept them honest with me, a born ringleader. My group always managed to win, so the others had to stay after school and wash the blackboards and clap out the erasers—busy work the nuns didn't want to do. I had more chores than I could handle at home.

The games always changed, like the seasons, and the gardens held mosses and ferns in late spring, and in the fall the colors of the leaves were a painter's palette to gladden my heart, because autumn was the saddest season, the season of dying and transformation. I always sensed a great loss when summer ended. The only redeeming part of fall I loved were the splashes of colors when the leaves changed and those strange and wonderful Indian summer days.

⁓✣⁓

IN THE MORNINGS WE WOULD attend Mass, or the nuns would lead prayers in French, or we'd spend an hour reading in French, studying etiquette, or practicing penmanship. If you had a good voice, you got to sing in Chorus, and with an exceptional voice, like mine, you sang in the elite Choir. That's how I learned Gregorian chant. It is at once sacred and mournful, with no music accompaniment, yet for some reason it never failed to uplift me, making me want to be a better daughter, sister, or friend.

There were also plays and performances held by the students, but always inside the cloister. I wanted to sing and dance and act, but I hated when in fourth grade I was forced to dress in a nun's habit, six times too large for my skinny frame. I hated the play and never learned the lines for spite. I had given fair warning to the sister in charge that this wasn't something I wanted to participate in. I learned a few lines at the beginning, but who cared about a religious person founding a convent in some remote part of Spain or France or wherever. So when it came time for the play, I just kept repeating the same two lines over and over until I finally shrugged my shoulders and put up my hands in surrender. Mother Superior finally indicated to me that I was to sit down on the sidelines. I almost shouted for joy, though wearing the most remorseful puss I could muster. Heading toward my castigated seat, I glanced at Mother's sprawling bottom on that rattan chair and knew for sure I'd never make a nun.

My poor Papa had to go see Mother Superior to make amends for my outrageous behavior. Naturally she was positioned behind the bars of a double grate. Students could see the sisters face to face, but no one else. I wasn't upset about the scolding from the nun, but I was more than distraught because I'd wounded my father who paid so much money to send me to the private, expensive school. I made up my mind then and there, with the very jowl-faced and obese nun continuing to badger and harangue Papa about my comportment, that I'd finished with the hypocrisy of pretending to want to be holy, a martyr, a saint, or a sister of the cloth. I stood, faced my father, and said in Italian, "*Questa suora ha parlato troppo. Non voglio sentire un'altra parola. Non voglio vernire mai più a questa prigione di scuola e non posso supportatre il fatto che tu paghi troppo, non soltanto per la scuola ma anche per l'uniforme che io detesto, quando la Mamma e la nostra famiglia avrebbe bisogno di questi soldi!*"

My father burst out laughing, asked pardon of the nun, and said, "We're quite done here. It seems my Marcella has fired you. She wants to go to public school. Thank you and good day." That said, he cocked his hat at a jaunty angle, took my arm, and marched me toward the door. The flustered nun had no choice but to pull the cord that rang a bell for the outside sister, a postulant, to open the exit door to the world beyond and let us out onto the street. *Arrivederci! Au revoir!*

"It was too far to travel back and forth every day anyway," I said and squeezed his strong hand.

⌘

GRADUATION OVER, WE WENT HOME to celebrate, and sure enough, a nosegay of late spring flowers awaited me at the door. I didn't have to read the card to know who'd sent the flowers from Chase Florals on Eighty-Sixth Street. Gianni was away with his brother Franco, helping him restore the front porch of his country home in Gardiner, and couldn't attend my graduation. I opened the small cream-colored envelope and read the card. *Auguri!* "Happiness," I said aloud. He signed the card, "Always, Gianni." I wanted to cry but instead waved the card at everyone and sassily said, "A good gal is hard to find. Guess he misses me."

⌘

THE WEEK FLEW BY, AND at the end of June the hydrangeas were in bloom, huge bushes of ivory, raspberry, and what I called Virgin Mary blue for the color of Mary's mantle. It seemed that these flowers were always the biggest and stayed in bloom the longest. I was not making this up; I actually did a study, and Valentina, who has very little faith in me and my hair-brained schemes, verified. When Papa wanted to change the color of the blue to make it more intense, he would add some of Mamma's steel wool to the earth surrounding the plant. He knew so much about gardening, another thing I wasn't keen on learning, but nobody in the family loved books the way I did and the way Jack and I loved sports. The lovely flowers reminded me of Gianni's nosegay, now dried and sitting on the top shelf of the étagère in the attic hallway. Why had I kept it?

The hydrangea bushes accompanied the long walk all the way to the house, which was set back, its dominant chimney proudly displaying the huge black iron initial "S" that Papa had hung there. I often wondered if it was a matter of pride or possession, or the accomplishment of an immigrant. Whatever it was, our house was the only one in the neighborhood distinguished and consecrated in this manner.

On a huge piece of property, our sprawling house sat on luscious lawns with huge trees. At night the family would sit out on the porch sipping lemonade, with the picture windows thrown open. Fireflies abounded, giving off their little flashes of love signals. They hovered near the white flowering hedge with the sweetest-smelling tiny buds. The privet hedge acted like a fence, bordering and separating our property from the street.

At times our family ate dinner under a huge, square, blue marine umbrella in the backyard or in a white-latticed gazebo my father and Jack had built. My favorite summer dinner was comprised of thin beef or veal cutlets, a tomato salad loaded to the gills with fresh, pungent basil and fat, red summer onions, awash in gold-green extra virgin olive oil. For dessert, Mamma always made a *crostata* of some fresh fruit. My favorite were blackberries, which we had picked wild, inking up our hands on Staten Island, near Grymes Hill, where Mamma's relatives were and where we'd picnic by Silver Lake. I got to play *bocci* with the boys, ride English saddle horseback with the adults, and even frolic with the girls on the badminton court—naturally, I always won.

I loved to go to Staten Island. I'd watch Papa sometimes help relatives with gasoline-powered traction engines they called tractors. Once I watched Papa spend most of the day fixing a tractor—well, trying to. After losing a lot of skin off his knuckles and banging and tweaking, it finally worked. Though I think the fact he threatened to cut its breaks and push it down a hill made it decide to run again.

Mamma's sister had such interesting friends. One of them, named Gertie, would have socials on summer mornings. She started neighborhood gatherings and called them the Old Ladies' Knitting Club. Apart from my Zia Nunziata, who was a mere baby compared to the others, the next youngest member was sixty, and the oldest, Gertie, was seventy-five. They talked about patterns and stitches, recipes, sometimes even a book they'd read, while Papa fixed things for them like washers, doors, broken steps, or screen doors. I would sing for them, and they'd all tell Papa that I should sing on the radio, and he would give me that exasperated look. Then they'd feed us yummy homemade cakes and tell the most fascinating stories of when they were young. Bea's story was my favorite. When she was young she had exchanged letters with an American sailor during WWI. His name was Eugene. One day she received a letter from Eugene's sister Didi saying he was killed in action. He told his sister if anything should happen to him, she was to tell Bea. I found this so sad, but what was even more heart-wrenching was that Bea never married. She said every man she met never measured up to this sailor. She still had all his letters and let me read them. Such a privilege. What a great love story. I thought about it for the rest of summer and even wrote it down in my diary. Love, like life, doesn't always go the way you want it to.

⸙

BEFORE WE LEFT FOR UNCLE Carlo's cabin for the rest of the summer, we enjoyed our own surroundings. On our front lawn in summer Papa would set out U-shaped metal croquet hooks or wickets. These he positioned into different shapes, with variegated, colored stakes at each end. We'd play for hours on end, and sometimes Mamma would even join in—it wasn't physically taxing. I loved to hear her laugh when she would actually hit the ball correctly. She would then serve chilled glasses of water with a few drops of *Anice Unico,* which was an old Sicilian tradition of adding *anice per aqua,* which turned the water milky and gave off a sweet and delicious taste of anise.

⸙

SOME SUMMER NIGHTS GIANNI JOINED us for dinner, but when Gianni made himself scarce, I'd think about him and what he'd be doing at that precise moment. Some evenings I'd walk our dog, Patches, over to Eighty-Fifth Street just to walk by Zia Grazia's house to see if the lights were on or if anyone was sitting out on their front terrace. Many nights I heard voices and laughter and longed to be part of it. I'd hope to glimpse him, but never did, and would walk back home thinking of him.

When I returned home, trees shadowed the alleyway the entire path to the garage. We were the only household in the neighborhood that had a two-car garage but only one car. Papa used the other half for the lawn mower, rake, shovel, spade, spare tools, and other sundries and parts for the car.

In the backyard, we grew peach and fig trees, flowering dogwoods, and on the garage wall rambling in profusion were pink tea roses. Lily of the valley, begonias, and every color geranium one could imagine grew along this rose-covered wall, and at the ends of the flower rows were bushes of rosemary. Mamma always had a spice garden somewhere with basil, parsley, and mint growing. In autumn, I always looked forward to blue wood asters blooming out in a shady spot.

I loved our gazebo. Even in winter, when it was covered with snow, it was splendid, prompting me to think about dachas and horse-drawn sleighs in Russia before the Russian Revolution. Papa also built us a stone summerhouse, not unlike the one at Visitation Academy, only a bit smaller, out in the back near a pergola of clustered apricot trees—huge, sprawling, spreading apricot trees, branches intertwined. Here's where Mamma canned the tomatoes at the end of summer when the price came down—our garden supply wasn't sufficient for preserving.

A hose extension led all the way to where Mamma did her canning. When Mamma canned tomatoes and put up preserves and jams, Papa, who was so ingenious, built her a big fire pit with bricks. He said that in Sicily, they'd put a huge oil drum, like the one Val and I scrubbed clean, stacked up on bricks and start a fire under it after all the bottles of tomatoes were wrapped in newspapers and submerged in water. The fire would burn for several hours to boil the water and hermetically seal the bottles. We used any bottles, like for beer and soda pop, and some other wide-mouthed ones that would close with a rubber ring and a cinch metal top. Into each bottle we'd put a little salt and a leaf or two or more of freshly harvested and washed basil—the smell was intoxicating, like licorice or that same sweet, almost anise smell from anisette. The bottles stayed in the water all night, and nobody could touch them until the water had cooled; taking a bottle out beforehand could be dangerous—I've seen some explode in cool air.

When Mamma was canning, she always talked about Sicily and her childhood and the beaches, with the magnificent color of the water so turquoise it shimmered like jewels cast out of a storm-tossed, sinking Spanish galleon. I could virtually see the white froth of the breaking waves crashing on shore in the wintertime, reminding her of snow on Mount Etna.

∗∗∗

WE GOT TO UNCLE CARLO'S cabin sooner than I expected. I went around to the fancy restaurant and got a job bussing tables. When I wasn't there, I pretended to be, but instead sneaked around to the Little Red Theater nearby, a small playhouse where they were doing some summer stock. I got to know everyone right away and made a meteoric rise from Girl Friday when the director heard me sing Ethel Waters' song "Am I Blue" from *On With the Show.*

I sang in the shower, in front of the bathroom mirror, on the lake-front, and hummed while I was bussing tables. If Mamma knew, she'd annihilate me with one swift blow. I was exhausted, and when I needed to be at the little theater, Val covered for me in the restaurant. I practiced and practiced, rehearsing lines. Why was it so easy to remember song lyrics when I had such a hard time remembering dialogue and lines? I stayed up late reading and studying with a flashlight. I could barely drag myself out of bed in the morning. Mamma was worried I was sick, but I just said it was the summer lazies and I needed to rest from the past year's work at school. Had she fallen for it? Anyway, she'd let me sleep in till almost eight o'clock for a week. Instead of boating or taking a swim, I'd take a nap under a tree until it was time to go to work or show up at the theater.

The director was a handsome man with salt-and-pepper hair. He was on crutches and couldn't work at the Forestburgh Playhouse in Sullivan County, where he usually directed summer productions, but he promised me that if I could get there next year, he'd have a part for me. He was a nice man, but Val said be careful, he might be interested in more than my singing. Of course I prayed for a big-shot Hollywood producer to be in the audience the night I was going to sing, but as fate would have it, there was nobody. However, the next day, a man who was supposedly a talent scout handed me his card and said, "Look me up when you turn eighteen."

WE RETURNED FROM UNCLE CARLO'S cabin in what seemed a flash. Our pet, Patches, was overjoyed at seeing us, jumping up and down and twirling about. Papa said the dog had moped about the whole time we were gone. Papa, too, was thrilled to have us back in Brooklyn and even promised to help with Mamma's late summer canning.

I decided to look for a job in Little Italy, as my father had gotten a job there building a back extension to one of his friend's restaurants. I convinced Mamma I'd travel with him every day and meet him for lunch, then continue my search for a job and meet up with him to take the subway home. Although Mamma was not wholly convinced, Papa stood up for me and approved. I asked my father for money to buy a couple of new dresses appropriate for work and also a new pair of shoes. What I got was one store-bought dress for three-fifty at Monte's Dress Shop on Fourth Avenue that Valentina said was chic, smart yet simple, but not the swanky wool getup I saw with the hefty price tag of ten dollars.

Valentina accompanied me to shop and made a clever observation. "You may be Papa's favorite, but you're going to be a working girl now," which meant I'd be paying for more of my own clothes, especially now that it seemed Papa wasn't working as much as before. We'd seen worried looks pass between Mamma and Papa, but he'd always managed to allay her fears with his handsome smile or by twirling her around the kitchen in a dance with unheard music.

While making a banana curl with her hair, Valentina told me to take the cheaper, more useful dress because it was the smarter decision. I did so but extracted a promise from her to make me a new gabardine skirt and two blouses, one sky blue silk and a white piqué cotton, because I'd learned that the other word for piqué is *marcella*. When I made some money, Mamma said, I could buy new shoes, but for now I was to wear my sensible ones as I'd be doing a lot of hoofing—and she didn't mean dancing.

For the first couple of days in September, I met Papa for a lunch pail break in the back of the building he was renovating. Mamma made us sandwiches of peppers and eggs one day, and tuna fish the next. I told her to skip lunch for me the next day, as it was such a trek to get back to where he was and I lost a lot of time. Instead, I packed up a small brown paper-wrapped package of biscotti and an apple. I eventually found a job, not in Little Italy but in Chinatown. I started as a bookkeeper for a small importing business.

⚜

IT WASN'T LONG AFTER MY first job that I decided I wanted more money and to be less in the service industry. I can still see Mamma and me sitting in the downstairs parlor in front of the fireplace—a comfortable and easy space because on the mantel there were so many pictures of our relatives in Sicily. There, I voiced my desires to her, and then we went upstairs to the kitchen where we began to cut and wash vegetables for soup.

Mamma said, "I want to talk to you seriously." She wrung her hands on her white apron. "You're not going to work in the Garment District. I forbid it. My cousin Gertie had a cousin whose friend got caught in that awful fire and jumped to her death. I'm not going to lose a daughter over a few dollars."

"Mamma, don't be silly, They don't lock the doors on workers anymore. These are different times."

"I remember the tragedy of the Triangle Shirtwaist fire," Mamma said.

"That was forever ago before I was born. Things are different now—no sweatshops like in the old days. There's even the International Ladies' Garment Workers Union." I wanted to put my arms around her to allay her fears, but when Mamma gets like this, I knew the only thing I could do was to stand my ground.

"You know so much, why did they lock the doors and kill those poor souls?" She took a wooden spoon from a painted ceramic pitcher full of utensils.

"Because the bosses thought the girls pilfered and took unsanctioned breaks—you know—time off."

"I know time off—what's pilfer mean? *Rubacchiare?* You mean steal the lousy cloth they made them sew on?" She waved the spoon at me for emphasis.

"Precisely." I opened my eyes large in agreement to her disbelief.

"Say what you want about the old country, but we lived a healthier and a different life." She walked to the stove, took the lid off a pot, and began to stir minestrone soup.'

"Mamma, I never said anything about Sicily. In fact, I want to go there on my honeymoon."

"*Luna di miele?* The way you treat Gianni, that golden-hearted boy?" She put the spoon down on a rest in the form of a large spoon and popped the lid back on the pot at a jaunty angle so the steam would filter out.

"Yes, Gianni's sweet, but he's not the only fish in the proverbial sea—"

"Maybe so, in your young eyes, but in mine, I know he's the best catch! The only one for you." She bent slightly, lowered the flame beneath the pot, and stood to face me.

"You're so old-fashioned—I can take care of myself. Do you really think I'm a 'dumb Dora,' stupid enough to work in a place where they lock doors? Besides, I won't be sewing, I'll be selling, doing the books, and maybe even some modeling."

"Modeling what? I don't want you involved with someone who'll take advantage of you."

"I wasn't born yesterday—I'm on the ball."

"You can use every modern expression you want, but you're still my baby girl, and I have a right to worry. I know something about the world—how men think and act with young girls."

"It's not the Middle Ages. You want me strapped in a chastity belt. No one's going to dare attempt anything funny with me." I left the kitchen and took hold of my hat on the attic stairs and came back. "Look at the size of my hatpin." And with that, I brandished it like a fencer.

"Oh, that's some weapon, all right."

I put the pin on the table, made a face, and drew my hands up into claws. "How about these deterrents?" I said, indicating my bent fingernails by shaking my head side to side.

She shook her head in wonderment, but at least I got her smiling.

⸎

MY FIRST FEW DAYS ON the new job flew by and seemed easy enough, as I did a lot of running around picking up sample books, showing illustrations, and dividing my time doing accounts, checking merchandise coming in, attending to people delivering, assisting with the sending out of packages, and sundry other things.

By the end of the third week, I'd made friends with Benjy, Mr. Coopmann's son, but I always called him Benjamin, as I thought the nickname took away from the respect he wasn't getting shown by the boss. In my eyes, Benjamin was not always treated the way a young man in his father's business should. For one thing, the boss called him on the carpet for the most insignificant things and actually scolded the boy, mostly in Yiddish, but I got the gist after a while. In fact, I was starting to learn quite a few Yiddish words, like *dumkop,* meaning dumb, and *a groyser tsuleyger,* which sarcastically implied "a big shot." The other words I learned I kept to myself but didn't use them for fear of insulting those whose language it was.

At least this was my opinion of Benjamin, who was nothing like his father—especially not in looks. He didn't resemble him at all, and at first I thought he might have been adopted, but then I saw a picture of his mother, and there was the likeness. So I assumed he had his mother's sweeter side, for he was docile. He had a discerning manner when it came to making decisions, most of which his father overlooked, vetoed, or simply tapped his temple and called him "*richt in kop,*" crazy in the head, or "*meshuga.*"

Every night I'd write in my diary all the interesting occurrences at work. Mamma did not know, nor did I inform her, that the particular garments involved in my work were brassieres. She would have gone into paroxysms of fury, and I'd be out of work before I could spell the word.

By the fourth week, something strange occurred. My boss, a tough-minded, belligerent, frenetic man, built like what I'd imagined Napoleon to look like, asked me to model two of his new brassieres, one a soft pink satin, the other made of white cotton lace.

I was a bit embarrassed at first, but the model that usually does this, Margie, wasn't in, and he needed to show off some of the merchandise on a real, live model. Behind the curtained area that served as a changing room, I felt odd. I yanked my shirt out of my skirt, unbuttoned the cuffs of my sleeves, and worked the shoulder straps of my own bra down my arms. I unhooked the back and slipped it off from under my blouse in front. I put on the model bra by fastening the hooks and eyes in front of my waist, swiveled it around to the back, and then pulled it up to cover my breasts. I unbuttoned my blouse and put my arms into the straps and pulled them up. Neat job without showing too much flesh before I was into the brassiere. As I was adjusting my breasts into this pink satin affair, I realized how high and forward my breasts were. If I donned a sweater,

I'd look the spitting image of one of those "sweater girls" I'd seen in magazines. I turned this way and that, looking into the mirror.

My boss barged into the small area designated as a dressing room—walked in without even knocking on the crooked posts that held the curtain. Taking me by surprise, he said, "*Krassavitseh, di:* Beautiful."

First it seemed like I was in a dream, but he was coming toward me with his cupped hands outstretched, reaching toward my pointed breasts. This wasn't a reverie but reality, and I was not a protagonist but a young girl in great danger.

Naturally, I balked, but then I began to think of a possible entrance to a modeling career, which might lead me to a singing career—my mind whirled in a flurry of pink and lavender puffed-up clouds, which obviously took over my good sense. How could I have been so blind, so misguided, such an ingénue, after all my mother's warnings? But there I stood, semi-nude in a dressing room with a balding Napoleon ogling me, advancing with outstretched paws about to ensnare me. I had no choice. I slapped his face and screamed for help.

Next thing I knew, I was out on the street, fired, ashamed, and worst of all, knowing that I'd have to face Mamma's "I told you so." Crushed beyond belief, I realized that not only hadn't I been paid, I hadn't even had lunch yet and my stomach was churning, yearning for sustenance. Did I have the courage to reenter the building and go up the elevator to the eleventh floor and demand payment for services rendered? The hell! I did not! Another realization hit. I wasn't only given the boot, I was a coward who couldn't even demand what was my due. Another life lesson I certainly could never admit to Mamma.

As I approached the subway station, Benjamin ran after me, calling my name. He was red in the face, but I couldn't make out if it was the exertion of the run or embarrassment at what had just occurred in his father's upper office. He stammered an apology and handed me a piece of blue stationery with his name and number on it, and beneath that was thirteen dollars, my weekly pay. "Benjamin, I didn't work the whole week."

"Consider it severance pay from a grubby old man."

"And this?" I asked, pointing to his name and number.

"If you ever need a friend."

And for the first time, I answered in Yiddish. "*Dank.*"

I turned, and a thought came to me. At least I didn't leave that place without learning that without even trying to beguile, one could make a man look like a wolf yearning after prey. And just maybe another thing—like my Papa, I was beginning to "read" people. I'd been right about Benjamin—he was a *mensch*.

⤐❦⤎

VALENTINA STOOD IN THE DOORWAY, and I couldn't contain my happiness, so I blurted out that I'd quit my job.

"This makes you happy? It's terrible news." She reached for a hank of hair.

"Not because of that, silly girl, which by the way, if you'd even bother to ask what went wrong, was a horrible experience of almost rape—"

At that, she opened her big brown eyes like saucers. "What do you mean?"

"Forced, unconsented sexual intercourse!"

"I think the word is nonconsensual, and aren't you being a bit overly dramatic?"

I nodded and in a calmer tone, I explained what had transpired between the lecher, Mr. Coopmann, and me.

"So basically you didn't quit—you were fired."

"Yes, but Benjamin, his son, followed me and thrust into my hand my pay for the week. In the meantime," I said and heaved a sigh, "this may not be a problem after all, because I saw an ad for a salesgirl in Macy's which I'm going to apply for tomorrow."

"How do you know you'll get it?

"I don't, but it's a lead. Please stop fussing with your hair. Are you ever going to get over that habit? Anyway, since at that point my day was shot, I used some of the money to splurge—Papa was too busy, so I went to lunch by myself in Chinatown."

"What's so great about that? You go there a lot with Papa."

"Hush up and listen! I was about to walk by a new Chinese restaurant—Wo Kee's or some Oriental name like that—when this handsome man walked by. He was carrying a bunch of books and papers and accidentally dropped some and said, '*Merda*,' and I almost keeled over. So I asked him if he spoke Italian. He said he did, and I told him I did, too. One thing led to another. He introduced himself as Bao and encouraged me to try the restaurant. It was incredible—you walk down this narrow, tiny staircase and almost plunk your head on every step, having to arch your back to keep from smacking your forehead, step by step. I had a rough time getting down so I wouldn't lose my balance."

"Marcella, I have to pee. Get on with it."

"By the time I got to the last step down those slanted stairs and entered the dining room, I was shocked to see a huge space. It opens up to this enormous dining room. It's so large, and there're a million waiters serving every dish you've never tasted—some sweet yet sour, picante but smooth, so many different foods you recognize but don't. They bring one dish after another to the table. You don't know where to begin first. There are no forks; you have to use tiny wooden sticks to pick and choose the things you want to taste."

"Now, I suppose, you'll give me the whole menu. Thrilling," she said, twisting a thick bunch of hair into a coil.

"I've never had such cuisine before, although some of the delicacies seem to be Italian because they have spaghetti or some other kind of long pasta, noodles in certain hot soups, with lots of vegetables, such as carrots and onions and even bean sprouts. Basically, darling sister, I wish I wasn't so tired, because I don't just want to tell you about everything I ate when the one thing that's most important is the wonderful man I met who joined me for lunch—he's Chinese, but could pass for Italian. I know it sounds strange, but it's true. He's so European. Older and mature. Big brown eyes, almost like Papa's. I swear to you! Did I say his name is Bao? I think I'll be awake all night thinking about him even though I'm so exhausted."

"And Gianni?"

"In my heart, I've not stopped thinking about Gianni since my party, but maybe this was only a ruse to shelter my heart."

"You're not serious."

"Like Mamma always says about first meeting Papa and he says about meeting her—I may have been struck by lightning. I think I'm falling in love with him and know him like he's part of me. I love him. I actually do."

"Marcella! You've lost your mind. You're out of your head." She twirled her finger at her temple.

"Indeed, I have. Over him," I said. "You don't know the first thing about him."

"Nor do I want to. It's not possible. You love Gianni. You're just too pigheaded to admit it."

"Who can say what love is? How can you ever know if it's genuine, verifiable, actual? And I don't need a lecture from you, baby sister," I said, trying to provoke a fight with her.

"Okey-dokey, we'll talk in the morning over a nice bowl of Cream o' Wheat. Nighty-night. Pina brought over bananas. And by the by—I do know what love is." She blew me a kiss.

Now that gave me pause. She wasn't offended, sensitive, annoyed, outraged—what's with her?

CHAPTER 10

Giacomo

A MONTH AFTER THE FAMILY came home from Lake George, Giacomo ran into Jan de Graaf coming out of an Italian restaurant near where Giacomo was working. A close acquaintance of Giacomo's, they hadn't seen each other for over two years. But de Graaf immediately said he was in need of a good man, and by summer's end, Giacomo had joined a construction crew that was building the new Downtown Athletic Club.

Giacomo had never considered de Graaf, whom he'd met the year Marcella was born, as a friend, as they lived on too different a social stratum. But Giacomo knew that despite his accented English, de Graaf liked him and valued his opinions and him personally as a hard worker. Jan de Graaf was a club member and worked as a civil engineer for the architectural company of Starrett & Van Vleck.

Giacomo thought of de Graaf as a good sort, a "big tycoon" getting ready for retirement, but he never quite understood why the man bothered to talk to the likes of him. Giacomo put together that the man was playing the stock market heavily, and Giacomo, who wasn't the least bit interested in finance, warned him. The old-fashioned ways are the best: Put your cash in a sock under your mattress or behind a brick of the chimney.

They had many on-the-job discussions about what Giacomo called the art nouveau design from these architects. He told de Graaf the style had started with the world *Exposition Universelle* of 1900 in Paris. Giacomo had been in China back then, but had heard about the designs when he returned to Sicily after the Boxer Rebellion and never actually had seen this style until coming to America. Giacomo discerned respect in de Graaf's eyes when they spoke.

"It's a shame you couldn't have studied to become an architect or engineer," de Graaf said.

Giacomo laughed. "Architects draw and don't get their hands dirty. I love to build."

"I understand." Jan de Graaf held his palms open.

Giacomo nodded, and knew the man was sincere and not scoffing at him and that the respect was reciprocal. "I have an idea, although you may think it's preposterous. I don't have the capabilities to draw, but I can explain a kind of internal vision that I have and perhaps you can put it on paper."

De Graaf invited Giacomo in his work clothes to his office. There de Graaf offered Giacomo a whiskey neat and told him to settle himself into a chair at his desk, thrusting some paper, pencils, and erasers in front of him.

Giacomo made a very crude sketch, but as he was drawing, began to explain some of the things he imagined. Hovering over Giacomo's shoulder, de Graaf worked with his own pencil, filling in and completing the rough design.

"Like this?" de Graaf asked as he proportioned lines and gave depth to the sketch.

"Yes, that's it," Giacomo said.

"If you were to see this building being constructed and be a part of it, would you be able to tell me if we were going in the right direction?"

"I believe I could."

De Graaf straightened and slapped Giacomo on the back. "And I believe you will. How would you like to be the foreman of this project?" De Graaf tossed back his drink and smiled.

"It'd be an honor, sir." Giacomo stood and held out his hand, while de Graaf reached into his breast pocket and pulled out a wad of cash and slapped it into Giacomo's hand.

They shook hands, the money falling to the floor.

CHAPTER II

Marcella

THE "HELP WANTED" SIGN I'D seen in the paper had caught my eye, but what if they'd already filled the position? I looked up at the dauntingly huge department store and the Macy's logo with the red star, wondering what it stood for, but decided I'd have to find out. I entered the building in my nifty outfit, thanks to Val, armed with the newspaper in which I'd seen the ad. I looked about for a sign to indicate which floor I was supposed to go to. There it was by the escalator: second floor, Intimate Apparel and Foundations. I took the escalator, looking at my feet, covered in polished shoes, as I hopped on. I'd heard horror stories about people riding escalators and not paying attention. I reached the second floor and meandered my way past lovely dresses and frocks to reach the foundations department. I looked about and saw a customer eyeing a fox-trimmed night sweater and seemingly considering lace and silk nightgowns that I knew held an exorbitant price tag. Way toward the back stood an interesting woman in a dark man-tailored suit and a crystal blue blouse with a man's tie denoting a position of authority. I knew immediately that this was the boss.

I approached her and asked if she was the person in charge.

"My name is Elaine Weiss—may I help you?"

"Yes," I said. I wasn't about to beg for a job, but what immediately struck me was there's no going back. I'd have to come across as a capable person who could handle anything and not be timid about it. She looked me up and down.

She had extremely dark brown hair, almost black, cut short, but not a bob—more of a barber cut for sure—so sophisticated and New York chic. Her vibrant eyes shone, although I couldn't note the color in this lighting.

"I've come—"

There was a distracting noise over by a sign for dressing rooms.

"Excuse me a minute," she said, and barely giving me a glance, she brusquely strolled over to a young saleswoman bawling her eyes out. The girl was young and blond and didn't stop sniffling. I felt sorry for her.

At Elaine Weiss' approach, the tongue-tied girl burst into a torrent of tears, while the other saleswoman, who had been next to her, turned around, took a deep breath, and pointing to a paper in her hand said, "She'll have to go, Miss Weiss. She makes too many mistakes."

Elaine Weiss considered the girl, the paper, and the other saleswoman and then walked back over to where I stood.

"Well, well, look at you! What have we here?" she asked as she pulled the newspaper advertisement I'd circled from my hand. "Mmmm," she said, "are you here for the sales position?"

"In fact, I am. Yes, ma'am."

"Call me Miss Weiss. You're a knockout. What's your name?" she asked, inspecting me again from head to toe.

"I'm Marcella Scimenti—"

"I was hoping for some miracle but I didn't expect such a looker. Aces," she said. "I can use you. Are you ready to start?"

"You mean right now?"

"Yes, as it seems this young lady and I are parting ways." She indicated the shaking blond held up by the wall. "Bye, Miss Friedman, I wish you luck. Pick up your paycheck downstairs."

I was flummoxed. I couldn't possibly have caused this girl to get the heave-ho.

"Close your mouth, dear, you can't subsist on flies. Have you eaten? I know a great little place around the corner for bagels and lox. Are you Jewish?"

"Me?"

"Do you see someone else I'm talking to? *A brooch!* You mean to tell me you're a little *shiksa?*"

"Oh," I blurted—"*mit yiddeshe kop.*"

"*Got in himmel,* I think I'm in love. Who taught you Yiddish?"

"No one. I picked it up."

"What's your name again? Where have you worked?" she asked. Not waiting for my answer, she told two women to watch the floor because she was going out to eat. We went to a deli around the corner. She ordered what she called brunch—not breakfast, but not quite lunch: toasted bagels, cream cheese, and lox. Fine with me, as I was starving; I only hoped I could afford it.

Elaine Weiss interviewed me as we ate, half the time with my mouth full, but I was able to croak out my name, and once, almost choking, to answer about my previous work experience. When it came time to pay the bill, I reached for my purse, but she raised a hand, palm toward my face. I felt like our dog Patches being told wordlessly to stay. She took the bill, paid, and left a big tip. I gulped the rest of my coffee, and asked to use the ladies', wishing someday to be as suave and self-assured.

⁓⋇⁓

BACK WITH BRASSIERES, CORSETS, AND garter belts, I was shown the layout of the floor with the dressing rooms; the fitting rooms; where the extra garments in different sizes were stored; where other intimate apparel, such as camisoles and chemises were housed; where nightwear including negligees and dressing gowns, peignoir sets, and other bedtime items, including try-as-they-might-to-be-alluring bed jackets were stocked; where the measuring tape was kept and how to measure a woman's bust, waist, or hips; where the pin cushion was to be found at all times and how to pin a slip or petticoat so it could be hemmed without ruining the lace; where the key was saved under the cash register in case there was a problem and the drawer wouldn't open; and where the order slips were and the catalogues stowed. I caught on fast and learned that very day that Elaine Weiss did not suffer fools.

⁓⋇⁓

WEEKS LATER, I KNEW SALES work suited my personality, and when you're good at something and it comes easy, you begin to like it even more. It was effortless. I warmed to it and wanted to excel even more.

One evening leaving work, I kissed Elaine's cheek and said, "Thanks for everything."

She looked surprised. "What about a real kiss?"

I kissed her other cheek and dashed off.

Three months into the job, I finally learned what the red star outside Macy's symbolized. The logo came from a tattoo that a teenaged Macy got working on a Nantucket whaling ship, the *Emily Morgan.* I discovered that romantic bit of the store's history from an elderly saleslady in Perfume on the first floor. Sometimes I'd spray myself with a free sample, luxuriating in something expensive but forbidden to be purchased, as my meager purse held no money to weight it. Besides, how could I spend lavishly on an extravagance when we needed bread on the table at home and Mamma was now using one tea bag for two cups of tea.

Every day, right after I'd meet Apple Mary on the corner and give her the nickel I'd saved from my subway fare by walking, the first person I'd see when I entered the store was the perfume lady, and we'd exchange greetings. One day I told her it was too bad Mr. Rowland Hussy Macy didn't live long enough to see the department store's meteoric rise. She agreed, and as I walked away, I said, "Hats doffed to you, Mr. Macy!" and as I saluted, heard her giggle.

⬦

IT WAS ALSO FIVE MONTHS into the job when Elaine Weiss invited me out for a Sunday. I knew she liked me with what I perceived as sisterly fondness, and offered me invaluable constructive criticism when selling. She'd mentioned several times the idea of some college courses to help me advance in the business world. Elaine said it would be lunch in the city, and then we'd go to tour the Metropolitan Museum. Arriving at the museum, Elaine bought the tickets and made a generous donation besides. I tried to look blasé but didn't know if I was pulling it off, though she had to call me away from intently looking at a poster.

It had been raining all afternoon, so we took our time visiting the many different exhibitions. It was fascinating, and I enjoyed it immensely. We were sitting on a bench together in front of a painting when Elaine said, "You're a natural when it comes to selling. Where did you learn the knack?"

"Maybe from Mamma, who always says you need to gain someone's confidence before you buy or sell."

⚜

TOWARD LATE AFTERNOON, WHEN WE were about to leave, Elaine said she wanted to freshen up. I waited for her in the crowded ladies' room of the museum. The stalls were all taken, but eventually, the ladies exited and I was still waiting. It was getting late. Finally the crowded bathroom thinned out to just Elaine, still in a stall, and me.

Waiting made me anxious.

"Elaine, are you all right?"

She came out of the stall and looked around. It was so quiet after the crush of all the women. She washed her hands and stared at me strangely in the mirror. After she dried her hands on paper towels, she tossed them into a bin and walked over to where I leaned against the wall and put her hands on either side of my head. She bent her head and I knew she was going to kiss me. I felt curious yet repulsed, so I turned my head, but she took her hand and forced my chin around to kiss me smack on the lips.

I shook my head like a wild colt. "Elaine! Are you crazy?"

"As a matter of fact, yes—for you."

I pushed her away.

"I think I love you," she said, her voice matter-of-fact and devoid of passion.

I waited a few seconds before saying, "I love you, too—like a sister."

"No. I mean I'm in love with you," she said, stressing the "in."

"Well, get over it, because I'm in love with a man," I said, stressing the "in" the way she'd done.

"You've never been with a woman, have you?" She stepped into the perimeter I'd deemed safe.

"Of course not. I've never been with a man either—if you mean slept with someone."

"I'll love you the way a man doesn't know how to and can't because he doesn't know what a woman desires. Only another woman knows that."

"Why're we even talking like this, and in a public toilet?"

"You're right. Why don't we go to my place? I can make dinner."

"Are you mad? I quit." I pushed her away from me.

"You're not serious." She grabbed my arm.

I looked down, put my hand on top of hers, and wrenched it off. Through my teeth I said, "Let go of me. You're my boss, and if you're going to behave in this unseemly manner, you leave me no choice. I can't work under the threat of a possible attack."

"I'm not assaulting you—"

"What do you call what just transpired?"

"An exchange of an affectionate kiss with somebody I'm falling in love with."

"Don't banter about it. Are you sure you know the meaning of the word? In my world, it's a family word—we have true, deep sentiments for each and every member of the family. But if it's outside of family relationships, then it means feelings between a man and a woman. Your kind of affection doesn't exist in my world."

"You can't be serious. You need this job."

"Oh, I need the job all right, but I need my sanity more. I'd be petrified you'd jump out and grab me in a dressing room—like Mr. Coopmann did."

"Who?"

"Forget it. A ghost of Christmas past."

"You're serious, aren't you? You'd leave a good job like this in times like these."

"Damn straight, I am. You give me no choice."

"I'll back off. I can't afford to lose you at work—you're my top salesperson. You already know—"

"Know what?" I shrugged my shoulders.

"The sales business inside and out. You've learned so fast, and what's more, you're fabulous with people and know how to deal with customers, even difficult ones. Why that woman with big breasts and huge hips who came in last Friday—she positively beamed when you said she was well-proportioned. You could sell anyone the Brooklyn Bridge."

I gave a little laugh. "Funny."

"What is?"

"You sound like my mother, only she says I can charm the painted saints off the wall."

"She's right, and I'm serious. I'd like you to start taking courses at NYU."

"University?" We'd talked about taking courses, but this was new.

"Yes. Let me mentor you. They've got a program in marketing and business."

"I work because I need the pay. I can't fling it away on college. And anyway, I just signed up for singing lessons with a voice teacher. Eventually, I want to go to Hollywood."

"Quite. I'll help you. In fact, I'll pay for you to start studying right away—this semester. You can take one voice lesson a week and practice singing at home. And you can take one course a week and study at night."

"You're kidding. I couldn't accept your payment for my schooling. Never. I'd be indebted to you. You'd like that, wouldn't you? But I'd hate it."

"No strings attached, I swear. You've got no other option. You intend to go forward and advance—I want you as a buyer, and I'll give you a raise so you can afford the voice coach. You've got excellent taste and know what kinds of intimate vestments women like and need, and you know what men like to see their women sauntering around in—"

"Something for everyone." I couldn't control myself or my brash tongue, but it was tempting.

"That's right," she said, as if we were coconspirators.

I beckoned her close with my crooked, pointing finger, and when she was close enough for me to kiss, I whispered, "Go kiss off in Macy's window," and walked away.

It wasn't enough apparently, because she followed me out, hailed a cab, and shoved me in. I created such a fuss that she dropped me at a nearby subway station.

I thought of Benjamin catching up with me on the move from that other unpleasant situation.

"Will I see you on Monday?" she said, her voice pleading.

I shook my head but never answered. I stepped out and slammed the door. Rushing my pace, I grabbed hold of the subway station handrail and hurried down the steps. I heard her call my name as I reached the last step.

It was unusually crowded for this time of day on the subway. I sat in the station considering all that had happened. I was drained. When I heard the train coming down the tracks, I stood with a crush of travelers and got on the next train. I didn't want to go home after all that had happened and kept hopping on and off trains when I realized this train was just beginning to come up for air around Eighth Street, cruising along the El. The autumn season was under way, and shoppers weren't going to be denied the pleasure of an outing just because of water falling from the sky and a slate-gray day. They toted umbrellas. Some wore work shoes, others boots. Everyone looked sodden. It'd suddenly become cold, and I was surprised the weather hadn't turned to freezing rain. People's coats and jackets steamed in the close atmosphere—sardines in a can of warmed olive oil.

At the last stop I noticed that a stylish man had entered the car. He was clean-shaven and a dead ringer for Jimmy Walker. I was tempted to say, "Why, hello Beau James," but was jostled into my seat. My thoughts led me to think about the good our New York mayor had done. He'd created a board of sanitation—so needed! He'd helped improve hospitals, upgraded many parks and playgrounds, worked on the construction and expansion of our subway system, and somehow managed to keep the five-cent subway fare despite a threatened strike by workers. Papa called him *l'irlandese*, the Irishman, but not in a derogatory way, only as a means of differentiating between his people and ours. Papa liked what the man was doing for New York.

The Jimmy Walker double squeezed past some workers and a gaggle of giggling teenage girls and slid into the vacant seat next to me. He wore an expensive-looking cashmere coat. My thoughts ran along the lines of: *Not such a gentlemen if he didn't tip his hat, and why isn't he in a chauffeured Rolls Royce instead of on a crowded subway train?* He removed a black leather glove from his left hand and placed it in his pocket. Why not remove both? I thought that a bit strange, but perhaps something was wrong with his other hand—deformed, misshapen from a terrible burn—there I went off again, carried away into a short story of a dapper-looking gentleman.

I was bored with the Tolstoy novel I'd lugged with me. Mamma had read it in Italian, *La Guerra e la Pace*, but it was bad enough in English. I could never have poured through it in flowery Italian—all those war scenes! I carried the British translation in my purse, and it weighed me down—certainly not a book to travel the Second Avenue El with. Live and learn, Mamma always said. Anyway, how could I concentrate when I kept replaying the incident with Elaine and what I'd said to her. How could I quit knowing I wanted to take voice lessons, couldn't ask my folks for the money, and was on the verge of signing up for them next week? I'd have to make her understand I wanted her friendship only. I genuinely liked her for so many reasons—she was smart, sophisticated, and a terrific boss. I'd learned so much from her in so little time.

To distract myself from my real-life problems, I glanced about at people, read a few advertising signs, and then with a start, I gathered that the stylish man was playing *mano morta*. Mamma and Pina had both warned me about men who casually slip or drop a "dead hand" in your lap—in movies, on buses, and on trains. I tried to remain still, but his left hand was on my right thigh, resting, not clasping, pressing, or clutching—simply positioned there. I made no swift move. Instead, just as casually, I removed my dark green felt-and-velour cloche hat, placed it on my lap, and with my left hand beneath it, drove the huge hatpin into his hand. He squealed like a pig, an abattoir-stunned animal, loudly and frantically jumping up. I did the same and shouted, "Masher! You should've taken your expensive car, traveled like a patrician, instead of riding a train with the common folk!" Everyone around us howled. He stooped forward to stand by the door and got off at the next stop, and I hoped he learned a lesson from a working-class girl.

Mamma and Pina would've died of sheer embarrassment. Why am I like this? Who do I take after? Maybe Mamma's right—I read too many books, see too many films. I thought of the glorious actresses Lily Langtry and Louise Brooks and recalled Wordsworth's tragic Evangeline searching for Gabriel; Edgar Allen Poe's "Annabel Lee"—why is that? Do I think I'm a heroine, a forlorn and abandoned creature in my own life story, a tragic figure? I could've kicked myself for all these senseless reveries, because they always led me inexorably back to one name—Gianni. Sensible and sweet. He kept me a flightless, earthbound bird.

I smiled to myself, thinking of Papa saying I'm too modern even for these times. What if he knew of Elaine's strike? These things happened, to be sure, even in the olden times. Oh well. But what was I going to do come Monday? I needed the money, especially now as I'd secretly begun taking voice lessons—thank heavens, close to home. I stopped off around the corner from where I lived one evening a week after work. I fancied my position at Macy's enough to know I wouldn't be likely to find something comparable anytime soon. I also knew I'd just have to learn how to fend off Miss Weiss, who had mentioned that raise before I so rudely told her off. I needed to continue working at Macy's even if I had to eat crow—a disgusting idea, as crow eat carrion. I'd have to think of a way to apologize to her. People can't help their feelings, and with that I pictured Gianni putting his strong, protective arm around my shoulder at the cinema.

⁓⋅✦⋅⁓

BUT THAT DIDN'T STOP ME when I began seeing Bao on occasion. It's a wonder I had time to breathe between my job and singing lessons. Bao was tall and lean and had a thin moustache. He was so interesting and wore tight-fitting dark suits with white shirts that had highly starched collars and elegant silk ties. He almost looked like a young seminarian, except for the tie, and one day when we met for lunch, I said this to him with a wry smile.

We sat at a crowded dinette near Macy's, and I asked him about his life in China. I learned his original name was Zhou Cheng-Gong, but originally Zhou was spelled "Chou," closer to the way Western missionaries called Chinese names back when he was born. Zhou was a family name, although he had no family.

I had finished eating a tuna fish sandwich on rye when I asked what his name meant.

"The name Cheng-Gong was Tseng-gong, meaning 'important subject of the emperor,' or someone who has a higher ranking in society due to his contribution and wisdom," he said.

He sipped his tea and pulled a face. "Not as good as ours, that's for sure." He put the cup down and told me he didn't know why he'd been given this name and the only thing he could figure out was the priest who raised him at the monastery wanted to give him an important-sounding name as the portents weren't in his favor.

On another occasion, a mere three days later, we met after work and took a walk. I didn't complain that my feet were killing me from standing all day, I was so happy to be with him and talk about his life.

We found a squat stone wall in front of a restaurant to rest awhile before I had to catch the train home.

"What I know is that I was born of a difficult childbirth that caused the death of my mother, so probably the priest wished to give me some luck to change my humble status. The outcome of all this is that when I came to America, I renamed myself Bao, meaning precious treasure, because that's what I hope to become one day to someone and because I liked the sound of it." He smiled, and then added, "It has another meaning for eunuchs, but never mind that."

"I like your name. You tower over me—probably got your height from your European father, who must've been tall."

"I believe so. Most Chinese women are petite, to say the least."

⸰⸱⸰

TOWARD THE END OF THE next week, it was Bao's night off—actually, I believe he took off, as nobody ever seemed to have days off in Chinatown. We were on our way to have dinner in a place near where he worked but which he said was cheaper and had better food. I couldn't help but think of Gianni and how he always wanted to take me to the best little restaurants in the neighborhood, and since there weren't many, we often went to Coney Island or Avenue U.

I wondered if Bao was taking me out on the cheap because he didn't have enough of the jingling stuff in his pockets. But how was that possible when he kept talking about going back to San Francisco to see friends and possibly traveling to the Orient for some business? I tried to engage him in conversations about this, but he always seemed to clam up or change the subject. In other words, it was none of my business to pry, but he was too kind just to say, *butt out of my affairs.*

That evening in Chinatown, Bao cajoled me as we passed some food stands, and I pulled a face. "What? You've never eaten a meal on the street, served by vendors packing their food stuffs and serving-ware?"

"This is America, remember? Yes, I've eaten street fare of all kinds at the Festival of San Giuseppe in March and the Feast of San Gennaro. That's a huge fair and has *zeppole*, which are tiny balls of fried ricotta—like doughnuts dusted with powdered sugar—and all sorts of other food. Everybody talks at once, eats, drinks, and the next Sunday in church, the Monsignor chastises everyone—but only after his pockets and the church coffers are full of coins from the fair. Or so I've heard, but we don't go to that parish—it's in New York."

"You haven't lived, young lady," he said to me like a venerable old grandfather, and I had an intense urge to pinch his cheek like Papa does to me.

At that point I thought I'd follow him anywhere, even to the bowels of Hell and for all eternity. I was smitten. We went to a tiny restaurant—I mean our upstairs bathroom had it over this, tenfold. Bao introduced me to a bunch of people who spoke no English or Italian, and my Chinese was absolutely lacking, so we all bowed heads, and I felt rather ignorant, wondering why Papa had never taught us even the simplest phrases.

Bao had me sit on a stool near the kitchen, where woks issued forth pungent odors and where steam poured out of every gadget, huge pots of boiling water, and cooking devices. "I'll be right back," he said, disappearing behind enormous hanging pots. Some minutes later, he reappeared, a blue-and-white bowl in his hand. "This," he said with pride, "is a humble dish called *dàndàn miàn*, Szechuan cuisine. It's a noodle dish not on the menu. I prepared it myself, just for you." He wore a sheepish grin.

"Ah. What my mother calls 'peasant food.'"

I wondered if it was some kind of weird aphrodisiac soup with rhinoceros horn powder thrown in. Oh no, that's for guys to have erections—at least that's what Papa said, and certainly he hadn't been addressing me. I had overheard him say it to Zio Carlo, who really wasn't an uncle at all, but that's what you call older people as a sign of respect.

I looked at the dish. It seemed like our Italian *buccatini*, only softer or a bit overcooked, not at all *al dente*. It was served with various hot chili sauces, including an especially tasty one of ground pork and green onions or scallions, using also the soft tops cut into thin ringlets.

"The word *dàndàn*," he said, "refers to the balance pole street vendors carry. On one end hangs a server or saucer of noodles, and on the other is a platter of hot chili sauces, spicy enough to raise the dead. The noodles are sold on the street and served in wooden bowls in my country, and Heaven alone knows what cleaning process these have undergone or not, but if you're willing to take a chance on your health, well—"

I was suddenly at a loss for words and mumbled, "But here we are in this restaurant—of sorts."

"Dine! Indulge!" he said.

And I definitely did. I went along with whatever Bao said, mesmerized by his intense look. I burned the roof of my mouth and begged for cold water, but what I got was a cup of boiling hot tea, followed by another rich and heated dish loaded to the gills with red pepper, steeped in soy. I thought of all the *piccanti* Italian fish dishes Gianni had treated me to, but none were ever of this intense fire that made my insides feel like they'd been to Hades and back. I refused another bite, and Bao made me wash it all down with warm sake, though I craved something icy cold. I must have been as red as the enamel on the tips of my chopsticks.

AFTER HE'D ENTICED ME WITH a musical off-Broadway—how I loved the music—and an improvisational jazz concert in a small theater in Harlem, my idea of following him everywhere suddenly came to a screeching halt because he made the decision to leave for San Francisco in what he called a "fortnight." Lucky I read enough English novels to know that I had exactly fourteen days to try to dissuade him. When I tried to dig for some information about this improvised trip, he went mute—shut up like a clam, and there wasn't a thing I could do to force him to talk about this mysterious trip. At one point, he asked me to stop badgering him like a younger sister!

CHAPTER 12

Giacomo

THAT YEAR THE CIRCUMSTANCES ON Wall Street went from bad to worse from August to October, but when Giacomo came home on Tuesday, October 22, he called it a black day. Over the next two days, business matters looked even more serious, and by the following Tuesday, the twenty-ninth, people ruined in the stock market were not jumping out of windows, as had been reported in the news, but some people reading those newspapers wished they had. The situation on Wall Street that month of October would be the end of the Roaring Twenties and ominously would soon be hailed as the beginning of the Great Depression.

Work had slowed on the frigid days before Christmas, but as soon as the weather broke, the men were back on the job. Giacomo was reading the newspaper in the living room with warm slippers and a knitted shawl thrown over his broad shoulders when he heard on the radio that a certain Jan de Graaf, lately of the architect firm of Starrett & Van Vleck, jumped out of the forty-second floor window of the Old Athletic Club. At first, Giacomo was stunned and disbelievingly called to Angelica, who came in from the kitchen.

"Not your friend de Graaf?" she asked

"He must have over-invested and lost everything," Giacomo said. He thought of his own loss, relatively small in comparison although substantial to him, which he'd riskily invested also. Guilt washed over him for not having told Angelica of this.

He cleared his throat. "When I saw him last month, he went like this," and with that, Giacomo drew his pointing finger across the front of his neck. "He was about to retire and become a consultant for his son's new firm—another Dutch name that I can't remember. Both of his boys graduated Harvard. Jan was so proud of them. It's wrong to think that a man has had an easy life just because he's made a success of himself. I know how hard Jan had it growing up. He worked to achieve all he wanted. What a shame."

"Suicide is such a loss of hope." Angelica sat on the sofa beside Giacomo's easy chair.

"I feel so helpless."

"In the face of death, *caro*, we all are."

He was quiet and pensive for a few moments.

Angelica bent toward him and said, "I can almost hear you thinking. What is it?"

"I read something about suicide in a magazine not too long ago. Where was that?"

"When you accompanied Pina and took Elena to that new pediatrician? The fancy one who won't make house calls."

As the room became shrouded in darkness, Angelica switched on a table lamp. "That's it. The article talked about people wanting to take their lives. They do it only when they discover a way. All that talk, all those fake reports in the newspaper of people jumping out of windows was not the case, but it gave Jan a means."

❦

THE NEXT MORNING AT BREAKFAST, Giacomo told Marcella he was concerned about her dating the Chinese man, Bao.

"I'd hardly call it dating, Papa. I see him once in a while." She dropped a heaping teaspoon of sugar in her café latte.

"I think I should meet him," Giacomo said, trying not to show he was insisting.

"Oh, you will, I suppose," she said, stirring her coffee absently.

"Eventually, if I continue to see him. But he's leaving for San Francisco for an indefinite amount of time."

Giacomo asked her what he was going to do on the west coast. She shrugged her shoulders and said, "He wouldn't tell me. Business, I think. He mentioned the Orient. Several countries with exotic names, but if you asked me right now, I couldn't come up with a single one of them, except, of course, China."

He kissed her on her way out the door, but the preoccupation stayed with him. Why did his daughter always find excuses not to bring Bao around, saying their relationship was nothing serious?

Giacomo wondered if it was "monkey business" and if his daughter was going to come out of this unscathed. Marcella explained that the man was a bit older, but dashing, and could possibly be involved with another woman. He might have been only toying with Marcella, but she didn't mind because he was interesting. But was she captivated by him? The way she'd said it didn't convince Giacomo and certainly didn't assuage his feelings about the situation, knowing how alluring an Asian could be. Bao would be gone for a while, but he'd return sooner or later. Giacomo found himself absently touching the jade Buddha he wore on the chain around his neck, his mind thousands of miles away, his heart racing when he pictured Lian's serene and exquisite face. Do you ever forget your first love?

On Sundays, Giacomo went to the basement and took out Lian's picture and chronicle. How many times had he watched her draw or write in this book? How many times had she said to him, "One day, you'll have this translated and know every thought I've ever possessed, but for now, you must be content with what I tell you." With that, she'd close the book.

He placed them both on his counter workspace and sat on a high stool, leafing through the pages, studying her artwork, and sometimes tracing the dragons she'd drawn. He considered the women's script, Nüshu, graceful and was pleased to have had Lian explain it to him as the key to fully understanding what their relationship had meant to her. After that he would replace these objects in the bottom drawer and tinker with some piece of furniture that needed fixing or continue with some woodwork.

His concern for Marcella was relieved when he found out Bao was leaving on a business trip and the date of his return was unknown. How alluring Celestials could be—of this he had little doubt. He reproached himself for his emotional infidelity. He adored Angelica, but he carried Lian within, like a tracing of his own soul.

CHAPTER 13

Marcella

I WAS MISSING BAO AND all the fun and fascinating activities we'd enjoyed together, but the holidays were keeping me busy, and I intended to make them as happy as I could for my family. On Sunday, in the late afternoon, Mamma and I were going to go to Fourth Avenue for a cup of hot cocoa, but she thought better on it. After all, Christmas was near, and she said she'd rather spend her money on presents. Instead, we stayed home and she made us cocoa. She had skimmed the cream off the top of the milk bottles delivered to the back door for two weeks and now made it into a delicious whipped cream. She always added a smidgeon of vanilla, and she used powdered baker's sugar instead of granulated so it was never gritty—as if we could taste the difference—so it melted right away. Things were going to get tougher—she meant monetarily—and said she believed even foodstuffs would begin to get scarce. This frightened her and I tried to allay her fears, but by her look, I saw she was determined to take action before a problem or something drastic occurred.

She said, "Take a piece of paper and one of Papa's lead carpenter pencils from the table drawer and write me a list." While she beat the cream, she dictated: "Sugar, salt, olive oil, pasta, rice, butter, and flour. We will make an extra storage place here under the kitchen sink."

"But not the butter, right?"

"Of course not, but butter freezes well. The rest of the foodstuffs will go under the sink," she said, washing the egg beater. "Tell Valentina to take all of these cleansers, like Old Dutch Boy and such, and scrub this cabinet out with Gevelle laundry bleach. Then keep the doors open to allow it to air. I think we should line it with shelf paper. I have some saved in the pantry downstairs."

"I'll do it now, Mamma, but remember we put the ammonia, borax, and lye all down in the basement for the wash?"

"Whatever's left."

"Nothing."

"Make sure. I don't want to contaminate our food. Take these blueing agents. Save me some steps. Carry them down to the basement to store near the washing machine and the mangle."

I took the package down two flights, Patches following close on my heels. I stacked the items on the shelf by the window opposite from where Mamma had put an old cabinet that held odd dishes, antique pots, and some silverware. It was dark and dank, and I felt chilled, so I hurried back upstairs.

When I entered the kitchen, Mamma asked, "Where's Patches?"

"With Valentina in the basement. We've got a problem. Val is sitting on top of the machine, holding on for dear life—she isn't even curling her hair! The machine's dancing and walking away." We all knew that our Gyrator was dying a slow death. The attached wringer was all corroded. Maybe it had been fine semisoft rubber, but now it was crumbling and we needed a new one.

"You have money to pay for this new one?"

"Mamma."

"Exactly."

⟞⟐⟜

THE FOLLOWING WEEK, MAMMA WAS still in her bathrobe when I came down for breakfast.

"Something wrong, Mamma? It's the last Thursday before Christmas. You never shop on Friday or Saturday, because many shops close for the Sabbath. Pina went to Orchard Street, early, like you taught us—first customers of the day get the best prices."

Mamma sighed. "I'm getting so forgetful. Lately my dreams are upsetting. Maybe my *cari morti*—dear dead ones—are trying to communicate something."

"Like what? "

"Last night I dreamed I opened the outside bulkhead cellar door and walked down the stone steps into the laundry room. The small window above let in a smidgeon of light, and that's when I saw an enormous black crow sitting on top of the china closet where we keep the old pots and pans, dishes, and jars for canning. He tried to flutter his wings but couldn't—he was caught. It seemed he was either too tired to fly or had a hurt wing. I looked around to see how he'd gotten in. I entered Papa's workroom, feeling terrible for the bird. I didn't want him to die in the basement. In Papa's room, the open window screen had broken, and apparently he had gotten in that way. I went back and miraculously he fluttered his wings, revved up, and took flight, soaring above me, but then he transformed into the most beautiful black horse with wings—I didn't know how he was going to fit through the window, but I followed him and the window turned into a door. Aren't dreams miraculous? Anything can happen. But then I was left once again with my curiosity and thinking what it meant."

"You're petrified of birds and love horses. Speaking of the basement, what can we do? We need a new machine."

"Wait. We'll see what we will see. Papa's working, and he talked of some kind of bonus. The builders are making something secret."

"A bomb shelter?" My remark went right over her head.

"We need to keep the Gyrator alive and well until we can shop for another. See if Jack can oil something or put a weight on it, other than Valentina. Don't say anything to Papa. He's got enough on his mind— all those casements, cantilevers, ceiling joists, and caissons he's always talking about. What's that other thing he's always talking about with the letter 'c'?"

"Caulking?" I offered.

Then, out of the blue, she changed the subject. "A few days ago I dreamt of making vinegar with my mother, which reminds me—I've got an hour now. Help me prepare some. If you want to make some new bottles, you've got to wash them and sterilize them by pouring boiling water into them. Then let them dry."

"Now?"

"First, take Patches out for a quick walk, and when you come back, finish scrubbing the bottles." Mamma nodded, which meant *indeed*.

When I got back, she asked what took me so long.

"I played ball with Patches," I said. I put water on the stove to boil, and then I washed bottles.

"Hand me that leftover wine," she said, drying her hands.

I did and watched as she added it to her vinegar, then left it uncorked but covered with a linen handkerchief.

"What else can I do?"

"Watch and learn."

"How long does it take?"

"About ten days. You just have to watch the process, not keep vigil for ten days. I usually leave it two weeks. To make vinegar, one must leave the dregs—the 'mother.' Sometimes from store-bought vinegar, the mother appears naturally. I save it!"

"What's the mother?"

"Look here. See that viscous glob?" She pointed.

"Slimy."

"Think of it as a miniature placenta."

"If I did, I'd probably never eat salad with vinegar for the rest of my life. What if there's no mother?"

"Make it." Mamma took a damp cloth and wiped the outside of the bottle.

"How?"

"With an uncooked *perciatello*—a long, fat *spaghetto*."

"*Buccatino*—"

"Get me one out of that open box in the pantry."

When I came back, she said, "Literally, a little hole—for that's what this pasta has—a hole in its center. I place it in an uncovered bottle and lightly cover it with cheesecloth—something that 'breathes'—usually a two-liter bottle with some dregs of real vinegar. A number of years ago, before Prohibition—"

"Before Prohibition, Papa told me when he had no time to make wine or didn't have the grapes, he'd have wine delivered by a horse-drawn cart—demijohns he'd pour out into two-liter or liter bottles and cork himself."

"If you'll stop interrupting, *Signorina*, I'll get to my story. Years ago someone gave your father a bottle of Sicilian wine, *Nero d'Avola,* made from hearty, deep ruby-red grapes and very pungent—I filled it to the half mark. The pasta disintegrates, but not totally, and forms the afterbirth-looking gobbet. I still have some. Look in the china closet. There's a cut crystal cruet my sister Rina gave me. It has that vinegar. Go and sniff it."

I did what she said and was overwhelmed by the essence. I came back into the kitchen and asked, "What if you leave it for too long?"

"I think it perfects itself into something special."

⌁⌁⌁

I FORGOT TO CHECK THE bottles long after two weeks had passed. I searched all over the house while practicing singing scales and humming tunes. I remembered Mamma had put some in the basement. I found a few in a mahogany cabinet in the basement. Papa had restored the cabinet when I was a baby.

Perfect, I thought, as I withdrew the bottles. Mamma said you can't hurt vinegar; it's acidic and a natural preservative. I collected from different locations all the vinegar we'd made and brought the bottles to Mamma, two in my apron pockets and a bunch nestled in my arms.

I trilled notes gingerly, making my way upstairs to the kitchen, where I found Mamma. I stopped practicing and told Mamma my throat felt a little raw. She told me to gargle straightaway with warm water and salt.

When I finished, I handed her a particular bottle of vinegar wrapped in cork. "I found it in that old cabinet with the mottled-gray marble top in the basement."

"It was never lost. I put it there."

"Oh, right. I hadn't seen that cabinet for so long, I thought we'd given it away."

"I wanted Pina to have it, but Papa was fond of it and moved it to his basement workroom. As you must have seen, he stores nails, screws, hammers, and such in it."

"I love that workroom. It's mysterious. The china closet with little opaque glass windows—always locked. I looked inside the wavy glass but can only imagine what Papa has in there."

"Construction tools and other equipment, and you shouldn't snoop."

"The drawers on the bottom are unlocked."

"Meaning?"

I wanted to say I peeked inside them, and there was more in there than just equipment—a handwritten book in what looked like Chinese, and the picture of an attractive young girl in a Chinese dress—but I didn't want to hurt Mamma's feelings and let her know that maybe my darling Papa wasn't always loyal to her in his memories, so I bit my tongue. "Nothing." I shrugged my shoulders.

Mamma looked at me as if I were hiding something, which I was, but I pulled an innocent face, eyes open wide, a half-smile.

"Vinegar's existed for centuries. You could even have gargled with that, but I wouldn't want to waste it." Then she began to recite. "From the darkness emerged the beginning of a good vinegar, the mother, floating like a sailor's safeguard from drowning—a caul purchased from a *strega*, a witch with magical powers, the production of vinegar."

"Where did you learn that?"

"Can't remember now. Maybe my mother." She handed me a washed bottle.

I wiped it off and placed it on the counter to the left of the window, out of harm's way. "Papa has a bottle of Strega in the cabinet next to the radio. It's a yellowish liquor."

"Slightly sweet, a little minty, and pine-scented—it comes from Benevento, a place that has a history of witchcraft. It's liquor not wine. For vinegar, I keep adding the remains of whatever wine your Papa drinks. In ancient Roman times, wine was diluted with a little water from the aqueducts and served even for breakfast, although it wasn't the good wine we have today. There was always plenty of the nectar of the gods."

"Bacchus! I remember getting sick on Papa's *vino*. What happens when you make too much vinegar?" The thought of the wine in the basement somehow triggered my mind back to the book in the drawer in papa's workroom. Suddenly I realized that one of the pictures of a dragon was the same one tattooed on Papa's arm.

Mamma had been talking, but I lost the thread. "What did you say?"

"Where are you, girl? I repeat, you can never have too much. You give it to friends and family members—like we're going to do for Christmas—making sure a piece of the mother goes in the gifted bottle so they can continue making their own."

I reached for another bottle. This one was sticky, so I rinsed it under the faucet. The water ran milky for about a minute and then pure and clear. "What do people do who don't have wine to make it?"

"Apple cider can be used."

The word *apple* kick-started my musical mind with the old song "I'll Be With You in Apple Blossom Time," and I hummed it as Mamma said, "There are many types—rice, black fig, white, malt, probably many I don't even know. Vinegar, if well "mothered," goes on for years and years, continuing for generations, reminding us that being a mother, while bitter at times, also ensures the continuity of life. Making vinegar has varied and symbolic levels, emerging into a poetic mix. Some recipes cry out to be made into poetic forms. Making vinegar's a prime example. You're always singing and writing. Write lyrics and use the recipe to begin."

I stopped humming when a splash of vinegar I poured from a larger bottle into two smaller ones spilled. There it was again, the image of the dragon in red on the sink. I washed it away quickly as though she'd catch on to my thoughts about Papa's secret stash.

"How do you know so much? You don't even drink." I rinsed the dishcloth.

"I pay attention. Something you, my lovely daughter, should learn to do. Quit preening in every glass window you pass by—oh, and there's *balsamico*. It started way back before the 1700s, and the name probably derived from the therapeutic uses of vinegar at the time."

"What's so special about it?"

"The vinegar starts with very sweet grapes and it takes years and years, at least twelve, to make a fine one because it's put into different wooden casks."

"What kinds of wood?"

"Cherry, acacia, ash, chestnut, juniper, mulberry, oak, walnut—the traditional method must use at least five of these barrels—the *solera* system."

"Mamma—"

"Now you want to know what that is and how I know so much, right?"

"*Certo.*"

"You remember my mother's side of the family originated from Spanish Jews. My grandfather made wines to sell in the cities. *Solera* is a wine-making method using sweet wines to make sherry. Small amounts of younger wines housed in an upper row of casks are methodically mixed with more aged ones in the casks below. Did you know I got very sick on wine from my father's shed when I was about eight years old?"

"Younger than me when I did."

"I had had an accident—a runaway horse threw me, so I wandered into the shed thinking wine would ease the pain. I was also curious about wine changing into the blood of Christ. I was about to make my first Holy Communion."

"Aha! You weren't the angel you purport yourself to be—eh, Mamma?"

"You're so bold!"

I laughed. "Bold as brass, but very shiny. Then it's the same process, but with vinegar instead of wine, right? How big are the wine casks?"

"A cask holds four hogsheads."

"Not very kosher. Perhaps monks made it in monasteries—"

"They weren't very Jewish either. That's the size—they didn't really put hogs in them—they were only used for wines."

"Or vinegars."

"Always have to have the last word?"

I nodded. "I try."

"One day you'll learn that honey catches more bees than vinegar."

⌁⌘⌁

I'D JUST FINISHED READING A book when I heard Papa's heavy footsteps on the stairs coming up to tell me something important, otherwise he'd never have mounted into our "inner sanctum," as I referred to my sister and my upstairs quarters.

I was sitting at my desk in the *antecamera* when Papa said, "You, me, and Jack will go for the Christmas tree on Sunday, the twenty-second, because by then the prices of trees will be reduced for sure."

"Papa, that's a heck of an expense right now. Maybe we could just buy some cuttings to decorate."

"No, I want Christmas to be Christmas despite the country's misery."

"If we wait till Christmas Eve, I bet we'd get it for half price because I've heard that things are slow in the tree-selling business this year."

"I don't want to wait—your Mamma needs something to lift her spirits."

⌁⌘⌁

SO ON THE TWENTY-SECOND, JACK, Papa, and I went to buy a Christmas tree on Fourth Avenue just as it started snowing. "Couldn't be more Christmassy if we'd planned it," Jack said. Big wreaths were everywhere, and I knew Valentina would be able to work her magic and make one for us with the bottom cuttings from the tree we selected. A guy wearing a plaid shirt under his lumberjack jacket, with dirty-blond hair dusted with snow, smiled at me with a twinkle in his sky blues and said in one of those "wheaty" western accents, maybe from Wyoming or someplace near the Canadian border, "Ma'am, would you like some extra branches I cut off some other trees?"

"Would I? Why, I'd love them! My sister may even come here in person to give you a peck on the cheek for them!"

"Do I have to wait for your sister?"

"How forward!" Jack hissed between his teeth. "Mamma's going to kill you."

I blew out a huge breath. "What did I say? I was only being polite."

"Flirt!"

"Okay, Jack, I owe you, *ricattatore*—you little blackmailer."

"Let me think about what you owe me," he said and winked.

I wished him to take all the time in the world and hoped he'd forget it.

Meanwhile, the cowboy brought out a bunch of cuttings. He stood a head taller than Jack and practically threw them at him. It seemed to me Jack grew a tail between his legs and meekly went to put them in the car trunk, and while he was busy arranging them, the cowboy presented me with his five o'clock-shadow cheek. What else could I do? I stood on tiptoes and kissed him. Where the hell was Papa when I needed him? The cowboy smelled just like I thought an outdoorsman would—of pine and some lemony aftershave. He flashed a smile with a set of snow-white teeth. Anyway, I knew this guy for sure wouldn't go home to mamma and kiss and tell.

Thinking of the day before, when she was cooking tomato sauce, I remembered that Mamma had accidentally burned her long-handled wooden spoon. She said it was through inattention and was so aggravated at herself that she was on the verge of tears. She scraped and scrubbed off the burn, and Papa sanded the now-disfigured and somewhat lopsided spoon, but she wouldn't throw it out, saying, "It's got personality, don't you think?"

Because of that, I knew what to get her for Christmas, and after we bought the tree, we went shopping. I bought her a big stainless steel spoon. The wooden handle was painted a bright, enameled emerald green. Stamped on the underside of the extended handle was "Genuine Stainless Steel Throughout." I knew she'd use it, but not with the affection she had for the old spoon she'd brought from Italy, as if coming to America meant leaving all the kitchen tools behind in Italy.

⌒⟡⌒

AT HOME LATER, MY TALENTED sister Valentina took the branches we got from the bottom of the huge tree and the ones the cutie-pie salesman had given me and formed them into an arch for the doorway. This festive garland she decorated with tiny red bows, tinsel, and shining silver Christmas balls to look like something out of a fashionable magazine. And indeed it did. People in the neighborhood stopped to compliment us on how original and "old world" our decorations looked. Val beamed when she was in earshot of all the hoopla! Truth be told, I would've too!

Mamma had found two old wooden candlesticks in the basement. When she came back upstairs, she looked as though she'd just won a lottery. "I don't know where these relics come from," she said. "Valentina, will you paint them for us?"

Val looked them over and said, "Maybe ash white with tiny streaks of gray to make them look antique and cracked—they'll look like precious family heirlooms." She enlisted my help, and we went to work around the kitchen table, which we covered with old newspapers. When the candlesticks dried, she decorated the bottoms with sprigs of holly and tiny pinecones. When she finished, she said, "Mamma, what other treasures are hidden in our basement?"

Mamma shrugged. So Val and I went to search, and we found an old oblong wooden table. Valentina and I carried it upstairs, washed it down, and then she dressed it in a many-ruffled skirt, covering the top with a hand-embroidered cream-colored cloth.

On the mantle downstairs in the living room she placed three wreaths. Mamma gave her the huge pinecones she'd brought from Italy, the pine nuts all gone or dried up. They were from enormous secular umbrella pines. Pinole. She'd told us how when she was a girl, she'd gather the pine nuts from inside the cones, crack them open, and save them in a jar so her mother could use them for baking and cooking. They were an ingredient in her specialty—her famous *caponata*, a delicate eggplant dish served as an appetizer. She made some to bring to her friend Caterina because they were invited over to spend the evening—the men would play cards and the women would share an evening of chit-chat. On occasion, Mamma brought knitting or crochet work. She hated wasting time, just talking. She was fond of saying: "Idle hands are the devil's playground."

Valentina painted the cones to look like miniature trees—some green, some red with tips of white for snow, and each of these she decorated with glittering bits pasted on the tips with glue. I knitted a rug for Patches, our bicolored little mutt with one black eye and one white, whose ears were always flapping from joy. Not a mean bone in that spirited little pup—and Mamma sewed a new cover for his pillow bed.

⁘

CHRISTMAS AND NEW YEAR'S HAD come and gone, and all the celebrating was over, too. It was a bit of a sad one this year, because Papa usually brought home fireworks from Chinatown, and after we had all exchanged kisses and hugs and toasted in the new year, he'd set them off in the backyard. Then we'd all come traipsing back in, bringing the cold and a sense of joy.

But this year we had no fireworks. Even sadder, though, was that Papa didn't distribute the adorable little Chinese red envelopes with money in them he always gave us. Things were tight, and he was feeling the pinch. But he made a good show of covering it up by giving each of us a delicate wooden ornament with tags written in Italian. "For when you have your own family and tree," he said.

I was so touched by this sweet token that I excused myself and ran to the bathroom, where I sobbed like a baby. When I returned to our meager celebration, I said, "Sorry, must be my time of month. I'm so sensitive." Papa looked at me with an odd expression. I think he thought I missed Bao, but I dared not defend myself and say I didn't for fear that mentioning his name would cause suspicion that I was trying to cover up my true feelings. I did miss him and looked for the post every day hoping to see some faraway stamp on an envelope, but none came.

Nor was there any hot chocolate. Mamma was saving milk for Elena. Nobody wanted hot chocolate made with Brooklyn water! To compound misery upon misery, instead of having *La Befana*, the little witch, bring gifts on January sixth—the three wise men's or kings' Celebration of the Epiphany—our Patches ran into the street, barking at something or someone, just as a car was passing. Patches died instantly. What was the likelihood of that on our quiet street, where cars passed so infrequently? When Mamma finally stopped crying, she said, "*Era il suo destino.*" It was his destiny.

We all suffered the loss and moped about and probably still would have done so for the rest of the day, but Papa picked up our house mascot and Mamma helped him wrap Patches in an old sheet. Then Papa said, "There's a spot in the backyard—still soft enough to bury the pup. He deserves a decent burial. We all loved him."

He went right to work and made a tiny casket out of a small wooden crate. We lined it with the pillow and cover and went to the gravesite with red eyes and noses. What a finish to an already dismal holiday season. I visualized other years when Mamma tossed out an old tin pie plate from the window and said, "*Auguri di Anno Nuovo a tutti*! Happy New Year to everyone! Out with the old, and in with the new!"

I sure hoped and prayed that 1930 would usher in some good luck.

CHAPTER 14

Giacomo

GIACOMO MANAGED TO HIDE THE loss of the investment he'd made with de Graaf by taking on any and every job he could find. He even became a bouncer in one of Carlo Albano's speakeasies, working mostly on Sundays with a promise from Carlo that he'd never mention it to his own wife or to Angelica. It was only temporary, Giacomo said. He didn't need any risky business with a wife and family, but he did need the extra cash.

Giacomo had been friends with Carlo for many years. He lived in the neighborhood and not in an ostentatious house or in a display of any great wealth. There were rumors of Carlo being in the Mafia, but Giacomo never questioned his friend. The story circulating was that Carlo had been a soldier and had killed a *capo*, or the boss of a rival Mafia family, to get promoted to *capo* himself.

Giacomo had never before asked anything of Carlo and valued his friendship—something understood from the old country. Under no circumstances did you ever interfere with another man's business. Besides the illegal speakeasy, the truth was that Carlo had a legitimate manufacturing business. He owned a small factory and paid a flock of thirty Italian, Irish, and Jewish immigrant women to sew skirts, dresses, and blouses. That's how he met his wife, Caterina. The clothes were sold to local businesses all over Kings County. He also kept a car for several years before buying a new one. His 1927 black Cadillac La Salle could be seen all over town with his license plate from Kings County, which read: K4219. Giacomo wondered, "K" for king? "K" for *kapo*? What did this represent and how did you read those numbers: 4/2/19, 4/21/9? What they signified Giacomo wasn't sure, but he knew they meant something.

When Carlo needed a driver, Giacomo gladly substituted for the regular chauffeur and preferred it rather than having to stand as guard/doorman and "cooler" of undesirable types and drunks. Most of all, he hated having to adopt aggressive behavior to enforce the establishment's rules. He was given a leather billy club, a wooden blackjack, and a pair of brass knuckles that up until now, he'd never had to use. He was taught to hit skull, sternum, spine, or groin to settle down a rowdy customer before tossing him out into the back alley. Giacomo didn't use any of these weapons, although they were stored at arm's distance from the entryway. Instead, he'd started practicing the martial arts he'd learned in China, plus a few more tactics he'd recently picked up in a local boxing club in Chinatown. In the meantime, he kept looking for work that would afford him enough money to leave the underworld life.

⌐⌐✿⌐⌐

IN EARLY SUMMER, GIACOMO READ in the newspaper that an unnamed man meeting Carlo's description had either hurtled from or been thrown out of a speeding car on a downtown Brooklyn street, his hands tied behind his back and a rope around his neck. Retaliation? Revenge? Reprisal? The man managed to escape, but sketches that fit Carlo perfectly had circulated in the newspaper. These had been given to the police by some observers unwilling to leave their names. Others said that was not what he looked like at all, but these were most probably Italian immigrants, including Giacomo, who recognized a failed hit.

⌐⌐✿⌐⌐

ANGELICA HARDLY EVER WENT WITH Giacomo when he played poker with the men, but she had nothing to do and Caterina told him to bring her along. Caterina, Carlo's pregnant wife, always prepared pick-on food for the men when they were playing. There was also quite a bit of whisky on the table. Giacomo noticed that every once in a while, Carlo rubbed his left arm and winced as though in pain.

Someone banged on the door. "Cops," Carlo's brother Tony said.

Caterina whisked the bottles off the table, moved back the rug underneath it, and lifted two floor boards to deposit the bottles. She poured all the liquor into one glass and flung it out the open window, then nodded to Angelica. They took all the glasses to the kitchen sink to suds them up, then came back and sat with the men. Tony had opened the door.

Caterina passed around homemade *caponata* and little pieces of toast.

"Officer," Tony said, loud enough to wake the dead.

Giacomo and Angelica's eyes arched to their eyebrows as they watched Carlo take his pistol out of his belt and hand it off to Caterina, who bent and put it between her very pregnant breasts then casually rested her hands on her protruding belly.

The cop entered, bringing in the cold night air with him. "Evening, folks. Sorry for the bust-in, but at the precinct we heard there was gambling and hard drinking going on here."

Caterina said, "Just a little gathering of old friends. Can I offer you some *caponatina*?"

Tipping his hat, the cop said, "Mind if I look around?"

"Got a warrant, officer?" Tony said.

"Tony, *per favore*, please, Officer Kelly is only doing his job," Caterina said, struggling to rise from her place, keeping one hand at her breasts as if she suffered from indigestion and wanted to burp. "I'll show you around. Where would you like to begin? The children's rooms? They're all sleeping, so we must be quiet. Do you have a flashlight? I don't want to turn on the light and wake them."

With a smirk from Brooklyn to Queens, Kelly said, "That won't be necessary, Mrs. Albano. Oh, Mary told me to ask you to come at nine tomorrow to watch the kids, she'd appreciate it. Her mother's ailing and her sister ain't too good, neither."

"Of course." She patted his arm. "Now, Tony, please see Officer Kelly out," she said with a honeyed voice.

☘

WHEN ANGELICA AND GIACOMO WERE ready to leave, Carlo saw them to the door. He opened the door and switched on the overhead light of the doorway, fished an envelope out of his breast pocket, and handed it to Giacomo. Carlo asked his friend to mail it for him from Manhattan. Giacomo hesitated at the strange request but didn't see why he should or could object. Carlo would have done the same for him, if he'd asked the favor. They bid each other farewell, and Carlo stood watching as they walked down the pathway to the street. Angelica looked back and waved, and still he stood there, not closing the door.

The air was fragrant. A slight breeze blew in the green plane trees and horse chestnuts. Walking home, Angelica asked about the envelope. It had a company name on it that Giacomo didn't recognize, with a P.O. box number in the Bronx. "For some reason," Giacomo said, taking Angelica by the arm to lead her across the street, "Carlo wants me to mail this from the city tomorrow."

"Strange. He goes often to the city. Why didn't he mail it himself?"

"I've no idea but saw no reason to refuse."

"A little odd he waited to give it to us in the front vestibule instead of earlier in the evening?"

"Not really," Giacomo said, with a twinge of annoyance. "Maybe he didn't want Tony to see, or maybe—"

"What is it?" Angelica asked, adjusting the collar of her blouse.

"*Niente.*"

"Doesn't seem like nothing. You're preoccupied." They crossed the street and turned right.

"It was like he was posing for a picture, don't you think?"

"He wanted someone to see him give it to you?"

"*Forse.* Maybe."

"I didn't see anyone in the street."

"You never do."

CHAPTER 15

Marcella

AFTER SEVERAL SERIOUS TALKS WITH Elaine, she promised to behave strictly as friend and mentor. I was relieved, and she seemed pleased I wasn't abandoning her because of one incident. What I discovered was she was an easy friend to talk to and so encouraging. Sometimes I said the most outlandish things, but she never criticized me, she'd hear me out, and then only if I asked, would she make a suggestion. I had begun taking a night course at NYU at Elaine's urging—she paid for my first course, saying it was an advance. An advance on what? I didn't like the sound of it and tried to pay her back as soon as I could. She refused to take my money, saying I should consider it a gift, as I wasn't that keen on going, and I could pay her if I continued. In the meantime, I worked and handed over my "dole" every week to Mamma, except for the small amount I took out for the voice lessons and subway fare. Mamma was against the late-night classes, but it was a perfect alibi for the little extra I took out each week toward what I called my "college fund," meaning Elaine's classes and my secret singing lessons, and I put it in a purse along with the business card from the talent agent I kept as a talisman.

After talking to other working girls trying for acting roles in the theater, it occurred to me that the piano teacher I had around the corner was just that—a pianist who allowed me to sing along with her playing. She wasn't a singer herself, so what could she teach me? I stopped going to her, with the extraction of a promise that over my dead body would she ever tell Mamma when she met her at Mass or on Novena night. Did she really believe I'd kill myself?

On the advice of several other Macy's salesgirls, I found a teacher who had been a singer and knew what the score was—tonally, musically, and otherwise. She also cost double that of the piano teacher. No more lunches out in cafeterias. I carried a lunch satchel and drank water, not coffee. These lessons also meant I was getting home later because I was coming from Manhattan. I told Mamma on these nights not to wait dinner for me. She would leave me what I called a "blue plate special," then explained what I meant, though our plates didn't have a blue willow or anything blue on them, nor did they possess the three separate sections those plates had that were used in local diners and cafes.

In the evenings for the last two weeks, I had the distinct feeling I was being followed. I kept turning around as if I were being shadowed. I thought it odd and mentioned it to Valentina. She actually started looking out the window and said she saw a man who seemed to be studying the outside of our house. She'd seen him several times, so I decided to pretend he was an architect or someone interested in the outside of our home or the structure of it to allay my fears.

I wondered if it was her ex-lover, Vic, because he had a similar build and light-colored hair, but she swore to me she'd never seen him again and now never wanted to for the rest of her life.

My parents were worried about me working and taking night classes. I fibbed and told them I had two night classes—not quite an outright lie—to cover for the night I was at my voice lesson.

Those lessons were proving more difficult than I'd anticipated. I practiced audio-vocal control. You don't just sing with your mouth but govern the management of your voice through your ears and what your mind and body experience as the notes float up, pour through you, and out of your mouth. My teacher tried to convince me that my voice was like a spirit that should hover above me yet surround me at the same time. All I wanted to do was sing—belt out tunes like I'd heard other singers do—but she was adamant about discipline, constraint, and manipulation. *Dio mio!* I hated it! It was more exhausting than my night class at

NYU and more debilitating than standing all day long selling corsets and brassieres to picky women.

Seeing the dark circles beneath my eyes and the weight that had slipped from my once shapely figure, my parents whisked me off with them for a weekend. Gianni's sister-in-law, Zia Grazia, had invited my parents for a weekend trip to their wonderful eighteenth-century house in Gardiner, so they made me take off Saturday and we left for Gardiner right when I got off from work on Friday. They literally dragged me along with them, saying I needed a rest. I had been so preoccupied with taking the busy day off, but had I thought about it earlier, I would've realized there must be an ulterior motive behind why Zia Grazia invited us. The reason, of course, had to be Gianni. We had a rollercoaster romance. Was his sister-in-law's aim to get Gianni and me back together again and on solid ground? On impulse, I knew I'd resist, but what did I really want? I had a connection with Gianni that went far deeper than superficial feelings, and I knew in my heart's heart he felt the same. It seemed there were always outside influences keeping us apart. Certainly not his dear sister-in-law or her mother. His brothers irritated me, and I knew I got under their skin, too. Perhaps it was mutual—I was as much a dominant force in Gianni's life as they were.

It was about forty-eight miles from New York City, sixty miles from the Catskills, to Gardiner. New Paltz was only seven miles to the hamlet of Gardiner. I wouldn't call it a city, as there were less than a thousand people living there, and it was quite quaint.

Our trip should have taken about two hours, but we had car trouble, and it ended up taking almost three. We reached the Red Apple Rest on Route 17 in Southfields about an hour and a half after our departure from Brooklyn. I always loved to stop at the Red Apple Rest—I'm the only one in my family who eats hamburgers, and I love catsup.

I enjoyed riding in the car, thinking and daydreaming, speeding past farms and houses, trees, and overgrown and derelict barns, properties left in disrepair. Before I knew it, we'd arrived at the big white house with no address. It was on Route 44/55, also the name of the highway near Gardiner. When we pulled into the long driveway, apprehension left me, yet I felt as if ace pilot Amelia Earhart, in some tiny dust-buster, had saluted with wing tips—an erratic flight pattern in my belly. Who came running down the steps and out to welcome us? He looked so dashing and fresh, I wanted to take off and fly with him. Control was the word I thought of—and I'll not lose it.

"Why hello, Gianni," I said. Miss Theda Bara herself couldn't have played it any smoother, and here I was thinking her famous line: "Kiss me, you fool."

"You look swell. I'll get the luggage." And he was gone—round to the back of the car in a flash to collect our bags.

He escorted us into the house as the phone rang. The maid answered. They had a party line, which was three short rings. I used to love to answer the phone and pretend I was someone else, confusing the poor, bedeviled operator. The house sat on twelve acres of land and had thirteen rooms. It was three stories high: a main living level, basement, and upstairs that begged to be made into a separate apartment. Gianni showed us our rooms and told us to freshen up and meet everyone downstairs.

I was enamored of this century-old house and all of its thirteen rooms, with its secret ghosts and many stories, and I was in awe of Zia Grazia for making Zio Franco buy it for her. How did she convince him? Zia Grazia adored the house on first sight. She made many renovations without diminishing the integrity of the old, stately home. She left the beveled paneling and took down the ceiling to expose wooden beams. Huge trees surrounded the house, and maples were numerous in the backyard. I liked to climb one and sprawl out on a thick branch, leaning my back on the sturdy trunk, and read, trying to catch the slight breeze. They also used the backyard for growing vegetables, mainly plum tomatoes, which Signora Laura, Gianni's adopted "grandmother," canned, bottled, and jarred into what he said made the best sauce for pasta in the world—but I knew differently. My mother's beat hers any day. The name of the kitchen stove was so old and burned, you couldn't read it. The stove burned coal and wood and anything else combustible you threw into it and was as black as the coal it burned. I thought it was so wonderfully old-fashioned that I asked Mamma if they had something like this in Sicily. Yes, some people had similar ones, but what she recalled was a wood-burning oven built into the wall of the kitchen. How great that must have been. But I was content with this stove as it was marvelous to cook on, especially scrambled eggs in a huge cast-iron skillet. I could make believe I was a six gun-toting mamma for a western cowboy, naturally one with great songs to sing.

There was a tool shed with an attached doghouse, and a beloved *bocci* court where the men gathered in the early evening or late afternoon for drinks and sport. The property had an abundance of fruit trees, including cherries, apples, pears, and plums; a gravel pit where the outside cooking and grilling was done; and lots of land for hunting. Way back of the house loomed a mountain, majestic when capped with snow.

Zia Grazia had the upstairs renovated, and the many rooms were a delight. My parents stayed in one of the larger rooms downstairs. I was put into a room near a huge dressing room with small windows that looked out on the dirt road that snaked from the highway all the way up to the house. Part of the adjacent dressing quarters had been converted into a bathroom, complete with a huge copper tub, a basin, and a pitcher always magically filled with fresh water. There were handmade linen towels edged with long, braided silk fringe. There was indoor plumbing, but only on the first level. All the rooms had chamber pots, which while having a certain charm that made me feel like I was living in the past century, were not exactly convenient. Someone had to remove them and their contents and wash them out. I always used one of the downstairs commodes.

There used to be a tenant the year before, but he'd vacated the downstairs room he occupied. He had worked at the college in a nonteaching department as custodian. We heard he eventually married. He seemed like a queer duck but was always polite and never made a disturbance. I saw him once or twice since he'd moved. A young girl, supposedly his daughter—but one could never tell as there was such a great deal of inbreeding—always helped him wash the car outside of a tiny cabin they'd rented on the far side of town. Why this odd detail of inbreeding struck me now was because Mamma had recently told me about a sad case of incest where she acted as midwife for a young girl who had to give the child to her mother to raise. I said a prayer for all involved in these wretched, sordid, criminal affairs, and one for me, so fortunate to have loving, respectful parents.

The neighbors were dear friends, the *simpatico* pair Fabio and Josefina di Nicolas. She was lively and he was a bit on the cheeky side, but that never bothered me. When I'd visited before, Gianni and I often walked to the rustic country cabin, especially on rainy days, and played cards, *mah-jongg*, or checkers. She always asked me to sing and accompanied me on a guitar, as she was quite accomplished.

One of my favorite activities was to go to the nearby Minnewaska Falls. There was a hotel that overlooked the lake of the same name, and on weekends a piano player was hired, and sometimes I'd sing along with his music. There was also a tower, hotel, and lake nearby called Mohonk. Both places were run by Huguenot brothers named Smiley. No liquor was allowed to be served there, Zia Grazia said, even before Prohibition. I was always enthralled with the old stories about the place. There had been a peace treaty between the Indians and the Huguenot settlers, who were all French Protestant refugees living in the area of New Paltz. The Esopus tribe was an ethnic group of the Lenape, a people who were native to upstate New York, specifically the Catskill Mountains. Their lands included modern-day Ulster and Sullivan counties. At the end of the Esopus Wars against the settlers from the New Netherland colony, the tribe sold them large expanses of land. It was difficult to fathom, but so fascinating, that some of these people had originated from those first settlers in the 1600s.

Down the road not too far from the big house, there was a natural pool behind Emil's Tavern. There were some cottages for rent, and there were always some summer residents. The tavern, known as Travelers, was situated just beyond another neighbor's, Ugo Quarta's house, where I'd sing along with the records on the old nickel-in-the-slot jukebox on weekends, and then Ugo always welcomed us and we'd go there to sip iced tea.

⊷⊱✿⊰⊶

SATURDAY MORNING GIANNI WAS UP early and pouring coffee. I was dressed and ready to go off hunting with the men. Gianni warned me to stay close to him, but I wouldn't hear of it and therefore suffered getting my ears chewed off by Zio Franco. I got a lesson and more information than I needed from him about his guns, or rather rifles. The Winchester Model 21 was a deluxe side-by-side or double-barreled shotgun; and Model 21 grades were chambered in twelve, sixteen, and twenty gauge. On Saturday morning we hunted with sixteen, twenty, and twelve gauge over and under shotguns. We also used a .22 caliber for target practice. Zio Franco told me that during open season, he hunted deer with a 30/30 and a 300 Savage, his special and favored gun. I was thankful we weren't going to hunt those vulnerable animals with huge brown eyes. Instead, we stalked grouse, pheasant, rabbits, and squirrels.

The men began to tease me that I'd become a "crack shot," which I didn't quite understand but knew I could shoot darn well, especially compared to some of Zio Franco's old cronies. If we bagged enough, Zia Grazia would make a great squirrel and rabbit sauce with onions and peas, which was delectable over *pappardelle,* homemade wide pasta noodles. We always went home with a trunk load of goodies made by this sweet auntie. I thought about her tasty venison stew. In fact, like my mother, give her an onion and she'd make you a meal. I learned a great deal from both of them, but I lacked the fantasy they put into every meal they made.

After early Saturday morning hunting, we returned and ate lunch—a late breakfast of bacon, eggs, fried potatoes, and buttered toast. Everybody disappeared for a siesta. Gianni and I decided to go horseback riding, but instead of going to Sunnipee Ranch, we wanted to use the familiar horses in the barn. Not only were there hills, dales, rivulets, gullies, and creeks, there were apple orchards, a huge industry in the area, that we wanted to see.

While finishing up the meal, I let my mind wander to the times I spent here when I was younger. I recalled the walks down by the gap, where the creek water flowed so swiftly in springtime after snowmelt; the smell of wildflowers in the back fields; the perfumes emanating from the kitchen while someone was cooking. Back then there was a handyman who wore loose overalls with no underwear and was constantly bending forward to mulch, cut, or prune in close proximity. I'd dash away, but it seemed he always followed me to work on something in the garden wherever I was. Upset and fed up, I finally reported his actions to Zia Grazia and told her I didn't appreciate the view he afforded. By week's end he'd been replaced, and although in a way I was sorry he got fired, an older but hard-working, more couth individual took his place. The truth was I was more than relieved that Mr. Loose Overalls lost his occupation.

⁕

AFTER I WASHED THE DISHES, I walked to the barn to meet Gianni and saddle the horses.

I let my mind travel backward, closing my eyes for a minute to see if I could remember where all the items in the barn were stowed. Sure enough, I was on the money. In the tack room, we picked out and carried the rough Indian blankets to put beneath the saddles. We saddled our horses, Gianni helping me with mine, but he was so intent, he hardly spoke to me.

That afternoon Gianni and I rode for about a half-hour. It had rained before we mounted up, but later two rainbows appeared and seemed to float in the sky, one above the other. They shone in a double-arched halo of colors splashed upon a blue-gray sky canvas—seven arcs altogether: red, orange, yellow, green, blue, indigo, and violet. At the top edge of the rainbow was a fiery red, at the bottom verge was the violet of lilacs, and all the other colors streamed in a hazy flow in between. I wondered if Bao was seeing something like this in San Francisco.

Gianni sat high in his saddle and pointed upward. "Rainbows are created both by reflection and refraction, or a bending of sunlight in raindrops. As sunlight enters a raindrop, it curves and splits it into its elemental colors that comprise white light."

"Ah, a lesson in rainbows," I said and immediately wished I hadn't spoken. I looked at him, and he seemed bereft with sorrow. I'd hurt him. Why was I so mean when I knew he couldn't harm a fly, much less toss a rude remark back at me? I could've kicked myself but didn't know how to rescue the situation for the life of me, so rode on. After a while I started a conversation about movies and books, and then it was time to head back.

⌐⊂❊⊃⌐

IN THE LATE AFTERNOON AFTER we'd bathed, everyone wandered out to the veranda to relax and sit around a rock-centered fire pit. Many of the older folks covered up with quilts and blankets, some sipping cocktails, until it was time to go in for dinner.

Zia Grazia asked me to fetch her two hermetically sealed wide-mouthed jars of tomatoes. She tugged me aside and said, like a conspirator, "I hope you and Gianni will have a chance to talk and make up over your silly spat."

She'd taken me off guard. At first I almost said, "None of your business, and stop meddling." But I knew she meant well and adored Gianni. So I guess that meant she cared for me by past association. I patted her hand. "We'll see."

"You're a generous, talented, and loving girl. He couldn't do better."

Hunting the tomatoes in the huge basement, which was for storage—loaded with shelves filled with jarred tomato sauce, jams, and homemade canned goods—I spotted one of my preferences, wild mushrooms under oil. Yum. So I took one of those as well. There was an abundance of tools, even more than Papa had, and a coal-burning heater with a coal bin housed near it.

There was an exit from the basement to the side of the house, and from there I entered the kitchen, where the coal stove sat on the left. A long table banked the window on the right. At one time the dining area had been separated from the rest of the kitchen with an entrance from the cooking area. Two ice boxes served to keep things cold. I put the tomatoes and the mushrooms on the table and told Zia Grazia I just couldn't resist nabbing them. "Great idea," she said. "Open them and we'll put them with some black olives, carrot sticks, and celery stuffed with cream cheese and a sprinkle of paprika for the drinkers to munch on."

"I'll carry the tray outside for you," I said.

Before she finished the platter, I wandered out to the front porch. I never remembered anyone entering from the front, although we sometimes used the porch, and in a flash, I remembered a costume party we had there when I was fourteen. I must have blushed recalling the huge crush I had on Gianni. I came back and helped her make little salami baskets filled with thick beaten cream and pimento.

Outside, friends of the family that lived nearby on another adjacent property in a small cottage were visiting. I said hello to Ugo Quarta and his boisterous wife, always fun and gregarious. Ugo was rather dour, maybe because he owned and operated a funeral parlor in Brooklyn but always said he wanted to buy a beauty parlor instead. I couldn't imagine the way his wife would let him touch her after he'd handled all those dead bodies. Creepy.

⸙

THE EVENING WORE ON AND everyone moved inside for dinner, after which they played cards. Gianni asked me to go for a walk, but I begged off because we had to go to early Mass.

We stood at the bottom of the stairs, my hand on the banister, and he put his hand on top of mine. "Going to bed with a book on such a beautiful night? Grab a wrap and let me escort you to the main road. That won't take long, and you can breathe some fresh air instead of all that cigarette smoke from the card players."

I wiggled my hand out from under his and said, "Sure. Just a sec." I flew up the stairs and picked up my white crocheted shawl and was down the stairs before he'd had time to get his jacket.

The walk was pleasant. We talked about the stars and constellations and the magnificent moon. He asked me about work. And I confessed that I'd been taking singing lessons, found a new teacher, and now was studying voice in the city.

He stopped on the gravel pathway and looked at me with a quizzical face. "Do your parents approve?"

"They never have. They won't start now. Are you going to turn traitor on me—"

"Marcella, I'd never do that. You know me better."

"Do I?" I turned to start walking back.

"If you don't, maybe we should do something about it."

"Like?"

"See each other more often."

"I don't have a great deal of time. I'm also taking a business course at NYU."

"You can always make time when you want to."

We'd reached the steps leading into the kitchen.

He leaned over and kissed my cheek. "Your skin smells like summer. See you in the morning."

⸎

ON SUNDAY WE ATTENDED MASS at a darling rustic white church set farther into the country. The windows were open, and the breezes carried the voice of the priest and his Latin words. I drifted off somewhere that was not in these United States of America. Light winds made the branches of the huge trees sway, like the movements of fat men suddenly graceful and seemingly weightless on the dance floor. Mamma always said wind in the trees means souls are in flight. My ears attended the wind's whistling canticles through the window fittings, bringing with them the scent of flowers. Somehow Gianni sat next to me, and I had the feeling he wanted to hold my hand. Had we done that when I was sixteen? His thigh was smack up against mine, and I didn't make a move, but when we stood, I shifted over a little so there'd be no contact. Sure enough, when we stood again, he'd moved a little closer, and there we sat, snug thighs all but rubbing. I looked up at him, down at his thigh, and he coughed that little embarrassed cough he has and gently scooted over, but he'd succeeded in making me feel his wanting of me physically and emotionally.

⋄

AFTER CHURCH AND A LOVELY family meal, we changed for archery. The targets were set far away from the back of the house and over toward the right. Quivers, bows, and arrows were lined up for the picking. I had shot some at Riis Park when we had picnicked there last summer, but my skills were mediocre at best.

I wore tan jodhpurs in case anyone suggested another horseback ride, and a white cotton blouse, a bit too gauzy, I realized. When I walked into the sun, it revealed the outline of my brassiere in the light. I should have worn a camisole, but no way in hell was I bothering to go change and lose out on the sport. I'd wait till later. Instead, I sought out and stood in a veil of shadow whenever possible.

When it was my turn, Gianni handed me the bow, snatched an arrow from the quiver, and very gently armed the bow and handed it to me, arrow pointing downward. I stepped up to the position, turning sideways so that my left shoulder faced the target. All of a sudden Gianni was behind me, his arms around me as he guided my hands, the left turning the bow into position straight up and down, the right pulling the string back toward my cheek.

"Hold," he whispered in my ear, "and when I say, 'release,' do it, but don't take your arm down, and leave your curled fingers next to your face. Now look at the target and imagine the flight of the arrow. Ready? Release!" he said, and I did, remaining in the stance.

I put down my arms and squealed for joy as I watched the arrow hit a hair's breadth from the yellow bull's eye. I spun around with the bow still in my left hand and did the most natural thing in the world. I hugged Gianni with my right arm and kissed him, right on the mouth.

We received a round of applause as my face turned hot—probably the color red of the two circles close to the bull's eye.

⌒⟨✿⟩⌒

AFTER ARCHERY, GIANNI ASKED ME to go for a walk. It was too late to go horseback riding, and though I was disappointed, I knew this might be what my heart yearned for—an opportunity to heal the open wound that was keeping us apart—so I accepted.

We walked toward the gorge above the creek and followed a hilly trail. The sun filtered light down through a coterie of leafy trees, forming a coppice cover and a great deal of shade. I felt chilled and shivered. Gianni took off his jacket and laid it on my shoulders. "You're a *Madonna* in sunlight and seductive in shadow. I've missed you."

"Why, Gianni, I've never heard you speak like that." I'd picked up a leaf which I twirled in my right hand. "You must come for dinner some time like you used to. Why did you stop?"

He took the leaf from my hand and blew it away. "I've needed time to think and dwell on what I want out of life."

I looked up at him. "Which is?"

"I'm not sure about a lot of things, but one is for certain: I want you in my life, and this time I won't let you scare me away with a trifling. Or bully me away because you don't like my brothers and they don't approve of you." He stepped down to the ledge of earth I was on, put his hands on my shoulders, and pulled me toward him. He leaned down, and the soft eagerness in his lips thrilled but also frightened me. Was this the same Gianni I'd sent running?

We walked toward a flat boulder, where we sat. Gianni took my hands in his and said, "I feel comfortable around you. Like I know you from another life."

I smiled. "You're easy to talk to. Like Papa. He's always ready to hear what I've got to say and he listens, even if what I'm thinking seems preposterous, even to me."

"We go round and round, never saying what we mean most of the time."

I reached up and circled his head.

"What're you doing?"

"Measuring you for a halo. I swear you have an aura of goodness—"

"I love you."

I dropped my hand. "I know. But why?"

"That's like asking the moon why it hangs in the sky."

"Why?"

"To govern the tides, of course." He kissed the top of my head. "It's a feeling. You know. Why do you like butterscotch, and I like fudge? You're the whipped cream and cherry on top of my ice cream sundae."

"And for the third time, I'm asking—why? I'm far from perfect."

"Maybe because you're not, but you've got grit. You persevere. I can't think of me without you."

CHAPTER 16

Giacomo

GIACOMO LEFT GARDINER IN THE early evening, toward Brooklyn. He drove Angelica and Marcella home without stopping at the Red Apple Rest, making good time. They snacked on Zia Grazia's *pannini*, home-baked cookies, and a thermos of coffee. When they reached home, he pulled the car into the long driveway. Giacomo got out, opened the garage door, and pulled the car in. He turned off the engine and said, "We're home, my sleeping beauties. Wake up."

They got their bundles and stepped outside of the garage while he closed the door. They walked to the front of the house, where they saw every light in the place lit. Why hadn't Giacomo noticed when he'd driven toward the garage? The front door was wide open. Something was amiss. Giacomo said, "Stay here," and ran into the house, calling for Jack and Valentina.

"Jack's not home," Valentina said in a muffled, frightened voice from where she sat huddled on the staircase.

"What happened? You're shaking." Giacomo put his arms around his daughter.

"We were robbed!" Valentina stammered.

"Robbed?" Giacomo shrieked.

"I went to open the door because I thought it was Jack, but the odd thing is, we never lock the door. A man pushed me aside and held a gun to my head. He said, 'You're alone, right? But if you say a word, you're good as dead, sweetheart.' He had an accent."

"Foreign? What did he look like?"

"No, an accent like from Boston, or somewhere—not New York. He was bulky and wore a mohair duster like chauffeurs wear, and a cap like one, too. He had goggles on, so I couldn't see him good. I was so frightened. I stayed cowed on the floor. He ran in and searched the rooms downstairs but only swiftly, but then he took the stairs two at a time and entered the kitchen. I heard him rooting around in the pots and pans; it sounded like he threw the silverware to the floor. That's when I saw an opportunity to flee and ran outside. I couldn't protect the house, Papa." She sobbed.

"Of course not, you did the right thing." *Self-preservation,* he thought.

"I cut through the hedges on the side and ran over to the Zaidans. The son—you know, the tall, skinny one—answered the door."

"Omar?"

She nodded. "He let me in, and as I sat with his mother, he called the police. When they came, Omar and his father went with them to search, but I was so afraid for them, too, and begged them not to go. His father loaded a hunting rifle, which the policemen made him leave behind. I beseeched them to be careful. Both officers released their holster closures and drew out flashlights and off they went.

"Mrs. Zaidan said, 'You should never interfere with fate. What will be, will.' I must have been screaming. She kept shushing me and trying to feed me dates and figs, but I couldn't eat. She made me tea."

"Did the cops and Zaidans come back right away?" Angelica, who'd followed her husband inside, asked.

"No. They must've searched the whole house and thankfully gave me the all-clear. Mrs. Zaidan wanted me to stay, but I said I had to get back or Jack would worry when he got home. So the policemen ushered me home and told me to lock all the doors. I was scared, so I turned on all the lights, locked the front door, and checked the back one, too. But when I heard you drive down the alleyway, I ran down and opened the door."

"Did the police or Zaidans find anything stolen?"

"They said they couldn't tell but didn't think so. They assumed the man was looking for something hidden, because the flour canister was thrown all over the upstairs kitchen and the sugar, too. The ice box door was left ajar, cooking stuff all over the place, the oven door open. Is that where people hide their valuables?"

"Maybe the thief wasn't looking for money or jewels. I'll go thank the Zaidans tomorrow morning—too late now."

Giacomo left Valentina in the care of Angelica and Marcella and went upstairs, like he had all the time in the world. He went into his bedroom and into the closet where Angelica's dresser stood on the left. Giacomo opened the bottom drawer and riffled it, wondering if this thief was after something in particular, other than their valuables. He held up a brown leather wallet with three hundred dollars in it. Then he pulled the dresser out, and behind a picture of the holy family, he opened a wall safe that contained his passport and important papers, his wife's small diamond earrings, a gold chain with a medal of Santa Rosalia, and a silver chain purse with several hundred dollars. Untouched. He closed the safe and pushed back the dresser. He heard his women move to the kitchen and followed them there, where Valentina sat with a cup of tea.

Marcella was making a valiant attempt at cleaning up.

"*Camomilla*," Angelica said to the unasked question. "I made it extra strong and put honey in it. She's had such an awful fright. Look at this mess. Anything missing?"

He shook his head, indicating nothing of their small treasures was gone. "Marcella, go up to the closet in the bathroom and look in the back of the bathtub underneath the floorboard. That's where I put anything extra from your and Jack's pay in hopes I can give you something back."

"Oh, Papa," Marcella said and hugged him from behind where he sat. She ran up the stairs and called down immediately. "Nobody's been here; nothing's been touched." She came down to where the family sat at the table and picked up the broom.

"Maybe the guy had the wrong house," Marcella said, sweeping flour into the dustbin. She stopped abruptly. "Come to think of it, no, he didn't."

"What do you mean?" Giacomo asked.

"I think I've been followed several times, mentioned it to Val, but I should have told you. I thought it was my imagination. Even Val saw someone watching the house a few times. It all seemed so odd, yet unimportant."

"That's right," Val said. "We didn't give it much importance, but he must've been waiting for an opportunity—"

"I'll look into this further," Giacomo said. His thoughts hurtled back to the night that Carlo gave him that fat envelope. He would go to see his friend early tomorrow after he thanked the Zaidans.

⊱⋅☙⋅⊰

GIACOMO WAS PLEASED TO SEE that Marcella and Gianni were once again courting on Sundays. They went ice skating in Central Park. Marcella had a jovial look in her eyes when she'd told him of how Gianni had been skating backward and trounced into a couple trying to keep their balance. He pictured his daughter laughing out loud. And when the weather permitted, they went cycling along Narrows Bay. Marcella confessed to her father that she had made Gianni wheedle a Sunday off from his brothers. The couple enjoyed ferry ride jaunts to Manhattan and Staten Island. She had dinner at his house, and he came over to theirs. After the Christmas holiday, there was a lull in sales at Macy's and sometimes she'd get another half-day off during the week.

Giacomo sat one night waiting for Marcella to return from a show she'd gone to with people he didn't know. When she got home, she confided that she now had established a good friendship with her boss, who was educated and cultured and a person that Marcella wished to emulate in all but one thing. When Giacomo asked her what that particular thing was, she simply demurred, "Never mind." But when he insisted, she said, "It's a strange Greek practice from one of the islands."

"Which one?"

"Lesbos. In the Aegean Sea."

Giacomo wondered if she meant what he thought.

It was shortly after this discussion that his lovely daughter started attending radical and Communist Party meetings with her boss, Elaine Weiss, on Saturday night. At first Giacomo and the family didn't think much of it, and Marcella acquired the nickname "Midnight Molly" from them because she started to break curfew so often that Angelica complained to Giacomo. Beyond annoyed one night, she waited up for her daughter seated in one of the porch chairs. When Marcella opened the door, Angelica popped her one over the head.

Marcella's sole utterance was "Ouch."

"This is the last time. I don't intend to spend my nights waiting for and worrying about you." But the very next night, when Angelica went to pop Marcella over the head when she came in late again, Marcella ducked and protected her head with her purse.

In bed a few nights later, Giacomo was angry rather than annoyed, because Angelica had broken a good umbrella over Marcella's head and made him buy a new one. He said, "Angelica, this has got to stop. I can't afford to buy new umbrellas every week, and I don't want that scamp of a daughter of ours hanging out with that crowd in New York."

Angelica sat up, leaned against the bedstead, and folded her arms across her chest. "Well? What're you going to do about it?"

⚜

THE FOLLOWING SATURDAY NIGHT, LATE into the season, Giacomo set up a comfy chair behind the door on the drafty covered porch, complete with several handmade quilts and a crocheted blanket, to wait up for his daughter. While he waited for Marcella to come home, his thoughts drifted and ran to springtime. He was daydreaming, wondering when it would finally warm up so that heavy racemes full of purple and violet wisteria flowers could bloom. How do you define its scent? What does it evoke? It's similar to freesia but not nearly as strong as gardenia. He'd pruned the thick, entwining bushes in back, wondering how old the stalks were.

Just then he heard Marcella jauntily march up the steps and was about to open the door. The look on her face spoke volumes of how surprised she was to find her father waiting for her. No umbrella over the head, but he grabbed her forcefully by both arms and said, "*Che cazzo stai facendo?*"

"Papa!"

"Now there's an end to it, as your Mamma says. You cannot be a party girl and be faithful to Gianni." Giacomo released her arms and slammed the door shut.

"Shush, you'll wake everyone."

"You care? Why aren't you seeing Gianni on Saturday nights? Going to the movies. Taking walks down by the Narrows."

"Gianni's sweet but sometimes boring—he doesn't like to have fun."

"Really? You've never given him a chance. Why don't you do some of the things you did in Gardiner? Or do you really want to be a heartbreaker? Go horseback riding on the weekend. Go picnic in the park instead of practically living in the city."

"It's exciting."

"Take a horse carriage ride in Central Park. That should be thrilling. I only wish I could take your mother."

Giacomo folded the covers and placed them on the chair. "You've been singing that song so much you believe it, don't you?"

"What song?"

"The song 'Life is Just a Bowl of Cherries'—my foot it is! Life isn't like that. I've never raised my hand to you, but if I hear one more time from Mamma you made her lose sleep fretting about you coming home late from one of these parties, I'll make sure you never dance again, never mind sing."

"Papa!"

"Marcella! *Basta*! Enough!"

She cowed toward the door, a puppy with a tail between her legs.

⌥

ON A SUNDAY AFTER MASS three weeks later, Angelica and Giacomo confronted Marcella, ecstatic because she'd defied her father once more and got away with it, as usual, unscathed.

"But Mamma, it's thrilling. They give speeches. There's all kinds of strange food like caviar and tiny blini and other foods, too, and vodka and people all talking at once and ladies smoking cigarettes with long filters so elegantly. The clothes the women wear—so dishy—and some places where we meet have a stage, where I sing a song or two, or sometimes there's a police raid that breaks up the party, like last night when the cops came in and someone yelled, 'Hey, remember—don't give your right name!' A friend of Elaine's dragged us out by some back, winding staircase. We had to climb out a window onto the ledge to get to the fire escape. A guy named Joel lowered it, and we were running down an alleyway just as the cop sirens came blaring down. We hid behind some garbage and watched as the cops parked, leaving their car doors open, and entered the way we'd just escaped."

"Marcella! Stop! Do you hear yourself? You're reciting a movie script," Giacomo said.

"This is serious and perilous. These people are anarchists," Angelica said.

"Don't think so. They're card-carrying Communists and want me to join," Marcella said.

"Dangerous and foolish," Angelica said.

"Are you out of your mind? I forbid you to go out any more with your boss or I'll come to Macy's and see her myself," Giacomo said, red-faced.

"And you'll apologize to Gianni," Angelica said. "He comes to pay call and sits moon-eyed waiting for you, but you never show up till after midnight. Do you make dates with him?"

"Of course not. Well, I did say maybe I'd be free this Tuesday night and possibly Friday. But maybe isn't definitely."

"Marcella, do not abuse his sentiments for you. One day you'll find out what you're throwing away and will regret it. Mark my words," Giacomo said.

"I think Gianni followed me after work tonight." Marcella looked at her feet. "I'll tell him I'm sorry and couldn't make it."

"He'll know you're lying. Tell him the truth. He's hurt and maybe jealous. Be careful not to trifle with his heart," Angelica said.

⌒ℭ✹ℜ⌒

GIACOMO WAS WALKING HOME. HE stopped to light a cigarette and thought back to a few weeks after the attempted robbery, when he'd gone to see Carlo. He'd stood where Carlo had given him the envelope, and he asked about it. As soon as the words were out of his mouth, Giacomo could have kicked himself because he realized it was a payoff for a job.

Carlo patted him on the shoulder. "*Fatti i cazzi tuoi,*" he said, menace in his voice, telling Giacomo not to butt in and mind his own business. Giacomo knew enough to leave it at that. Carlo offered him his hand, and they shook—a promise not to mention it again.

Giacomo put together that he'd been seen receiving the envelope. That's why his home had been burglarized, but Giacomo had already mailed it.

CHAPTER 17

Marcella

I THOUGHT ABOUT WHAT MAMMA had said and knew I had to apologize, but how do you do that without actually coming out and saying you're sorry? Somehow I'd do it. Gianni was easy prey, and sometimes I felt like a shark. Where did that come from?

It was a warm June evening and Gianni and Jack came back inside for a glass of cold lemonade after baseball practice. Hot and sweaty, they settled themselves at the downstairs table while I poured from a pitcher into frosty glasses I'd kept in the downstairs fridge.

I looked from one to the other. "How would you two like to see Babe Ruth and Lou Gherig take on the Cleveland Indians Saturday?"

"The twenty-eighth?" Gianni said.

"What about the rest of the Giants? Are they going to sit the bench and watch?" Jack asked, and gulped his drink.

I swatted him playfully on his arm. "You know what I mean."

He rubbed his arm, "Hey, easy. Watch out, that's my pitching arm."

I reached into my skirt pocket and pulled out two tickets and fanned myself.

"You mean you're not going to horn in and come with us?" Jack said, and flashed a smile.

I shook my head. "Boys only.

"So what's the trade?" Jack said in his shrewd businesslike voice.

"Just bring me home the play by play," I said.

"A loaded hot dog, too?" Gianni asked.

And with that I knew I had him back. "Nah. Just peanuts," I said and licked my lips.

꧁⚹꧂

ANYWAY, IT WAS TIME FOR vacation and I was excited to be at Camp Isida with a bunch of other Macy's girls. There was a main building at the camp. The rooms were shared by two, three, and four girls. Some had four-poster beds. Two other girls shared the ample room with me. Each room was close to a bathroom. The vanity of ours held three French-cut glass, opal, spray perfume bottles with long forest-green tassels, plush towels, and talcum powder with a puff in a round green onyx bowl—total elegance.

There was a dancing hall with tufted covered benches all along the walls beneath charming old stained-glass windows. Chandeliers hung above wooden parquet floors that gleamed in the fading sunlight streaming through the open windows.

In the mountains on cool summer nights, it was lovely to knit with light strands of pink and white wool, making a crib blanket for Elena. The *clack-clack* of the needles, the unthinking process of knit a row, purl a row, gave me time to let my mind wander.

Before I left for camp, Jack had told me the next time he saw Pina with any kind of mark on her that shouldn't be there he was going to have a conversation with her husband. Pina had come to dinner the night before he wrote me the letter. He noticed she had bruises on her wrists again, and this was going to be the last time. He didn't need to tell me more. I pictured Jack, lean and lanky, standing up to Bruno and telling him to keep his grubby mitts off of our sister, except to love her to bits. Jack could be such a tease about Gianni, and so generous like Mamma, but when he got that look in his eyes like Papa—I wished I could have been a little bird flitting about when he faced Bruno, a head shorter. I remembered Pina saying Jack was like Mamma. Pina said she didn't think he would ever stand up for her or champion her in any cause. However, I'd seen ferociousness in some of his looks that made me understand he would defend his family at any cost. I was hoping for a letter from Jack, but instead Pina rang me up. I was about to hang up the phone when she said, "Bruno's turned a corner"—and I knew she'd always be all right from now on. Jack was no longer my little brother, but my sister's protector. *Bravo*, Jack!

⁓◦⊰✸⊱◦⁓

LATE THE NEXT DAY, THE afternoon sky was overcast and threatened to rain. My work friends Jane Hadley-Foss, Cathy Cappi, and I sat on the veranda sipping lemonade. Jane dreamed of becoming a writer. How dull! Although I loved to write, I couldn't think of anything worse than doing it full-time and under a deadline. Imagine what it's like being cooped up all day in a small alcove with a desk, a dim-lighted bank lamp, and a typewriter whose keys stick. She wanted to write a love story based on the couple Isidor and Ida Strauss. While I thought this sweet and noble, Jane didn't know anything at all about writing fiction—although she was a voracious reader, I'll give her that, more so than me!

"But think," Jane said. "How brave and romantic of Ida to cede her place on the lifeboat of the sinking Titanic to her new English maid, Ellen Bird. She even gave the girl her fur coat, saying, 'I won't need it anymore.'"

"For one thing, that might only be hearsay." I poured more lemonade into my perspiring glass.

"It wouldn't matter, it's fiction." She continued in that same dreamy tone she affected every time she thought she was spouting writerly speak. "Isidor was offered a seat in a lifeboat to accompany Ida, but he had refused to abandon ship while there were still women and children aboard."

Cathy said, "He wasn't the captain—"

Jane turned to her with an air of haughtiness. "No, but he didn't want to be an exception. My mother said she read in the paper after it happened that a friend of his, a colonel who survived the ordeal, reported that Ida refused to leave her husband. I think I'll title it 'Lifeboat Number Eight.' Can you imagine Ida saying to her husband she wouldn't be separated from him, that they'd lived together and now would die together?"

Cathy said, "We've all heard the story, and while it's highly romantic, I don't think it's a good idea to make such a tragic event into fiction."

"Why not?" Jane asked.

"The family might not like it or approve. Why not write nonfiction? You could tell the story of how this place was made into Camp Isida." Cathy pulled her long hair off her neck and let it drop again. "Muggy, isn't it, here in dear Camp Isida?"

"I don't know that story," Jane said, dejection in her voice.

"I do." Cathy and I said simultaneously, and looked at each other.

"You first," I said.

Cathy cleared her throat as if she were going to sing an aria. "In the 1800s, the property was owned by the Diets family—it was a tannery. They owned a lantern-making company, too. Think how romantic lanterns are! From what I heard, leather from the tannery was used to make boots for Union soldiers during the Civil War."

"Never heard that about soldiers' boots," I said. "Sure it's true?"

"Indeed. Next the property was sold to Benjamin Todd, who owned hotels and inns, and he made it into a summer resort," Cathy gave her reportage quite expertly. "And around 1904, Todd sold to R.H. Macy Corp., the self-same year that Macy's department store moved to Herald Square. After Isidor and Ida Strauss, Macy's owners, succumbed on the RMS *Titanic* as it sank to the depths of the ocean in 1912, the foundation designed Camp Isida to allow all the Macy's employees a place to get away from the noise and stress of city life. And here we are—beneficiaries of their great generosity."

Just then it hit me that the camp name was a combination of their first names. Now that was romantic, but I didn't say anything to interrupt.

After our long discussion about the property, its owners, and the grounds, we talked about our fantasies and dreams. I naturally spoke of my ambition to sing professionally. Jane looked at me as though I'd grown an extra head. Seeing as they were not buying into it, I changed the subject lest they squelch my fondest hope.

We decided to have a stroll before dinner. On the main road outside the gate we met a bunch of young actors from a summer stock production asking for directions. I wanted nothing more than to hop into that roadster's rumble seat and drive away with them. They were so kind. They gave us their names and said to look them up at the theater that Saturday afternoon at the matinee performance, and that they'd leave tickets for us at will call. Afterward, we'd all go out for a bite to eat and talk about the show. I felt I'd become a tiny-winged creature flying in heaven.

I was a working woman on vacation, and it was a hot month of July in the city, but not here in the Borscht Belt. The Catskill Mountains were a delight, even more so after we'd met the actors. Cool mornings and evenings, and days to bask in the sun, play sports, or swim. And now a Saturday afternoon show to look forward to.

After the stroll, I sat down on the window bench and bent my legs. An old song was playing on the radio, and it reminded me of a day in Point Lookout two summers ago. I started to hum along with it and propped my diary on top of my knees. The first thing I started to write about was that remembered day on the beach.

⌐⌐⌐

WE HAD BEEN STAYING IN the cottage in Point Lookout. It had been hot and sultry for almost a week. The next day it was overcast and threatening to rain, so I asked Mamma if I could ride my bike to the beach and take a walk, promising not to swim although I wore my bathing suit under my shorts. I took a yellow slicker with me, rolled and tied onto the back of my seat. I asked Valentina if she wanted to come, but she had her nose in some magazine, fiddling with her hair and listening to old phonograph records. I sang along with one song, then asked her again if she'd like to come, but she said, "Another time."

Other people and huddled shapes bicycled past me. When I reached the beach, I put my bike in the stand and placed my sandals in the basket. I'd brought along a tuna fish sandwich and a thermos of warm milk and sugar, into which I'd poured a tiny pot of espresso. I always get hungry at the beach. Mamma says it's the salt air.

I walked along the beach, the surf crashing over my feet, the water so much colder than the day before. I picked up some shells, but tossed them one by one into the surf.

I went back to my bike, got out my towel and food provisions, and put on my jacket. I walked toward the surf, but not as close as before, spread out the towel, and sat down Indian-style. While munching on the food and occasionally sipping the hot café latte, I began to think about what my parents' lives had been like in Sicily, living on an island surrounded by water. No wonder Papa had become a sailor. The wind picked up, so I scrunched up the waxed paper that had held my sandwich and put it in a paper bag that I secured under my bottom so it wouldn't fly away. I remembered pulling up my knees to the same bent position they were in now, encircling them with my arms and clasping my hands. I closed my eyes, listened to the wind and the crashing roar of waves, and pictured some photos I'd seen. My mind began to trip over the many stories I'd heard, and I tried to weave these all together into a fabric I could grasp with understanding. I opened my eyes and looked out toward the frothing sea and passed into a meditative state. My eyes grew heavy, and I curled up onto Val's towel, placing the scrunched-up paper bag into my jacket pocket. I pulled the hood up and was instantly asleep and dreaming.

I can't recall for sure how long I'd been there, but raindrops were beginning to fall insistently, and finally I awakened from my dream. I could swear I'd seen and heard Mamma's girlhood laugh and even got a glimpse of her grandparents in their garden. They spoke fast in a language I didn't understand, perhaps dialect or even Spanish.

When I got back to the cottage, Mamma was furious because I'd been out so long and it was raining quite heavily. I distracted her and diffused her wrath. As I took off my slicker, I began telling her of my dreamlike imaginings and how I saw her in a garden talking a foreign tongue to her grandparents.

"My mother's people had been from Spain, and there are many Spanish-sounding words in our Sicilian dialect," she said.

We sat down and I began to tell her about the garden I had seen and her little grandmother, and she began to cry. "You saw so much. How is it that some of us are so attuned to the lives of others?"

"Curiosity?" I asked.

"I think it's knowledge handed down, but you're open to receive it, aware, and therefore ready for reception of thoughts and times, a world gone by. You're special, Marcella. You should try to develop this gift you have. It's inborn, an intuitive nature. Don't disregard it."

⌒⊂✿⊃⌒

BUT I DO DISREGARD IT, don't I? I wrote and underlined this phrase to bring it to my attention the next time I opened the book. I hadn't thought of that for a long while. Where had the time gone? I hated losing track of time. Why hadn't I tried to be more perceptive? Opportunities for this presented themselves all the time with Gianni, Val, and even Elaine. I closed my book and went to bed, hoping for a dream. Mamma always said ask for the dream, and it will come to you.

⚜

THE NEXT MORNING WHEN I awoke, I realized that instead of dreaming of Mamma and her family in Sicily, I had dreamed of Gianni and our weekend in Gardiner and how Val living up to her Valentine name had played cupid when I came home. She wanted Gianni and me to make amends from forever—such a romantic! In the dream, I held the movie theater tickets she'd given us, and as naturally as bees take to honey, Gianni and I were back to being the sweethearts we were meant to be. I still had those tickets in my Missal.

Now months later, I was comfy-cozy off in the summer camp, a Garden-of-Eden spot, glad to be away for a brief spell with time to think—of Gianni and my family. A little distance, I decided, was a good thing and I was in the perfect place. I loved everything about it: the huge wrought iron entrance gates; the stately outdoor lamps on red-brick columns; the rustic cabins; the barn, horses, and tennis courts; and the fir tree-lined pathways going toward the wishing well with its pointy roof made out of shingles. Outside in back of the main building was a terrace encased by a rock slate wall.

That afternoon, I went walking and thought over our discussion about writing the Macy's story, the story of Isidor and Ida Strauss' tragic deaths and the founding of our camp. I took a woodsy path so beaten it wasn't even a direction, but I circled back and somehow ended up down by the tranquil lake bordered with weeping willows trailing their branches into the water, stately magnolias, maples, evergreens, and syca-mores. After I'd been sitting, watching the ripples on the water, I finally decided I couldn't wile away my time. I retraced my steps and went to my room to pick up some writing paper and a pen. Then I followed a pretty row, concealed between hedges and huge trees, all the way to the gazebo. I took my time walking among the urns, planters, containers, tubs, and jardinières—someone had a green thumb and a great love of gardens, flowers, and shrubs and had dedicated much time to planning out this one. It teemed with every color and species of summer flowers one could image to delight a lonesome heart—mine. Equipped with blue stationery and a two-cent red stamp—I remembered that Papa told me in China red means good luck—I decided to write a letter.

July 7, 1931,
Camp Isida, Burlingham,
Sullivan County, New York

Dear Gianni,

Received your sweet letter and enjoyed it immensely. So you miss me just a little, huh? Well, I don't miss you at all—Ha! Only kidding.

My family was up to see me Sunday and we had a lovely time. They liked the place very much. It rained here yesterday and this morning, but it's all clear now and hot as Hades.

My mother was surprised to see me so fat and tanned. She was just crazy about my friends and I know you would be, too. We all enjoyed Grazia's candy very much. Believe me, these girls up here are always hungry.

I wish you would come for me Sunday, as I don't feel very much like riding in a stuffy, hot train. I hope your brother Giuseppe likes my card and maybe he might want to come when he hears of the lovely girls here. One of the girls, Marie, and I go around with Dottie—she's Italian, too, and lives near you. The other is Pat, and she's just grand. We have loads of fun all together.

Everybody is going swimming, and it's so hot I'd better go just as soon as I finish this letter to you, dear. Pina says she might come, but they got a flat going home last Sunday, and they sorta think they might get another if they do come.

Please call Pina up and tell her you can come for me. I just got some letters from home and from a girl that lives in Jersey. There isn't more news to tell you except that some of our friends left Sunday night and we all had a very good cry. It was a very funny sight, I must say.

Please give my love to everyone, and thank you very much for the kiss you sent me via Pina.

I must admit I wish I were home tonite 'cause this is your nite to come over.

Well, goodbye for now and be good and don't work too hard and don't call me chubby, darling. Loads and loads of love.

As ever,
Marcella

As soon as I finished writing that letter, I began another.

July 7, 1931, Camp Isida, Burlingham,
Sullivan County, New York

Dear Bao,

Even though I haven't heard from you in a very long, long, long time, I've decided to write anyway to tell you how busy I've been. I sang in a talent show here at the camp, and every one of the camp girls and all the staff loved it. The directors, too! I was oohed all over the place and asked if I ever thought of singing professionally. I couldn't exactly say yes, since I'm working at Macy's and here I'm surrounded by all Macy's people, but my heart burned to say, yes, absolutely.

One evening while we were out walking, night-blooming jasmine and honeysuckle combined to make the most luscious perfume, and as luck would have it, I also met a bunch of actors in a summer stock production who invited me and two friends to a matinee and then out for hamburgers and shakes. It was such fun! This one gal takes singing lessons from the same woman I do in Manhattan. Can you imagine that?

The time here is flying by, and I can't believe I'll soon be packing up and heading for home. I'm not disappointed to be leaving because I've decided to double up on my voice lessons and look up some of the actors I met. Won't that be fun and exciting?

Time's fleeting, and I must get down to dinner. Don't bother to write me here at camp, as I'll be leaving so soon. Write me at home, if you care to, that is.

Love from your friend,
Marcella

❦

SUMMER FLEW BY, AND I never did get to meet any of the people connected with the theater that I'd met at camp. But I doubled up on my lessons, and before I knew it summer was over and we were into fall. On one of those weekends that everyone called "Indian Summer," Gianni invited me to go horseback riding in Prospect Park on a Sunday afternoon. He was an incredible horseman. We rode all around, and at one point he suddenly reversed his position and was riding backward.

"What're you doing? You'll kill yourself!" I shrieked.

"Tame beast. I can handle him. I've been riding since I was fourteen. My father kept horses when I was studying in Sicily for a summer. Watch this," he said, and the next thing I knew he was in the proper position and cantering along. My eyes must have popped out of their sockets when I saw him slide off the horse, hit the ground with his feet, and then hop back onto the saddle. He gave a little whoop, turned around, and came back to me.

"Valentino, the sheik, has nothing on me, young lady."

"You bet he doesn't. I was terrified. You took my breath away."

"Thank heavens something can."

"You do, Gianni, more than you know."

❦

BEFORE I KNEW IT, WE were deep into autumn leaves and it was the evening before Thanksgiving. I got out of work early so I could help with the preparations, promising my boss that I'd stay late on Friday since it's always a busy shopping day.

I ran into Lucille that evening in Carmine's while I waited for Jack to give me a package that Mamma had ordered. Lucille seemed upset, and when I asked what happened, she said she'd been laid off her job as a temporary fill-in secretary and was looking for new employment.

"Why not try Macy's? They're looking for bundle wrappers now that the holidays are fast approaching. That'd hold you over the Christmas holidays at least, and then with the new year you can start looking in earnest for a permanent position."

"How come you're not working?"

"My boss gave me off this afternoon because I'll be working late on Friday. Why not come to work with me Friday morning and apply for the position?"

"Okay."

"Never know—they might hire you on the spot. If not, we could meet for lunch. Bring a sandwich. I've got a half-hour break at twelve-thirty."

"Sounds great. It's tough getting a bum break like this right before the holidays," Lucille said.

We both were seated on wooden folding chairs, and I noticed we were doing the exact same thing with our right feet—drawing and doodling with our shoe toes in the sawdust.

Jack came to the front of the store in his bloody apron and handed me a package wrapped in butcher paper and twine. "Hi," he said to Lucille.

"Thanks," I said and noticed he was blushing. I wouldn't embarrass him now, but later I'd ask if he was sweet on my friend. Jack said he had to get back to work.

"See you," Lucille called to his back.

"Want to walk home with me?" I asked.

"Would love to, but I'm waiting for Carmine to finish mother's order and I still have to pick up a few things in the grocery store."

"Come to the house early so we can have a cup of coffee together beforehand. Don't eat too much bird."

Lucille laughed. "I hate turkey. I'd rather eat your mother's pasta."

♦

GIANNI AND I WENT TO the Macy's Thanksgiving Day Parade in Manhattan, and it teemed with onlookers. He and I both loved the fall season with its crisp air, changing leaves on the trees, Halloween, and Thanksgiving—it was the season that heralded the soon-approaching Christmas and New Year's holidays.

This year the parade fell on a bitterly cold day, but that didn't stop people from inundating Times Square—the throngs of people and excitement kept us warm. The parade featured a variety of floats—helium balloons of a huge dragon, Felix the Cat, a Jerry Pig balloon, and others. Everybody loves a parade for sure! This one featured a large assortment of papier-mâché heads and more huge balloons of clowns and a hippopotamus. Marching bands lent an air of colorful and joyful festivity. At the end of the parade, the arrival of Santa Claus announced the beginning of the Christmas season and the time for shopping.

Gianni read that over a thousand people had volunteered to help organize and plan the parade, and I believed it when we were in the crush of families, jostling and maneuvering for a better view—not even the police barricades could stop children from sneaking under and even adults from overflowing from curb to street.

Some of the balloons were crowded by trolley cars! We heard some of the floats dwarfed Broadway and had to squeeze in the "lane," as the Knickerbockers and highfalutin' New Yorkers had to cede their aristocratic places for us plebeians.

We learned the next day that aviator Clarence Chamberlain flew over NYC and lassoed the Jerry Pig balloon in midair in an effort to collect the reward money for doing so—we never heard if he got it or not.

⚜

THANKSGIVING DINNER WAS AN INTERESTING project, because Gianni first had to eat at Zia Grazia's in the afternoon and then save room to eat more at our house for dinner. Gianni had come early after he'd eaten with his brothers. We waited for the company to arrive and were sitting on the downstairs sofa by the window that faced the backyard.

I pulled the curtain aside and said, "Look. The poor birds can't even bathe in the birdbath because the water is frozen. I love it in springtime when it is ringed with purple iris. Mamma said that iris grow wild in Sicily and the lemon blossoms are so pungent they make a kind of perfume out of it."

Gianni picked up my wrist and kissed it. "You smell lemony."

I withdrew my hand.

He leaned close and said, "When we're married—"

"Hold up a sec—I'm too young. Mamma was twenty-three. I'm in my teens," I said.

Valentina walked over to us and said, "You know I love you like a brother, Gianni, but watch out she doesn't fall in love with someone else in the meantime."

Gianni bristled but didn't have time to answer, as Jack, walking into the room, said, "She's so fickle."

"Who invited you? Nobody asked your opinion, pipsqueak," I said quickly.

Gianni stood, shook Jack's hand, and then tousled his hair. Gianni looked at me. "Leave him alone, he's going to be my partner in some wacky wonderful business get-rich scheme. Wait and see."

"If I wait that long, Hell will freeze, and I'll have gray hair like Mamma." I began to set the downstairs table. Gianni leaned over to me and whispered, "I'd wait that long for you. I'm sure you'll let me know when you're ready." I was tempted to say something about the way Jack blushed when he'd seen Lucille the night before in the meat store, but I decided to let him off the hook.

The doorbell chimed and guests were arriving, each couple laden with what they referred to as "some American dish." Set upon the table were covered dishes of mashed sweet potatoes with marshmallows, green beans with dill, fresh cranberry sauce, and cornbread. Mamma made a turkey filled with what she called Italian stuffing—manicotti overflowing with spinach, ham, and three cheeses, and a tomato sauce made of sausage and pork ribs for *penne*. First she'd serve the pasta dish and manicotti, followed by the turkey with the trimmings, and lastly a huge mixed salad, which she wouldn't dress but would set out after the meal, as that's when we eat salad to wash everything down. She would toss the salad only with olive oil and our homemade vinegar.

Papa's brother, Ned, and his wife, Lia, were coming for dinner, as well as Carlo and Caterina without their children, as they had secured her mother and her sister Vera to babysit, and Pina, Bruno, and baby Elena, who was now getting into everything and talking.

Mamma and I had served an antipasto, and we'd already finished and awaited the next course. Valentina cleared off dishes and silverware like a restaurant pro, and Pina had gone to the kitchen to help Mamma so I could entertain our guests. We weren't even finished eating the pasta when Gianni received a phone call. Apparently, by the way his faced blanched white, Mamma and I knew that something unfortunate had occurred.

He hung up the phone, came back to the table, and looked at Mamma, then me. "My sister-in-law Grazia has taken an overdose of sleeping pills. I have to go. Forgive me."

"Do you want me to go with you, Gianni?"

"No. Forgive me, I have to leave. They're walking her back and forth and giving her black coffee to drink. I think my brother is ashamed to take her to the hospital. Perhaps I can convince him it'd be best for her."

"I didn't know she was so unhappy," Mamma said.

"Good God. I never realized it either until just now," Gianni said.

I helped him shrug into his coat, struck dumb by sadness and fear. All I could say was, "Such a sweet woman."

I handed him his hat in the vestibule, and he pecked my cheek. "I'll call you," he said.

"Please let us know. I'll say a prayer for her," thinking, *dear God, don't let her die like this, giving up hope and wanting to end her life.*

I made some stupid excuse to the guests for Gianni's departure, and the festivities continued.

CHAPTER 18

Giacomo

THE WEEKEND RIGHT AFTER THE Thanksgiving Day parade, Giacomo started drawing ideas for a Christmas window in the porch. He gathered all his materials, took measurements, and went down to his workroom, where he built a wooden platform to hold a winter scene and crèche. Jack helped Giacomo mount it and did whatever else he could whenever he could, but now he was working even on weekends delivering Western Union messages on his new bike. In his stead, Valentina and Marcella volunteered and became Giacomo's helpmates. They gathered all sorts of materials to possibly use in the construction.

From the window to the wall in back of it, Giacomo mounted a wooden platform and another one that sloped at a forty-five-degree angle. He set up lights that would shine down on his Christmas scene. These he covered with red and green cellophane. Then he began to cover the platforms in papier-mâché. Giacomo used a composite of different materials made up of paper pulp and glue. He strengthened his papers with bits of old cloth, felt material, cotton threads, knitting yarn, and fragments of rags and fibrous materials, such as jute and hemp, and assembled the whole thing with starch and flour paste for putting up wallpaper. The effect was a mountainous incline, made bumpy and smooth into hillsides and plateaus. He used little hand mirrors that were sequestered from various purses and pocketbooks to make lakes, and designed and painted blue, silver, and white squiggles to form streams. Gathering stones from the garden, he painted the larger ones to look like gray boulders and the smaller rocks black. Valentina suggested using rough sandpaper painted variegated shades of green for fields, browns and tans for deserts and wastelands. Tiny trees and bushes were made of pine branches, and figures of people and animals made from wooden clothespins dotted the landscape. He built miniature houses and tents and fires of matchsticks with tiny flashing lightbulbs beneath, some yellow and some red.

Valentina added to all of his skills with ideas for color and design. Giacomo assigned tasks of fetching various articles from all over the house to Marcella, as she was not inspired by the building process, although she lent an air of festivity by singing Christmas carols. Angelica came to inspect the progress from time to time, admiring their handicrafts and serving them all hot drinks when they took breaks.

⸙

AFTER ONE BREAK, WHILE RUMMAGING around in Giacomo's workroom, Valentina found Giacomo's stashed chronicle in what looked like Chinese and began to ask her father about it. Marcella grabbed it from her sister's hands and said, "Oh, careful there, that belongs to Bao. I was just holding it till he got back from San Francisco and thought to put it here out of harm's way because you always seem to get into everything."

Valentina started to protest. "In Papa's workroom?"

Giacomo gently removed it from Marcella's hands, giving her a thankful look for her intuition, and said, "We're keepers of Bao's family's history," Marcella lied. "He had no place to store it."

Valentina looked at her father queerly. "I thought you didn't particularly like him, Papa."

Giacomo placed the book reverently back in the bottom drawer that housed it. "It's not that. It's just that I worry about your faithless sister, who should be thinking only of Gianni," he gently chided. "When, in fact, she's a terrible—what is it Jack calls her?"

"A flirt," Valentina volunteered.

"Precisely," Giacomo said.

Marcella stood up from the stool she'd been sitting on next to Giacomo's. "We've had enough drinks to drown an elephant. Shall we take a lunch break now? I'm starving and don't want any more accusations about my moral character. I don't appreciate being spoken of in the third person when I'm standing right here in front of both of you."

When Valentina was out of earshot halfway up the stairs, Marcella put her hand on the banister, and before mounting the first step, turned to her father and said, "I'm a flirt? How do you explain that book in Chinese? And the tattooed dragon on your arm? It looks exactly like the one in that book."

"Why did you poke your nose into my things?" he asked without a hint of anger in his voice.

For once, she didn't answer.

He shook his head and then looked up.

"Papa, a look of sadness has crept into your eyes."

"Can you imagine me a young sailor in love for the first time? It's a long story, but over and done with before I left China."

From the top of the staircase, Valentina called, "Hey, what's keeping you two? Thought you were starved?"

"How did you know the book was in there?"

Marcella looked at her father. "I didn't snoop. I was looking for something for Mamma. Can't remember what it was. She was canning or bottling something. But we need to talk. Another time?"

"*Certo.* Certainly."

Marcella called back up the stairs to Valentina, "We're coming." To Giacomo, she mouthed, "When? This can't wait."

"Soon."

"Not good enough. Tonight? After dinner, let's take a walk."

"I don't owe you an explanation of my life before this family came into being. Who do you think you are to question me?"

"Your daughter, who loves you and wants to be closer to you."

⁓⁂⁓

AFTER LUNCH, WHEN THEY FINISHED setting up the nativity scene and villages, Giacomo congratulated the girls and said it was time for a toast. They were just about to leave the porch with the lights shining on their ingenious work when there was a knock on the door.

Giacomo hunched his shoulders, as if to say *who is it at this hour, and why not ring?* He opened the door without looking and was shocked to see Józef Brodzik, a man he'd worked with on the docks. Giacomo's first thought was *trouble*, remembering the incident of the man he'd accidentally killed. But Józef seemed pleased to see him and smiled. He stuck out his hand, and Giacomo shook it and invited him in.

He turned to the girls as he was shutting the door. "Go on up, and don't wait for me. Mamma has something ready for you."

"What brings you to Brooklyn?" Giacomo asked.

"Looking for you," Brodzik said.

"Me?"

"Remember those years ago you promise me work? I come to ask you now."

"That was Piero, not me."

Józef took off his hat and toyed with it in his hands, turning the cap round and round. He looked sheepishly at Giacomo. "I'm in bad way, Jocko. Wife, she sick. Babies need food."

"Where're you working?"

"No work now for two months. You work?"

Giacomo thought how fortunate it was he had a job. "Part of a New York construction crew."

"Ah! I knew. I says to Beata, if anyone of old crowd work, it's Jocko. He help me."

It was cold on the porch, and Giacomo was no longer moving and working so he felt chilled. "Come in, Józef."

"No want to bother. Just a name. Please?"

Giacomo opened the vestibule door and motioned the man to follow him. Once they stepped inside, Józef said, "Nice house. Big. You build?"

"Wish I had. This was here when I came from Italy."

Giacomo took Józef's coat and hung it up on the coat rack, took the hat from his hands and plunked it on top. "Come this way."

They went upstairs to the kitchen and the sound of the girls' laughter. Giacomo presented his former coworker to his women and made him sit at the table.

Even though it was close to dinnertime, Angelica offered the man some tea or hot chocolate.

He didn't answer, but Giacomo noticed that he looked as shy as Jack did sometimes.

"Józef is out of work. Maybe my boss could hire an extra man," Giacomo said.

"Wife sick. Babies hungry," Józef repeated.

"Oh, dear." Angelica caught Giacomo's eye, and he nodded. The man hadn't answered when asked, so she put a cup of hot chocolate and three cookies in front of Józef. "Perhaps we can send some food to your family. Would that be all right?" she said.

"I no beg," Józef said, with such alacrity that Giacomo understood he was offended.

"Not for you—your babies," Angelica said in a soothing voice.

Józef shook his head.

Giacomo took a piece of paper and a pencil from the center drawer of the table and wrote something. He handed it to Józef. "This is where I work. Meet me on Monday at seven sharp. The boss will be there to distribute—I mean, give out the work schedule for the week. He might take you on. Now drink up."

Despite his refusal, Giacomo saw Angelica put together some provisions in a sack: pastina, rice, half a loaf of bread, and a bottle of milk. "How old are your babies?"

"The boy, he seven years. The girl, she five."

"What's wrong with your wife?" Angelica asked.

"She cough. All the time, cough." Józef sipped from his cup.

"Can you get her to a doctor?" Angelica reached for a small jar of honey.

"Not money for this." He bit off the end of a cookie. "Now blood. Chills. Skinny."

Angelica almost dropped the jar. Her hand flew to her mouth. "Tuberculosis?"

"Józef, listen to me," Giacomo said. "You must get her to a doctor. Can you bring her here tomorrow? Angelica will take her across the street to our doctor. He has medicine for your wife."

"Beata," he said, his voice plaintive. "Can't pay."

"Don't worry. He won't charge," Marcella said. "Papa does work for him all the time."

Giacomo silenced her with a look.

"Sorry, Papa." Marcella got up and cleared away the cups, and Valentina joined her at the sink. Marcella washed, Val dried.

"It's settled then. You come tomorrow with your Beata. Monday we'll see about getting you work."

"Sunday?"

"Yes." Angelica wrapped a jar of beef broth in newspapers and put it into the sack. "For Beata. Make sure she drinks it. And put this honey in her tea or hot water to ease the cough."

Downstairs, Giacomo helped Józef with his coat. When they reached the door, he turned and faced Giacomo. He proffered his hand.

"You hold no grudge?"

"A waste of time. Life's too short." He patted Józef's shoulder and opened the door to the frigid night, and saw Jack, slip-slide racing toward the house.

"*Ciao*, Papa," Jack said, nodded to the man, and raced upstairs.

Giacomo closed the door and trudged behind Jack with a heavy heart, thinking how blessed they were and how someone is always worse off than you.

After dinner, Giacomo told Marcella they'd take a walk another evening.

Marcella patted his hand. "Sure, Papa, you're tired and upset about your friend. It can wait."

⋰⋰⋲⋇⋳⋱⋱

THE NEXT MORNING, A SUNDAY, Dr. Amanti examined Beata in the doctor's kitchen and in Italian explained to Giacomo there was nothing he could do for her except send her to Waverly Hills Sanatorium in Kentucky or she'd die, and most likely she'd die anyway, but at least she wouldn't infect the rest of her family.

Giacomo took a minute to digest the information before he translated, easing and erasing some of the doctor's words. Then he answered the doctor that Józef couldn't afford to pay.

Switching to English, the doctor said to Józef, "Can you pay the train ticket to get her there? I know doctors who would care for her, but she has to make the trip."

"What are her chances?" Giacomo asked in Italian.

The doctor looked at Józef and Beata but answered Giacomo in Italian, "If she doesn't leave by the front entrance cured, she'll leave by a 'body chute,' which deposits the soulless bodies to a train car for removal so the other patients won't see how many corpses there are—for the mental health of the remaining patients."

"Come," Giacomo said to Józef and Beata. "I'll explain more at home. The doctor is busy. He shook hands with the doctor, who escorted them out the house's back entryway, where his office exited.

Józef and Beata went back to Giacomo's, where he explained the situation as gently as he could to Józef while Angelica gave Beata a spoonful of honey and put more in her tea.

Leaving out the last things Giacomo heard the doctor say, he informed Józef, who broke down but said he would pawn the family jewels and silverware for her trip. Beata cried, too.

It was agreed. Beata would leave on Tuesday, after Józef had seen about getting new employment and hocking what he could for a ticket to Louisville.

When they left, Angelica boiled water and soaked the cup, saucer, and spoon that Beata had used. She looked at Giacomo. "You did what you could for them. Will she be cured?"

"Amanti didn't sound hopeful. But there's a chance, and she'll have a clean environment and hot food."

"And she won't be a danger to the little ones," Angelica said. "How will you repay Dr. Amanti?"

"He asked me to make a rocking horse for Albertino, his four-year-old. I'll start on it today."

"That'll cover the visit, but how will you pay the sanatorium?"

Giacomo shook his head. "I've no idea. Maybe he has."

"I do," Marcella said.

"Where did you come from?" Angelica asked.

"Sitting at the top of the stairs, listening to Papa talking about that poor man and his wife." She sat at the table and took her father's hands in hers. "Papa, you know how Mrs. Amanti loves to dress up and lord it over the neighborhood."

"Marcella!" Angelica exclaimed.

"Truth hurts. She does. Everyone knows it."

"Your plan?" asked Giacomo.

"Valentina could make her some of those new frocks from France. She's got some McCall's patterns and could create something fantastic. She could whip up some snazzy outfit for the old windbag in a minute."

"Not quite a minute," Valentina said, standing in the doorway. "Who pays for the materials? And thanks for volunteering me. Why don't you bring her a fancy negligee from Macy's?"

"I may just do that. Along with the dress you'll make her, the doctor will be repaid in spades, and have her Christmas present besides," Marcella said, enthusiasm pouring out of every word.

"Valentina?" Giacomo said.

"Of course, Papa. But the *stoffa*?" Valentina put her arms around his neck and kissed the top of his head.

"You have plenty of material tidied away," Marcella said.

"Not silk," Valentina said.

"I've got something you may be able to use." Angelica went to the cabinet on the left side of the window where the bread drawer was and opened the hodge-podge drawer to the left where she kept sundries. She took out a small antique rose-velvet package, unwrapped it at the table, and eight tiny mother-of-pearl buttons surrounded by gold toppled out.

"Where on earth—" Giacomo started to say.

"Mr. Blitzer was here before Chanukah and sold these to me at a bargain price—as always," Angelica said.

"Real gold? Let me see," Valentina said.

Angelica nodded, pleased, a smile playing about her lips.

"How delicate and lovely. What a gorgeous addition for a blouse," Valentina said, her voice filled with excitement. "Are you sure you want to part with them, Mamma? I wouldn't. Do you think she'll know they're gold?"

Angelica nodded. "She'll know."

"That woman is never even cordial with you. She barely greets you on the street with those two yapping Yorkies of hers," Valentina said.

"Doesn't matter. But what I want to know is just how the Miss Queen-of-Ideas here," Angelica said, pointing to Marcella, "will pay for the silk fabric and fancy boudoir set?" She pulled out a chair.

"Simple," Marcella said with confidence. "By the good graces of Elaine Weiss."

"Your boss?" Valentina all but shrieked. "What will your payback to her have to be?" Marcella shot her a look, and Giacomo wondered but wasn't quite sure if Angelica got Val's inference or not. Valentina sat down next to Giacomo.

He watched Val mouth "Sorry" to her sister. Marcella cleared her throat. "Elaine gets samples all the time. I'm sure I can get her to part with one if I bring her home for dinner to meet the family, and Mamma'll make her something very Italian and un-Kosher. She loves pork almost as much as Papa. She also said she loves Christmas trees—maybe because she grew up without ever having one."

"And the silk fabric?" Val asked.

"Our darling Mr. A. will make us a special price," Marcella all but sang, and everyone laughed knowing he always made them a *special price.*

Angelica smiled. "Settled then?"

"All in favor, say aye," Marcella said.

"Wherever do you get these sayings?" Giacomo asked.

Valentina smiled. "Aye."

"You too?" Angelica shook her head.

Marcella asked, "When, Mamma?"

"When what, *cara?*"

"When can I invite Elaine over for dinner?"

Angelica looked at Giacomo.

"Next Sunday," he said and looked at Jack, who hadn't said a word all this time. "Jack will bring home sausage and pork ribs and a cut of loin for Mamma to make sauce." Giacomo thought about his wife always cooking a delicious pork sauce but never eating it.

Val said, "Mamma, if you want, I'll help you make homemade fettucine. We have enough eggs from the chickens."

Giacomo couldn't help but think of his daughter Pina and all the weekends before she married helping her mother make homemade pasta or ravioli.

"Good idea," he said. "We'll have Pina and Bruno over, too." And it seemed to him that everyone present had guessed his thoughts.

CHAPTER 19

Marcella

SO MUCH HAD HAPPENED BETWEEN Christmas and Valentine's. Lucille had gotten the job at Macy's and was hired on permanently. Zia Grazia had gotten better and seemed much less depressed because Zio Franco had quit drinking. Elaine fell in love again—this time with our whole family. Mrs. Amanti loved her Christmas presents and started saying hello to Mamma. Józef worked with Papa, but sadly, his wife, Beata, had passed away. His children were in school all day, and after school let out, they were being cared for by his Polish landlady, who Papa said had a "twinkling in her eye for Józef."

I was feeling low—what Mamma called—"the slough of despond." Although I actually tried, Gianni and I had broken up again. This time it was more injurious than the plate affair, or any other falling out we'd had in the past. Mamma, standing in her chenille bathrobe looking in the fridge for something, said to me, "You two are getting too old for this nonsense. This time he won't be back any time soon, so don't hold your breath, Missy."

❧

THE AFTERNOON HAD STARTED OUT delightful. We walked to the bakery, and Gianni bought his favorite Napoleons for everyone. While walking back to the house, we had an argument. It came about like this. I opened my big mouth and asked, "I thought you'd changed. Why are you so meek with your brothers?"

"I'm not. I respect them, that's all."

"You never exert your will or personality. When they tell you to do something or to snap to it, you do—isn't that the truth?"

"My strength of character doesn't mean I have to 'tell them off,' as you say." He switched the pastry box to his other hand, stopped, and faced me. "They don't tell me, they ask me."

"You're completely subservient to them. 'Gianni, do this, and Gianni, do that.' Then you even have the audacity to tell me that Giuseppe preferred you stop seeing me. What was it he said? Probably, 'Marcella's no good for you—too strong-headed and stubborn.' So I guess he thinks you need someone more flexible?"

"He said you talk too much, and he wants me to start seeing his future wife's sister. She's been pushing him. He wants to keep peace in the family—"

I interrupted, "At your expense and mine. Talk too much? Not good for you? I'll say, because I instigate you to answer back and tell them in various shades of no that you won't do their bidding! I didn't expect a derring-do kind of boldness, but I do expect spine! And I do presume you'd stick up for me rather than acquiesce and go out with Giuseppe's mousy almost-sister-in-law."

"Whew. That's a mouthful. Calm down. I never said I would. Come on, it's freezing. Let's stop in here for a cup of coffee." He nudged his head toward a small café.

"You're not going to mollify me with a cup of anything. I'm done talking about this. Keep the pastry and go visit what's-her-name."

"Marcella, be reasonable."

"No. We want different things. What's worse, we can't even agree on little things that will grow into major issues."

"Why are you always argumentative?"

I shrugged. "My nature, I guess—although this time, I'm right."

⁓❦⁓

ONE SATURDAY MORNING, A FEW weeks after Gianni and I had cooled our relationship, I cobbled together a new self. Not so much from my wanting it, but from Val's demanding it. My bedroom was clogged with books, ephemera for writing, 78 RPM records, a phonograph, and movie magazines. It was beginning to look like a writer's music office/studio, and Val had enough and began a cleanup campaign. Holding two books or objects at a time, she barked, "Which one? And only one." I understood her seriousness about this ritual cleansing. She wanted me to rid myself of skewed memories tied to these books, which she said influenced my notions about acting in movies and shows. Most especially, she wanted me to give up records and the voice lessons, which cost me time, energy, and money.

"I can't," I begged.

"Okay. You will, or I toss both." She put the books down and picked up my Duke Ellington record of "Mood Indigo" and a used and abused copy of *Wuthering Heights*.

"That's not a choice—it's a total impossibility."

The miserable, miserly morning passed as I unhinged myself and formed three piles: "Give Away," "Keep," and "Sell." I could sell the books to a used bookstore on the corner of Eighty-Fourth Street, I reasoned, and that would give me the means to buy some lessons. But what was I to do with the other stuff? I decided to give Jack some records to pawn, sell, or trade. I kept the business card from the agent I met at Lake George and the names of the actors I'd met in the Catskills.

After this ordeal, it was close to midday. Val had showered and gone down to help Mamma make lunch. I came downstairs, probably looking my sheepish best, clean and wearing my pressed pink piqué blouse.

"Why are you wearing such a pretty blouse? Go change so you can help me." I'd worn the blouse in hopes of getting out of helping Mamma, but my ploy didn't work. Obviously.

⌒⥁⌒

WITH THE CHRISTMAS HOLIDAYS ENDED, sales slowed noticeably, not only in my department but the whole store. My nine-teenth birthday had come and gone without fanfare. After all, the money situation was, as Papa often told us, "tight," and we had to watch frivolous spending.

Business picked up around Valentine's Day and on the blustery day itself I had a hunch it was going to be a banner day for sales. I also had the feeling someone I hadn't seen in a while was going to show up. I wondered if this was what Mamma meant about being open to knowing things before they happened. Going about my business, I straightened up a showcase and looked up. A sleekly dressed customer was browsing, and to my utter shock, I recognized him. What I didn't expect, though, was the surprised look on the customer's face when he noticed my approach, pencil tucked behind my ear and sales book at the ready. I walked up to the salesgirl waiting on him and said, "Do you mind, dear? This is a very old friend of my family. I'd like to assist him personally, if I may." She looked like she was going to object, but I patted her hand. "Ms. Weiss would appreciate it."

The sweet retiring violet slipped away, and I asked a very flustered Bao, "When did you return from San Francisco?"

He exclaimed, "I'm shopping for my sister."

"Really?" I said, honey dripping from every syllable of the word, which I'd made into exactly three. I repeated, "Re-al-ly? That's strange. You told me you were orphaned, had no living relative, and were raised by a priest."

"I was embarrassed to say. Actually, I was shopping for my, uh, auntie?"

"You buy ladies' unmentionables for your aunt?" I stepped behind a small glass-topped counter displaying lace panties and a brassiere in black Belgian lace that could entice even an octogenarian to become inflamed with passion. "You left me with the impression you were going to get in touch when you returned."

"Actually, I just got back."

"Recently come again to New York, and shopping for delicate intimates in the boudoir section of Macy's. Me oh my, you really do things differently in China. Have you made your selection then?"

"This set here," he said.

"Size?"

He raised both of his hands as if to grab apples, but since I knew Chinese girls were all slender, I said to him, "More like apricots, no?"

His head bobbed vigorously.

"That's the cup size. Now, for inches?" I held up my tape measure and circled my breasts, wondering if he'd ever encircle me this way. "No, no. This will never do. Way too much, I think, for an Oriental auntie,"

I said and yanked the tape around so it squashed my breasts. Then I whipped it away from my body with one quick, smooth move, looking at the number. "Of course, 32, not my robust 34, don't you agree?"

By this time he was Chinese-apple red—even the whites of his eyes were the color of pomegranates—and he was practically going into apoplexy. I released him from the invisible dangling line I'd roped around him. "I'll take you down to Wrapping, where my friend Lucille can bundle these up for you. Will there be anything else?" I draped the tape measure around my neck and had the distinct feeling he wanted to strangle me with it even through his embarrassment.

Apparently he gathered a bit of poise, enough to say, "You must excuse me. I will call you soon."

Under my breath I murmured, "I won't hold my breath." To Bao I said, "Follow me, please. The escalator is this way."

When we got to the wrapping desk, Lucille, pretty as a picture in pink, had just come back from a break. I introduced them, leaned over the counter, and straightened her name tag.

"Plenty of tissue, Lucille," I said. "Please make sure to crimp and tuck, sweetie. It's for his little old auntie. Goodbye, Bao."

He stuttered something that sounded like "Thanks. See you soon?"

I turned on my heels. "Auntie, my foot," escaped my lips. Walking away, I waved backward over my shoulder and called out, "Toodles."

⌒⋐✿⋑⌒

ON THE TRAIN RIDE FROM Manhattan, all Lucille did was rave about the handsome man who purchased the lovely undergarments. How did you meet him? Where does he live? How long have you known him? Why hadn't she ever met him before? At one point, I wanted to either tape her mouth or sock her, but I did neither, tried to change the subject umpteen times, and finally gave up and listened to her squawk all the way home.

The minute I got in the door, I called out for Valentina. Mamma called down to me, "What's all the fuss? She's upstairs."

I tossed my coat on the rack, yanked off my scarf and draped it over, then took the stairs two at a time. I kissed Mamma on the landing and headed to our attic bedroom.

Out of breath, I announced the return of the prodigal. "He's back."

"Who?" She looked up from the *Life* magazine she was reading on the bed.

"Bao." I kicked off my shoes.

"Where'd you see him? Not Chinatown?"

"Shopping in my department for small clothes."

"For what?"

"Lingerie. Sexy lingerie. For his 'auntie.' Ha! Thinks I was born yesterday." I took off my earrings and a bracelet and put them in Mamma's ceramic keepsake ashtray that she'd gotten on her honeymoon as a souvenir—she'd actually asked for it—from a hotel in Mondello.

"He just got back and he already found a girlfriend? You've been betrayed before you even had a chance to begin a romance? Good for him."

"How can you say that? I'm your sister. And don't you dare twirl your hair."

"My point. Stick with Gianni. He'd never buy that stuff for anyone but you."

"We had a fight."

"When?"

"Does it matter?"

"What could you possibly argue about?"

"His family. They think I'm a hussy."

Somehow she'd looped her hair into a fat banana curl. "Well?"

"Valentina! You're horrid."

"Truthful. What did you do to provoke Gianni's family?"

"Nothing, I swear. The only thing is—"

"Here it comes."

"We were having dinner. When we finished eating, I helped Zia Grazia clear off the dishes, and then I sat back down with Gianni's two brothers."

"Not the one you hate?"

I nodded. "Giuseppe. He's getting married. And guess whose future bride doesn't like me? All I said was a woman should be allowed to work if she chooses after she marries."

"You said that? To those old-fashioned Sicilian men? Practically straight off the boat from the *latifondo* and each one still carrying a *lupara*? Proud men who'd rather starve than see their womenfolk work? Are you out of your mind? That can't be all of it. Fess up, Sis."

I stood and took off my belt. "So then I got up and walked to the vestibule to cool off, and Gianni followed me."

"And?"

I unzipped my skirt and dropped it to the floor, picked it up with one toe, and tossed it upward to catch with my hands. "As soon as we were alone, he took both my arms and shook me. Really hard. He said in a hoarse whisper, 'I love you in spite of yourself—but you're a difficult girl to love.'"

"That's for sure. What did you say?"

I hung my skirt in the closet. "You don't know how to love."

"You didn't really say that?"

"I'm afraid I did. When I fall in love, I want to give myself—all of me—to someone someday. I'm not sure it will ever be Gianni or a guy as sweet as he is. Maybe I'm looking for a bad boy. I've read in some novels that good women like bad men."

"And what did he say to that?"

"He gave me that look—you know, with those soft eyes of his—and said, 'What do they say when you point the finger of accusation? You've got three fingers pointing back at yourself.'"

"Yipes," Val said and almost jumped off the bed.

"So I said, 'This is a pointless discussion. I'm leaving.'"

"And then?" Val asked.

"'Goodnight,' he said very firmly and opened the front door."

"I asked him if he was going to walk me home, but I already knew the answer to that one. It didn't take too much intuition."

"So dish. What?" Val said.

"He said, 'You're enough company for yourself—in fact, you're six people in a room all by yourself. Half the time, I don't know who you are.' Can you imagine?"

"Oh Lord, you've really gone and done it this time. Congratulations. You lost a fine man," Val said.

"I walked inside, grabbed my purse, and said goodnight to his family. He'll be back."

"Put money on it? Here's one of your own fancy words—you're supercilious. You're too big for your own britches."

"You don't mean that. Well, anyway," I said, changing the subject, "Elaine took me to a music studio after work last Friday. Her friend owns it. I recorded two numbers. I've got a copy of the records. Want to hear them?"

"Are you bonkers? Papa will murder you. Forget the Simoni brothers. Child's play. He'll have you drawn and quartered."

"Stop it, please." I sat on my bed next to hers, separated by a nightstand.

"No. Why did you say it, and where do you come up with this stuff? How are you so intelligent for everything else but don't have enough brains to keep your pretty lipstick-painted siren mouth shut? Bet they hate that, too, don't they?"

"What?"

"Your red lipstick." She began to curl her hair.

"I take it off when I go there. And I wear my longest skirts. That's the point, Val—what I'm trying to tell you. I can't be me when I'm around his folks, and I hate it."

"They must really love your thoroughly modern hair bob, too. But I say, 'Love me, love my dog.'"

"Why bring up Patches? Hey, what does that mean?" My feet hurt from standing most of the day. I put my right ankle on my left knee and began to massage my foot.

"Simple." She stopped fussing with her hair and sat up, propped two pillows behind her, and punched them until she was satisfied. "His family might, if they love Gianni enough, although it seems to me they don't care about him the way he reveres them—they *might* accept you for the brash, outspoken person you're trying to become. Or you could behave and learn to tolerate his family the way they are—or break with Gianni. Permanently. Come to think of it, you don't have to worry about that—you already did."

That's when I cried.

"That's right, cry it out. Not going to help. I cried until the salt burned my eyes, and still feel miserable when I think of how stupid I was to fall for Vic Piccolo."

That's when I blew my nose. "I told that bum off."

"What?"

"I didn't carry your gentle, sweet message to him that you couldn't see him anymore. I threatened him, said our cousin was Carlo Albano, and if he ever came within a block of you ever again, he'd be ground into sausage."

I never expected the reaction I got from Val. She burst out laughing. And so did I.

"Seriously?" Val said.

"Worse. You know how when we read about the disappearance of a Mafioso, Papa always says, 'He's swimming to China.' I gave Vic a choice: a forever swim or a concrete foundation burial."

"Marcella! How could you?"

"Easy. I'm Papa's daughter, but I don't quite recognize who you are."

⁕

THE FOLLOWING EVENING WHEN I got home, flowers awaited me. Mamma had put them in a vase by my bedside. When I'd changed into something more comfortable and put slippers on my aching feet, I came down into the kitchen and kissed Mamma. "Thanks for putting the flowers in your vase."

"Remove them when you go to sleep. They rob the air of oxygen." She stirred something that smelled scrumptious.

"Old wives' tale."

"Tale or not, do it just the same," she said. "Were they from Gianni?"

I shook my head. She looked at me, waiting for an answer.

"Bao."

"He's back?" She was standing at the sink washing vegetables.

"Can I invite him for a Sunday dinner?" A vision of Papa's Chinese book popped into my head, and I wondered if I could ask Bao to have it translated for Papa. Who was I kidding? I meant me.

"What about Gianni—"

"Out of the picture unless he stands up to his brothers."

She whirled around and gave me a look that said, *speak up!*

"It's nothing. Honest Injun."

"Remember, he's not like you. He picks his arguments, and he doesn't expect you to disrespect his older brothers."

"Me? Disrespect?" I guffawed.

"Nobody else in the room getting all excited for nothing. If it really was nothing as you say."

"The truth is I'm hateful, and I said hateful things, and I don't blame him if he never talks to me again."

"You've got a sharp tongue and need to curb your temper. The world doesn't spin just for you or only around you."

"Oh Mamma, why am I like this?"

"You shouldn't ask 'why am I like this,' but 'how can I change?'"

I took the silverware out of the drawer and started setting the table. It was the second time in two days that I cried my eyes out, but Mamma didn't comfort me. She chided me the same way that Valentina had.

"Make amends."

"Impossible. How can I?"

"Swallow your pride. Apologize."

⸙

AFTER DINNER, I WASHED THE dishes and Val dried. Mamma disappeared downstairs to talk to Jack. I went to the telephone table in the alcove by Mamma's room, sat down, and looked at the ugly black apparatus sitting on a crocheted doily. It loomed like a miniature monster, a daunting presence. After a full three minutes of trying to figure out what I'd say and rehearsing it in my mind, I picked up the receiver and started dialing Zia Grazia's number, releasing the rotary dial each time it clicked a number. Courage failed me, so I recradled the receiver before it started to ring on the other side. I sat there staring until I felt I'd hypnotized myself, thinking *coward* and trying to convince myself this wasn't the right time. Finally I got up and walked into the living room where Papa was reading. I asked him if I could turn on the radio.

"Keep it low. I'm trying to concentrate on this article." He looked at me over the top of the newspaper.

"Never mind." I didn't have patience to sit and listen to anything when my head roared with the insults and aspersions I'd cast at Gianni and couldn't undo.

I decided to go to my room and write in the diary, but upon passing a hall mirror, I stopped and made the observation, *pretty on the outside, rotten inside. No wonder Gianni said I'm hard to love*, and feeling miserable and sorry for myself, I trudged upstairs.

I put on a record of "Smoke Gets in Your Eyes" and sang along with it as I took out the diary from its new hiding place, in open view on the bookcase, knowing Val would never want to read a book. I stopped singing and wrote: *Marcella! You'd better take stock of yourself, like Mamma says, and try not to be so selfish. Easy to say.* I crossed out "say" and scribbled "write." I thought of the humble old priest I saw at last Sunday's Mass. Maybe I should ask him what he did to attain meekness, or does it come with the cloth? I listed seven instances where I could try on this new penitential hirsute of humility. Typical! I couldn't even name ten. But the first thing on my inventory wasn't something concerning Gianni. Instead, it had to do with Val. I would stop trying to always "best" her and be the "bee's knees." A start, anyway. Just as I closed the diary, Jack stuck his head around the door.

"Hey, how many times are you going to play that record? Feeling sorry for yourself again?"

"If I didn't love you, I'd hate you." I stuck the book under the coverlet.

"Saw Gianni delivering to Mrs. Amanti across the street." Jack flicked his head like a horse, so the hair falling in his eyes whipped backward.

"Did he ask about me?"

"As a matter of fact," he drew in a huge breath, "he did not. What hateful little thing have you been up to lately?"

"What makes you say that?"

"If Gianni Simoni, who is insane about you, doesn't even bother to ask if you're living or dead, I figure some sort of storm's brewing. But I wasn't going to play Monkey in the Middle, thank you very much."

"Come here, you little urchin, and let me kiss you and smack you and beat you."

⇜❦⇝

I COULDN'T BELIEVE IT WHEN Gianni came the Sunday before Easter and brought Mamma's order and supplies from Simoni Brothers. I thought surely he'd send awful Alfredo, but he came himself, of all times on a day when he knew I'd be home. I stood behind the vestibule door trying to get Jack's attention as he was opening the front door to tell him to say I wasn't home, but the poor darling innocently said, "Sure, she's home. Right here in the hallway." He snatched the packages away from Gianni. "I'll run these up to Mamma. She'll need them for *Pasqua* and *Pasquetta.*"

"Right, for Little Easter, too," Gianni agreed, seeming to forget we celebrated both Easter and Easter Monday.

"Come on in, Gianni. Can I get you anything?" Jack, ever so helpfully, asked.

I thought for sure he'd say, "Oh yes—your sister's head, like St. John the Baptist's, on a silver salver, or maybe bronze as she doesn't deserve high-quality metal." But he didn't answer, and the next thing I knew he was standing in front of me, saying, "You look pretty this evening, Marcella."

"You look worn out. I see the slave drivers are overworking you as usual? Don't they know today is Sunday?"

"Holidays always mean extra time. Today when I was delivering olive oil, I showed your picture to an Arab lady from Sicily. She said the mark above your lip is a beauty mark, and you should never touch it, so don't fret about it anymore. She called it a *beauté*—a sign of beauty."

"And just when did I ever worry over it?"

"Last time we had dinner and my future sister-in-law made a comment about it. You flushed beet red."

"Can't remember. That was eons ago." I swung the door forward and back.

"Are you going to stay mad at me forever?" He stepped into the vestibule.

"I'm not mad, for Pete's sake. I'm, I'm—"

"Gorgeous in this light."

"Stop saying things like that!" I closed the door.

"Why? It's true. The silver streak in front of your hair looks thicker and more pronounced. Bleaching it?"

"It's almost an inch wide. I want to cover it up, but Mamma would slay me. Everyone's calling me 'skunk' lately. I hate it."

"Not me. It's unusual. Attractive."

I folded my arms in front of me in case he decided to grab my hands—a possibility as he was most demonstrative, and my hands were shaking and I didn't want him to see that I was nervous. Maybe he showed affection because he was raised without a mother. He held my hand in the movies or put his arm around me as if to protect me from invading hordes. He was bighearted, but for some absurd reason, I thought I should show myself as inflexible. After what seemed forever lost in my thoughts, I said, "Go soak your head. Clear the cobwebs."

"Be nice. I'm here to make up."

I looked him in the eyes so he'd know how sincere I was being. "I need time. It's no use. Your family hates me."

"You won't let them get to know the real you."

"Are you serious?"

"You say outrageous things without thinking of the consequences."

"I say things I mean. Why shouldn't a woman work after she marries if she wants to help her husband?"

"It's not just that—"

"That's it. It's over. I'm done. No reconnoitering on this mission."

"Where did that come from?"

"Just finished reading a World War I novel. Frightening."

"So are your dramatic expressions. Please don't do this. Say you care for me."

"I care. But consider it over and done."

"You pose so much, like a character in a play, but I see your interior—you're a better person than you show the world. Better than you even believe yourself to be. What are you afraid of? Exposing the real you behind all the showy stuff? Deep inside, for some reason, unbeknownst to me and half the world we know, you think you're not worthy of love, don't you?"

"Very poetic. And what have you been reading of late?"

"John Donne."

"The metaphysical poet?"

"And Shakespeare and the Renaissance poets. You're not the only one who knows how to read, Marcella. I read Dante, too, in Italian. Do you?"

I felt so stupid. He'd just smacked me with my own conceit. Good for him.

Just then, Mamma called to Gianni in the nick of time before I really uttered something obscene, like I love everything about you.

"*Vieni qui, caro.* Come up, I made some *malfatti*," Mamma said.

"Be right there, but I have to get something out of the truck first." He ran outside and came back carrying the most adorable little puppy. Without a word, he put him in my arms, kissed my forehead, and dashing upstairs, called out to Mamma, "Nothing you make could be 'badly made.'"

Mamma laughed. "They call them that because the form doesn't always stay together. They squash a bit. They're supposed to be finger-sized croquettes, but oh dear, some of mine look like malformed sixth toes."

"Bet they taste good and they squish in your stomach. Never had them. Grazia doesn't make them," he said, at the top of the stairs in a flash. "What're they made of?"

I stood there like an *asino* awaiting its master, cuddling the new pup and listening to Mamma explain how the dang things are made with ricotta and spinach, tossed into seasoned flour, quickly boiled in salt water, and then doused with butter, sage, and grated cheese. I fumed, yet I knew what Gianni said to me was true. I was afraid to show the real, emotional me to the world.

"Next time, please send Alfredo," I murmured and mounted the stairs to the kitchen like an overgrown snail.

In the kitchen, I said, "Mamma, look what Gianni brought us. What will we name him?"

"*O che bello!*" Mamma said when she saw the pup.

She thanked Gianni and continued ladling from the pot onto a serving plate the fat spinach fingers, dripping in butter and sprinkled with grated cheese. Gianni leaned over her shoulder and was positively ogling.

I couldn't resist, so I said to him, "You look like the cat that swallowed the canary. Quite at home, eh?"

"Marcella! Control yourself. Gianni's our guest." Mamma almost froze me with her look, but I still answered, "Your guest. I said goodbye to him downstairs, and then he ran out and brought in the dog."

My mother shot me a gaze—probably what Lot's wife saw when she looked back and turned into a pillar of salt.

"Gianni can't stay. He's working, right?"

"Marcella!"

"Mamma! I can't say anything."

"Bite your tongue if you can't say something nice," she said.

"*Scusi.*"

Jack came into the kitchen, saw the dog, and started fussing. "Got a name yet? Look, he's got a stripe around his neck. Let's call him Tiger."

"That's a name for a cat, silly," I said.

"Papa's home. Staying for dinner, Gianni?" Jack asked.

Jack was about to say something else, but I silenced him with one of Mamma's looks I'd been practicing in the mirror, and said, "*Et tu, Brute?*"

"What did I say?" Jack said, offended.

"Gianni's busy," I said in a know-it-all voice. "He's got to make deliveries."

"Not too busy to stay and try your Mamma's delicious offerings of something badly made," Gianni said.

Jack and Mamma laughed. I seethed, plopped the puppy into Jack's hands, washed mine, and set the table with an extra setting. I know when I've lost an argument, but to tell the truth, I was pleased he was staying and thrilled Mamma had a new puppy to love.

Valentina came rushing in, all flushed and happy to see Gianni, and gave him a kiss on the cheek. I wanted to strangle her with a *mapina,* Mamma's good tea towel. Then she saw the dog and went all sugar and spice, petting and scratching him behind the ears.

Papa came in, greeted everyone, and kissed Mamma. She gently shoved him with her hip. "We have a new family member. Meet Tiger," she indicated with her head. "Go wash, and be quick. The boys are starving."

Valentina took Tiger from Jack, plunked down next to him, and put the dog on her lap, so I had to sit next to Gianni.

Mamma looked at Valentina and shook her head. "Not at my table."

Valentina put the dog down. "But if he wets, Mamma?"

"Gianni will clean it up."

Papa barely had time to sit when Mamma said, "Now, Jack, say grace."

◦⟨✦⟩◦

I WALKED GIANNI TO THE DOOR.

Before he left he said, "When you fondle the pup, think of me."

"Ha!" I watched him walk to the curb and hop in the truck to start the motor. I thought of his laughter and knew he was my friend for life—which somehow my brain deciphered as being more important than the lover I often wished he'd become.

That night Jack claimed Tiger, got a box and some old rags, and made a bed for him in his room. I hadn't realized how much everyone had missed Patches.

When I'd finished my bath, I opened the door. I looked in the fogged-up mirror, wiped it off with a fluffy white towel, and said to myself, "Maybe I could be a better person if I took into consideration the outside forces working on Gianni and for once kept my mouth shut."

Val called from the bedroom, "Amen."

I had a fitful night, sleeping on and off. I must have gotten up to go to the bathroom at least six times and another six to drink water. The next morning, in the quiet of the dawn, I went into the hallway and looked out the landing window at the trees bursting forth in green finery. The sky was murky. My thoughts galloped like a runaway horse I couldn't calm down. An inner voice told me to still myself because I was living this moment—a moment to reflect, grasp, and comprehend. The universe is as large as a man's mind is capable of thinking and imagining. A moment in time—what was its significance? So fleeting that no matter how hard I tried to recall my thoughts, they evaded me. I'd come to like writing in my diary more each day—it kept my thoughts, like these, from evaporating.

I walked to the bathroom closet where I'd last left my diary but couldn't find it. I didn't want to lose my train of thought, so I grabbed a pad of foolscap and began to pencil in my sentiments and reactions to last night, intending to copy them into my book whenever St. Anthony decided to find it for me. I whispered, *Please, St. Anthony, come around, something's lost and must be found.* I wrote fast: Gianni's entrance. Tiger. Dinner. I'd asked Valentina to see him out, but by the way she scrunched up her mouth, I knew she wouldn't talk to me the rest of the night if I didn't do it myself.

Gianni saw right through my cold, insensitive farewell, grabbed my hand, put his arm around me, and inched me to the door, where he hugged and held me tight, and I wanted to melt. He kissed my lips sweetly, looked at me with great tenderness, and then put his cheek to mine. "Now, don't wash your face for a week."

Then I scrawled these words: *It's like you've got him in the pocket of your heart and you pull him out whenever you want or need him, but he sees through you, doesn't he, Marcella? How can he still love me? But he does, I know he does despite my flaws, sharp edges, and spiky angles. Why? I'm enthusiastic about getting to know people but afraid of actually knowing them. Except Gianni. Is it fear of learning their true opinion of me? I'm complex, conflicted, imperfect. Didn't he tell me that? One has to internalize who they really are inside before trying to get to know someone else. You have to be dang sure of who you are, Marcella, not to give a fig what they think about you. You're not there yet. Is Gianni?*

CHAPTER 20

Giacomo

SINCE GIACOMO COULD NOT AFFORD new outfits for his ladies, he asked Valentina to make over old dresses—and, if possible, something new for Angelica—two months before the holiday on April 20 in order to give her plenty of time. On the Friday before Easter, he came home at dusk and found Angelica lighting the Sabbath candles. He tried to recall how long she had been doing this. When had she started? Was it in Carini? He couldn't remember her ever missing a Friday. Valentina was with her, and after they'd said a prayer, Valentina told Giacomo she'd hand him the new outfits for the family tomorrow night.

THE NEXT NIGHT, GIACOMO CALLED everyone to the table early to ooh and aah over their new getups. The last one to receive her gift was his beloved wife. He was pleased to see Valentina hand Angelica a lovely new print dress with a sash. Minutes later, when Angelica modeled it for them, it absolutely hung on her. Angelica had lost weight, and Valentina seemed a bit mortified not to have taken that into consideration.

"I should have taken a final measurement, Mamma. I'm so sorry," Valentina said, looking upset.

"It's nothing, *cara*, you can take the seams in a bit for me. We'll go upstairs and you can pin it now," Angelica said.

Giacomo wondered why he hadn't noticed that his wife was down a complete size. Was it worry over finances? Wasn't she eating enough? Was something else on her mind? He would make sure to talk with her after dinner. Maybe he hadn't succeeded well enough in keeping things hidden.

That evening, when the dishes were being washed, Giacomo didn't leave to go listen to the radio or finish reading the paper. He gave the girls and Jack the night off from helping, and he dried the dishes so he could speak to Angelica about her weight loss. When he asked her about it, she fluffed it off. But he wouldn't let go of it, like a dog worrying a bone.

"*Basta*," she said, annoyance in her voice. "Enough. If you must know, I've been a little worried about something. Come into the bedroom and I'll tell you."

In the bedroom she explained that she had gone into menopause. She was skipping her monthlies and having hot flashes and becoming moody for no reason at all.

"Now it's your turn to see Dr. Amanti. I insist."

"I certainly will not. This is normal for a woman. It's just that it usually happens when one is older."

"Do you want me to find a woman who practices medicine?"

"You forget, darling husband, I practice women's medicine."

It was then, for the first time, Giacomo thought of the similarities between the women in his life: Lian, his first love, who was a healer; and Angelica, his forever love, who was a midwife—a practitioner who aided women in their travails.

She twirled around for him. "There's nothing wrong. In fact, I think I look better now that I'm a bit thinner."

"A bit? You've lost a whole you." He pointed to the dresser mirror.

"Silly exaggeration. Honestly, you'd think I looked like Valentina."

"Size-wise, you do."

"Stop fussing."

"On one condition."

"What?"

"Take off your dress and let me see you in the light. We're always in bed with the lights off."

"Is that how you know so much about women's bodies? You went to sing-song houses and kept the lights on?"

"Come here and let me ravish you." He took off his shoes and pants and sat on the bed with his arms open.

Angelica laughed but started unbuttoning her frock. "Really, at this age."

"I'll love you when you celebrate a hundred years."

"Flabby skin, loose muscles, and all?"

"*Certamente. Sei bellissima.*" He gently tugged her toward him until she fell on top of him.

⸙

A COUPLE OF DAYS BEFORE Easter, Angelica and Giacomo had somehow found time to go to a candy shop on Third Avenue that made milk chocolate Easter bunnies and magnificently decorated dark chocolate crosses, decorated oval eggs, and sold jellybeans as well. Whenever they were in the vicinity or down around Ridge Boulevard, they'd make time to go to the candy shop to buy red hand-shaped lollipops for the family. "The children loved these when they were little," Giacomo said of their purchases. "Let's spoil Elena and give her one."

"Pina will be cross at first but then overcome by your thoughtfulness."

On the opposite side of the street, a few blocks down from Eighty-Second Street, Giacomo and Angelica's friend Marco Pinto sold antiques and paintings. Giacomo would accompany Angelica there whenever possible on a Saturday because she loved to browse. When the girls were small, she bought pearl or coral rings, earrings, and bracelets for them. For Jack, she bought a gold chain and a cross. She declared often enough for Giacomo to almost believe that she always found inexpensive treasures, but he'd always say, "If you don't buy anything—that's a real savings." Once in a while she'd buy something extravagant and luxurious for the house. But now that money was scarce, she'd only go to chat and surround herself with fine objects.

On Easter Sunday, after Mass at St. Patrick's Cathedral in Manhattan, Giacomo took the whole family to New York's Fifth Avenue for the Easter parade. They came home hungry and tired. Giacomo anticipated this and had Angelica prepare in advance a baked lasagna dish made with fresh basil pesto, cream, mozzarella, and grated *parmigiano*. She'd seasoned a leg of lamb with garlic, rosemary, salt, and pepper and baptized it with white wine and lemon with a touch of one of her famous vinegars. She marinated the roast the day before and baked it in the oven before anyone was up for church on Easter morning.

There were three side dishes that Giacomo loved: string beans with slivered almonds, reminding him of the almond orchards in Sicily; onions cooked *agro-dolce*, bittersweet, like so many things in life; and a salad of young spring greens and *puntarelle*—little pointers, or inner shoots of a chicory plant—always harking back to life's theme of regeneration. These greens Angelica had sliced into thin pieces and plunged into ice-cold water until they curled, before drying and adding them to the greens. The salad dressing she made was lively, with garlic and anchovies in golden-green extra virgin olive oil, and only the first cold press would do for Giacomo's palate. And of course, some *balsamico*.

These accompaniments were no surprise to Giacomo, who expected nothing less than an Easter Sunday dinner fit for monarchs. However, what shocked the family was the unexpected buzz of the doorbell and the unannounced visit from Bao.

Marcella was all apologetic yet full of guile, ushering Giacomo aside to whisper, "Oh Papa, forgive me, it must have slipped my mind to tell you he was invited."

"By whom?" Giacomo asked, folding his arms across his chest, his demeanor not happy.

"Why, me, of course. I mentioned it to Mamma."

While Valentina welcomed Bao, Angelica joined the twosome and said between her teeth to Marcella, "Exactly when was that?"

"Back in February?"

"Of course, and I was supposed to remember?" Angelica murmured.

Giacomo stepped up to Bao and shook his hand. Bao grimaced, as Giacomo's handshake was more than firm. Giacomo looked at his hand, and there was an indentation of a pinky ring left by Bao's shake. Then he looked at the green stone in the ring on Bao's pinky. "That's an emerald, isn't it? Is that a woman's ring?"

"A family friend gave it to me. He was like an uncle to me."

"Who was he? Where did he get it?"

"I beg your pardon?"

"I said—"

"I understood you perfectly, sir, but I'm a bit taken aback by your—"

"Forgive me. It was a feeling of—" he hesitated and then said, "déjà vu."

Everybody in the vestibule seemed to freeze—Boa, with the fingers of one hand curved beneath those of his other hand, while the three females stood as mannequins and Jack posed like a jockey minus the horse's reins. All of them gazed askance at Giacomo due to his improper behavior. Giacomo, painfully aware of his mistaken tactic, didn't insist on seeing the ring.

The silence lasted for an uncomfortable minute that seemed like an hour. Finally, Angelica broke the embarrassing moment. "Why don't you men go into the dining room?" She turned toward the girls. "Marcella, Valentina, come join me in the kitchen before Papa passes out from starvation. Jack, please take Bao's jacket and get him something to drink."

"He doesn't drink," Marcella said.

Angelica looked peeved and addressed Marcella. "He has a tongue and can speak for himself, I'm sure. Now, march."

Giacomo put his hand to his neck and rubbed it as if he were in pain, then cleared his throat. "Why don't you ladies go upstairs and finish the preparations for dinner? I'm sure everyone wants to eat. I'll sit in the parlor with Bao and reminisce about China."

Jack said, "I'm in for that discussion, Papa."

"Get us some tea, son, and be careful with your mother's good cups."

Giacomo turned to Bao. "You don't take sugar, do you? It's jasmine."

Bao shook his head. By the look on his face, Giacomo was sure he felt awkward in this embarrassing position. One thing Giacomo knew for sure was that Orientals hated to be put in surprising or compromising positions.

Giacomo said, "Marcella says you've been back to Asia. Business or pleasure?"

"Actually, sir, it was business. I'm a painter, and I've gotten into buying and selling and auctioning here in the states. Mostly San Francisco, L.A., and New York."

"Where were you in China?'

"Not just China. Vietnam, Singapore, and cities like Rangoon and Kuala Lampur."

"Not Japan," Giacomo asked facetiously, knowing there was no amenity between the two countries.

Bao pursed his lips and shook his head slowly.

"What do you paint?"

"Mostly landscapes. Some portraits."

"What medium?"

"I think I excel most with oil on canvas. I've tried most vehicles: pen and ink, charcoal, etching, and watercolors."

Giacomo couldn't help but think of Lian and her drawings of dragons and the one she painted on his forearm before he went to have it tattooed.

After a moment, Giacomo said, "Marcella never mentioned you have this talent."

"I don't think I've ever discussed it with her, although I've taken her to some art exhibitions."

"Do you want this kept secret?"

"By no means. We just never got around to talking about it."

"From what I gather, most painters starve before they make a name for themselves."

"Too true. That's why I'm lucky to have friends in Chinatown who own restaurants, and I also now invest in other artists' work."

Giacomo nodded, appreciating this young man's vision and knowledge. He was pleased to have had this time to speak with Bao alone. They conversed easily in Italian or English. Giacomo had forgotten much Mandarin and felt too rusty to have a conversation. A word or two here or there always slipped in, but never full sentences. He was sorry to have lost so much of what he'd learned in China and what he knew of the language, but more hurtfully, he'd lost his first love and his child.

When they were called to dinner, Giacomo thought again about the ring. Why hadn't he pursued it when they were alone? Some other time, perhaps.

CHAPTER 21

Marcella

WHENEVER MAMMA FORGOT A WORD in English, she'd say it in Italian and keep talking, no matter who she was speaking to, whether they understood Italian or not. I got a big kick out of it most times, but now, in the kitchen, the atmosphere was fraught with her anger. It was palpable.

Mamma said to me, "We'll have your guest here with us today and we will be polite to him, but this is never to happen again without our permission. No arguments or objections. *Hai capito?*"

"Understood," I said.

Wringing her hands, she said, "Look at what happened to your sister Valentina." She winced after she said this but continued on her rant. "There's something odd about this man. Not because he is Chinese—he has suffered a great deal of loneliness. His eyes are so much like—I don't know. He carries the weight of sadness. He's much older and terribly mature, and you are gullible—"

"I'm not like Valentina, and I am not naïve. She was only fifteen. I'm nineteen and have a head on my shoulders."

Valentina, looking quite peeved with her hands on her hips, said, "Does this sound familiar? Did it ever occur to either of you that I don't like being spoken about when I'm standing right here?"

❦

THE DINNER WAS FRIGID. NOT the food, of course, but the manner in which it was served by the hostess. My mother's attitude toward the situation was less than cordial. I blamed myself for being so egotistical as to think I could blindside them into liking this new choice of mine. He was as genial as could be, and my parents were like the Great Wall of China—stony and very present, but implacable. I understood that my parents would not be accepting of Bao unless I absolutely insisted. Did I want to do that to oppose them? Did I really want him in my life? I was so confused because I felt a strong connection to him.

When Mamma served the dessert, I had an awakening. If I really was falling in love with Bao, I'd have to make my family understand I couldn't live life without him. When I looked in the mirror after he'd left, I asked those magic words to determine who I really was and where I was heading. I didn't know my own heart. Was Bao just another bauble to dangle on my chain of triumphs? Did he matter to me? What was important to me was trying to seduce him, trying to make the conquest, trying and winning, but could I seriously see myself with him for the rest of my life? How much would I have to alter? What if he wanted to return to China? Could I give up my family? My roots? Bao was astute, beguiling, compelling, deep, enchanting. I had to stop myself from finding a word for every letter in the alphabet to suit him, so I came up with the next letter of the alphabet, "f," but this one was for me: falling—for him.

I realized then that Gianni had been too easy a conquest for me. Why? Because I was sure of him and maybe because he really did love me. I was secure in his love for me. He knew me too well. Is that what made me want to distance him all the time?

Every other man seemed like a challenge, and that's what I loved— the game, the battle to attain, the fight to glory, a victorious win. That's when I understood what a shallow person I was becoming, and I figured I'd better change quickly or else be an insubstantial and one-dimensional woman. How could I when I'd just cast Gianni aside once more to go after Bao? I flirted and cajoled and primped and sashayed like some fashion plate, a bird pluming feathers to attract him.

⚬◦⊱✿⊰◦⚬

TO MY SURPRISE, MY TACTICS worked. Bao and I actually started dating. I was petrified at first, as I felt I'd never really dated Gianni. Oh sure, Gianni and I went to baseball games, movies, and horseback riding, but this was different and I knew nothing about the process. Bao no longer worked in restaurants. He was in a partnership with someone and had started an import/export business, which apparently was very lucrative. He escorted me to art exhibitions and always seemed to be taking me to art auctions and galleries. He was rather receptive whenever I hinted that I wanted to attend the opera, ballet, or theater, hoping to enhance the cultural side of me that I'd missed out on by not attending university for a degree—but Bao had studied art. When we went out to these artsy places, he was almost always recognized, and I felt admired. Is that what he wanted, to be escorted by a good-looking Caucasian? Could he be that shallow? When I wanted to go to movies or out to dinner—and not Chinese—I merely said so. Either the poor sap fell for me and all my hysterics—at least I thought he did—or he had money to burn, which meant he couldn't be saving anything for a rainy day. What about the future? How could he spend so lavishly and not save money in these terrible times?

Little by little I discovered he was intrigued by my American outlandishness but was nevertheless considering a move back to China to run the business from that end. Would this mean he would expect me to go back with him? Leave my family and everyone and everything?

After several weeks of dating, I was moon-eyed and constantly gushing over everything he said and did. My parents got used to him coming around occasionally. Papa always seemed to speak to him in Italian rather than English, but I didn't find anything particularly odd in that. He talked to Bao a great deal about China and how things had changed since Papa was there.

A rustle of doubt seemed to be knocking on my door. I began to distrust myself and my sexual attraction, for it seemed I didn't appeal to him as much as I thought I did. He was never forward or physical with me in any way, to the point that I wondered if he was a male version of my dear friend Elaine Weiss, who had finally found someone to love. Her name was Shoshannah but had changed her name to Sara as a newly arrived model from Paris. Sometimes we even got together with them, but always somewhere private, like their apartment, for drinks or dinner. Elaine cornered me in her kitchen nook and asked me, *sotto voce*, what was my intention concerning Bao? It was obvious to her that I was pushing, whereas he was being more than standoffish. He was polite, but cool. She said as a warning, "Perhaps there's someone else. Look into it." Then she served us overcooked pot roast, but I admired her effort. After dinner, she said, "I should have ordered out from that little French place on the corner."

"Next time, *chérie*," Sara said, rubbing her thumb up and down Elaine's bare arm, an indication that it was time for her guests to leave, or at least I took it that way.

⋅⋅⋆⋅⋅

A WEEK WENT BY. I confided in Pina, who threw my words back in my face, saying, "Confront him." How could I? Here I was waiting for a further commitment and a step up to our romantic life. I didn't want to cause a rift.

One night toward the end of June, I asked Bao to take me home with him after the theater. He flat out refused and said he couldn't as he had a roommate, but what he didn't tell me was that the roommate was a lithe and lovely Chinese girl with blue-black long, silky hair. This I didn't discover by accident. How do I know? I spied on him. I called on him one afternoon after work. She spoke hardly any English, but I got the drift and she showed me a dazzling ring on her finger. I walked away from that meeting and, not even a block away, got sick in the street. How could he?

That wasn't the worst of it. I had already invited him to dinner the next night, which was a Saturday, and I couldn't reach him to cancel. He showed up at the door with red roses for Mamma and a bottle of some kind of plum wine for Papa.

I had to bide my time and tongue and wait until after dinner, when we went to sit in the gazebo in the backyard, before I challenged him about his "roommate." Apparently, I had raised my voice.

Of all times for Papa to come walking by!

"What's all the fuss?" he asked. "You're so angry, Marcella. Your voice can be heard a mile away. Mamma asked me to tell you to settle down, or take your aggressions out on poor Bao inside the house and close the windows."

I turned as red as one of the beauty roses he'd brought home for Mamma, but thank heavens it was too dark for him or Papa to notice.

"I'm sorry," I said, on the verge of tears.

"Come inside, please," Papa said.

And so we went. I'd calmed down, but what I wanted to do was empty the vase of water and roses and break it over his head. As soon as Papa left us alone, I said through my teeth, "How dare you take me hither and yon and spend all that money on me, making me think we had some serious connection, while all the while you have a girl sleeping with you? I thought you cared for me, and I was willing—yes, willing—to submit to your every whim!"

He looked surprised. Had I shocked him? It undoubtedly wasn't the Asian way to be so forward and daring.

"She isn't my girl; she's my friend's fiancée."

"A likely story."

"Believe it or not, that's the truth. I had to take her in, as my friend still lives under his father's roof and couldn't very well have her move in there. She's recently come from China"

A mail-order bride for his friend. I was a bit mollified because I wanted to believe him.

We finally made up. He was a smidgeon disgruntled that I should have doubted him, but the next time he came for dinner, he brought a picture of the girl with his friend and their arms entwined. Was it all an act? Some theater prop? We were sitting on the front porch swing after dinner when I hoped he'd finally kiss me the way I wanted him to, when along came Lucille and the dynamics changed. I felt like a fifth wheel—an oddball not only in my own family but with my friend.

"You're the guy I wrapped the lingerie for in Macy's. Remember—it was Valentine's Day?" Lucille asked.

"That seems long ago. Ah yes, you did a superb job," Bao said.

Superb? A little paper and a bow?

All of a sudden, I was witnessing Lucille being unabashed, outrageously flirting with Bao, and he liked it. When she left, I was furious. He didn't seem to care. He really liked her. More than me?

Papa came in to say goodnight to him, and when he shook hands, he said, "Ah, that little ring again. You haven't worn it in many months. May I see it now?" Papa proffered his hand to accept it.

Bao took the ring off and handed it to Papa, who turned it around in the low-lit lamp, then faced the window and held it to the moonlight. His face changed.

"What is it?" I asked.

Papa's face was ashen.

He handed back the ring and said, "Marcella, say goodnight to Bao. Please excuse us."

I was miffed by the seriousness of his pronouncement, although I didn't make a fuss, kissed Bao on the cheek, and said goodnight to both of them.

I took my time walking upstairs, hoping for an airy drift of their conversation, but they had stepped outside, and I heard Papa wish him a good night.

⸙

THE NEXT MORNING, I AWOKE after an odd dream and wanted to tell Val. As soon as she came out of the bathroom, I made her sit on the bed so I could relate the strangeness of it.

"What were these curious happenings?" Val asked.

"I was in a faraway place."

"Where?" She pulled on a sweater. "Coney Island?"

"Don't be fresh. Seriously. I think it was Tibet."

"Tibet? Not China?" She rummaged around in the top drawer of the dresser.

"Mmm. What are you looking for?"

"My white slip."

"In the wash. I wore it, okay?"

Her hand flew to her hair and yanked a thick strand into a fat curl. She said, "Now what am I supposed to wear?"

I flung a slip across the bed. "Here's my pink one. Don't get mad. Listen. Here's what happens in my dream: I write a prayer on a silk flag, then another and another until I can string them all across an old bridge—a rust-colored wooden bridge high above a ravine and a frozen creek. Red, yellow, green, blue."

"Do you always dream in color?" She'd finished dressing and sat back down on the bed. "Are you going to name every tint and shade imaginable?"

"Hush up. The winds took them, one by one, and scattered them over the scarred land strewn with tracks and paths. Burned gouges. On some of the boulders and rocks, I painted images and scenes. Ice and snow covered the dark earth, and large plots of ground had frosted over where the wind had licked off the snow. A temple drum sheared the quiet and sounded in the distance. A path was laden with drifted snow, and on the rocks could be seen the remains of a sky burial."

"What's a sky burial?"

"You're squeamish and don't want to know." Then I said in a dreamy voice, "The world will never be the same."

"What do you mean?"

"The world is in flux and changing. There'll soon never be a place for kings and tsars, and—"

"You read too much."

"Not enough. I would've loved to have lived in Tsarist Russia, gliding over snow in a troika, going to a dacha filled with warmth and balalaika music, everyone dancing, singing, drinking vodka, and eating caviar."

"You'd like to have been served hand-and-foot by serfs? Heavens no! Maybe you're spending too much time with those Commies, my darling sister."

"I mean I love thinking of the Old World—it's so romantic. Not quite like taking the subway to Manhattan."

"Or perhaps you would've liked being the serf, chased by some big handsome lord of the manor."

We both laughed.

"What about the dream?"

"I woke up."

"You've been seeing too much of Bao."

"Like reading, not enough. We do such interesting things. He took me to see an art exhibition of this famous Rangoon artist, Aza somebody-or-other. These names sound so exotic, don't they?"

"I suppose. What did he paint?"

"Oh, not only him. Though he stood out, there were many others."

"Like?"

"I noticed when I looked at the artists' representations that they're basically all poets. Their ideas are communicated through images—it's their heritage. We saw a fishing village painted on batik and a seascape on silk. Extraordinary. Breathtaking."

Val stood. "You're getting way too intellectual for my taste."

"Are you afraid of classical learning?"

"Don't be bratty. Just where will you use all your smarts selling underwear?"

"One never knows."

"Or with Gianni?"

"Why do you keep bringing him up? When, well, the thing is—Bao doesn't seem to want to be more than friends, and I'm crazy about him. What can I do to entice him?"

"Come on, we'll talk over breakfast," she said. "I smell coffee, and it's inviting me."

CHAPTER 22

Giacomo

NOT LONG AFTER GIACOMO HAD seen Bao, and knowing Marcella wouldn't be home till late, Giacomo called to invite the young man over for a talk. They went into the living room, and Giacomo asked politely if Bao would let him see the ring again.

"I didn't mean to embarrass you, but when I saw your ring, well, I had that familiar feeling as though I'd seen it before."

"So you said." Bao handed over the ring and sat on the sofa.

When Giacomo took it in his hands it seemed as if they were on fire. How could this be? He scrutinized the ring, holding it this way and that, turning it beneath the table lamp's cut-glass colored shade.

"Please tell me," Giacomo said, handing back the ring, "how did you come to have this?"

"I thought you knew. I told Marcella I was raised by an Italian priest because my mother died in childbirth and my father was an Italian sailor."

"*Dio Cristo!*" Giacomo felt his insides quake.

"What did I say?"

"Tell me, please," Giacomo said and began to pace.

"Father Giordano told me my mother left me this ring and my father had been called back to Italy, and—"

Giacomo stopped pacing. "Father Giordano? That's all he said?"

"Why are you so interested?"

"I believe I knew this priest. So that's why you speak Italian." Giacomo pulled out a handkerchief and dried the perspiration from his hands. His thoughts all but choked him. *How on all of earth, in the entire world, was this possible?*

Bao's expression changed from placid to surprised. "You did? How?"

"I'll tell you later. Continue, please." Giacomo sat down heavily, his hands in his lap, his thumbs circling one another in ceaseless motion, forward and back.

As Bao's story unspooled, Giacomo remained more than alert, looking for any nuances that might hint at the truth or a lie.

"When I was older, Father Giordano told me that the sailor would never look for me. Father Giordano thought it would be best to inform the man that I had died along with my mother in childbirth. At first I was furious, but then I realized he couldn't have done anything else. To save this sailor more pain and suffering, for I was told that he loved my mother as with his own life—"

"True," Giacomo murmured before thinking. He put his face in his hands and shook his head.

"How would you know?"

Giacomo uncovered his face and looked at Bao. "Please. Go on, please. Resume your story."

"Father Giordano said he told the sailor that I died with my mother so he could live in peace and never worry about me again. Otherwise, Father said, if the sailor had known I was alive, he would have returned to China. "

"Bao." Giacomo was overwhelmed with sensations of belief yet disbelief. How could Bao's story also be his? How could Giacomo tell him the truth? Abruptly Giacomo was on his feet. He took hold of Bao's shoulders and held him for a minute.

"Yes? Sir, why are you looking at me like this? Did you know my father?"

"Bao, this is an impossible dream." Giacomo dropped his hands, unbuttoned his cuff, and rolled up his sleeve. "Your mother drew this dragon and I had it tattooed—"

"That's impossible—only my father—"

"A forever mark stamped on me, real as the invisible one she imprinted on my heart. Bao, you are looking at him."

"Beg pardon?"

Giacomo watched his son's expression change from incomprehension to understanding of what he had just heard. They stood in silence for a long time. Then Giacomo broke the quiet, and in a hushed voice, said, "Now I understand why I didn't want Marcella to fall in love with you. I couldn't put my finger on the reason. Now I know it is because you are my blood. It would be incest."

Bao jumped back. "I love her, but only like a sister. I am fascinated by her, that's true and maybe I didn't clarify, but, sir—"

"Please, call me Giacomo. Your beautiful mother did."

"This is some fantasy. A fairytale. How can it be true? Then again, this had to be." Bao sat down pensive for a moment, gathering his thoughts. Changing from Italian to Mandarin, he said, "There's an ancient Chinese legend that goes something like this: According to myth, the gods tie an invisible red cord around the ankles of those destined to meet under a specific condition to aid each other in a particular manner. I don't know the author, but the expression is close to this—'An invisible thread connects those who are destined to meet, regardless of time, place, and circumstance. The thread may stretch or tangle, but it will never break.'" Switching back to Italian, he asked, "Have you ever heard it?"

"I believe the rest of it is: 'May you be open to each thread that comes into your life—the golden ones and the coarse ones—and may you weave them into a brilliant and beautiful life.' Am I right?"

"That's it exactly."

"I know for certain that Lian, your mother, knew she would meet her babies in a life to come. Although I believed you perished with her, I have no doubt she trusted in a perfect universe where we would all meet, where she'd gather her loved ones and you on the other side."

"Please, I beg you, tell me about her. I know so little."

Giacomo sat and wiped his eyes with a handkerchief. "Lian. Lian," Giacomo cried. Then he was quiet for a time, gathering his thoughts. Of course, he'd noticed many times there was a familiarity about Bao. Giacomo found it hard to concentrate. *Think*, he commanded his brain. Ah, memory—how sometimes thoughts can be rogue and feral. He didn't want it to be true. Yet here was this handsome man—so like Lian in ways difficult to name. Giacomo's heart began to race until he thought it was about to split open. He must cut down on drinking *vino*. No, that wasn't it at all. He was afraid because he knew it was true.

"Bao, you are my son. The priest told me you died with your mother in childbirth. He lied to me. At the time, I felt so in my gut, yet couldn't understand it. Only now do I grasp why and value his bravery. He was a unique and learned man."

"I must hear about my mother. Please share her with me."

Giacomo recounted the story of his life in China with Lian and said how she had left him her chronicle.

⌒⋐✿⋑⌒

AFTER A LONG DISCUSSION, GIACOMO said, "Bao, please accompany me to the basement." Giacomo flipped through the pages, stopping at the dragon drawing. "So precious, yet I couldn't read it. It's in Nüshu, women's secret language." He handed his son his mother's chronicle.

Bao stood holding the diary. "This to me is a sacred artifact to treasure."

"Can you have it translated?"

"Possibly. I will certainly look into it and let you know. It's yours—are you sure you want me to have it?"

"It's ours—Lian's gift to both of us."

Giacomo embraced his son and then bowed.

Bao also bowed, his head touching his father's.

Giacomo asked Bao to leave and he agreed, although his face was perplexed. At the front door, Giacomo said, "*Abbi fede.* Have faith and trust me. I will tell Marcella and the family."

Now with this certainty, most of all, he didn't want to break Marcella's heart but knew he had to tell her: *Bao is your brother, dear child. You cannot love him romantically. It would be a sin.*

CHAPTER 23

Marcella

I BOUNCED INTO THE KITCHEN excited because I remembered my dream, which was quite strange. I wanted to tell Mamma right away to see if she could make sense of it and translate what it meant. She always said you should speak about dreams in the early morning.

Mamma was sipping cappuccino. A plate of *biscotti* and *regina*, those little fat cookies loaded with sesame seeds that I love, were on the table, along with a fresh loaf of Italian bread, butter, and homemade grape jam. I kissed her cheek and plopped down in the chair.

"Mamma," I said a little breathlessly, "I must tell you my dream."

"Have something to eat. Do you want juice?"

"I dreamed of Nonna. How many years has she been gone? In the dream, she was young and happy for me. We were going out for dinner— I never remember going out to dinner with Nonna, do you?"

"Once or twice in Sheepshead Bay for seafood." Mamma poured me a cup of coffee.

"There were some people I didn't know in this strange white stucco house. It was like a country house at the beach."

"You mean like the summer beach house we went to in Point Lookout?"

I nodded. "There was a blue bedroom I'd forgotten about, and the door to the outside back courtyard wasn't locked. There was a ripped curtain to keep the rain out, useless as it came in torrents—the kind of tarp Papa uses in construction.

"Nonna was about to change into a beautiful filmy blue blouse. I'd never seen anything so gossamer—long puffy sleeves—and then at one point I felt frightened and began to shake. There was a storm outside, so violent, and in the front of the house a man on a black stallion was arguing with a mean-faced thug who seemed to cast a spell on the horse and petrified me when he turned to stare through the window. The look on this hateful, scarred man's face was scary! A woman with long blond hair like Lucille jumped off the back, and then the horse started to rear. I stood frozen, though I wanted to scream for someone to call the cops. Perhaps he wanted to steal our money hidden in three pink ballerina shoes hanging from the horse's mane. You always say if you dream money, it doesn't bring any, but I didn't actually see any bills or coins. But the number three is good, isn't it, Mamma? The horse was exquisite, almost dancing in the rain."

Mamma drank her coffee unhurriedly, then she poured more for me, adding heated milk and sugar. She stirred it, pensively, and handed it to me. I dunked the end of an anise *biscotto* into it and bit down. "Mmm, *delicioso*! Delish."

Mamma said, "Beware or be aware of someone, perhaps Lucille, I'm not sure. But I do know positively that to dream hair means treachery. You dreamt of Lucille's hair and the horse's mane."

I must have looked afraid because she said, "Don't be frightened, just pay attention to the people around you. Not family."

Not long after the discussion with Mamma about my dream, I decided to quit night school after having attended NYU on and off for two years. Many of the courses were dry and boring. I had no desire or inclination to finish a degree. I needed challenges in real-life situations, not dull classes with homework papers and reading till my eyes fell out. The material didn't stick half the time because it wasn't applicable to what I really wanted to do—retail and sales to pay for singing lessons. I also figured that if I could continue to work in Macy's as a salesgirl or get a higher position, maybe even as a buyer, this would be a perfect hold-over post until I decided if I wanted to look into something else when the nation's fiscal problems settled and the economy started to improve. For the moment, I was happy where I was and I was good at my job.

Elaine wasn't happy with my decision, but I informed her that I couldn't sponge off her and didn't want to be a pitiable case, running to her if I needed money to pay for a course that was superfluous to my current existence. At first, she was furious, then she appeared hurt, but she heard me out and finally said she'd help me train for a buyer's position. We became quite close, and I confided in her that I was interested in singing and curious about photography, because if I were to someday be able to appear in public I thought it might come in handy. Anytime I'd pass a photographic studio, I'd walk in, pretend I was a customer so I could ask a great many questions, and look at all the equipment. Once I even got to peek in the dark room. I got so that I could ask intelligent questions about angles and lighting and learned how to pose with my chin down and my lips moist. If I never got to go to Hollywood, at least I'd know how to look good in front of a crowd.

To shake the blues and get back into life instead of mooning about like a lost kitten, I went Christmas shopping—not that I spent any money. I'd go "window shopping" in Manhattan with Lucille on her dinner break, enjoying all the wonderful store decorations. We were doing this one evening when in an instant, like Cinderella, Lucille had to hurry or her carriage would turn into a pumpkin—she had a date to surreptitiously meet a guy she said she'd met working an extra evening in Men's Haberdashery, a Christmas job at Saks. She was going to get laid off after the holiday and threw caution to the wind, telling her boss she felt nauseous and feverish. I was a bit concerned, but she swore he was a total gentleman. I had a feeling she was lying, but why? I asked her if he was an Ivy Leaguer in New York for the holidays to visit his aging grandfather. It seemed as though I had caught her off guard. "No," she said, "he's local and we're going to a party in Chinatown."

"Chinatown?"

She looked away, mumbling, "Yes. I don't go there often."

"That's a surprise. Who do you know from there?"

"Oh, nobody you know."

I didn't swallow an inch of it. She was jeopardizing her job, losing money, going out with a complete stranger—or was he? And she was leaving me flat. I did the only thing I could—told her to keep her legs crossed, like the nuns used to tell us, and started making my way toward the theater district, where I had scored a weekend Christmas job as coat check girl through my father's Mafia "cousin." When she pecked me on the cheek and turned to go, I had this awful niggling feeling. It couldn't possibly be Bao she was seeing—or was it? He'd broken our date because he had a previous engagement in Chinatown. Of course, he knew how I loved to go to Chinatown with him. A princess in a fairytale, left in the tower, I invented the most fantastical things, and they all seemed real and pinched like thorns.

The last time he'd escorted me there was incredibly magical. We went to a restaurant where there were nine lanterns of red, green, and gold silk strung across from the building to a high wooden fence. I felt as though I were dream-walking in a fantasyland. Somehow atmosphere adds to a certain moment in a way that becomes unforgettable. I recalled seeing a tiny pool with lotus leaves and koi swimming back and forth. In back of it, toward a crude rock wall, was a stone pagoda with a statue of a fat, happy Buddha and a tinkling waterfall. The statue was garlanded with small white flowers, especially fragrant when the wind picked up. His legs enfolded, and in that pouch were nine little children. On a rock nearby was a silver cup.

"Pick it up," Bao said. "Scoop up some water and pour it on top of him." He indicated toward the statue.

"Why?"

"For good luck. Do it three times," he said.

I figured one should never flout smugness or test destiny. I picked up the cup, my hand a bit shaky, wondering if I were committing some mortal sin for bathing a statue of Buddha. I doused the statue, then rethought my action. Since seven is my lucky number, what harm to douse him with four more cups? So that's what I did with a baffled Bao looking on.

Inside the restaurant were two Chinese silk scrolls hung on either side of a fireplace. One had beautiful characters. Bao said that an artist can spend up to a year simply practicing eight strokes in the air without ever putting his brush to paper. As if it's not enough to learn thousands of characters, one must also learn eight basic brush strokes that comprise dashes, down strokes, twists, and hooks.

The second scroll was a wonderful painted drawing, haunting and forlorn. It was of a fishing skiff with a lone coolie-hatted fisherman steering the boat. It was full of pathos, saying so much with a mere few strokes of an artist's brush.

Bao had come up behind me and said one word: "Guilin."

His voice had surprised me. "What does it mean?" I asked.

"It's a city near a river, surrounded by mauve cliffs. Where my ancestors are from—my mother's birthplace. It wounds me to look at it for too long," he said, ushering us to a table outside near the tiny pagoda with the Buddha. It was then that I noticed the statue was carved of the greenest jade.

Pointing to the second scroll, his eyes went suddenly dim, as if the scroll was a torture device and he was made to look at it by men who were about to inflict great pain on him.

Something in his past was making him suffer, and I didn't want to be a part of it. I knew only one thing—this man had undergone something I hadn't, because he didn't know his roots or from where he had come. I felt enormously sad for him—in some respect, sorry for what I knew and understood of my own beginnings and background but worse for what I didn't understand, couldn't know, and never would.

I think I gave a little shriek as if I'd seen a mouse dart over my shoe, but I can't be certain. Whatever happened had brought him back to the present.

"You want to touch the paper, but please refrain," he said in a somber tone. "It's Xuanshi, from the Tartar wingceltis tree. Calligraphy paper is also made from other materials, including rice straw, the bark of mulberry, bamboo, and hemp."

"So knowledgeable," I said.

"I studied a little in China, but it wasn't for me. I don't have the temperament to do this kind of art."

I remember wanting to pursue the conversation, but the way he tilted his head and the way his shoulders slumped, I thought it best not to intrude on his thoughts.

⟡

WALKING AT A BRISK PACE as the temperature had dropped and thick swirling snow was coming down with the intention to stick, I hopped on a crowded Fifth Avenue bus. As we passed Rockefeller Plaza, I caught sight of the huge Christmas tree all lit up as the bus whizzed by. On the bus I felt as if I'd entered a Turkish steam bath. Heat poured from my woolen coat, and the air was muggy, filled with warm passenger breath and closely pressed bodies coming in from the cold, snowy day. I wanted to swoon. An old woman loaded down with packages wedged between two big oafs, and nobody made a move, so I stood to offer her my seat. She could've been my grandmother, a tiny thing with more wrinkles than a road map, but her smile lit up her dreary face and her eyes twinkled. I felt like Mrs. Claus had just accepted my place with her bundles of already made toys from the Arctic but with no Mr. Claus in sight—probably home in the snowy fields tending reindeer and giving tasks and candy canes to the elves.

I turned, leaving my fairytale musings, and reached up for a grip just in the nick of time, as the bus driver slammed on the brakes, muttered something along with some of the other male commuters, then put the bus into first gear to continue the journey. Why are some men so short of patience when Papa is a virtue—or is it because I love him?

The bus driver hadn't gotten very far when *wham*—I was thrown off balance, but this time landed right in someone's lap. All I could think of was "M" for Marcella in an alphabet soup. The blond-haired, blue-eyed man looked at me, said, "Ma'am," and doffed his hat. I was too stunned to move, and besides, who wanted to rise from this cozy position facing a Norse Viking!

"Oh, I do beg your pardon." Not one bit, I thought.

"All right, Ma'am?"

With my arms still on his shoulders, I asked, "Do I seem that old to you?"

"Why no, Ma'am—I mean, Miss. Only being polite."

By then I'd recovered my poise sufficiently and stood up alongside him, at which point he also stood and offered me his seat. I wondered if he was Harvard or Yale, if I'd missed my stop, and if the universe had planned in my future destiny for me to ever see him again. I had a feeling our paths would cross again. Just something the cosmos planned for you, and you know is going to happen.

He smiled, flashing a perfect set of pearls, reached up, and pulled the cord. At the next stop, he made a slight bow, raised his collar, and turned his camel-color coated back to me, stepping off the bus. He turned and mouthed, "Merry Christmas," and winked, making me feel that the holiday season wasn't going to be that bad after all.

NOT LESS THAN A WEEK later, the guy from the Fifth Avenue bus appeared in my department looking around for a salesgirl, but everyone was helping customers.

I had just finished putting stock away from the dressing room when I saw him and said, "Well howdy, sunshine!"

"Is it really you, the girl who captured my heart and I foolishly left sitting on a bus?"

"Smooth." My eyelashes all aflutter, I said, "Is it you, Yalie, the heart-breaker?"

"You're cute as a bug's ear."

"I'd know that line anywhere—well, well, if it isn't Hollywood Handsome personified, fancy twangy diction and all."

"Do you just flirt, or do you sell sexy lingerie, too?"

"For your sweet Mamma at home?" I stepped behind a glass showcase.

"No, actually, it's a parting gift for an ex-girlfriend. She's leaving for Paris, and I figure she'll need something to snag someone new in the Land of ooh-la-la."

I smiled and began to ask the usual: size, color, article.

After I waited on him, Elaine called me over and asked me his name. I said I didn't catch it.

"I only saw him from the back as he was leaving, but he looks like a friend of mine," she said.

"What's wrong?" I asked.

She shook her head. "I didn't see the entire exchange but a supervisor from another department stuck her nose in. It's one thing to be friendly and talkative with the customers, dear heart, but be careful not to cross the line. I wouldn't want it reported back that you were flirtatious." She took a pencil from behind her ear and placed it by the cash register.

"Elaine."

"No, this isn't about me. I'm serious. It's a cautious directive, I've had from up above—the powers that be." She tapped my shoulder. "You're top in sales—no need to gush."

"Coffee?" I put on my best contrite face.

"Sure. On me."

"Not this time."

CHAPTER 24

Giacomo

GIACOMO HAD LET A WEEK slip by thinking how best to tell Marcella, but this morning he was up early and sat determined with his third cup of coffee and with thoughts of Angelica's reaction to the news that Bao was his son. Giacomo had spoken to her the night he discovered the truth, and had been grateful for the dim light in their bedroom so he didn't have to see signs of hurt etching on Angelica's face as he spoke to her—of what? He couldn't call it a betrayal, because it all happened before he knew Angelica existed, although in a strange way if felt like unfaithfulness.

Angelica sat up in bed and said in a voice barely above a whisper, "I wondered about Lian for a long time, and then one day I shut her out of my thoughts. She was your past. I am your ever-present and future. I may have even said that to you long ago in Sicily. I can't say I'm not jealous because I am, as absurd as that may be—envious of the time a dead woman shared with you. But she must approve of me from the other side to entrust this son of hers to us now, don't you think?"

Giacomo could almost feel her injured heart as he took her in his arms and held her tightly, leaning into her shoulder and crying.

THIS MORNING ANGELICA HAD GONE to Mass early to begin a novena for Marcella, and Giacomo served the family breakfast, at which Marcella was noticeably absent. Giacomo asked Valentina why she hadn't come down with her.

"She didn't sleep well. Was up half the night and just dozed off now, so I didn't bother her."

Giacomo seized the opportunity to repeat what he'd told Angelica about Bao. This time he said it addressing Valentina and Jack. Valentina was visibly upset, first asking about her mother's reaction and then saying she was worried, concerned about how Marcella would take this news. Jack, instead, took it like a light chuck on the chin, saying something more profound than anyone in the family might have expected.

"Isn't this something—a miracle that you found your son, Papa? What a blessing for you. And our family. I now have another brother."

"What do you mean another?" Giacomo asked.

"Why, Gianni, of course," Jack said, heaping another teaspoon of sugar into his cafe latte.

When breakfast was over and the dishes done, Jack went off to work, hugging his father and telling Val she looked like a knockout. Naturally, Valentina beamed.

Angelica came back from church and had another cup of coffee and tidied up the kitchen. Giacomo suggested that Angelica go shopping with Valentina so he'd be able to speak with Marcella alone. Before Angelica acquiesced, she turned to Giacomo and said, "You're very brave to face this alone. Perhaps it's best. We'll go." She stood and said to Val, "Wait for me downstairs. I'm going to change into something more suitable for shopping."

⋘✵⋙

GIACOMO SAT READING THE NEWSPAPER when Marcella came in for breakfast.

"I'm sorry I'm late and missed everybody." Marcella poured herself a cup of coffee, made a face, and threw it out. "I'll make fresh. Want some?"

"I could float away with all I've had." Giacomo got up and washed the coffee pot. "Use the smaller one," he said. He was in no hurry, for he didn't know how to begin, but he was grateful that he'd waited and had first explained everything to Angelica concerning his conversation with Bao. He saw his brokenhearted wife take courage and consolation in the fact she'd become his wife and shared all these wonderful years with him raising their family.

But this was different. Now he had to tell his daughter something horrific and dreadful.

He was thankful that Angelica had taken Valentina out so he could speak privately with Marcella.

He sat down at the kitchen table again and took her hands in his. "I don't know how to say this to you except to say you were prophetic when Valentina found my chronicle, or rather Lian's, in my workshop. Do you remember what you said?"

"I invented something about Bao because it was written in Chinese."

"You told your sister that we were custodians of the journals of Bao's family. You were so right."

"What are you talking about, Papa? The book was your sweetheart's."

"I have to tell you about my time in China."

"I know. You were a sailor and probably had a girl in every port."

Giacomo shook his head. "Perhaps at the beginning. But then something happened. A miracle. I was a young sailor, and I fell deeply in love with a healer. Her name was Lian, and she was of mixed blood—Chinese and Swiss. Her father was a doctor who taught her about medicine from both Europe and China, and she spoke Italian." His voice was tender and silky, like a new scarf at Christmas.

"Was she as beautiful as Mamma?"

"She was every bit as striking as Mamma when I met her. I loved Lian very much, and then the winds of war conspired to separate us. I looked for her everywhere I went, and she searched for me. Finally, when we found each other, we were together as often as we could be. Numerous times I jumped ship and risked imprisonment to be with her. Do you understand what I'm telling you?"

Marcella dropped his hands, took up her spoon, and started to play with it.

"Please stop fidgeting," he said.

She dropped her spoon into the saucer and looked at her father, astounded. Her look seemed almost childlike—her countenance painted with shades of disbelief.

"Lian and I lived together as man and wife, and the union produced a baby. I thought that the baby died in childbirth when she died. I was devastated by her death. There was a priest friend of hers with her when she died and when our son was born. I had given her a ring that she wore always, but when she died, the priest who'd been with her told me there was no ring. I have just discovered that Bao has been wearing his mother's ring all of these years. The priest lied to me when I asked him for it, but now I understand his motive. He gave it to Bao."

Marcella's mouth fell open. Her eyes darted back and forth like someone possessed. She stood up and shouted, "Please stop! He's not your son! You're mistaken!"

"Calm down. I asked Bao a favor with your mother's permission. My love for Lian died with her so many years ago, but I feel it's my obligation to her to learn what was in her heart and what she wrote about in her treasured chronicle. She was so young and she risked so much for our love. I asked Bao to have it translated for me—for us."

"Papa! Did you tell him that? That he's my brother? How could you! I'm in love with him. I want to marry him."

Giacomo looked intently at his daughter. "Marcella, you cannot entertain thoughts of romantic love for or marry your brother."

"I didn't know he was. Oh, Papa my life is ruined."

"Why?"

Silence reigned for a long time, and then he took her by the shoulders and shook her. "Have you had relations with him?"

"Papa!"

"Well, have you?"

"No, of course not."

"Though you thought about it, right? You considered giving yourself to him, didn't you?"

Marcella nodded. "Oh, Papa," she said, her tone mournful and remorseful.

"My wild, precious child—so much like me. How could you want to make love with Bao when you and Gianni belong together?"

"Gianni's predictable. He admits to being a romantic who believes in the power of his love to make me love him back."

"He's compassionate and understanding. Concede that."

"I do. He loves me, I know he does, but that doesn't mean I'm going to prance down the aisle with him. I read somewhere recently that love is equal parts the pursuit of passion and the passion of the pursuit."

"Makes sense, I suppose."

"What kind of life would I have with him? His relations think I'm brazen—too outspoken."

"True. You'd have to curb your temper and tongue." Giacomo sighed and thought how hard it is to tame a racehorse. He'd been too lenient with her. How could he have been otherwise, this thoroughbred filly?

"Everyone keeps telling me that. I'm sick of hearing it. I've got a mind of my own. A heart of my own, too."

"When I spoke to Bao, I had the feeling he loves you, too, but he's not *in* love with you. It's not a romantic love. Not like Gianni's. Bao is what his mother would have called a wayfarer, and I think his wayfaring days are over now that he's found me, you, and the family. Can you be a sister to him?"

Marcella cried, and her sobs wrenched Giacomo's heart. He felt her hurt, damaged psyche and feared this adversity would crush her spirit.

To console her, he said, "Love begins with a dream, poetry, but those are abstract things. In order to love, you need your feet on earth and your ideas centered. You must be willing to sacrifice yourself and compromise. Your heart's willing, but not your head."

"Gianni's a poem. Maybe he isn't real at all."

"Maybe he's an old soul."

"Oh Papa, I want to die," Marcella said and ran from the room.

CHAPTER 25

Marcella

ABOUT THE TIME I QUIT taking courses at NYU, I was offered a bit part on stage. Recently I'd run into one of the actors I'd met at Camp Isida who was now directing an off-Broadway play, and he gave me, without even a try-out, a singing part in the chorus. Of course, I couldn't take it—it would mean being out every night of the week and for matinees on Saturday and Sunday. I became overwhelmed with a shroud of frustration and sadness, because at the same time, I learned about the tragic life Bao had lived and the awful facts surrounding his birth. The unspeakable truth was that my darling father was Bao's father, too. I had fallen in love with my brother. Even more grave was that I insisted I'd marry him just the same. Mamma and Papa tried to explain to me after hours of meetings and conversations with Bao that he wasn't interested in me as a lover or as a wife. In fact, he'd never entertained the idea of marrying me, and now that he knew of our relationship, the idea was appalling and repugnant. I insisted that he face me himself to say this. I wanted to look into his face.

⁓⚘⁓

A FEW DAYS LATER, BAO came to the house, hat in one hand and Lucille's hand in the other. Mamma had changed toward him, I noticed, and now greeted him as a son, and I almost died. With all the courage I could muster on shaking legs, I followed as she escorted them into the downstairs parlor. What was going on? I had to sit for fear my knees wouldn't support me and watched Mamma close the double doors.

What is the most horrible thing a person who believes themselves in love can hear? He simply said, "I love you like a sister. It has never been passion on my part, and I think you know that. I'm in love with Lucille."

I looked from him to her. How it all fit now, yet I couldn't help myself from pleading. "But surely there were moments," I interjected, trying to defend my pitiable case, "when you were close to—"

"Forgive me if you felt differently or thought that I did. As you know, I've only just learned the truth that you are my sister, but I never cared for you in any other way than that. Forgive me." He looked at Lucille and said, quietly, "Forgive us."

Even so, I thought, a bit thunderstruck by his words, but said nothing. All I could do was look at his exotic features and cry silent tears.

In a lowered voice, as if not to frighten a child, he said, "Please, I beg you, don't make this more difficult than it has to be." He kissed my cheek and then he was gone. I had said nothing on my own behalf. To lose him and to be betrayed by my best friend was exceeding any past sorrow I'd ever known.

⌒⟨✦⟩⌒

WHEN I WAS ALONE, I thought back to the time in the city when Bao had walked me to the corner to catch the subway and handed me a parcel of fresh vegetable foodstuffs. Embarrassed but pleased, I didn't know how to thank him so I reached up and kissed his cheek. He blushed pomegranate red and said, "No need." I wanted to kiss him again, on the mouth. But we were in the middle of a busy street with passersby jostling us as they hurried past.

"Oh, but I want to thank you," I said, but thought *in a most physical way.* "Because I can't repay you for your generosity. Things are getting tough. At first they cut Papa's pay by forty percent, but now he's been laid off. Valentina's not getting any work from her usual customers. People are making do with the things they have, washing and ironing their own clothes and not paying her for alterations. She's not able to contribute to our household anymore. All she can do to help Mamma is clean the house and do whatever meager shopping to save Mamma the walk and carrying bundles. And she cooks," I indicated the packages, "thanks to you."

"The Chinese are frugal."

"So's Mamma—she makes salad with plain old weeds like chicory and dandelion from the garden."

"The Chinese eat every part of the fish—love the tails and cheeks—and every part of four-legged animals. In the restaurant where I work, they braise, poach, boil, simmer, steam, broil, bake in clay or salt, or they pot it."

"What do you mean? Isn't everything cooked in pots?"

"No, I mean they cook it but then they can, cream, mince, chip, or cook it in a soy sauce with different spices, and it's sort of 'mum,' as they use it from one dish to another. We eat everything of the pig except its grunting, oinking yak—and we only pay a groat."

"A what?"

He smiled. "You know, a small sum. As I said, we're frugal with money except when it comes to gambling, which appears to be our greatest vice. But here are some vegetables. I'm sure your mother will know what to do with them if you say she's such a good cook. They are different than most vegetables grown here, but she'll make good use of these."

"What are these gifts?"

"Some *bok choi*. It's Chinese cabbage of a variety with tapering leaves."

"And these look like broccoli."

"Flowering broccoli— skinny and deep green, full of nutrients."

"Leeks," I said, happy to recognize something else.

"For soups."

"Snow pod shoots—" I shook my head as I pointed to but didn't recognize some dark things.

He said, "Dried dog-ear mushrooms—"

"We use dried mushrooms, too, only not this kind."

"These," he said, taking hold of some skinny greens, "are flowering chives and silk squash."

"Aha! Like our zucchini. Oh, and I recognize these, though a different variety than we use," I said and counted aloud six purple lovelies. "They're a kind of thin eggplants. I love eggplant." I wanted to add *I think I love you, too.*

"Make these cut long and fried, add minced pork, hot pepper, garlic, a bit of soy, some tomato, and—"

"Are you a chef?"

He shook his head. "There's not a person in China who doesn't understand the value of home-grown vegetables and basic cooking. Even children."

⚬⚬⚬

ANOTHER TIME HE'D WATCHED MAMMA cut the chicken into several parts and put it in the boiling pot of water for soup. He asked her why she didn't use the feet, liver, kidneys, or ovaries. "Not in soup," she said. "I make a sort of pâté with the chicken livers. The only internal organs we use are for a sauce to make with tomatoes over pasta."

He looked over her shoulder and said, "In China, we use every part of every animal."

Then Mamma didn't know what to say due to embarrassment, but in some way she wanted to thank him, so she leaned in and kissed his cheek and said, "No different than my Giacomo's skin."

He laughed. "Did you imagine us Chinese different?"

She looked shy. "I didn't want to embarrass you, but we Italians are very demonstrative, and you may not be used to such behavior. I didn't want to offend you."

Maybe because he didn't want any more familiarity than the level they seemed to have just achieved, he asked her to show him the garden.

Marcella knew Mamma had been more than pleased to receive such abundance and to be able to turn the veggies into minestrone soups, stews, and mixed dishes.

⚬⚬⚬

NOW MAMMA WELCOMED HIM INTO her home and became quite attached to him because of his gracious manner and the fact that she saw much of Papa in him.

Thinking back on it, I'm not sure how we got through the initial Depression years, but it was not just by prayer alone. We were fortunate to have a great ally who gave us wonderful offerings when food was so hard to come by, even if we had money to buy it.

At the time, I'd hoped Bao was completely smitten with me, but I never could tell if he was flirting with me or if he held me in some weird revered position for some unknown reason. It was because he considered me a younger sister. Ouch!

Food was sustenance, and somehow we managed to slide through those beginning Depression years with help from our garden, help from others, and dumb luck. Jack always brought us bones that Mamma put in the soup to give it strong flavor and to nourish us.

Once he brought home a few slices of *pancetta*, a gift from his boss. The small portion wasn't enough to make a whole breakfast. Mamma snatched it midair and said, "Not enough for everyone, but enough for all if I add it to minestrone for flavor or to a pot of stew or sautéed veggies—a taste beyond compare—or toss with eggs into *carbonara* sauce for pasta."

"I'm for soup!" I piped in.

Jack seconded the motion.

Papa vetoed us and we got pasta.

⁂

I DESCRIBED ALL THE ATROCIOUS events to my diary as "The Bao Affair and Its Aftermath." I had caused such a terrible upset in the family. The subsequent breakup made me violently ill. I couldn't eat, couldn't sleep. How could I possibly have had a sexual attraction and romantic feelings toward my own brother? Just wasn't normal. I didn't know he was my brother, but even so, shouldn't something in my heart or soul, my inner being, have averted me?

I confided in Val. "I guess I fell for him more than I thought possible."

"Kind of neat finding a brother. I always liked him. Hope Mamma will still let him come to visit. I wonder if she's jealous. Papa had a lot of courage to tell her of his first love, don't you think?"

"Mamma's already accepted him as a son. She told me that when I dreamed of hair, what I should have been aware of was the fact that Lucille and Bao would be getting together. My quasi-intended and my best friend."

"Maybe that's meant to be." She began to curl her hair. I grabbed her hand. She yanked it away.

"All of a sudden you're so wise, while my ego has been shot to hell—where's your sympathy? You're not a bit helpful," I said.

"I didn't invent this tragedy. Anyway, I never thought he was for you. You know that."

Discussion over. I began to wonder about myself. Was I on a road to discovery?

I went to the bathroom, threw a cup of salts into the tub, and adjusted the water using both taps. As the water rose higher and higher, I considered drowning myself. Just not my style. And truly, was he worth it? I'd rather suffer the consequences than end my life—a lack of hope and faith and plain old desperation.

That afternoon, Pina came to see me, and Val went downstairs so Pina and I could talk privately and to watch the baby, who was now talking and getting into everything. At times Val could be so attuned, and these delicate acts of hers always took me by surprise. I pictured her laughing eyes when she played with Elena.

Pina hugged me in the living room. We sat down on the sofa, and she initiated the conversation. "There's plenty of time," she said. "Why do you seem so rushed and in a great hurry? You don't have to get to work."

"I'm still upset about Bao."

Pina took my hands in hers. "You've got to let this go and embrace the fact that you now have a brother. This wasn't your destiny."

Pina and I talked until dinnertime.

⌐℃⌐

AS THE DAYS PASSED, I was having a hard time handling work due to terrible lethargy. I missed work so often that Elaine Weiss came to visit and told me not to worry, but that no man was worth getting sick over. She'd cover for me, but please, get back to work pronto. There'd be time enough over summer to make up the college work if I had a change of heart, but I answered, "No more school." My mind was made up.

We were having tea and cookies in the living room. Val was being sweet and solicitous and also eavesdropping on our conversation.

Elaine sipped some tea. "Take as much time as you need, but make sure you come back to Macy's. I'll hold your position open."

I was being my usual self-centered self and hadn't even inquired as to her special friend. "How's Sara?"

"No longer in my life." She bit into one of Mamma's cookies.

"I'm sorry."

"I'm not. Besides . . . " she trailed off.

"Besides what?" The words were barely out of my mouth when I realized I should never have asked.

"She wasn't you."

I was mildly surprised, having thought she'd long given up on the idea that I could be part of her life in that way. The expression on my face gave me away.

"Did you think I'd gotten over you? Seeing you every day, being close to you but you being off limits for me?"

"There was never a *me* to get over. I could never—"

"Just because you could never doesn't mean I stopped caring for you."

"Elaine," I said as softly as I could.

"I know," she said and patted my hand. "I know."

⌒⟨✦⟩⌒

I RAN A LOW-GRADE FEVER FOR close to a week. It would range between 99.6 to 100.6. Mamma was short-tempered with Val and Jack—that's how I understood she was worried about me. After a few days of the low-grade temperature, Mamma went across the street and asked the missus to let Dr. Amanti know how sick I was. When she came back, I knew Mamma was really concerned. She never cared for Mrs. Amanti's snobbish ways, so for her to ask a favor was a huge sacrifice—although Mrs. Amanti was now quite civil to Mamma ever since the gift of the blouse with the gold buttons Val had made her.

The doctor arrived on Saturday evening after everyone had eaten and I'd thrown up for the second time. He discussed the previous weeks with my mother. Drifts of their conversation made it upstairs. I heard them talking but was too weak and too apathetic to listen. Val came skipping into the room and said, "Hey, pretty girl, you need to brush your teeth and comb your hair for the doctor."

"I can't. Where's Papa?"

"Had to work late, I guess. Now up you go."

She practically dragged me from the bedroom to the bathroom and sponge-bathed me and made me do what she said. She brushed my hair and changed my nightgown and pillowcase and propped me up looking like a diva in a romantic scene on the silver screen.

The doctor trudged upstairs, and by his heavy tread on the stairs I knew the man was exhausted. He sat on a straight-backed chair that Val placed near my bed. Following a time of probing and questioning, he finally got around to saying that my condition may be due to a panicky feeling over losing this boyfriend. Then he said, "Maybe guilt has a part in all this, too."

"What do you mean?" I said, sitting up straight.

"The fact that you found out that you're related could be the cause of making your immune system low." Why did Mamma tell him? He went on to explain how he'd heard of these kinds of situations. Not precisely like mine, but that some shocking occurrence had made girls sickly, feverish, and anguished.

Mamma came into my room. She begged him not to say anything about this in the neighborhood. She couldn't stand a scandal. I heard her implore, "I beg you, please, please—not even to Mrs. Amanti. Promise?"

"Rest assured, Angelica, I won't divulge a thing. It's nobody's business."

That wasn't enough for Mamma, who made him swear on his children's eyes.

The weary doctor swore he wouldn't say a thing, like a priest in the seal of the confessional. His prescription for me was rest, good food, plenty to drink, fresh air, long walks, and a change of environment as soon as possible, which we could ill afford.

Walking with the doctor down the stairs, I heard Mamma ask if there was anything that Papa would be able to do to repay the doctor's kindness. "Not now," he said, adding that she shouldn't fret, he'd let her know.

Mamma said I'd made myself sick. Can a person do that? Run a fever? She said I brought the sickness on, and she was furious with me because, as she said, sounding exactly like Elaine, "No man is worth suffering like this. Bad enough women have to suffer through childbirth and every other thing."

Then all of a sudden one night the fever spiked, and I must have been hallucinating, because I said I'd walked with Jesus. I told Mamma the story, insisting that it wasn't a dream because it was real—about baskets and someone hiding me and the soldiers in sandals and short skirts running around the courtyard trying to find me.

She called in the older priest to bless me, hear my confession, and give me Communion.

⌐◦◍◦⌐

I WAS HAVING DIFFICULTY, and often I couldn't keep food down. If this is what love did, you could keep the whole idea of it. Each time after I was sick, I flushed the toilet, washed my face, and brushed my teeth. I'd look in the mirror to see a very haggard girl. At the beginning I thought it was one of those weird mirrors at Coney Island that made you fat or skinny—who was that creature?

I had made myself ill over this whole circumstance with Bao but kept insisting I craved company. How absurd. All I wanted was to be left alone and not be getting all of this negative attention. When vacation time rolled around and it was getting close to time to make a decision, Dr. Amanti suggested to my parents that it would be better if I didn't go with the girls from Macy's to camp, but vacation alone. He told them I needed the solitude—away from not only the family, but everyone—time to reflect and to heal. Mamma agreed, as she was afraid that I'd confide in the wrong person and the whole sordid business would leak out. How could she think I'd tell anyone? Papa insisted that instead I should go for a few weeks to stay at his friend Carlo's bungalow on Lake George, even if taking an extra week off meant no pay.

He sat me down in the living room and explained I'd have the whole place to myself this summer. I could read, take walks, sun, and swim. The Albano family would be traveling in Europe and taking an extended Mediterranean cruise. Mamma didn't want me to go alone, but I said, "Alone, or I'm not going." I could fend for myself.

Papa said, "You look skeletal. Promise me you'll eat three meals a day."

"I will." I'd swear to anything just to be by myself and not have the whole family hovering over me like I was on my deathbed. Anybody can open a can of tuna packed in olive oil and squirt some lemon juice on it and call it dinner. I could cook eggs and boil water, so I figured it wouldn't be difficult to cook pasta, add salt to the water, drain it, and toss in some butter and grated cheese. I'd survive. Who cared about food or eating? I seemed to have survived this terrible tragedy, hadn't I?

I looked forward to basking in the sun and swimming. I would be able to read to my heart's content and wouldn't have to socialize with anyone. It was the best solution. Mamma worried that I'd be lonely by myself. She called me a person who thrived on company; how could I face such solitude?

The day before I left, Elaine sent a car for me and took me out shopping in the Village. Elaine wanted to get me a special going-away present to cheer me because in such "lean and wan times," as she called our sales days, I'd increased sales for the month despite my days off more than on and being morally and emotionally depressed. We walked into a boutique, and she purchased a French peasant blouse with billowy sleeves in black chiffon with a small Mandarin collar and an opening that reached the breasts. Not even that lifted my spirits. We went to an Italian coffeehouse where some guy played guitar and sang with a melodious voice. His poignant words brought tears to my eyes. Elaine leaned over and patted my hand, asked me to translate and when I did, she said, "You'll get over him. You'll fall in love for real—a lifetime love awaits you. I have a surprise for you. Someone's coming to meet you."

"Who?" I thought of all the girls on the floor with me at Macy's, but I couldn't imagine one of them Elaine would invite.

"Here he is now—the tall man wearing a hat and sunglasses. He's just had an eye operation and must wear them to shade his eyes," she said. He walked over to us and smiled at Elaine. Where had I seen that smile before? We both stood up. "Marcella, meet my friend Al Lentz. He's a film producer from Hollywood."

"Pleased to meet you," I stammered like an awestruck movie fan. He looked vaguely familiar.

"Marcella," he said. "What an unusual name."

I all but fell into my chair, because for some reason, I hadn't paid attention to his name.

"She's not only my top salesgirl and beautiful, she can sing and act, too."

He looked apologetic as he said, "Elaine, you're going to have to forgive me, but I can't stay as I have an important meeting at the 21 Club." He turned to me and said, "Forgive me. Here's my card."

I knew his voice, but from where? "So nice to meet you," I said, fingering the card like it was a precious jewel.

I don't recall much of the rest of the day, but I know I thought it was lovely, and, by way of apology for his quick departure, I rode home in Mr. Al Lentz's hired car, which was divine to say the least.

～⟶⟵～

THE TRAIN TRIP THE NEXT day to Lake George didn't take as long as I thought it would, but then again, I had my nose in a good book that was well-plotted and had great characters. Carlo Albano's caretaker met me at the train station, picked up my bag, and escorted me to the cabin. I was surprised to see it stocked with provisions. He saw the expression on my face and told me to help myself to whatever I liked. I asked if there was a can of tuna fish.

After he'd gone, I sat on the comfortable chintz-covered easy chair with my feet propped up on a cross-stitch-covered footstool, finished the novel, and must have dozed. When I awoke, it was beyond twilight. I stood, stretched, and looked around, tossing my white piqué jacket with fine ribbing on the chair. I stepped onto the pavers of the screened-in porch and looked across the lake at the twinkling lights. I unzipped my linen skirt and let it fall to the floor, unbuttoned my blouse and dropped it. I approached the screen in my silk full slip and listened to the croaking sounds of a summer night in the country. I felt sapped of every bit of energy. Picking up my clothes, I wandered into the kitchen and let the tap run until the water felt cool, splashed my face and neck, and dried with a tea towel. I drank a huge glass of water, which I convinced myself would make me feel I had eaten a full meal. In the guest bedroom, I hung up my clothes, slipped off my bra and panties, and got into bed, covering myself with the chenille bedcover. I traced the fabric and recalled what Elaine had said about it. *Chenille* is the French word for caterpillar. I rubbed the fur-like raised material, the yarn resembling just that—a caterpillar.

～⟶⟵～

THE NEXT DAY, I WALKED down to the shore with a small volume of *The Prince* in my pocket. I spread out a red-and-white-striped bathing towel, sat in my navy blue shorts and polka-dot halter top, lathering up in baby oil, and tried to look like an overworked bathing beauty in need of a suntan. Swimming in the lake far out by a raft was what looked like a huge fish until I remembered this wasn't the ocean. It was a big-built man, and when the blond Viking stepped out of the water and shook off, he reminded me of Patches when he'd come out of his bath. The bronzed man, as big as a statue, had a musculature I never knew existed, although for some odd reason I felt as though I'd seen him somewhere. *He must be a movie gladiator or a wrestling coach or—*

Just as I was sizing up his occupation, the little man who had picked me up at the station tipped his hat, blocking my view, his withered body shading the sun. He asked if I needed anything.

"No thanks," I said, shifting my gaze back on the Adonis in his well-fitting bathing costume.

"I'm in the number three cottage over there to the right if you need anything. I'm Pasquale, remember?"

"Oh, forgive me. I'm Marcella."

"Yes, Miss, I know."

"Of course. How silly of me."

"There's a get-together dance in the recreation center at seven-thirty for the young crowd, and there's also a restaurant in the back right on the water. Beautiful view, if you'd care to—"

"No thanks. I'll be going to bed early."

He tipped his hat. "If you need to phone, there's a public booth just down the road. You can get change at the desk in the recreation center."

I smiled and shook my head, and still he didn't budge.

"Would you care to join me and my wife for dinner this evening, Miss?"

I shook my head. "Another night, perhaps. Thanks." I waved my fingers and put my beach bag in back of me, laid my head down, and opened my book.

⚜

ABOUT AN HOUR LATER, A shadow loomed above me, and I wondered if a huge cloud had covered the sun and it was suddenly going to rain. I looked up and a deep voice said, "Close your book and come along to take a swim. The water's fine."

"Really?"

"I josh you not."

"You what?"

"Wouldn't kid you," he said with a Western twang that I recognized. He took off his sunglasses and looked so familiar, but I didn't want to say that. "How would I know, Mister—hey—what'd you say your name was?"

"I didn't. Forgive my manners—in such a hurry to get into the water." He extended his hand. "Alistair Lentz, formerly from Texas and now California. Please call me Al."

"Elaine Weiss's friend?"

"The very self-same."

"Too much of a coincidence—Fate must be playing games with me. I'm Miss Scimenti, from Brooklyn, New York." I shook his hand, thinking of Papa always saying a handshake should be firm. "You have an unusual name."

"Alistair is Scottish. It means 'defender of mankind.'"

"Impressive. You've got a lot to live up to."

"I'd rather be a defender of the damsel I'm gazing upon right now." He shaded his eyes with his hand.

Oh dear, I thought. *Now that's a bit of malarkey from a Scotsman.* "Good idea. I'll just run back and get into my costume, and then let's swim. Niccolò Machiavelli is more boring than a business course and such a controlling, inhumane individual."

"Who?"

"*The Prince.*" I turned the cover of the book for him to see. "He believed that humanity ended when you became a prince," I answered, quite disbelievingly—hadn't everybody heard of him? Right then and there I should have known this man didn't use his brain as much as his brawn, but he sure was pleasing to the eye in that Nordic Viking kind of way.

"Ma'am, forgive me, but you look so awfully darned—"

"Familiar?"

"Yes, and you mentioned Elaine. Don't I know you from some-place else?"

"Is that your best pickup line? We've actually met several times. I didn't recognize you at first because when I met you with Elaine, you wore a hat and glasses."

"You're the girl on the bus in Manhattan. The salesgirl in Macy's."

"You're the Yalie Bulldog with a twang. Oh my, oh me—when Elaine Weiss introduced us, you were incognito."

"Of course! You're the girl with the beautiful name. Marcella."

"The very self-same," I mimicked, but I'd already been seduced by his twang and blue eyes. Were the stars finally aligning for me? I suddenly remembered his calling card. Why hadn't I looked to see if it was the same man I'd met in the Catskills? Too much coincidence—it couldn't be.

⁕

I RETURNED IN MY ONE-PIECE navy blue swimsuit with the white trim decked out in a white lace cover-up that I'd received from Elaine as a parting gift, along with her counsel to take the cover-up off but keep the suit on when I went bathing. I took off the tunic-style button-down shirt and dropped it dramatically on my towel. Apparently I had his attention, for Mr. Alistair Lentz was almost drooling with approval. I'd gotten not only a validating glance but also a fixated one remaining for some time on my breasts—or was I being paranoid? I reached into my tote and pulled out the cream Elaine also gave me. I slathered my arms, legs, chest, throat, and face with Dorothy Gray Sunburn Cream, thinking of Elaine, whom I'd teased, saying, "Why are you interested in keeping me fit and tanned when you'll never succeed and you know it, darling?" She'd laughed and said, "No matter. Where there's life, there's hope, eh?"

We swam out to the raft. I did a crawl and Al did a show-off butterfly which doused me to the point that I slowed to turtle pace. He gave me his arm and hoisted me out of the water, seeing to it that my bonny feet never touched the cord ladder. We sunned for quite a while. He was handsome and looked as though he could hurl a huge boulder into the water with no effort, just to make a splash. He made small talk, and I must have dozed because I lost his gossamer thread. I sort of shook my head in agreement till I could catch up.

⁕

AFTER OUR SWIM, HE INVITED me out to a nearby country diner for ham and eggs. Sounded good to me. I hadn't eaten any breakfast except for a glass of iced tea so that I could get down to the lake early, wanting to finish reading all about the flamboyant Florentines and end my misery. Why couldn't I have tossed it away? Why did I have to finish reading books, even when I detested them, yet it seemed everything about my life, especially my supposed love life, was so unfinished and always in such upheaval? Where had I picked up this book? Oh yes—I'd found it in the train station. Should have left it there.

We crossed a footbridge over a small pond and breakfasted in an airy country inn decorated with calico curtains and red-and-white checkered tablecloths with matching napkins. The hostess sat us by a window so we could look out on the surrounding gardens. There was a rocking horse for kiddies, a seesaw, three swings, and the pond we'd crossed with ducks and swans. I was starving and ordered eggs over easy, bacon, and buttered toast. Add two pancakes and two sausage links to that and that's the breakfast Al wolfed down with several cups of sugared coffee and enough milk to feed a calf. When he'd finished, he nursed a last cup of coffee and chewed my ear off about how the east is nice, but there's nothing like the great big state of Texas, or the west for that matter. As he droned on a bit, my mind leaped to New York City's Chinatown, where currently Bao was investing in real estate. I had to stop my wandering thoughts and drag them back to Al's surge-and-wave discussion about bluebonnets, barbeque, friendliness, and open skies. He finished his sermon, which did not sway or convert me, by saying, "Why, sitting out on the veranda I can look out—the size of our ranch is acres and acres, and they're all mine."

"Really?" I finally asked. His shocked expression caught me up short and made me realize that I'd not only committed a major gaff, I'd stung and hurt his blustering, wide-open prairie feelings.

⌗

LATE IN THE AFTERNOON WE walked to the tennis courts. After about a half-hour of me lobbing the ball and Al chasing after it, he said, "I'll treat you to an hour with the tennis pro—you'll at least learn to hold the racket correctly."

"I don't understand. I played badminton with Gianni at Zia Grazia's, and I was pretty darn good."

"Who's Johnny?"

I hesitated a second and then looked away. "My brother," I said, thinking *Liar, liar, pants on fire.*

"Both games are played with rackets—the similarities end there. To begin with, the tennis court is larger and the net is lower. There are different moves altogether. Badminton is all wrist action with lighter rackets. The cock is almost featherweight—"

Not so the cock-tutoring swain admiring me at the moment, I thought.

"Are you listening?"

"By all means, a cock is nothing like a tennis ball."

⁎

THE NEXT AFTERNOON WE DECIDED to make a picnic and took one of the rowboats out. Al rowed us to a secluded sandy bank. When he'd beached the boat, he suggested we take a swim before eating. I almost dropped dead when he suggested a swim in the altogether.

"Nude?" I screamed. "I can't. I'm from Bay Ridge." Al laughed out loud. Needless to say, I'd be writing this occurrence in my diary. He stripped off his shirt and dove into the water minus his swimming trunks. I took the rowboat back and made him swim across the lake.

After his long swim and a quick apology, I tossed him his trunks, and he struggled into them in the water. He proposed dinner and an evening stroll, but I had had enough company for the day and needed to be by myself. Did Al always propel himself onto a girl he'd just chatted up lakeside, despite a brief introduction?

I got back to the cottage, and a letter was stuck into the screen door. Lucille. My heart sank. I dashed inside and ripped it open. I sat down and read it over and over, tears streaming down my cheeks. She and Bao had gotten engaged. That was enough of a horror, but then she asked me if I'd consent to be her maid of honor. I gagged, wanting to vomit. How could I? Even worse than these two horrors was the absurd betrayal I felt at Papa's now reading the translation of Lian's chronicle with Bao. There it was in blue ink written with a fountain pen on stark white paper. Why would Lucille think that would sound like good news to me?

⁎

THE NEXT MORNING, SOMEHOW FEELING better after practically memorizing Lucille's words, I walked down the road to a little inn and asked to use the phone. I plunked my money on the counter and asked for a soda pop. I hoped that Val would answer. Not that I didn't want to talk to Mamma, but I needed to talk to my sister.

"*Pronto,*" Mamma said, as though she knew the call was from me, then switched quickly to English, saying, "Ready. Hello?"

"Mamma, how are you? Papa? Everybody?"

"Oh *bella gioia*, we're fine. Good to hear your voice. How are you?"

"Swimming every day. Reading, hiking. I'm brown as a sun-dried berry. Sleep like a baby and eat like a gorilla." I was pretty sure that Mamma didn't know gorillas only ate vegetables, berries, and nuts. But just in case, I added that Carlo's neighbor-watchman looked in on me and brought me pies and cupcakes that his wife baked fresh.

"Eat but don't gain weight," she said, anxiousness in her tone. "Did you hear from Lucille?"

"I did, Mamma. I'd love to speak to Val. Is she around?"

"Standing right here. I'll pass her the phone. *Baci.*"

"*Ciao,* Mamma. Kisses to you and Papa, too. Oh, and Pina and Jack."

As she passed the phone, I swear I heard her say, "It was for the best."

"Val, I've got to talk to you. I need to come home." I twisted the black cord.

"Honey, in time you'll get over Bao."

"It's not that. If I write you a letter, Mamma may ask to read it."

"What?" she said a little too loudly. She lowered her voice. "You're ready to leave idyllic Lake George? That bad, huh? Lonely?"

"Hell no! I'm having a hard time fending off a guy named Al. He seems taken with your sister, and he's big and strong—I mean built like King Kong."

"What's he like?"

"Good-looking. Seems as though he's from Texas money that smells of cows, horseshit, and oil. He lives part-time in California—he's a movie producer—and I think he wants me to act in a film. Only I'm not sure what kind of film. It may be one that's made for his eyes only, if you get my gist. Tell Mamma you miss me and need me to come home."

"Are you sure you want to toss away this chance?"

"Start crying when you get off the phone."

"No, you're a brave girl. Do it yourself. And remember, opportunity only knocks once."

That threw me for a loop. I hung up the phone with the operator's voice in my ear asking for more coins.

⸻

AL AND I PLAYED MINI-GOLF one day and he beat me; croquet the next with some of his neighbors, and we beat them. We were invited to a hoedown where we would square dance and everybody was supposed to dress western, which I thought was pretty dumb as we lived in the east. Al picked me up in a rented Ford roadster and drove me to a little nearby town that had a secondhand store. He went slicing down country lanes eating up the sedge on the side of the road with his spinning tires, but he seemed not to care, choosing speed and daring over sane and safe. He bought me a red-and-white checkered blouse, a kerchief to tie around my neck, and a full skirt that looked like an old-fashioned cowgirl outfit. We had a hot dog lunch with lemonade at a roadside stand that sold summer fruit.

After that, we went back to our respective cabins to shower and dress. He was early, so I had him sit in the itsy-bitsy parlor and gave him iced tea.

"Got anything stronger?"

"Not sure. Uncle Carlo may keep something on hand for medicinal purposes, but you do know it's against the law, don't you?"

"So are a lot of things, but wouldn't it be a dull life if we all adhered to the rules."

Oy vey. A rule breaker.

I looked in Carlo's cabinet, took back the tea, which I drank, and went to the kitchen. When I came back, I handed him a jelly glass filled with ice chips as there were no tumblers. Then I gave him a bottle of Scotch.

He nodded his approval, and I watched him pour what I'd heard was called a "stout drink." Then he took out a flask and poured some of the Scotch from the bottle into it. I wondered if he'd keep this drinking up all night and if I'd have to fight him off. Then I wondered if I'd even want to. I'd seen his physique when he swam naked, but when he pulled himself ashore to towel off, he was chastely covered in his bathing trunks. He was well-endowed, and I fantasized what it would be like making love to him.

I went to finish dressing but had the distinct feeling that he'd maneuvered his chair so he could peak through the partially cracked door, which didn't close completely. I leaned over the sink and combed my hair in the mirror and applied a light coat of red lipstick, which I smoothed around with my pinky.

When I came out, I twirled around and he said, "You're a fine specimen of a girl."

He sat on the overstuffed chair, and when he stood up he had an obvious bulge in his pants. He met my eyes and then grasped my hand and forcefully put it on his crotch. Hard. "It's been that way the whole time I've been watching you lean over the sink putting on lipstick and combing your hair."

I screeched and wrenched my hand free of his private parts. "You are not the gentleman you purport to be. Now let's get out of here."

I grabbed a sweater and off we went to the dance, where I learned to do-si-do, promenade, allemande left, and fall on my ass as gracefully as a gazelle. Two sets of hands dragged me to my feet, and I swiped at the skirt flecked with pieces of hay that had been strewn on the barn floor along with sawdust.

At one point I told Al I'd love to ask the bandleader to play a song that I could sing for him, and he gave me a ten-dollar bill and said, "Hand him this."

I did and sang "All of Me," ending to thunderous applause and a wink from the bandleader.

Al continued sipping from the flask all night, and when he said he'd drive me home, I said no. "I'll drive or we'll walk or hitch a ride with another couple." I'm not sure he even knew it was me who had been singing.

When his neighbor let us off at the cottage, I said goodnight and quickly went to let myself in. But Al waved off the driver and called out loudly, "We'll be all right. Don'tcha worry."

I didn't want to let him in, but he followed me and sat in the easy chair and pulled me down on top of him. He started kissing me and holding me to him. I felt like I was in a vise, locked in his strong arms, and although I squirmed, I really wasn't doing it forcefully enough to break free. I could get out, but I was feeling as though I wanted to lose control. I'd kept physical emotions so tamped down until now. He nipped my shoulder gently. I pulled away, and he released me.

"I'm sorry, but you must understand. I can't be constrained. If you want to have a relationship with me, it'll have to be my way. Slowly. I don't know you. You're strong, handsome, but what makes you think you can man-handle me?"

He got to his feet. "I apologize. I got bad news today and drank too much. I was upset—like sticking your head in the sand like an ostrich," he said, shamefaced and sheepish.

"You have to face up to the harsh realities life presents you with," I said in that know-it-all tone I use with Val. How dare I say such a preposterous thing when I'd just been slapped with one of life's rude realities with Bao and knocked down with an unseen wallop coming from Lucille's letter?

He left. Somehow Gianni came to mind, and I doubted he would've ever taken such liberties after drinking.

The next morning went by before I saw Al again by the lake. He was reading, spread out supine on a plaid blanket, shading his eyes with a book, and I had to laugh because it was *The Prince*.

"Well, what do you think?" I asked.

"Your review of it was perfect. Can you forgive my bad behavior last night?"

"We'll see." I sat on his blanket. "Where did you find a copy?"

"It's yours. It was on top of your garbage pail."

"Well hello, Jack."

"It's Al." He scooted over to make more room for me.

"I know, but you remind me of my brother, Jack."

"Hey, how many brothers do you have?"

"Just one."

"What about the other one?"

"What other one?"

"Johnny?"

"Oh him? Doesn't count. He's adopted. What were you doing snooping in my garbage?"

With an embarrassed chortle, he said, "I wasn't actually snooping. Came by to see if you were up and about."

"Stalking me?"

"Listen," he said with a hangdog look on his face. "I'm sorry. Maybe we got off on the wrong foot. But hey, you and I, what a great project we'd make. Shall we give it a go? What d'you say?" He smiled his rakish best, and it made me feel somewhat flattered, but then I was immediately struck with the image of this big, oafish guy squeezing my mother's hand in greeting. I winced.

⁓❊⁓

ON THE DAYS THAT FOLLOWED, we hiked, biked, fished, and boated. I got too much sun on a windy day. After a cool shower, I slathered on as much moisturizer as I could. But I glanced over my shoulder into the mirror to find my back red and blistering. I went to Pasquale's and asked his wife to assess the damage. She took a gander and told her husband to get the doctor. I could barely keep the light, gauzy blouse on my skin, but I braved it. I had barged in on them at dinnertime, and I couldn't very well go over there in a bathing suit. I thanked her and walked back to the cottage, and Pasquale went for a local doctor to tend to my sun and windburn.

⁓❊⁓

LATER, THE DOCTOR TOOK ONE look at the blisters on my back and said, "Tea."

"You want a glass of tea?"

"No. I want you to make strong hot tea, cool it, and then apply it to your back or have someone do it for you. The tannic acid will calm this immediately. And get that oily stuff off of your skin as soon as I leave. Take a cool bath and add baking soda. Soak for fifteen minutes, no longer, or you'll turn into a lizard. Do not dry off with a towel. Air dry your body. Tomorrow pour in a cup or so of oatmeal into the bath water. Soak for ten minutes and rinse in tepid water. Never use cold water. You can go into shock."

So that's what I did the next day. Bathed and soaked in gloppy water, rinsed in lukewarm, waltzed around naked to air dry, and then threw on a loose-fitting nightgown three sizes too big that was in Caterina's dresser drawer. Mrs. Pasquale, whose first name I never did learn, came in three times a day to daub cold tea on my back and fan it dry.

Al came around morning, noon, and night. He brought me fresh peaches, a candy bar, and flowers. I had the feeling he was hanging around the cottage even more than that, but I never saw a shadow of him when I went out to the porch to read or doze, hoping for a breeze.

⌒⟨❊⟩⌒

AFTER THE CALAMITY OF MY sunburn, Al and I resumed our outings but with more caution. We picnicked under large shade trees and pines, we went to an outdoor movie one evening, and another we got all gussied up and went to the club for a dinner of *coq au vin, sans vin,* that was more like a dried-out old hen. All I could do was talk about my mother's *pollo in bianco,* a wonderful, flavorful dish with a rich brown gravy to toss with pasta. Al ordered strawberry shortcake topped with a mountain of whipped cream for our dessert, which I devoured as if I were a prisoner on the gallows and this was my last meal on earth. When he walked me home, I didn't let him in.

Instead we stayed away from the porch light and sat on the swing chair and played a lot of kissy face.

"I know this sounds presumptuous, even irrational," he said, "but I'm falling in love with you." I was speechless for a few minutes, and the next thing he did was confess the bad news that he'd received from the doctor. How sad for him, but how unromantic could you get? At a time like this, here he goes into a soliloquy about his rheumatoid arthritis sickness. Hamlet, once removed, is what I thought, but I truly felt sorry for him—a young man facing such physical hardships. He was so young to have been diagnosed with such a crippling disease. I didn't know much about the illness, but I was determined to find out more concerning it.

Then, the night before I was going to leave, he became quite amorous, and I had to shove him off of me, with him begging me to be more passionate, groping my breasts and kissing my neck. Finally he fell to his knees in front of me, lifted my skirt and pressed his mouth against me.

I yanked down my skirt. "You can't be serious. We don't even know each other."

"I know enough. Will you marry me?"

"You're relentless."

He stood up and put his hands on my shoulders. "Love forces you into a mode of persistence. I swear I've never felt like this before or been so resolute about getting a girl. You're kind and generous and have a great sense of humor, and you'll take care of me. Oh, I'm dead serious. My folks'll love you. You're as pretty as a dappled pony learning to take those first steps."

This, I assumed, was the Texan way of saying he thought I was cute. *Mio Dio!* I removed his hands from my shoulders. "Whoa, cowboy! You're moving too fast," I said, but what I meant was *You're smothering me.* "I need to get some sleep. You'll have to leave now, Al."

"Consider my proposal, honey bunch. I can make you happy. You won't have to work at Macy's anymore."

Would he keep me prisoner in a Texas oil tower? I pictured myself, an Italian Rapunzel, tossing down a long black braid three years from now when my hair grew out. Would he ever let me act in one of the films he produced? Thinking back to the square dance, I wasn't even sure he knew I could sing he'd had so much to drink.

"You mean, I could sing and dance in one of your movie musicals?" I imagined the klieg lights, the megaphone on the director's chair, the glamorous dresses, the excitement of people recognizing me in fancy restaurants, asking me for my autograph on their menus.

He lifted my chin and I raised my lips to his. I let him untie the bow to my halter, and this time I did not resist.

⌇

WE PARTED THE NEXT DAY at the train station, but not before Al loaded my arms with a bouquet of pink roses, a box of chocolates, and a book about Texas. The conductor barked once, tipped his hat as he walked past us, and yelled again, "All aboard!" just like out of a movie script.

I stood on tiptoes and kissed his cheek. When I came back down to earth, Al handed me a light robin's-egg-blue box with a white ribbon, the size of which frightened me. It was so tiny it had to be a ring. How had he had time to go to Tiffany's?

"Not yet. This is happening at a gallop," I said, hoping he'd catch my horse metaphor just for him. I refused to open the box, saying he hadn't even heard me sing yet, which sounded absurd even to my ears. He took the box from my hand, tore off the bow, and opened it for me.

There in a velvet slot sat a diamond engagement ring the size of a chickpea, glinting blindingly in my eyes, and when I looked up, I saw his wet eyes, pleading. With my arms so loaded, I couldn't maneuver. He pushed the ring on my finger and stuck the Tiffany box in my bag.

Dumfounded, I mumbled, "Write me."

"Be in New York soon, I promise. I've got your telephone number already memorized: TE6-9052. Give me your address again," he said, fumbling in his jacket pocket for a pen.

I croaked it out somehow, while he scribbled it on a matchbook with a Mont Blanc fountain pen like the one I'd seen Elaine use. I was distracted by the pen, thinking how lovely it would be to use that to sign my name to a Hollywood contract.

While he was vowing to write and call me every day, I was chiding myself on how ignoble of me to be more interested in his pen than his promise. He swore he would come to see me in three weeks' time, after I'd had time to think over his proposal and talk to my family.

Al put my suitcase on the train, and I said, "Why not hold onto the ring for me? You'll have to ask my Papa's permission."

"No, you keep it, and oh, I'll ask your daddy for sure, little darlin'. I will. First thing when I shake his hand. See you next month."

Again I was seized by the vision of Al's brute-strength grip crunching Papa's hand as I waved from the compartment window and the train whistle blew.

⌐◖✿◗¬

GAZING AT MY RING FINGER, with the sunlight hitting it and dazzling me, I wondered why I hadn't been wearing those white lady-like cotton gloves that Elaine had given me. I leafed through the book Al gave me and conveniently forgot it on my seat when the train pulled into the station. I pulled off the ring and stuck it in the box in my purse.

⌐◖✿◗¬

WHEN I GOT HOME, AFTER visiting with Mamma and Pina and the baby, I said I was tired and needed to take a nap and asked Val to come help me unpack. As I put away my summer wardrobe, I told Val all about Al.

The next thing she said after she plopped my suitcase on the bed was, "Marcella, he's sick. He's riddled with rheumatoid arthritis. He'll be a bent old man by the time he's thirty-five. What're you thinking of? You're looking for love in all the wrong places."

I finished folding a pair of shorts. "He needs me and he'll help me get my career started."

"He's moving from California to Texas or Arizona—that's, like, where? The end of the universe?"

I took my purse and rummaged around till I found the ring, put it on my finger, and waved prettily for my sister.

Her eyes bulged and her hand went to her mouth to stifle a scream. She sat down next to me. "Tell me you didn't say yes. He needs a nurse. You'll be his Venus all right, but falling straight into a fly trap." Val snapped the two clamps on my valise.

"I'm looking for someone who can be more to me than just a husband. Maybe I'm looking for a lover who is a friend. He can make my career."

"Stop right there. You're thinking this guy is going to give you your dreams of stardom on a silver platter, and it's not going to happen, I'm telling you!"

"Don't be so harsh. Of course I'd expect him to help me—open a few doors, maybe—but I have talent."

"I know that. But you told me you're not sure he even heard you sing. Besides your enchanting figure and adorable face, what talent does Mr. Alistair Lentz think you possess?"

I stopped putting the last of my clothes away, a pair of panties held aloft in my hand.

"Are you really so blind? Gianni loves you for who you are, and he's so much more to you," Val said.

I guess this was a fairytale I'd scripted for myself. Did I always seek difficult relationships simply to watch them crumble and fall? Another slash on a page of two cross-outs already—when will I learn to face reality? I'd have opposition coming at me from all directions if I chose this path with Al. Did I know it from the beginning? Maybe that's what I wanted after all—someone like Val to slap me up the side of my face and say, "Wake up!" But what would I do now? He was coming to ask Papa for my hand and to be my escort at the reception of Lucille's wedding.

TWO WEEKS PASSED, AND ALL of a sudden Val and I and three other neighborhood girls were trying on gowns, long gloves, and hats with veils, princess tiaras and diadems. Lucille's wedding was soon approaching, and the girls in the wedding party were all in a flurry of excitement. At the last fitting, they all had tried on and had been pinned into their deep purple velvet dresses, when I finally went into the dressing room. I was the maid of honor, and my dress was the color of lilac in spring. One by one they'd finished, given over their dresses to be sewn and adjusted, and left. I was the last to leave, and when I came out all of the other dressing rooms had been abandoned and an eerie silence pervaded the back of the shop. Except for a choked kind of sobbing. I found the source. Lucille was hunched over on a large ottoman, crying.

I touched her shoulder. "Hey. What's going on here? What's wrong? Why are you crying?"

She could barely get her breath when she said, "It's all too much. I apologize for falling in love with Bao and hurting you."

"You can't help who you love."

"You forgive me?"

"It wasn't in the cards. Obviously."

She cried some more. "Good thing Bao's paying for the whole shooting match."

"What're you talking about?"

"Everything. The wedding, the flowers, my dress, my shoes, the reception. My parents are going to disown me when I marry him—they called him 'an Oriental.' Last night we had a huge row. I just want to die."

"No, you don't. You want to marry him, but you want your cake and want to eat it, too. You'll marry, and your parents will come around soon enough when there's a little one expected."

"Do you really think so?" She dried her eyes.

"Know it for a fact," I said. "Look at Pina." But that's not what I felt with all those squirmy things squiggling topsy-turvy in my innards. I was afraid that Lucille's father's Irish temper and Irish fist might land smack dab in the middle of Bao's handsome face. I pictured him dashing into the church and pulling off Lucille's veil.

"Dad slammed his fist down on the table, and the mashed potatoes and peas splattered all over the corned beef. He called Bao a chink. My mom agreed. She says it's a disgrace to intermarry. 'Her poor dear Da is going to turn over in his grave on that sunny slope of green grass facing the Irish Sea.' She ranted and raved and would rather see me become an old spinster maid or dead. Dead, so she could mourn me, rather than see me happily married. She's not even coming to the church, and none of her 'shanty Irish relatives,' as Dad calls them, are coming either. I'm heartsick."

"Hush now. No wonder you've got puffy eyes. You look like hell." I handed her my hanky. Would her father be audacious enough to come to the reception and yank the tablecloth off the dais and smash up the works?

"Thanks," she said and sniffled.

"Are you sure he won't relent at the last minute?"

"You know my father."

"Stop or you'll choke." I got up and asked for a glass of water from one of the salesgirls.

In the few minutes it took to bring the water back, I thought Lucille would've calmed down. Instead she cried and cried until she hiccoughed. I gave her the water.

She said, "He's not walking me down the aisle. He told me last night."

"Fine time to tell you. What about your brothers? Won't one of them walk you? Sean? Or Aidan? I guess Brendan's too young."

She shook her head mournfully. "Petrified of Dad. He'd wipe the floor with all three of them, one hand tied behind him."

I was pensive for a minute. "Lucille."

She looked up.

"I've got an idea. You think it'd help if Papa talked to your father? You know, man to man."

"You slay me! Do you know what Dad calls your father?"

"Mr. Scimenti?"

"Funny. Try 'that guinea bastard,' that's what."

"Well, there you go. I didn't want to suggest it, but since he feels that way, how'd you like 'that guinea bastard' Papa of mine to usher you to the awaiting priest and your intended spouse on your wedding day? Supposedly the happiest day of your life, I may add. I'm sure my passionate, deliriously happy father would love to escort you, especially because you were practically raised in our home and now—"

"Now?"

"My dearest Lucille, you're going to really be part of our family now that you're marrying my Oriental brother, Papa's son."

"He's what?"

"I gather he didn't mention that little factoid to you. Here's the thing—we don't exactly tell the *Brooklyn Eagle* journalists to spread it all over town, but yes, if you didn't know, you do now. Bao, your fiancé, that chink, dago, goomba, wop, is my half-brother. I thought he gave you this happy news at your engagement party. What's wrong with him?"

"Of course he told me." She laughed and shook her head vigorously. "It's just that you make every slur sound like dialogue in a movie script."

"Lucille, that may be one of the nicest things you've ever said to me. You're coming to dinner tomorrow night. We'll discuss it all then."

The look on her face was beatific. Two perfect celestial blue angel's eyes brightened as if she'd ascended into clouds, part of a heavenly host. The ironic word, *celestial,* was not lost on me.

It had gotten so late that the city lights were coming on, and the bustling salesgirl was making guttural noises, readying herself to get our attention with a visual expression on the verge of tears as she kept looking at her watch, opening and closing her sales book, about to speak.

"Lucille and I were just leaving," I called to the salesgirl, waving to her. "Come on," I said to Lucille. "Let's go to Hinkely's and have a cup of coffee and a cheese Danish. That'll perk you up, and I'm starving."

CHAPTER 26

Giacomo

GIACOMO AND ANGELICA HAD WALKED home from church the Sunday before Lucille's wedding. Giacomo's feet ached, and he slipped into his old, worn *pantofole* and turned on the radio. He was listening to music while reading the Sunday newspaper but decided to keep Angelica company as she had been in the kitchen since early morning, only taking time off for Mass. Now she went back to preparing a big dinner. A large pot of sauce bubbled gently on the stove, and a huge pasta pot was set in back of that burner with salted water to boil. Yesterday she'd made the pronouncement to Giacomo that she hadn't made stuffed ravioli or homemade fettuccine in a long time. So while Jack entertained Elena, Pina, whose husband was traveling in Europe, helped their mother. "Go see what I've done with our bedroom," she said.

Giacomo took one look in the bedroom and thought it had been invaded by ghosts. The room was covered over in white linen sheets, and long strands of wide noodles were draped over every available space to dry.

He knew he should retire once more to the living room but felt badly about leaving Angelica working. In the kitchen on top of every flat surface were tins for making ravioli. She made the pasta dough and lined tray after tray with square ravioli and filled the bottom of each with a scoop of ground meat or a combination of whipped ricotta and fresh grated *parmigiano* cheese. To this mixture she always added a dash of *noce moscato*, nutmeg, then covered these and pressed the sides, cutting off the excess dough to be re-worked for the next tin. Once Angelica had marshaled all of the family into a troop while she gave orders like the queen bee, Giacomo took one look at Marcella and they both skipped out, leaving Jack to play with Elena, and Pina and Valentina to be the worker bees.

To the soft strains of symphony music, Marcella initiated the conversation. "You know, Papa, I appreciate the beautiful life you have given me—us. Not everyone gets love and protection. I see the beggar girls, the street walkers, prostituting themselves. Papa, are you listening?"

"Of course I am," he said and folded a newspaper page.

"What a terrible thing for a woman to have to sell her body, to lose her soul and become degraded in such a fashion."

Giacomo thought of the sing-song girls of China and all the brothels he'd frequented before he'd fallen in love with Lian. He put down the paper. "What brought this on? Are you saying life is precious, but precarious, and we should learn to cherish the now, the present?"

"Life should be treasured. We should cherish the now," Marcella agreed and picked up a photograph from the mantel. "Look at this photograph with Mamma. You remember that windy day on Staten Island—"

"Many years ago."

"She's leaning into your chest, and the top of her head barely reaches your shoulder—our histories lie beneath us, difficult to reach, as if buried under an avalanche of snow."

"What you're saying is that I had a past you never knew I had." Giacomo ran his hands through his hair.

"Something like that."

"You think you know a person, but you really never do. Your mother's mother always said you have to eat nine dishes of salt to know someone. Can you eat nine dishes of salt?"

"What was Nonna Rosalia like?" Marcella asked.

"Strong like you, but shorter. And resilient."

"The way you'd like me to be."

"You are."

"Where's the proof of that?"

"You're going to be in Bao's wedding party. Proof enough?"

"You never call him my brother. You always say his name."

"I don't call him my son either. It's a touchy subject. Your brother Jack is still young and, although he seems to be accepting of it, might feel slighted. This doesn't mean I care any less for Bao. Why is it, do you think, that we are so companionable and I can talk to you?"

"For the same reason I can tell you serious things more than Mamma. She agonizes over everything. You can take or leave, keep or shirk. Besides, Mamma has a little bit of a jealous streak, like Val, that you don't have, and neither do I. Maybe not jealous, but rather possessiveness."

"So easy to speak with you," Giacomo said. "If only I could have talked to Pina this way before she married. Had I been able to maybe things wouldn't have gone the way they did, and she might not have married Bruno."

"Takes two sides, Papa. Pina couldn't voice to her own shadow what she felt back then. Mamma blames you for that, but don't beat yourself up. Pina consented. And now she's blessed with Elena, chunky thighs and puffy cheeks. So cute."

"I take responsibility for that marriage. It wasn't made in heaven. But Pina isn't you. She needed a nest of her own but wasn't willing to work for it to be a pleasant one. I thought Bruno was a different man—"

"Just because he has the same blood doesn't make him the man you are."

"With all the many people in the world, it will always come down to one man and one woman, but they have to make it work," he said, his wise, smooth voice warm as a covering shawl.

"How do you find the one?" Marcella asked.

"Valentina thought she loved that awful Vic. Attraction doesn't always mean love."

"Not everyone can have a love story like yours and Mamma's. How do you know when the one found is truly the one? I don't think being struck by lightning is going to work for me."

"I'm not rich, but I have wealth beyond compare," Giacomo said. "I've been blessed with not one but two great loves. Not to take away from your mother, but I did love before her. Your mother and I were destined for one another. Lian was too ethereal for this earth. She belongs in that other realm, whatever it is."

"I thought you'd never speak of her to me for fear of hurting Mamma."

"Lian," he said quietly.

"Bao said it means 'lotus flower.'"

"Why hadn't I remembered that? I know you'd never cause your mother pain. I have you and the family. Even though Pina resents me less now, I'm praying she'll come back into the fold and embrace me once more."

It was then that Marcella broached the subject of Lucille, her father, and the fact that he was adamantly against the wedding and wasn't going to walk Lucille down the aisle.

"A girl dreams of that, Papa, from the time she's little and goes from the princess stage to wondering who she'll marry when she grows up. I stuck my neck out and said you'd escort her in church if her father really won't. You will, won't you?"

Giacomo studied his daughter for a long time. "Lucille grew up in this house. She's like another child. I can't believe her father would refuse, although I understand his prejudice. Should I speak to him?"

"Heavens no. You've no idea what that man calls you or how he thinks."

"Sticks and stones," Giacomo said.

"He has a murderous temper. Don't do it. You can't reason with someone like him."

"Are you certain?"

"Ask Lucille yourself."

"If you say so. Now that she's decided to tie her fate with Bao—" Giacomo hesitated. "But of course, I'll do it. Did he tell her about us? Me?"

"He did. We spoke of it while we were trying on dresses. Have you seen how adoringly they look at each other? Or is it only me who notices?"

"Ah, my Marcella *bella*, you've got a lot to figure out on your own about the fact that your relationship with him was eclipsed."

"I was heartbroken and thought I'd never really ever recover. Lake George was the best cure for me."

⌒⟡⌒

THE DOORBELL RANG AND THERE stood the happy couple looking so in love, Giacomo wondered how blind Marcella could have been not to have seen it right from the beginning. They gathered in the living room and then as if on command, one by one the others vacated the space, leaving Giacomo with Lucille.

When the two of them came marching arm in arm into the kitchen for dinner, everyone gathered that the deed was done, and it looked as if they were already practicing for a walk down the church aisle. Marcella and Valentina served the meal, so that Pina and Angelica could relax and everyone felt quite content. Jack put Elena to bed and arrived last to the table, proclaiming the ravioli were the best he'd ever tasted.

After the delicious dinner everyone sat talking, and although the atmosphere seemed gay, Giacomo knew Lucille was hiding her sadness, wishing her own family could be as elated for her.

Everyone was surprised when the doorbell rang. Jack ran down to see who it was. When they heard a booming Texas drawl, Marcella blanched as white as her mother's bleached and starched tablecloth, and Giacomo wondered what his "Marcella *bella*" had gotten herself into this time. She tore out of the room as if followed by an incendiary torch and dashed downstairs, leaving them all quite in shock.

CHAPTER 27

Marcella

JACK OPENED THE DOOR, AND I saw Al and mouthed "hello." I quietly shut the door. "Jack, this is Al," I said. "Let's go." Al tried to kiss me, but I dodged, putting a finger over my lips and taking his hand to follow me upstairs.

I faced the sitting group, returning with a huge, broad-shouldered man with tousled, tawny hair who now filled the doorway. "Mamma, Papa, Val, Bao, Lucille—this is Al. From Texas."

In his boisterous twang, he said, "I'm sure Marcella has told you about us—our meeting in Lake George and all."

Right then I thought I'd faint from the closeness in the room, his very personage pressing against my side, and the odor of Mamma's pork sauce.

Val piped in and said, "Oh hi, Al. Actually, things have been a little up in the air over Lucille and Bao's fast-approaching wedding. Welcome. Marcella did mention you'd be arriving. She just didn't seem to know when to expect you."

Nice recovery, Val. I took the ring from my pocket and slipped it on my finger.

"A wedding is such a happy occasion. I was wondering if—" he began, and I could swear he was about to say, "We could make it a double ceremony," when I accidentally on purpose stepped on his foot.

"Ouch. What was that for, darlin'?"

"I'm so sorry. Here, Al. Come sit next to my sister, Val," I said, pulling out my chair. With shock I realized she was all agog over his broad shoulders and boyish grin. How was this possible? She was supposed to be getting me out of a raw situation.

Sure enough, without missing a beat, Mamma, ever diligent, saw my left hand all sparkling as I pulled out the chair. She grabbed my hand, miraculously without twisting it off.

"*Che cosa é questo?*" she nearly shrieked.

"*Niente. Mi fai spiegare, per favore.*" This I eked out like a mouse trying to extricate itself from a trap where it had glutted on a hunk of cheese, all the while straining to free my hand from her claw-like grip.

"Yes," she pronounced, dragging the word through her clenched teeth. "Do explain."

Mamma all but pulled my arm out of its socket as we left the room, everyone nattering at once.

When we were alone, Mamma asked me what the meaning of this secret engagement was all about, and I could barely look at her because I was so embarrassed. She began to grill me like a piece of raw meat on a barbeque. I divulged that Al had taken certain liberties with me, and I couldn't stop him, so I thought I had to marry him.

"Couldn't or wouldn't?" Mamma asked, her arms crossed and her foot tapping.

"Mamma, he's a film producer, and he's going to take me to Hollywood and—"

Her open-handed slap felt as if she'd socked me. "Forgive me," I cried, "but it's my life and what I want."

She handed me her handkerchief and pronounced my sentence. "You will never step foot in this house again if you marry him to become a harlot in Hollywood."

"You mean starlet, Mamma?"

"It will kill your father."

We came back into the kitchen, Mamma wearing a defeated expression. Lucille, Bao, and Jack excused themselves and went downstairs. *Aha!* I thought. *Rats deserting my sinking ship.* Al and I spent the next hour in sheer torture. Not even the Inquisition could hold a candle to the barrage of accusing questions I had to fend off. How could Mamma,

Papa, and Val all hurl questions that seemed perfectly innocent to Al's untutored ear but that I identified as having barbed innuendos?

As Al devoured two helpings of Mamma's leftovers along with half a loaf of seeded Italian bread and quaffed a liter of Papa's red wine, he managed to explain the reason for his visit, without, bless his heart, ever mentioning the fact of our engagement, holding true to his promise to ask my father for my hand before announcing our betrothal.

"I'm here to escort Miss Marcella to the wedding, of course, but I'll need to speak to you in private, Sir."

Everyone seemed to breathe out a collective sigh of relief.

The wine did the trick, and the next thing I knew, our guest was being escorted—half-carried—by Papa and Jack to Jack's room for a Sunday *pisolino*, a siesta.

"Jack, my sweet, kind, lovely brother, I hope you don't mind sharing your room with a cowboy."

"Sure, but it'll cost you. Does he snore?"

"How would I know?" I said and cuffed him one on the back of the head.

⁓

TWO DAYS BEFORE BAO AND Lucille's wedding, Mamma and I were in the kitchen starting to assemble all the things we'd need to make *pizza rustica*. My guest, Al, was bunking in with Jack, who somehow marveled each time the Texan opened his mouth to tell him about life on the open range.

To Mamma's credit, she never mentioned the guest occupying the spare bed in Jack's room as we proceeded to arrange the necessary ingredients for our work, although she made a remark about me having to return his gift. But I had full intention of wearing the ring to complete my outfit for Lucille's wedding.

As adept as Mamma was at switching a subject midbreath, I pulled a cutie on her and launched into a discussion of *pizza rustica*. "Mamma, you changed the recipe from last year. How will I ever learn to make it?"

"I make it differently every time depending on what I have, what I buy, and what's available."

"What're you using this year?"

"Can't you see? We have cooked ham, *prosciutto, Genoa salami,* hot and sweet *soprassata* from your father's friend in Little Italy, *provolone,* Swiss cheese, *ricotta, mozzarella,* grated *parmigiano,* and some slivers of *pecorino,* eggs, sugar, and black fresh-ground pepper."

"And for the crust?" I asked.

"I make it sweet, almost like for a *crostata.* Then I let it rest in the fridge. When it's set, it's easier to work with the *matterello* afterward."

"Which rolling pin? You have three sizes. I love the long one that fits in the holes underneath the table. How long is it, anyway?"

"Three meters," she said.

"But how much of each ingredient for the crust?"

"Al' occhio."

"'By eye' is not a valid measurement. People always ask me for your recipes, and when I give them they say, 'Don't you measure?' And I'm stuck. They think I don't really want to tell them, that it's some Sicilian secret you won't part with."

"That's why they'll never make great cooks or bakers," Mamma said.

"I'd add too much cheese—I'm a rat for cheese. How do you make the crust?"

"Weren't you watching Pina when she made it for Easter?"

"Sifted flour."

"*Doppio OO* is what we called it in Sicily."

"Some sugar, a whole egg, and a *tuorlo.*"

"Yes, it's important not to use two whole eggs," Mamma said. "A yolk from one and a whole egg. How much sugar?"

"About one-third of a cup?" I said, seeking confirmation.

"Calumet baking powder?"

"A teaspoon?"

"What else?" Mamma asked.

"A dash of salt, soft butter, and ice-cold water."

"There, see—you paid attention. After you prepare it, you let it rest in the *frigo* for half an hour or more. Easier to roll out."

As I watched Mamma, the battering fuss of her hands seemed to be taking out anger as they punched through the dough. She had something on her mind, and I'd soon find out what it was. After we got everything mixed and the dough resting in the fridge, we sat down and had a cup of coffee.

"Mamma, no one can say where their destiny will lead, where the paths of life will take them. I feel Gianni betrayed me, taking his brothers' side."

"Did you ever possibly think he was bragging about you? Or had to defend himself to them? Maybe he was surprised and shocked that an outgoing girl like you felt for him the way he feels for you? I never dreamed I'd fall in love with Papa and come to live in America."

"It's so confusing."

"Question all you want, but unless it's revealed to your heart, you'll never know. Time, nothing but time, brings answers to all you seek. Trust your soul." She wiped her hands.

"How can I when I make mistake after mistake? How could I have thought I'd fallen in love with Bao?"

"There's a close affinity of spirit with Bao because the blood that flows in both of you is your father's. When your father walked into our shop in Sicily, I wasn't supposed to be there. It was meant to happen. My mother always said, 'These things are planned in Heaven before you're even born.' But what about Al?"

A noise—I thought a frog croaked in my throat. "I don't know, Mamma. We met in Lake George. He's crazy about me." I held out my hand and looked at the glittering ring. "He gave me this as I was getting on the train to come back home."

This time she got a good look at the diamond and asked, "How large is that? It seems bigger than the ones Mr. Blitzer showed me."

"Three carats. 'D flawless,' whatever that means. He ordered it from Tiffany's and they delivered it to him in Lake George."

"I'm not impressed," she said. "Money can buy things, but it's not the only important thing in this world. Perhaps your womanly hormones were dictating a physical attraction, a feeling of curiosity—even lustful— but not love. Maybe it's attraction, bouncing off delusion or unrequited love. Some things even you can't confide in your dear Papa. Al was available, charming, and he appealed to you, made you feel special and like a woman, not a girl."

"How is it possible I keep messing up Heaven's divine arrangements for me? How can you know all this? It wouldn't be the worst thing if I settled for a man of means."

"From Texas? You'd actually consider living there?"

"I considered China, didn't I?"

"Bao," she said. "It never would have come to that."

"Maybe we'll spend half the time in California when he's working, and half in Arizona for the dry heat and for his arthritis."

"Arizona. That's far west. How much would he be able to work? Your sister said he was sick with a form of crippling arthritis. Could you see that huge man doubled over and in a wheelchair? Can you picture little you dragging him from chair to bed?"

"I haven't said 'yes.' He's going to talk to Papa."

"If he does, your Papa's going to introduce him to Carlo Albano, who speaks Texan with an automatic weapon."

"Mamma, you can't be serious."

"Don't ever doubt it. All those movies have gone to your head. Like that one with the riveter and the—"

"*The Hot Heiress*," I said, mooning. "And *Delicious.*" I started swaying and singing "You're So Delicious," but Mamma cut me short.

"You're practically swooning. It's not real life. You may find some universal truths in all those fictions you read, but that's not everything. What was the last one you read?"

"*A Farewell to Arms*. Beautiful but sad."

"Like life." All of a sudden, Mamma was speaking Italian. "I've lived. Life is a supreme master and teacher."

"You're furious with me."

"I've made my mistakes, but mine were all with one man—Papa. Not true—also with my father. His was a jealous, possessive kind of love. Your Papa loves with all his heart but understands you have to leave someday. You need to be allowed to make your own mistakes—that's how we learn and develop, make progress in our maturity. I had to accept the fact that your Papa profoundly loved another woman before me. How do you think that made me feel? I thought of myself as second best, a matter of his needing a wife, not choosing me as a lover."

"That was way before you. He was lonely in a foreign country," I said, realizing that she wasn't just interjecting a phrase here and there but having a complete conversation in her birth language.

She wheeled around. "Don't make excuses for the man I married. I know him as I breathe, as if he is the skin over my bones. He was young, hot-blooded, and sowing his wild oats, only he never dreamed he'd actually fall in love with—"

She hesitated, and in that slight passage of time, I understood how much it had cost her to accept another woman in Papa's life.

"Lian," she said finally. "I commune with her spirit sometimes. Did you know that?"

I must've looked mentally deficient when I breathed, "Mamma—"

"Close your mouth. In time and through prayer, and yes, even arguments over a dead woman, I persevered and in a sense won your father's heart with my tenacious and fierce love. In some ways, I think I must be like her."

I didn't know what else to say. After a time, I said, "You hardly ever speak Italian anymore."

She hesitated and switched back to English. "That's because I'm now American. I passed the test, and I'm proud."

"But doesn't being married to Papa, who has citizenship, make you American automatically?"

"You can understand, no? I wanted this for myself."

"You have no desire to go back to Sicily?"

"My life is here." Mamma sighed.

"I made you worry about me and made you sad. I'm so sorry."

"A mother's love is vast like the ocean, limitless like the sky." She hugged me as best she could, trying not to get flour all over my green sweater.

Mamma loved me unconditionally and would always forgive me even when I upset her.

She washed her hands, and I handed her a towel. "You'll find your great love if you listen to your heart and don't put pride above all else. Your voyage will lead you—I think even a backward journey is sometimes in store for us. Who can say? Not the dark of night nor the mountains high will be an obstacle to you. Your heart will soar when you realize a promise of what's to come, and maybe it's already a kernel within you. When Gianni looks at you—even now after you broke not only that dish but his heart time and again, even after all this time has passed—can't you see it, or are you being stubborn, foolish, afraid?"

"Why do you keep harping on Gianni? What am I afraid of?"

She hung the towel on the oven door. "Of life and of falling in love—it's demanding. It means putting someone else first, above yourself, your feelings, and your wants—above all else. Until you learn that great lesson, *figlia bella*, you'll never understand what love is. There's much more than liking a person for his good looks—you must fall in love for serious reasons."

"I know."

"You don't. You've got your pretty head in the clouds. It's the inside of a person that matters."

"I get that, Mamma, I do. But romance is important, too, isn't it?"

"Absolutely not. I would venture to say all that romantic business lasts only a little time before you settle into a real *collegamento*."

"Liaison?"

"Precisely," Mamma said. "Don't distract me when I want to tell you something significant—even vital—to a marriage."

"What's that?

"Both parties that enter into a marriage don't necessarily love equally. The dynamics of marriage are constantly changing. At times, I worship your father, but he's involved in so many things, he doesn't even notice. Friendship in a relationship is more important than all those "Loop the Loop" feelings—they don't last—that's a Coney Island attraction, nothing more. You need somebody with character, somebody who can be faithful, true, somebody who's honest and works hard, who'll love you and support you the way you should be taken care of. Why are you so flighty? Half the time you're doing aerial acrobatics like that plane in the open air field show in Staten Island we saw last year."

"Why didn't you want Pina to marry Bruno?"

"Changing the subject again? I'll allow this. She didn't love him, or have respect for him—she didn't even like him. More detrimental was that he didn't care for her enough to be the kind of man she needed. Pina was a convenience. Because she was younger, he thought he could mold her. You can't change a person. Never think you can. That's the most common mistake people make. A loveless marriage is a curse for both."

"I'm surprised you didn't say, 'And never fall in love with teeth or hair,' like you usually do."

Mamma looked wistfully out of the window. "And then she had Elena. She had no place to run. That's a different kind of love that binds two people for eternity."

"You and Papa?"

"Your Papa and I disagree on many things—it's only love that sees us through. A thunderbolt, the minute he walked in to buy some *vino*.

That's destiny. I wasn't supposed to be there. We were married in thirty-three days, the same number as the age of Christ."

"How romantic."

"Not if you'd seen my father's reaction, but we're not going into that now." She took me by the shoulders and said, "I truly don't think you love Al. He may be a good person, fascinating in his way, even charming, rich, and pleasant, but he's not for you. Give him back his ring and tell him to save it for a girl who'll regard him as special. He's not that to you."

"Why not? Why can't he be the one?" I asked.

"Because he's not Gianni."

"Gianni isn't the only man in all of New York state!"

"Go straighten your room and dust the living room, *per cortesia*," she said.

"Why do you think Gianni's so right for me?"

"He is goodness personified and he adores you. Simple as that."

"I don't feel that way about him."

"Maybe not now, but when you discover the key to Gianni's heart and soul, you will. Then your heart will wrench loose from your body to join his, and your souls will spark and unite."

I hated to disagree with Mamma because she sounded so sure, but I was tempted to say, "I doubt it." Although how could I? Hadn't she just drawn him on paper, cut him out, and made him the most perfect paper doll?

⸻⚜⸻

LUCILLE AND BAO CAME OVER again for dinner. I started to wonder if this was going to be a regular thing. Papa was so formal, it made me want to weep—the integrity of the man, taking on the responsibility of another man's daughter.

Bao came into the kitchen with Mamma, Val, and me. Jack was off to Pina's to help her move some furniture around with the help of Al's brute force, and I wondered how long that would last. Was Mamma right? Was Val? Would I be tending a sick man the rest of my days? In the depths of my core, I knew I could never be happy if I had to nurse him. Did that make me shallow or realistic?

Papa had asked for a few minutes alone with Lucille to tell her once more that he'd be honored to walk her down the aisle, but he wanted to make sure she'd have no regrets. I've never seen anything like it. Lucille walked into the kitchen holding Papa's hand, her face radiant through tears. She was another sister in so many ways—adoring Papa, loving Bao.

⸙

THE NEXT TWO DAYS FLEW by, and then I was donning a long-sleeved dress. I'd been selected by my dearest friend to be the maid of honor at her wedding to Bao, who was more than a brother—he'd become my dear friend. What I'd felt for him, Papa said, was that invisible red thread. It had drawn Bao back to Papa, and for this, both Bao and my father were eternally thankful. It shone in the light that emanated from their eyes.

The very night before the wedding, I felt like I was in a haze after dinner as I sat on the porch reminiscing. Al and Jack had gone to hit golf balls. Who knew Jack could hold a golf club? I was happy for the time alone and let my mind wander past summer moments spent in Gardiner, at home in Brooklyn, at Point Lookout, in Staten Island, and in Manhattan. I'd been so young. Closing my eyes, it's like I could walk around and smell the perfumes and odors. I let my hands, like a blind person, run over items in the rooms I'd shared with Valentina, in the basement with Lucille, in the shed with Gianni.

This brought me up short, and all of a sudden I was giving over to everything in me that I'd ever seen or heard, things so stored in my memory I couldn't believe the wealth of material that started pouring through the files of my mind. I listened, freely associating names, dates, descriptions, anything at all I could recall, and I had no power over it, like a wayfarer in a dream—the mind has a mind of its own.

It was not just me, myself, and I that my mind hit upon—oh no. I began to see things clearly. I understood why my mother loved Gianni like a son, almost as much as Jack, and even if Jack was a tiny bit miffed by it, he cared for Gianni like a brother. Jack got along with everyone. That's why he hit it off with Al. Mamma certainly didn't feel that way about the big guy. I pictured Gianni always sweet with Mamma, breaking off a piece of bread and dunking it in her sauce; she playfully hitting his arm, shooing him away with no real intent. The truth was she never minded with Gianni but would get angry if anyone else ever dared. After one such kitchen theft, Gianni even pinched Mamma's cheek in thanks and she giggled like a girl. Papa laughed, saying he could never get away with that.

When Jack approached the pot, Mamma shooed him away and took the dish right out of his hands. "Later," she'd said, "at the table."

"Gee, Mamma," Jack said, giving the offended look of a caught criminal. "You'd think he was your son."

Mamma wheeled about on him and said, "He is! That boy was raised without a mother—it's the least someone can do for him, give him a little mothering. God knows his sisters-in-law are all too busy raising their own broods. It doesn't mean I love you less." So that's how it was. Mamma, of the big heart, opening it up wide enough for Gianni and also for Bao, her husband's lover's son—how incredibly generous was that? How grand is a mother's heart? Could I ever hope to aspire to be like Mamma, even minimally?

CHAPTER 28

Giacomo

GIACOMO THOUGHT BACK TO THE night when Al had arrived, and he had watched Marcella tear out of the kitchen and dart downstairs. Val shrugged her shoulders, but Giacomo had the feeling that she knew exactly what was happening. And he was right.

Apparently, Giacomo was being barraged from all angles. Angelica told him that Al wanted to ask for Marcella's hand, so every time he cornered Giacomo, he'd found a quick escape. Al had already given her a big, expensive ring, which she wore sometimes but not always, which gave Giacomo the distinct feeling she wasn't at all sure she wanted him. *What is he doing in our home?* Giacomo wondered. Why had Marcella invited Al, and what was the vixen playing at?

Jack told Giacomo that Al was the nicest guy, who showed him his gun and how to clean it, promising that he'd take Jack target shooting just as soon as it was feasible. *Feasible!* Giacomo thought. *He could kill everyone in the house if we don't agree to the marriage*, which still, somehow was never mentioned.

Valentina, on the other hand, told Giacomo how insistent the cowboy was, and he'd never give up chasing Marcella, even though he was sick and would be riddled with some kind of ferocious arthritis that would eat and deform his body. She informed Giacomo of her opinion, which was that as nice as Al was, Giacomo should unleash a bloodhound on him, namely *compare* Carlo. Giacomo asked Valentina if she was serious. She shrugged her shoulders.

Giacomo tossed Valentina's words over and over in his mind, then told Angelica, who sat at the bedroom vanity, brushing her hair. "Al won't give up easily, but Carlo isn't the one who should talk to him, and by that I mean persuade him in a way he'll want to run back to Texas as soon as possible. That remains a job for our Marcella."

⌐⌐✿⌐⌐

THE HOUSE HAD BEEN FRAUGHT with excitement, rather emotional tension, because of Lucille's father refusing to walk her down the aisle and Giacomo being her choice for his replacement, because even her cowardly brothers wouldn't stand up to their father and step in for him.

Up until now Giacomo hadn't had a moment to discuss the matter of Al with Marcella. Finally, he cornered her.

"Oh, Papa." When she began like this, he knew there was going to be a yarn long enough to knit a sweater, and could put him to sleep if he wasn't diligent.

She asked her father to walk her to the bakery on Thirteenth Avenue.

On the downhill stretch of the street, Marcella reached for her father's hand and said, "Papa, I'm not sure how this is going to work, but there's a possibility that Al can foster my career in California."

Giacomo dropped her hand and faced her.

"What career? Salesgirl? Why so far?"

"Singing in movies. It's what I've always wanted. A movie set isn't like a nightclub, so you can't object, and I'd be protected because he'd be my husband, which would make it all above board."

"You can sing to your children, at your friends' weddings, in the shower. Isn't that enough? Must you flaunt yourself on the silver screen and embarrass or humiliate your family? And why would you marry a man you hardly know?"

"Papa, you married Mamma in thirty-three days. You hardly knew her," she said.

"I loved her instantly. I love her still. And she loved me. It was a lightning strike. You do not care for this man, and you certainly don't love him."

"How can you say that?"

"Because it's true. Look into your heart."

"I'm not sure what I feel for him, but I could learn to love him," Marcella said, sounding sensible, as if trying on Oxford lace-up shoes.

"No, you'll learn nursing and attend him as your patient. This man is sick with a debilitating illness. If you loved him, I'd give you my blessing. You don't. Have you heard yourself? You're talking about a possible career. If you loved him, you'd be moon-eyed about your upcoming marriage."

For Marcella, it was more wounding than the slap from her mother.

She leaned her head on Giacomo's shoulder, and he handed Marcella his handkerchief.

CHAPTER 29

Marcella

THE CHURCH WEDDING WAS SIMPLE and an evening service without a Mass. I sang the *Ave Maria* and saw my mother's shoulders quake and knew she was crying. In her heart, Mamma never wanted me to have a singing career—was that why she was upset, knowing how much I'd wanted it? Or was it because she'd wished me to be the bride, and the groom another? Maybe it was for a simpler reason—she always cried when she heard the *Ave Maria*.

⚜

AT SIRICO'S CATERING, THE RECEPTION hall was filled to the gills with flowers, music, and all kinds of antipasto on trays, being served by waiters in tails and white gloves to the gathered attendees. I was peeking behind a curtain watching the activity while the last photographs were being taken of the pretty bride and the gorgeous groom.

Soon the band struck up a song that was the signal for us to march in as couples, the groomsmen and bridesmaids and me, the maid of honor, with Jack, who'd shot up to Papa's shoulder, as my partner and the best man. We formed a tunnel into which the newly married couple walked, and everyone applauded. Their wedding song, "Dancing in the Dark," began to play, and Lucille handed me her bouquet, which I placed on the dais by her place in the center.

After the newly wedded couple danced, Papa exchanged places with Bao, and I took the bride's place with him. As we twirled around the dance floor, there was only one person in the room of any consequence for me, and Gianni's eyes were fastened on mine.

Al was seated at a table of young people because Jack and I were seated on the dais with the rest of the wedding party. I spotted Gianni, milling about with the other guests, and I was pleased as punch to be sporting my big diamond ring. I took off my gloves, left them near my bouquet, and pretended to be walking toward Al's table, when in reality I knew I'd run smack dab into Gianni's shoulder in my hurry. Why had I worn it? I knew Gianni would be there. Was it to shove the knife in a little deeper? Because that's the look he gave me when he saw it.

He stuttered and offered me his congratulations, but a minute later, I got my comeuppance, when at Gianni's side a skittish little thing in powder pink appeared.

"This is my fiancée, Oriana Grandine," he said, not a drop of smugness in his voice.

It took me a moment to stop reeling and to place the name, but then I remembered his sister-in-law Beatrice's maiden name and understood this was her sister—Beatrice was married to Gianni's brother, Giuseppe.

"So now it'll be two brothers married to two sisters," I said and felt the breath leave my body as I stood quaking. "Congrats," I called over my shoulder as I all but ran to Al's table.

I was taken aback, and knowing I'd behaved in a cool manner— barely civil, much less cordial—couldn't wait to get to Al.

"What's the matter, sugar plum? Looks like you've seen a ghost," he said, standing.

"No, only Oriana."

"Who?"

"A timid nurse with mousy brown hair."

After a waltz with Al, I did an about face and felt like a bolt shot through me as I returned to the dais, heart pounding, the blood in my temples thrumming. *God forgive me, what a fool I've been and what a mess I've made.* Approaching my seat, I murmured to myself, "I still have intense feelings for Gianni."

"What did you say?" Jack looked up at me.

I shook my head, and a truant tear rolled down my cheek.

"Are you crying?" Jack asked, amazed.

"It's nothing. I twisted my ankle coming back to the dais."

"You didn't. You're upset. What is it?"

"Leave it for now, Jack, please." I sat down next to him.

Everyone ate, and all around me I heard compliments about the wonderful food. I pushed the food around on my plate but couldn't eat a bite.

I saw Lucille get up to go to the ladies' room, and I followed her.

When she came out of the stall, I slammed the door and said, "Why did you invite Gianni with that—"

"I didn't. I invited Gianni with an escort. He brought her. What could I do?"

"He introduced her as his fiancée. Are they engaged?"

"Aren't you?"

"Heavens, no!"

"You're wearing Al's engagement ring."

"I'm simply wearing a ring. I never said I'd marry him." Looking in the gilded mirror, Lucille fluffed her hair and adjusted her veil.

"A ring? That just happens to be a huge Tiffany diamond betrothal ring."

I walked over to the sink and blotted my flaming cheeks with a wet paper towel, as if that would wash away my anger and quell the passion.

"I'm sorry," she said. "It was a tactical error to wear it if you still care for him, which you swore to me you didn't. Remember?" She patted my cheek.

"I've made a huge mistake." I flicked away a tear. "He's the only one. I'm in love with Gianni. I know it now."

"What are you saying? Marcella, look what you've done." Lucille shook her head.

She opened the door, picked up her train, and walked out.

I sat on one of the burgundy velvet stools and faced myself in the mirror. *What have you done, you haughty girl?*

<hr>

AFTER I DON'T KNOW HOW long or how many unwanted caresses and dances with Al, the music finally stopped and the announcement came that the bridal bouquet toss was about to commence. I no more wanted to be with a bunch of eager females than I wanted to walk to the guillotine. I stood toward the back of the cache of women. There was a drumroll and a countdown of three, and then I was pushed and knocked over by Oriana, who snatched the bridal bouquet from my hands, which had shot up more to protect my face than out of a desire to catch it.

Shocked and dismayed at how this irksome little girl had bested me, I fled the scene and went outside to cry my eyes out. I realized I'd never stopped caring for Gianni and always thought one day he'd become the father of my children because of his goodness, his gentle eyes, and his kind-hearted nature. Suddenly I knew that everything until now had been one infatuation after the other and that Gianni belonged with me.

I dried my tears and told myself to take my courage into my two hands and march right back in there and face the music. I went back inside and stopped by the band, congratulating the leader on his great music and choice of songs. I leaned in and whispered something in his ear. Then I did the boldest thing I had ever done in my life. I walked with determination toward Gianni's table and asked him for the next dance.

Oriana's mouth dropped, and Gianni suppressed a smile as I grabbed his hand and led him to the dance floor. I can't remember the song that was ending, but the song that began to play for us was an old favorite, "It Had to Be You," and Gianni held me just a little too tightly for a man engaged to another woman—and for a woman wearing another man's bauble on her left hand, I did the same. I smiled my perfect smile that Gianni adored, dimples at the corners of my mouth, and for him alone.

At one point he cracked a joke, and I tossed my head back to expose my neck in a move that was at once inviting and suggestive. I can honestly say I've never done that before or with anyone in my life. At the same time, I fluttered my eyelashes, and I can guarantee it wasn't due to the smoke in the air. I moved in closer, and my left hand slid from his back to his neck, but only for a few seconds. I wasn't brave enough to keep hold of him in that embrace. I can't remember much of what was said, but his lips brushed my hair and ear and I felt his hot breath, and I prayed Oriana Grandine would soon be history, but there was no leaving this up to fate. I stepped up my unexpected flirtatious program. When the dance was over, I stood a few seconds too long with my hand in his and then squeezed it, turned, and left him standing there on the dance floor as I looked for my escort, who had been dancing with Valentina.

Lucille had asked me to sing a few songs, but I had demurred, saying it was her day. In a flash I changed my mind, walked over to the bandleader for a second time, and asked him to play something for me— in fact, two songs for me to sing: "You Made Me Love You" and "I Can't Give You Anything but Love."

I stood in back of the microphone and adjusted it, waited until I'd connected with the object of my desire and sang for him.

When the reception party started to break up, I walked out of the hall holding Al's arm, but he wasn't pleased with me by any means or the fact that I had danced with Gianni, whom he now gathered wasn't my adopted brother.

"You asked him to dance. You're an outrageous flirt," Al said, hurt and shock registering in his voice. "And you sang those songs looking at him, not me."

"Please don't make a scene here. We'll talk at home," I said and ushered him out into the night and our awaiting ride. The doors of the reception hall had been flung open so the crowd of people could exit without being trampled. Two of the banquet hall owners were at the doors greeting people and handing out carnations and business cards, hoping to get some responses.

The minute we hit the fresh night air, the realization also hit me that I would now have to tell Al, but the timing was off. How could I? I was exactly what Bao had said I was and had once written on a restaurant paper napkin and handed to me: 主要要怨自己，自討苦吃. *Your own worst enemy.* He took back the paper and was going to rip it up, but it was too late, I was stunned and took the paper back. I had kept that scrap of paper in my diary and that night I looked at it when I got into bed and propped my diary on my bent knees. Then I read over the words I'd written about keeping Gianni in the pocket of my heart.

The night of Lucille and Bao's wedding, I wrote something new in my diary, and when I'd finished I noticed that a little unsure niggling worm had creeped into my oh-so-positive feelings when I'd danced with Gianni. What if this time I wouldn't be able to pull him out of that pocket. What if he stayed there forever? To what end? Maybe to make me ache for him the way he had been aching for me all these years.

I closed the book and walked to the open window, pushed the curtain aside, and leaned out. I'd kept the man with whom I belonged at bay. I was stricken with the crucial mindfulness of what it's like to be human. My heart, every fiber of my being, understood how deeply I loved Gianni. The wind blew through me.

I had left my beaded purse on top of the dresser. I took out a piece of wedding cake to place under my pillow, hoping to dream of the man I wanted to marry, Gianni. I felt he belonged to me, not that timid little nurse that his sister-in-law was hurling at him every instant and who almost knocked my teeth out in order to wrench the bridal bouquet from my hands. *How could I have let her beat me out? I'm a foot taller, for Pete's sake, and I'm no giant!*

I glanced at Val as I sat on my bed and mulled over the things I'd seen at the wedding reception that made me yearn for the moment when I'd walk down the aisle to become Mrs. Gianni Simoni. The dais had been set with glowing golden candles surrounded by lacy doilies. In the center were three floral arrangements of red roses and sprigs of fresh, tender eucalyptus—I recognized these because Mamma had it dried in the house along with some shafts of wheat, or money plants. They brought *fortuna.* Mamma told me the leaves are willowy, long and slender, before the tree grows to huge heights, and tisanes are made from this plant. There were other flowers, too, but Bao wouldn't hear of white, which, as I knew from Papa, was worn at funerals in China. Who would want a symbol of death on your wedding day? Even Lucille's dress was cream-colored, but I wondered if that was also a sign she was no longer a virgin. *Sour grapes, Marcella?*

Each place setting had a miniature picture of the bride and groom on a pack of stick matches. For wedding favors, I'd helped Lucille make the *bomboniere,* souvenirs with confetti. Bao had brought some fake Capodimonte look-alike ashtrays made in China to serve for this purpose. They apparently passed muster, because not even Mamma or Papa made a comment about them. Each ashtray was filled with a pink tulle sack that wrapped up five pieces of pink confetti and held a tiny cutting of parchment paper with the celebrants' names and the date in Chinese and English. These were tied with bows of a red satin ribbon. I'd asked Mamma why five and only five. She told me that her mother had said they stood for the five working days, Monday through Friday, for good luck.

I fell asleep and dreamed of making *bomboniere* wedding favors with Val in the kitchen. These would be for my wedding with confetti for the working days of the week. Into each tiny silk pouch, the color of a robin's egg, I dropped in five pieces of confetti and explained to Val why only five. I awoke in the middle of the night with the thought that Mamma always said dreaming numbers is good luck. It came to me the minute my feet hit the floor. I went to the bathroom and drank straight from the faucet. Then I padded barefoot down to the kitchen and cut a huge slice of Italian bread and buttered it, scooping on a tablespoon of grape jelly, like when I was a little girl and couldn't sleep or had wakened afraid of something—an impending storm, lightning, or the tree branches rattling the windows. What was I afraid of? I knew quite well as I ate my bread and jam sitting on the steps to the attic.

⌒⊂❊⊃⌒

I WAS UP EARLY, SHOWERED, dressed, and busily set the table. By the time everyone came into the kitchen, I was merrily making pancakes. Val asked for Mamma and Papa.

"Gone to Mass early," I said.

She gave me one of her looks.

"I doubt there'll be a need to contact Papa's friend," I said, hoping she got the inference. *To scare off dear Al,* for this was a task I'd have to face after breakfast.

She shook her head. She did her best to be attentive to, and at the same time distract, Al from me. Val poured his coffee, offered him milk and sugar, and asked Jack what he wanted as though she were a waitress in a diner used to taking everyone's requests at once, remembering everyone's order without writing it down, and delivering the food promptly and hot.

Jack looked at both of us and asked for eggs over easy, buttered toast and bacon. I happily complied—anything to keep me busy and forestall the moment when I'd have to face Al, the moment everyone left the kitchen.

I've never seen Val and Jack wolf down food so fast and vacate the premises, but I was ever so grateful and they knew it.

Alone in the quiet kitchen, I said, "I hate farewells, Al, but you can see it's not going to work out for us."

"What? After all that dancing hoochie-coochie last night? You're not being fair. Not giving us a try," he said. I watched his eyes follow my hands as I slipped the ring from my finger and tried to put it into his palm, but he closed it into a fist. "That damn Johnny's fault, but he already has a girl. Why, I never even got the chance to ask your father's permission," he said with a whiny tinge in his words.

"Al, remember when I left Lake George? You recall what I said to you at the train station? Maybe it was better if you kept the ring, but you insisted." I didn't let him get a word in or I knew I'd be thrown off-kilter. "I wasn't ready then, and I'm sure not ready now. There's too much party left in me. I can't settle down and know I'd made a mistake, and even more horrific, break your heart. I'm too flighty for a guy like you. You need a plain Jane sort of gal. Not a Brooklynite—we're much too close to Manhattan."

"But I—"

"Pack your bags, dear. Shall I help you?"

"What about me getting you an audition?" he asked as an objection.

"Dreams of Hollywood, stardom, singing, and dancing. If I'm honest, these are the things that interested me more than you. You're a fine man, and I hope you can forgive me someday. When Papa comes back from church, he'll drive you to the bus station." I took out my hanky and dabbed the corners of my dry eyes. I patted his huge hand, turned it over, and inserted the ring. I closed his hand.

"When you leave, I'll be going to Mass to pray you find the right girl, the one you deserve, because obviously this girl is the wrong girl for you." I almost hummed, but in truth, I did hope he'd find someone just as long as it wasn't me. I was out of that chair like a shot when I heard my parents' arrival downstairs, home from church.

⸛

WHAT HAPPENED NEXT WAS MY father bustling Al out the door. Al stood pat at the front door, still asking me to rethink our brief engagement and keep the ring, as he didn't want to take it. Though I hated to part with the beautiful sparkler, I insisted he'd need it for the right girl, the love he was going to find in Texas. A girl who, most likely, knew how to ride horses and rope steer. "Come with me for the car ride," he said, hat in hand.

"I must beg off. I've got a terrible headache that's made me very weepy, and I must go to church."

Mamma was so angry with me her flaring nostrils were practically smoking, so much so that she offered to go in my stead just not to face talking to me without Papa. Her eyes were murderous.

⟡

WHEN THEY'D RETURNED AND I'D come back from Mass with Valentina, Mamma said there would be a delay for lunch and told Valentina to excuse herself and Jack to go read some of his comics. Alone, facing Mamma and Papa without a single, solitary ally in the world in the very house in which I lived with my dismissed siblings, I felt extremely uncomfortable and mortified.

Mamma berated me and I took it. What else could I do? She told me how disgracefully I'd behaved.

Papa said, "To trifle with that poor man's heart was beneath you. He was truly captivated and allured by you, and you tread on his soul. Damn, you can be so charming when you want to be."

I agreed that my behavior was vile, but at the same time, I couldn't get Gianni out of my mind. My thoughts crowded in from all angles to form one huge question: How will I ever win him back?

After the balling out, I hopped up to help Mamma in the kitchen to show how contrite I was. Papa said he was going downstairs to the living room to get Val and Jack.

Mamma tied an apron around her waist and started to stir the sauce. The minute Papa was out of earshot, I confessed the truth of my intention to get Gianni back.

Mamma stopped twirling the wooden spoon, deliberately dropped it onto the holder, and turned to face me. "Do not think for one minute that you can enlist my help in your mad scheme. You've done so much damage at this point, Marcella. Don't you think you really should let it go?"

"Over my dead body. Mamma, please, I'm begging you."

"You created this mess. How will you clean it up?"

"How can you say that? If I can't curry favor from my own mother, who can I in this world?"

Val popped in and said, "You could try Signora di Maggio. She adores you and worships Gianni."

"Great idea. Thanks." I kissed Val and was ready to leave the room when Mamma grabbed my arm.

"Leave that woman alone. Don't you think you've upset her enough with your on-again, off-again toward Gianni?"

I was flabbergasted. "Mamma, how will I ever manage it without inside help?"

"You don't deserve help, and I'm beginning to think you don't deserve Gianni. He's too good for you."

She shoved me in a chair and walked out, visibly upset.

At this point, I'd never be able to hold lunch down, so I looked at my sister and said, "Val, please tell them I went to stay with Elaine in the city. I'll be back midweek when things settle down."

"Do you think that's wise after all the other incendiary bombs you've tossed their way this week?"

"No, I don't. But I don't know what else to do."

"I'll help you pack," she said and walked me upstairs.

⌘

I GAVE MY NAME TO the concierge of Elaine's building, a tall man with a moustache who always looked at visitors as if they were going to remove a potted palm and make off with it. Disregarding his distrust, I smiled and piped up with my name and that I was there to see Elaine Weiss.

I spent a nervous elevator ride up to the seventh floor wondering if she would let me stay with her. The next thing I knew, I was standing in front of her door about to knock when she opened it. "*Nu?*" she said, and that's all I needed. I dropped the suitcase and burst into tears. She took me into her arms. When I had calmed down, she took my suitcase, ushered me in, and sat me down on a chaise lounge. When I poured out my story, she looked at me with disgust written on her face and said one word: "*Feh!*" Elaine shook her head and then asked me, "Seriously? And this is supposed to be the dearest mother in the world? *A shandeh un a charpeh.* A shame and a disgrace."

Naturally, I went on the defensive, telling her I understood Mamma's position but felt hurt all the same.

"She'll get over it. You leaving and coming here is a statement of independence she won't like. But you're too strong to run away from things. Stick to your guns and go for the ring on the carousel if that's what you want. You may have to lean forward and off the horse a bit—are you sure?"

⌐◦ᶜ◉ᵔᵔ

MIDWEEK CAME SLOWLY. I CALLED twice, but Mamma refused to speak with me and passed the phone to Val or Jack. Val told me she was ever so glad I called to put Mamma's mind at peace. I told her I was staying at Elaine's and it was actually fun living the life of a New Yorker, getting up and having coffee and a bagel and dashing off to work, which was a hop, skip, and a jump in comparison to the trek that I made every day.

Val teased me, as always. "Make sure you keep your knickers on and legs crossed in that apartment."

"My darling sister, she could never—but she's every bit the friend you are to me and I'm blessed to have her."

"You're a lucky son-of-a gun."

"Why?" I asked.

"So many people care about you even though you're a devil sometimes," Val said.

"Well, you've got me there."

"It's your inside beauty they see."

I wondered if she were "joshing me" to use Al's colloquialism.

⌐◦ᶜ◉ᵔᵔ

ON WEDNESDAY EVENING, I DRAGGED myself though the front door and heard Mr. Blitzer, the peddler who sells everything from porcelain to sheets to diamonds, talking to Mamma. I wondered if I should wait for him to take his leave, but instead, I lugged my suitcase upstairs, and there sat Mr. Blitzer enjoying a cup of espresso with Mamma, whose eyes opened wide when she saw me. No wonder the man considered Mamma his best friend—she listened to all his tales of woe and had given him advice for years. The most recent dilemma, since his wife had died, was that his son was dating a *shiksa*. I thought he was an uncle when I was a little girl because most of the time he spoke Italian with Mamma.

"Sit," Mamma said, and it was like I'd never left.

⟨≈⟩

WHEN MR. BLITZER LEFT, MAMMA hugged me. "I forgive you, but please never run from me again. You're a woman now. Face your difficulties and talk things out. What's a family for? We have differences, of course, but love will see us through. Now come, I have something to show you. Here's the diamond ring I purchased for Pina—she never got one from her husband," Mamma said.

"How can you afford it?"

"I've been squirreling away here and there for years. Try it on."

"Perfect fit for me, Mamma. You'll have to get another for Pina," I said, holding my hand this way and that, pretending I had a headache so she could see it better.

"The stone's a good size, not overly large, like the one that dwarfed your hand before. Pina will like it," she said.

"It's more than a good size—it's beautiful—can't wear anything too small. She has large hands, like me."

I offered her my hand to remove it, but she said, "No. You slip it off." So I did and watched Mamma put the ring away. "It's elegant, Mamma. Pina will love it."

"Not as big as the one you gave back, nor as bright and white, but it's a good color with only very slight imperfections that aren't visible to the naked eye. It's over a carat."

"Since when do you know so much about diamonds?"

"Since I've known Mr. Blitzer and been shopping on Canal Street. You learn a lot when you listen and watch and wait. I've been taught what is called 'comparison shopping,' and I've studied how to equate the goods for prices."

"How will you pay for this? Where's the money?"

"Mr. Blitzer knows I'm good for it. I give him something every week."

"You can have my communion jewelry to trade up. I'll have extra money from my singing lessons—"

"What singing lessons?"

"*Mox nix.* Doesn't matter—I won't be taking them any longer."

I reached out and kissed her. "I'm so, so sorry, Mamma. I put you in a bad light and embarrassed the whole household." I burst into tears. "Forgive me for hurting you."

"You showed a despicable side of your character with Al. I had an urge to slap you."

"You did."

"I did? Sit down and write a letter to him. Right now."

"What for?"

"To apologize once more. In writing."

I didn't argue. She handed me a sheaf of good stock, cream paper and an envelope. I wondered if this, too, was a Blitzer special. While I sat writing the letter, Mamma stole up behind me and said quietly that she'd been invited to Grazia's by Signora di Maggio for Sunday afternoon.

My heart almost stopped.

"Do you still want to approach her? It's risky. She may refuse and spit in your face," Mamma said.

"She wouldn't, would she?"

Mamma waited.

"That's a chance I'll have to take," I said, feeling my face turn glum.

"Settled. You'll come with me, because you'll be able to speak to her and *la signora* di Maggio loves Gianni like a grandson. She told me once it always hurt her to see the way he'd been bounced from one brother's family to the other. I feel very much the same way. It's so hard to see someone suffer because they lack parental guidance in the world."

⌐✦⌐

THE WEEKEND COULDN'T ARRIVE SOON enough for me. I counted the days and marked each one off on the religious calendar hanging up on the inside of the bathroom closet door. I practiced every day in the mirror the things I'd say to her. I said it several times as sincerely, without artifice, as I could.

Then the day was upon me. Mamma and I walked over to Zia Grazia's house. We strolled rather than walked fast, trying not to rush anything. Mamma and I talked about so many mundane things, but I knew I wouldn't remember a single one of them. Zia Grazia greeted us and had us sit at the dining room table, where Signora di Maggio was already waiting in her wheelchair. She greeted us with kisses and smiles. She made chit-chat while Zia Grazia was in the kitchen preparing espresso and arranging a plate of biscotti. Mamma didn't wait and broached the subject of me getting back with Gianni with Signora di Maggio, a wise yet cunning woman.

When Zia Grazia brought in the coffee, the conversation ceased.

"Did I interrupt something?" Zia Grazia asked.

"Of course not," Mamma said.

But when Zia Grazia went back in the kitchen for napkins, Signora di Maggio whispered, "I'm positive Gianni still has feelings for you, Marcella. Beatrice shoved Oriana at him. After all," she declared, "he is a man and needs the company of a woman. However, I believe we are still in time, and Gianni cares for you—deeply."

Zia Grazia came back, and as she poured the coffee, she didn't bother to look up but merely stated as fact, "Yes, he does, but does that mean he'll break his engagement?"

"It's not official. What's-her-name wasn't wearing a ring," I said.

"You know her name is Oriana," Zia Grazia said with annoyance. "And no, she wasn't wearing one, but you were and he saw it." Zia Grazia set the coffee pot down and passed around the sugar bowl. "What can we do for you?"

All of a sudden, I stood up. "Ladies, I appreciate your wanting to help on my behalf, but I see clearly this is something that has to come from me, and me alone—no meddling, no interference. Thank you with all my heart." I kissed each of the ladies in turn and went to the door. At first my mother was speechless, and so were the other two, but they were smiling and understanding.

My mother stood up. "What are you doing? Where are you going? Have you lost your courage?"

"On the contrary, Mamma. I'm going to solve the dilemma that I've created." I blew everyone a kiss and headed straight for the front door.

Signora di Maggio said, "Let her go. She's determined, and nothing can stop her now."

From the corner of my eye as I reached for the handle of the door, I saw Zia Grazia take Mamma's hand in a gesture that said, "Don't worry."

CHAPTER 30

Giacomo

WHEN GIACOMO AND THE FAMILY finished dinner that evening, Marcella asked him if he wanted to take a walk, which he immediately understood to mean she needed to speak with him alone. They strolled around the neighborhood streets for quite some time before she built up courage. It was palpable.

"How do I solve a problem?" she finally asked.

"Depends on what it is. Does it involve people or things?"

"People."

"Men go about solving things in different ways than women when it comes to dealing with other people. Perhaps they circle and circle, and then they pounce. Women may do some circling, too, but they are sizing up the situation, inching closer with each circle. They approach stealthily until they come face to face. Like now."

"What do you mean 'like now'?"

"I would've already told you what my problem is, but you're circling. I would've dived right in and tackled it."

They stopped walking under a streetlamp. A cat swaggered by on the prowl.

"Let's say you find out that you've been wrong for a long time," Marcella said.

"What do you mean?"

"How do you rectify a situation? In other words, correct some things that you've tangled up badly into knots."

"Why don't you stop talking in riddles and tell me what's going on in that pretty head of yours?"

"Papa, I've been such a fool. It's taken me all this time to realize I love Gianni."

"Ah."

"That's it? All you have to say is 'ah'?"

"I'm thinking."

"What?"

"Are you sure?" Giacomo asked.

"Of course I'm sure."

"Or is it because he was at the wedding with another girl and you're jealous? You thought you had him tied to a string and could fly him like a kite whenever you pleased, but now you see someone else holds the lead."

Giacomo saw his daughter's eyes fill to the brim. "Don't," he said and handed her his handkerchief. "It solves nothing."

He told Marcella about when he was a sailor and was separated from Lian. He searched all over for her while she was searching for him. He said, "Against all odds, if it's meant to be it will be. But you must aid in the fight for your destiny, although I don't know how. Our society doesn't allow for or approve of a woman going after a man, but it seems to me you have no choice. Gianni is not coming back this time. Sometimes you must break the rules."

"But how, Papa? How?"

They started walking back toward the house. "I don't think I can tell you, but you will come up with a tactic. I guarantee it. We'll go home now and talk about it over a nice cup of chamomile tea and some of your mamma's cookies. Don't worry, Marcella—Val and Jack are all tucked in their beds now and won't hear us. That's the reason for this walk, no?"

Marcella nodded and her tears fell.

CHAPTER 31

Marcella

ONCE HOME, WE DECIDED TO get comfortable. I put on a pair of Chinese silk pajamas that Bao and Lucille had given me for being in their wedding party and went down to the kitchen, where I prepared the tea and set out a plate of cookies. Papa put on his old comfy bathrobe and slippers and shuffled into the kitchen. He was showing signs of a hard life. He was tired, and here I was giving him more concerns.

He had a strange look on his face. "What is it?" I asked as I filled the kettle and put it on the stove, turned on the gas, and struck a match. "I'm sorry, Papa."

He pulled out a chair and sat. "For what?" He pulled the collar of the bathrobe closer.

"Giving you more to worry about. You looked thrown by—"

"I was surprised to see the design on your pajamas. That color of blue silk and the dragons reminded me of something."

"Lucille and Bao gave them to me."

"Should have guessed. Lian gave me a vest like that. Did you see that Lucille now wears her ring? A miracle. Life comes full circle. A father should be able to counsel his loving daughter. The trouble with that is I don't think I can give you the advice you're looking for or need. Can't you just go to the man and tell him you love him?"

I shook my head, thinking *not even dead.*

"Maybe you should speak to Pina. Mamma seems to think she's fallen in love with Bruno and he loves her. Another miracle!"

I set the cups on the table and took a spoon from the drawer. "Pina. Mmm. That's an idea. I'll go over early tomorrow evening before she goes to bingo at church. I'm babysitting Elena—if you can call it babysitting. Elena will be asleep, I bet. I'm bringing along a new book I got out of the library."

Papa blew on his tea and then sipped some. He shivered.

"Are you all right?" I poured tea for myself, put in a cube of sugar, and stirred.

"Cold in here, isn't it?"

"I'll close the window." I sat back down. "Sugar?" I asked.

He shook his head. "Miracles come in threes, like births and deaths. It'll happen for you."

We spoke of banalities for a few more minutes, then finished our tisanes and cookies, kissed each other goodnight, and went to bed. Papa would probably be asleep as soon as his silvery locks hit the pillow. But me? I had some serious thinking to do.

⸙

I GOT OFF WORK A little early, went home to change into slacks, and dashed over to Pina's apartment a few blocks away. It wasn't like a regular apartment, and I loved it. It was an old carriage house on a huge piece of property set off way in back of an old, palatial Dutch mansion. It was surrounded by shrubs and trees, and I found it extremely romantic.

The first thing Pina said to me was, "She won't give you any trouble. She's fast asleep."

"Can you sit with me a minute? I have something to ask you." We sat on a loveseat that was covered with forest green, pink, and gold chintz with two puffy pillows leaning on the sides.

"Have you eaten?" Pina asked.

"Not hungry."

"If you want something, I made chicken cutlets. In the fridge. There's some *caciocavallo* cheese and apples, too."

"Maybe later."

"Help yourself. There's cider, too. Bruno brought it back from upstate New York."

"Pina," I interjected, "I've made the most drastic mistake of my life." I twirled the cording on one of the pillows.

"Another one?"

"Seriously." I smoothed the pillow and put it in back of me.

"Shoot."

"I'm in love with Gianni Simoni."

"Oh, that old song. I thought you were going to tell me something new."

"Didn't you hear?" I didn't wait for an answer but plunged ahead. "He's almost engaged to Oriana—"

"You're kidding! Everyone knows he's in love with you."

"Maybe so, but he was fixed up with Giuseppe's wife's sister. Gianni introduced her to me at Lucille's wedding as his fiancée."

"Oh, dear me."

"You see the problem now?"

"You said 'almost.' What's that mean?"

"She wasn't wearing a ring. Yet," I said.

"What are you planning to do?"

"Thought I'd ask you what you'd do if you were me."

"Give up."

"You can't mean that."

"I do," Pina said. "You can't go chasing him all over town. You can't call him on the phone, you can't go over to visit him. What can a girl do that doesn't appear to be hussy-like and forward? Maybe write him a letter? And say what exactly? So tacky."

"I could try to run into him accidentally on purpose, but I'd need help with that tactic."

"If you're so keen on it, what about enlisting Zia Grazia's help?"

"Actually, she's not wholly in favor of it. Thinks I should leave Gianni be at this point."

"Probably scared of what her husband will do or what the Simoni brothers will say. I always felt she was a kindred spirit," Pina said.

"You mean the way Zio Franco treats her?"

She nodded, stood, and said, "And Bruno treated me."

"Is that all over now?"

"He's possessive, but he's come a long way. I can't say I'm madly in love—he's too old-school to be romantic—but it's better as is."

"As is. I don't want to settle for that with some jerk. I know Gianni inside and out. He's the best thing that ever happened to me, but I was too pig-headed and blind to see it."

"You have to tell him how you feel. You told me that and I opened up with Bruno. It worked."

I wondered how much Jack influenced Bruno.

"What about seeing him at Mass?"

"Great idea! Oriana's in another parish."

"Got to go, kiddo, or I'll be late," she said. "Sorry I haven't been much help."

I pulled the book out of my bag.

"What're you reading?"

"*Magnificent Obsession*. Got it in the library," I said, wishing I could've bought a copy of my own, but the price of books is so dear.

⌒⊂⊅⌒

BY THE TIME PINA CAME back, I was asleep with the book open and a handmade crocheted blanket of "granny squares" thrown over me.

She called me from the kitchen and said she was making a cup of coffee. "Do you want some?"

I yawned and folded the blanket. "No thanks."

She asked if she should call Mamma and tell her I was going to sleep over, but I said no, I'd walk home. "The fresh air will do me good."

"Clear the cobwebs from your head?"

"You're in a good mood. Did you win at bingo?"

"Uh-huh. I saw the young priest who has become a spiritual advisor of sorts."

My ears pricked up at that. "How's that coming along?"

"Good. Things have calmed down between Bruno and me, if that's what you're wondering."

"Really? Because of this priest?"

"He's very worldly for someone so young. I have the feeling he had a wild life in California before moving east and taking his vows."

"Still have a crush on him?"

She shook her head. "He's truly devoted and has a certain aura about him—I think it protects him from womanly designs."

"I'll say this—you're much calmer and, maybe not happy, but at peace."

She accompanied me to the door. "Look around you. Don't have your head in the clouds when you're in the shadows. Now go on."

I got a sudden chill and pictured those boys circling me when I was young.

"Call me tomorrow," she said.

"Better yet, bring the baby over and I'll treat her to a story and homemade Italian ice," I offered.

"Are you serious? In this polar bear weather?"

"A kid is a kid is a kid. Ice is good anytime. Don't you remember?"

Pina kissed me and said, "Thanks."

"Let me babysit at least once when she's awake and we can play together. Jack says she's a riot and wants to win everything."

"Like her auntie."

"Who? Me?"

She gave me a gentle shove and stood in the doorway and waved to me. When I reached the gate, she closed the door. I had a hard time opening the gate, and when it slammed shut in back of me I jumped. Once on the street, I started working out what I could say as an opener to Gianni at church next Sunday.

I was a block away when I switched my shoulder bag to the left. It was the lightness of the bag that made me remember I'd left the novel I'd been reading on the loveseat. Oh well, I thought, she'll bring it tomorrow.

I'd been daydreaming for a block or so, trying to form an idea of how I'd go about meeting up with Gianni other than at church and make it seem coincidental. A few blocks farther, I decided to get my keys out of my pocketbook and have them at the ready. When I heard running footsteps behind me, I started to turn around, then felt my bag ripped off my shoulder. The next thing I knew all was total black.

⸙

I AWOKE IN A STERILE hospital room with what seemed to be distant church bells ringing, silverware clinking, and an overloaded trolley clanking outside my door.

There was a gentle knock, and a pretty nurse in a starched cap and pure white uniform entered the room and asked how I was feeling.

"You were dazed when they brought you in last night. Recall anything about that?" she asked, primping all around and plumping up my pillows.

I looked around the room. Nothing was familiar. Did I remember anything at all? I reached for the tissue box on the nightstand and blew my nose.

She shook a thermometer, stuck it under my tongue, and asked if I wanted to eat.

I was so nauseous, how could I even think about food? But I couldn't answer because she was measuring my temperature.

After a few minutes, she took the thermometer, looked at it, shook it down, and wrote something on my chart. My head swiveled left to right trying to follow her tennis-playing movements, making me dizzy. Hearing her speak was like listening to someone trying to communicate underwater. I became quite agitated and asked for something, but I think it wasn't very clear, because she looked at me and kept repeating, "What? What is it you want?"

"I've got a headache. Can I have some aspirin?"

"Oh, sure. I'll be right back."

When she returned with two white pills and a glass of water, I was about to ask how I got to this place when she offered me this bit of information. "You're here to rest from a blow on the head."

I must have fallen, but where? When? I had the feeling there was more to this than she was willing to say, but at the same moment, a tall, handsome man walked into the room. He had dark wavy hair, and at first I thought he might be a doctor, but he wasn't wearing a white coat. Then his face came into focus clearly.

"How're you feeling?" he asked, taking my hand very gallantly and kissing it. I felt like a high-born lady at court. But what I said was, "Higgledy-piggledy," and for some reason smiled at my own silly remark.

"Muddled in the head?"

"Precisely."

A young red-haired medic with *payos* wearing a *yarmulke* and a suit with a white coat over it came in and said, "You're confused, aren't you?" He picked up a chart at the foot of the bed and read it. The nurse signaled him and wagged her finger, some secret code for *don't say anything*. I knew that's what it meant because I wanted desperately to know what I was doing there in what seemed to be a hospital room and a hospital bed, with Gianni, so good-looking but wearing a worried expression, nearby after kissing my hand.

The red-headed man introduced himself as Dr. Miriam. "You're in the hospital—Israel Zion in Brooklyn. You had a concussion last night. Can you tell me what happened?"

I shook my head.

"Some neighbors heard a scuffle, then found you on the sidewalk unconscious. They called an ambulance, which brought you here. We assumed you had your purse stolen because you had no identifying information on you and your left arm was bruised. You must have fallen on it after the thief pulled your bag from you. Your concussion is not from the fall but from trauma. Someone hit you on the head with a dull object. Remember any of this?

"The police called this morning," Dr. Miriam continued. "Someone found your shoulder bag in the bushes and reported it, so it turns out our guesswork was correct. The purse had your name and address in it. We notified your parents, and they were here this morning, but you were sleeping, on the verge of a coma. Your friend's been with you ever since they left."

"Thanks so much, doctor," Gianni said, no longer a dark stranger to me.

I was bewildered beyond words but had to ask, "What was I doing, and why did I get hit on the head?"

Gianni, at my bedside, took my hand and stroked it. "You'll be fine." He had a reassuring voice, but somehow I didn't think that could be right if I couldn't remember things.

The doctor said, "Right now you should try to relax. Your memory will come back soon, and you'll recall everything and everyone." He said this in a cold, sterile, metallic sort of way.

I must have looked perplexed because Gianni's pleasing voice tried to soothe me. He called me sweetheart. Wasn't that a little bold in front of the doctor? Yet his familiar soft eyes were comforting to me.

The doctor faced Gianni and flung into the air phrases and expressions that were meant to be understood but sounded like gibberish to me: "islands of memory," "clouded consciousness," and "post-traumatic amnesia" seemed to be his favorites.

I wanted to ask him what it all meant, but all I could say was, "Where was I when the hit to my head happened?"

The doctor replaced my chart at the foot of the bed. "You were at your sister Pina's house, and then walking—"

"I'm trying," I said haltingly, "hard to remember where I'd been going. I believe I'd just promised myself to do something, but what?"

"Don't be alarmed," he said, taking hold of a pressure gadget and wrapping it around my arm. "I explained to your parents the type of amnesia you have is called anterograde, so if at first you can't seem to make future memories, don't be alarmed."

"Future memories sounds rather terrifying."

"It'll all come back, and you'll learn how to again. For now the future may appear foggier than past memories."

"What am I supposed to be doing?" I sat up straighter.

He was about to answer me, but we were interrupted by the presence of Val and Jack standing in the doorway. Valentina was visibly upset, wringing a hanky instead of curling her hair, and Jack looked like he'd seen a specter.

"Do I look that bad?" I said. "Where's a mirror?"

They both rushed to my side, almost knocking into Gianni, who adeptly shifted his position and stood to greet them. Val kissed me and then kissed Gianni. "Am I ever glad to see you," she said to him.

The doctor winked at me, said he'd see me later, and took his leave. Then he stepped back in the room, held up five fingers, and said, "Five minutes. Too many visitors."

Gianni shook Jack's hand and with the other one, ruffled up his hair. Jack's voice cracked when he said, "Missed seeing you around. What's it been, a year?"

"I'm driving a truck for my brothers now," Gianni said.

"Saw you in the neighborhood about a month ago and waved, but you were talking to a pretty little honey," Jack said, and Val elbowed him in the ribs.

Jack, looking quite offended, said, "What did I say?"

"Nothing. It was probably a customer," Gianni said, covering nicely I thought. I took that to be for my benefit and heard him continue, "I've been working hard and saving the greenbacks."

"For an engagement ring?" I asked, the words coming out before I had time to bite my tongue.

He turned to look at me. "Actually, I was thinking of buying my own place."

I cultivated a new respect for him, realizing he'd grown tired of being shoved pillar to post by his brothers, their wives, and their families.

"That's wonderful," I said and smiled.

"That's great, Gianni," Val said and winked at me.

My thoughts seemed to fly backward. I visualized the last time we'd gone to the movies on Eighty-Sixth Street. I couldn't remember what we went to see, but I recalled that on the way into the theater, I'd said to Gianni, "I love the way you blush when you get embarrassed," immediately planning my next assault. When the movie credits and music were over, Gianni took my hand, and we began to exit with the crowd.

Holding hands coming out of the show, I grabbed his hat and stuck it under my coat, making me look quite pregnant. I stopped dead still and yelled, "Masher!" pointing to Gianni, who was staring at my bulging stomach. It was almost the same scene on the train all those years ago with a real masher. I screamed again, "Masher! Help!"

I pulled back from Gianni, who dropped my hand and fled. I burst out laughing, covering my face with both hands. Suddenly I was the center of attention in the hall, although the men who'd encircled me didn't find it quite that funny and I had to apologize to everyone, explaining it was a joke.

⸙

WHEN I CAME BACK FROM my reverie, everyone seemed to be talking at once, and all of a sudden I felt exhausted. Luckily a nurse came by and shooed everyone out so I could rest.

Val kissed me, and Jack smiled and waved.

"Will you come see me tomorrow?" I asked Gianni.

"Count on it."

CHAPTER 32

Giacomo

GIACOMO GOT THE NEWS OF his friend Carlo's death in the strangest way. He and Val were sitting on the porch. There was a knock on the door, and Val went to answer it. Giacomo could tell by his daughter's expression she was taken aback.

"What are you doing here?" she said to the man at the door.

"I've come to deliver a message to your father."

"Who is it, Valentina?" Giacomo called.

"Someone for you, Papa," she said, standing aside to let Vic Piccolo enter.

"*Buona sera,* Signor Scimenti."

Papa stood and offered him a seat. "Have we ever met?"

"No, sir. I'm Vittorio Piccolo, a soldier for the Albano family."

With his hand, Giacomo signaled for Val to leave, and she gave the seated man a disgusted look and said, "I'm going upstairs, Papa."

"*Va bene,*" he answered.

They spoke in Italian for a while, and then Giacomo raised his hand and said, "Please, stop. Forgive me, but your Italian is atrocious. Let's speak English."

"I've come to deliver some bad news, sir."

"Spit it out."

"Your dear friend, Mr. Carlo Albano, was murdered last night in downtown Brooklyn."

"Where? When? How?" Giacomo was on his feet, brushing back his hair with his hand.

"He was having a late dinner—after midnight—with two other bosses. They were gunned down. It looks like it was a vendetta."

"Or all-out war between families," Giacomo said in a quiet, pensive voice. "When's the wake?"

"Tomorrow at Torregrossa's."

"And the funeral?"

"I think they're going to take him to St. Charles, out on Long Island. He had a marble mausoleum built for the family, and their name is already carved overhead. Carlo's brother is buried there."

Giacomo shook his head. "Who told you to come here?"

"His wife."

"Tell Caterina we'll be there, but I'll have my wife go and comfort her now."

Vic stood to leave.

"My daughter recognized you—like she'd seen a ghost," Giacomo remarked.

"She's seen me around the neighborhood. Then I was gone for a while."

"You're working for the family?"

"Only temporary. I'm going back to Boston. I'm only half-Italian. Mother's Irish."

Something clicked, and a memory spiraled in Giacomo's brain. "Sooner the better. Stay away from my daughter," Giacomo said, his voice menacing.

Vic put out his hand to shake.

Giacomo looked at it, then glared into Vic's eyes and opened the door.

CHAPTER 33

Marcella

I WAS HOME FROM THE hospital and getting visitors and flowers and cards from everyone, it seemed. Everyone but the person I wanted to see—Gianni. I was starting to feel my old self and didn't want to be petted and pampered. I needed to do something, but Mamma refused to let me go to work for the rest of the week. Elaine came to visit and agreed with Mamma.

I had picked up a book and started reading when, to my surprise, Gianni walked in carrying a nosegay of roses and a box of candy. I thanked him and accepted his lovely gifts. Val popped in and said hello and that she'd bring the flowers to the kitchen and put them in a vase.

"Are you up for a walk or to get some fresh air in the gazebo?" Gianni asked.

"I'd love it. They're keeping me under lock and key, and I feel like the prisoner of Zenda."

"Who?"

"Oh, it's a book I'm reading. I'm really quite fit. Mamma said I can't go back to work until next week," I said, and on and on I went, chattering away, until I realized I was nervous and stopped myself.

"Shall we go?" Gianni said.

He escorted me down the stairs and out to our lovely walkway studded with hydrangeas. We strolled around the block, and then we walked to the back of the house and sat in the gazebo.

Gianni did the strangest thing. He got down on one knee, took a ring out of his vest pocket, and held it up to me.

"Will you?" he asked.

I shook my head in disbelief but said, "Yes! With all my heart, yes!"

He stood and stuck a finger in his ear and wiggled it. "I heard you. The whole neighborhood heard. No need to scream."

He took hold of my left hand and placed the ring on my finger. It was a perfect fit.

We kissed. And then we kissed again.

"But Gianni—where? Where did you get this ring?"

"Your mother bought it for me from Mr. Blitzer."

"But you were getting engaged to Oriana."

"Maybe you were fooled into thinking so. Something had to make you come to your senses."

The sun was setting, and the fading evening light all around the garden glowed ripe apricot. I shrieked with joy and threw my arms around his neck and covered his face with kisses.

I pulled back my face from his, our foreheads touching, and said, "I guess now you'll have to ask my father permission to marry me."

"No. I refuse." He straightened.

"But it's only proper. That's not like you."

"I feel once is enough."

"What do you mean?"

"Everybody but you, Marcella, knows that I've had his permission since you were sixteen years old. I was going to propose on your birthday if it hadn't been for a broken plate over my head."

We were quiet for a moment, and then I said, "I've been such a fool. I want you in my life. You. Only you. Forever. I wish to give you all of me, and I want all of you. Loving doesn't seem enough—you're my beginning and end."

Gianni and I held each other. He breathed next to my ear. "To my very soul I adore you."

I might never understand the workings of a man, his heart, his emotions and intellect, but I knew one thing I didn't know beforehand. While this boy turned to man, this friend to lover, my guardian angel had watched over me so I wouldn't fall too far from grace. In finding Gianni, I finally found my center.

-Fini-

ACKNOWLEDGMENTS

WHEN I WAS A LITTLE girl, I was taught to offer "spiritual bouquets" of prayers, good thoughts, and aspirations for my parents and those I loved. I'm offering one now along with a thousand thanks to my husband, Felipe, for his encouragement and support during the past year devising, writing, and revising this novel.

I would like to thank my very exceptional readers for feedback during the writing process: Jane Brownley, Mona Birch, Rosalie Muskatt, and my writing group, but most especially Marni Graff, and Melissa Westemeier. And as always, my gratitude to John Dufresne.

Sincere thanks to Turner Publishing, especially Stephanie Beard, Jon O'Neal, Maddie Cothren, Kym Whitley, and Jolene Barto.

CPSIA information can be obtained at www.ICGtesting.com
Printed in the USA
LVOW08s2358270616

494335LV00004B/137/P